NATIONWIDE PRAISE FOR
PHANTOM FORTRESS:

About the Author

BRUCE LANCASTER is one of the most popular American historical novelists, respected not only for the swiftness and liveliness of his narratives, but also for the soundness and thoroughness of his research.

Mr. Lancaster did not begin writing until he was 40. Before his death in June, 1963, he had written and published 17 novels. He was also the author of all but one of the textual chapters in *The American Heritage Book of the Revolution.*

Other books by Bruce Lancaster soon to be published in paperback by Popular Library are: *GUNS OF BURGOYNE, TRUMPET TO ARMS,* and *BLIND JOURNEY.*

PHANTOM FORTRESS

By BRUCE LANCASTER

POPULAR LIBRARY • NEW YORK

Dedication:

to Roger and Brooks Holden

I have not the honor of your acquaintance, but am no stranger to your character and merit. Your services in lower South Carolina in awing the Tories and preventing the enemy from extending their limits have been very important. . . . I am fully sensible your service is hard and your suffering great, but how great the prize for which we contend.

—*Extract from a letter by Nathanael Greene to Francis Marion, December 3, 1780*

By the late summer of 1780, the American cause in the South seemed hopeless. Two Continental armies had been sent there. The first, under Lincoln of Massachusetts, had been forced to surrender at Charleston in early May. The second, commanded by Gates, was crushed near Camden in August.

Most of the South Carolina leaders of the Revolution were dead, prisoners or refugees. The main British army, under Lord Cornwallis, lay just over the North Carolina border where it watched the shrinking wreck of Gates's force and slowly prepared for an advance north into Virginia.

It is possible that even mild conciliation toward the defeated Colonists might have ended the last spark of rebellion in the South. Instead, extreme measures were taken. Property was confiscated in apparent violation of Crown guarantees. Former Rebels who gave their paroles to fight no longer against Royal power were not allowed to remain in peace. Often, they were called upon to take the field against their former comrades in arms, to hunt them down, to inform against them. Refusal on the part of the parolees was often treated as active treason. Helpless, without arms, dependent for life itself on the Crown, the patriots found themselves exposed to British and Tory raids, to virtual conscription, to exile to Jamaica and forced service in British regiments, to harsh imprisonment. These men turned and fought again. First as partisans harrying the British, then as indispensable allies of the third Continental army to be sent south, under the Rhode Islander, Nathanael Greene, South Carolinians struck, vanished into the swamps, struck again, until the British empire of the South vanished.

The characters of this novel, real and fictitious, participate in that uprising, fighting first as partisans entirely on their own, later with Greene's tiny force. They would have been helpless without Greene. Without them, the Rhode Islander must have failed. Together, after bloody months, they saw the last of the British sail from Charleston. There was, of course, a good deal of indecisive fighting after that last, formal engagement at Eutaw Springs in September of 1781. The British evacuation did not take place until December 1782. But that evacuation was made inevitable by Yorktown and Eutaw Springs.

Although Francis Marion has been selected as the actual character to carry the story of the partisans, there were many others of equal or nearly equal distinction such as Thomas Sumter, Andrew Pickens, the Hamptons, Bratton, Brandon,

Lacey and their fellows. Marion, however, served the purposes of this book best. Hence the full light has been thrown on him and his known followers—Peter and Hugh Horry, the Postells, the James brothers, the Conyers and the rest.

It is a loss to history that the story of Marion's men, and of other partisans, exists in such vague detail. Even the writings of men who actually served with him, like Judge James, are confusing as to places, dates and people. The trail is further obscured by the efforts of the well-meaning Parson Weems of cherry-tree fame, who wrote a life of Marion and attributed it to Peter Horry, Marion's closest friend. Despite the fact that Horry denied any share in the work, some writers have leaned on Weems's version, thus carrying on his errors. Nonetheless, the story of Marion, pieced out by known records covering his actual contacts with Nathanael Greene and Light Horse Harry Lee, is clear enough to be accepted in substance if not entirely in fact.

Nathanael Greene, best-known figure of this book, is splendidly documented. So is the career of Lee's Legion (commanded by Henry Lee, the father of Robert E. Lee), at least so far as the why's, when's, where's are concerned. Records are dimmer when they touch on the composition of his Legion, where its men came from, how they were raised, trained, and uniformed.

Whether in substance or fact, the records show clearly men fighting in a seemingly hopeless cause through sheer conviction and, under skilled leaders from many states, seeing that cause triumph.

BRUCE LANCASTER
Beverly, Massachusetts

I • The Upcountry Convoy, 1780

Through the haze of a South Carolina October, the upcountry convoy rolled slowly along the south bank of the Santee. Brass-helmeted dragoons of the escort turned from time to time to stare at the girl in the creaking cart halfway down the column. Slim and cool in green-sprigged muslin, she perched on a roped sea chest, her body yielding gracefully to the sway and pitch of the wheels. Wrapped in her own thoughts, she was apparently oblivious to the slow-passing landscape where sickly swamp alternated with lush groves and sluggish river—and as oblivious to the covert interest roused in the troopers by the startling contrast of blond hair, black brows and lashes and snapping black eyes.

A dozen yards behind her, the boyish officer in charge of the convoy sat his weedy, country-bred horse, immensely proud of his rank of cornet in His Majesty's 17th Dragoons and of the responsibilities of his temporary command. He kept glancing at the girl like an eager, wagging puppy, hoping for a word that would call him to her, yet not daring a rebuff by riding up to her without a summons.

A clatter of hoofs from the rear of the column made him turn. Then he gave a sigh that was half relief and half resignation as he caught the glitter of brass and scarlet emerging from a spongy side trail. Captain Bayne, his immediate superior, was rejoining the column and would assume responsibility. Also, he would assume command. As the cornet swung his horse to meet the captain and his escort, he wondered if his relegation to a subordinate role would lessen him in the dark eyes of the girl up ahead.

He reined in by his captain, brown eyes solemn with hero worship. Captain Bayne was short and stoop-shouldered. His pebble-hard eyes were set close to a predatory nose and his thin lips spread in a fox's smile as he acknowledged the cornet's salute.

"All in order, Horton?" he asked in a rasping voice.

9

"Oh, quite, sir."

"Good. Now I want you—" He broke off, then pointed to the girl in the cart. "What the devil's that woman doing in my convoy?"

Horton's young face lit up. "Prettiest thing I've seen in the colonies, sir. Really—"

"I asked what she was doing here."

Horton meekly accepted the rebuke. "The major at Georgetown authorized her to come with us, sir."

"Damned irregular!"

"Oh, he didn't want to, sir. But she kept at him. Jove! You ought to have seen those eyes and that smile! The major'd have given her a commission in the Guards if she'd asked for it."

"Who is she?"

Horton adjusted the chin strap of his helmet. "I didn't see her papers, sir, but I did hear her talking before the convoy started yesterday. Her name's Dorande van Kortenaer and her father's Dutch and her mother's French."

Bayne scowled. "Didn't that damn major know the French are at war with us and the Dutch are slipping that way? French mother, eh? That means she's Papist?"

"Oh, the major was most particular about that. Her father's Dutch Reformed Church and her mother's Huguenot."

"So *she* says," grumbled Bayne. "How'd she get to Georgetown?"

Horton grinned excitedly. "It's like something out of Defoe. She lives on one of those Dutch islands in the Caribbean and the blacks got nasty and slaughtered a lot of whites. She was hidden in the jungle and finally got as far north as Havana."

"Slaughter?" Bayne frowned. "That would be the island of St. Eusebius."

"That's it, sir. Well, most of her friends were killed, but her mother and father were at that Dutch mainland station, Surinam, so they were safe. When they found she was in Havana, they wrote her to join her uncle who lives up the Congaree and they'd join her when they could. She couldn't get passage to Charleston, so she landed up at Georgetown."

"Uncle? Up the Congaree? Who is he?"

Horton shrugged. "Another of those French names. It's Paul—Paul St. Auburn, or something like that."

Bayne narrowed his eyes, nodding. "Paul St. Aubin. That explains why the major let her come with you. St. Aubin's a Frogeater, of course, but he's done good work for the Crown. Has the girl made any trouble?"

"Oh no, sir! Wait till you talk to her. Speaks English and

French and I heard her say something that must have been Dutch."

Bayne laughed coldly. "These damn West India colonials *have* to speak about seven tongues if they're going to get along with Europeans. Never mind about her prettiness. St. Aubin's always turning up with new nieces and they're *all* pretty." He eyed the cornet coldly. "Don't get any idea about getting closer to that prettiness. St. Aubin's made powerful friends here and he'd have you thrown to the alligators quick as winking."

Horton flushed. "Oh sir! I wouldn't think—"

"The devil you wouldn't. But don't let it go beyond thinking. I'll have a word with her. After that, I'm riding ahead with a few troopers. There's work to be done upriver."

"Work, sir?"

Bayne smiled and a hard glitter came into his eyes. "Essential work for the Crown. You'll catch up with us later. Come on. Let's see this current niece."

Reining in by the cart, Horton stammered through the presentation of his captain, while Bayne coldly appraised the unexpected passenger, whom the cornet had certainly not overpraised. Masses of very light blond hair showed under the long-vizored poke bonnet with its green ribbons. Startlingly dark eyes under black brows and lashes surveyed the captain calmly. An impudent nose accentuated the rebellious red lips and round chin, and her pink and white complexion struck him as unusual for a tropics-bred girl. "Fine figure, too," thought Bayne. "Could make trouble among the men if they see too much of her. Have to watch that. Something almost frozen about her. Shock of that St. Eusebius business, I suppose." Then, having thoroughly assessed the girl, he raised his hand to his helmet and cantered off, some twenty scarlet troopers behind him.

Horton babbled on. That was *his* captain, a fine hard man. The Rebels would run the length of a shire to avoid him. They were almost as afraid of him as of Tarleton and Wemyss. What? Miss van Kortenaer had never heard of *them?* Amazing. Why, Banastre Tarleton commanded all of Lord Cornwallis's cavalry and twice he had cornered hundreds of Rebels and cut them down like sheep while they bleated for quarter. People called him Bloody Tarleton. And Major Wemyss of the 63rd! He had hung traitors by the score and had burned so many farms that you could ride through his area for a day and never see a whole roof! And now people were beginning to mention Bayne with Wemyss and Tarleton.

Dorande van Kortenaer held up her hand as though in protest and Horton broke off his recital, worried. Had he offended her? It seemed to him that she had grown pale. He bent toward her. "I trust I've said nothing—" he stammered.

She shook her head. "It is only that I do not understand." Her voice was low and rich and her English, though fluent, was markedly alien in accent. "I do not understand this talk. At Georgetown, the major told me the war was over. He spoke of peace everywhere. Then why do I see new-burned houses? Why do so many guards ride with us? And why do you talk of butchering and hanging and burning?"

"Oh, the war's over in the South," exclaimed Horton. "But there were proper bad Rebels about here and some of them still may be bunnying about, you see. We never caught the worst of them and Lord knows what he may be up to. Had a name like a girl's. Maude? Maudsley? No—Marion, that was it! Fancy fighting with a name like Marion!"

"And you have fought against him?"

Horton flushed. "Ah—no. Not exactly. I didn't come to the Americas until we'd thrashed the last Rebel army. That's why I'm down here instead of being with the rest of the regiment up in North Carolina."

Dorande closed her ears to the cornet's talk of war and slaughter and fastened her mind on her journey that would take her, as she knew from the careful instructions she had received in Havana, along the Santee and on up the Congaree. So deep was her abstraction that she was barely aware of Horton's departure in a cloud of apologies. The road to the Congaree would be tedious, but quiet, despite the cornet's words. In any event, troubles in the English colonies did not touch her. In far-off St. Eusebius she had vaguely known that there had been disturbances in North America. But of their extent and whom they affected and why, she knew little, in common with most inhabitants of St. Eusebius.

St. Eusebius! Her hands tightened in her lap as her memory repeated sounds and sights that for weeks and months she had been trying so stifle, repeated them from the past and into the present. Booming drums and scarlet fires in the sullen tropical night. People who looked fearfully from darkened windows to the jungle hills where drums and fires raged. A hot glare at midnight, heat and smoke in her room. Then musket shots and a howling that echoed in her mind above the grinding wheels of the present. A moment of terror as a black hand reached for her. Fathomless relief as she recognized the voice of her maid, Sophie. Garden shrubs ripping at her as other black hands guided her into the flaring night. Dutch soldiers dead in the alley that led on from the hidden gate into the hills. Deep voices in a courtyard and screams of Dutch women. Her guides knew how to find protecting shadow, but they could not blot out the pools of firelight that showed her the van Steen girls trapped against a wall by a mob that swept toward them. Nor Hilda van Os, nightdress burning as she jumped in terror from a window into a hedge of black arms. Dorande's hand clenched tighter. She would think of all this no more.

Slowly she began to notice the country through which the convoy rolled. Stands of oak and hickory loomed cool to the south and sometimes she saw white houses with girdles of lawn and garden. Here and there, blackened chimneys reared stark among charred timbers. To the north was the sullen Santee cutting its channels through the gray-green swamps that spread deep on each side. The wind brought the musky reek of alligators, and poison-green grasses stirred to reptilian passage.

At a crossroads more troopers joined the column, men in green jackets and black helmets. At Georgetown she had seen the uniform and heard the wearers called Tories or loyal Americans. Why? Weren't they all English, as the people of St. Eusebius and Curaçao and Surinam were Dutch? But again, it was no concern of hers. Green jacket and red, she would ride with them to the Congaree and then be done with them.

To the Congaree. How long was the road and, once there, how long must she wait in the care of this uncle whom she had not seen since earliest childhood? How long? Her eyes misted and her throat tightened. When would she see again her French mother, always tender and gay? And her father, big and blond and laughing, showering on his only daughter treasures from a dozen West Indian islands. But it was to her mother that her thoughts turned more, for Syvert van Kortenaer, ever-prospering trader, was always sailing away to Havana, to Jamaica, to the South American mainland, leaving the two on St. Eusebius, where people looked upon them more as elder and younger sister than mother and daughter.

Dorande started as people ahead called out, pointing to the left of the road. Her cart topped a shallow rise and she saw gardens off to the left, a row of tulip trees, smooth grass that swept up to a solid white house. It was a pleasant spot. No wonder that even the rough teamsters exclaimed over it.

Then she saw the saddled horses, held by men in red and men in green. The road swung nearer, showing the wide door hanging from a single hinge, and splintered windows.

Somewhere inside the house a woman screamed; then came a child's high thin wail. Dorande swung to the ground in one swift motion. Heedless of shouts from the column she raced up the slope as troopers called harshly after her. Her slippers clicked over the threshold and she stood looking into a deep hall where stairs of dark wood rose gracefully. To the left of the stairs a knot of green and red coats clustered. In their midst sat a tall woman, her strong comely features contorted with pain and her graying hair hanging over her shoulders. She was bound to her chair, and one arm was held out rigidly.

Dorande tried to call, but her voice died. She took an uncertain step and the group swirled before her. The thumb of the woman's outstretched hand was wedged in the lock of a carbine from which the flint had been removed. A man in green slowly turned the screw above the lock. A voice that Dorande recognized as Bayne's said coldly, "One more turn, ma'am, and you'll hear your thumb bone crack. I give you five seconds to answer. *Where's your husband?*" He began to count slowly. The woman writhed in her chair and shook her head.

Dorande felt hot blood rush to her head. She snatched up a riding crop that lay on a table and slashed at Bayne's head. He whirled about, eyes blazing. His hands caught her wrist and twisted the crop free. Then he released her, choking back his rage. "Here! Can't have this. You—Selkirk, Fordyce! Get her out of here. Don't hurt her. She's something to Major Carey."

Two dragoons caught her by the wrist and elbow, guided her out of the door as she struggled helplessly. One of them said soothingly, " 'Ere, 'ere, Miss. Whatever would the major say did 'e 'ear you was interferin' with one of 'Is Majesty's officers a-doin' of 'is duty?"

She panted, "Let me go! At once. That woman—"

There was a stir inside the house. The dragoons looked to the west where shouts sounded, and Dorande looked with them. Green riders cantered toward the house and in their midst stumbled a bound man. From the door, Bayne's voice trumpeted, "Fetch him here, Conway. You! On the road! Keep those carts moving. We'll catch up!"

Dorande saw the riders come on, cutting at their captive with switches when he stumbled. Bayne, rubbing his hands and chuckling coldly, moved out to meet them. The prisoner, panting, tried to draw himself erect. He was a tall, slim man in his late thirties, with proud, hot eyes and a defiant chin. Bayne said tersely, "You broke your parole."

The prisoner's eyes were steady. "I gave my parole not to resist the Crown on the understanding that I and my family would be left in peace and my property secure. Those were the terms of Sir Henry Clinton's proclamation. What happened? I kept my part, the Crown did not. Within a week, my house was plundered, my wife and child ill-treated. My slaves were driven off and more stores were burned." He paused for breath.

"Go on," said Bayne, lips compressed.

"That alone freed me from my oath. But there was the second proclamation that said everyone who'd taken Crown protection would have to fight or face charges of treason. My oath did *not* touch that."

"No?" asked Bayne with mock politeness. "Then why did you hide in the swamps when you saw us coming?"

"Why? Because of the way you've treated others who took the oath. Yes! I *have* gathered arms—to protect myself and my neighbors, since the Crown, despite my oath, would not or could not protect me. I'll go peaceably with you before any Crown court you name. They can hold me as a prisoner of war, but as a traitor, by God they can't!" He shook with the intensity of his words.

Bayne gave a barking laugh. "Court? Ha! I know your record. You served with that damned Marion before we chased him out of the Province and you'll go back to him the first chance you get. *If* you get one." He called over his shoulder. "Fetch the old hag out. And the cub, too." Then his eye fell on Dorande, who stared at him, white faced.

"What are you going to do?" she said huskily.

Bayne turned furiously on the dragoons. "God's bones! I told you to get her out of here."

She felt their hold tighten on her, felt herself marched swiftly down the sandy path. There was a cry from the house, high and piteous. "Ronald! They took you!" Then a steady answer. "No fault of yours, my dear. Chin up! Our flag's still flying north of the border."

Dorande tried to kick at the dragoons' high boots, but her feet swung helpless. She cried, "I have guilders, gold, Holland guilders. Let me go. I will pay you."

One of the guards hesitated, but the other growled, "Bayne'd follow a man as took a bribe through 'ell's blackest pits, that he would."

A confused babble broke out by the house and she tried

to turn her head. The taller guard said not unkindly, "Best not look back, Miss, not unless you're 'ardened to it, like."

She had to look back. From a tree close by the house, a man's body dangled and spun. The woman had fainted and lay by the shattered door, and a little boy ran toward her screaming, "Mama! Mama!" Bayne had turned his back on the dangling body and was watching the upper windows where ruddy smoke coiled, thick and oily.

Dorande choked back a sob and let herself be led along the column where men stared down at her, wondering at her uncertain gait and at the clumsy solicitude of her escorts. Then for uncounted miles she jolted on her cart. She stared rigidly forward, finding a sort of mesmeric relief in the slow-turning spokes of the cart ahead. She was oblivious to the triumphant sweep and clatter as Bayne galloped his red and green men along the column. A single thought flowed through her mind. The Crown had hanged a man because the Crown had broken its word—a sentence that became blended with the jolt of the cart. The *Crown* hanged a *man* because the *Crown* had broken its word; the *Crown* hanged a *man*—

She was vaguely aware of Horton reining in beside her and managed to say, "What is it?"

He bent from the saddle. "See here—not getting a touch of the sun, are you? You look pale."

"I do well," she said mechanically.

"We'll have the sawbones at Nelson's Ferry see to you. Now Captain Bayne sends his compliments. Regrets that you were distressed at the Colclough place. Military necessity, you know."

Military necessity! Dorande was shaken by a feeling of nausea. "Go away," she said in a flat voice. Then she shrank to the far side of the cart as Bayne cantered up, red plume flowing jauntily from his brass helmet.

"Horton!" he snapped. "Do you see that?"

His tone was so sharp that Dorande looked up in spite of herself. From the crest of a long, gentle hill she saw more carts and the red dragoons in the lead. To the left of the road was a broad savannah where feathery grasses waved, then dense woods at the distant foot of the slope. To the right, the Santee swamps crowded close. A quarter of a mile beyond the leading trooper a single horseman waited, broadside to the column. He wore a black helmet with a white plume, a white jacket faced with red, and white breeches.

Bayne rasped, "That's no uniform that I know. Take six

troopers, get that man and bring him here. It'll be easy. He's only riding a tacky."

Horton leaned forward eagerly, his hand on the hilt of his sabre. His face glowed. "I'll bring him back unharmed."

"I didn't say unharmed. Alive is enough. Off with you." Horton shot down the column, Bayne following.

Dorande's hands opened and closed as she stared at the white horseman. If he would only go, while there was time! She saw Horton gather a few troopers and race away. The man gathered his mount, swung it about and shot off into the woods. The troopers whooped like hunters, swerved into the fields and made for the trees that soon swallowed them up. She found herself on her feet, trembling. The column had halted and a dead hush hung over the road. There were scattering shots from the tangled oaks and then silence fell again. She could hear the sigh of a tired horse as it shifted its feet, the mutter of aimless voices behind her.

Red showed on the road, far beyond the spot where the white horseman had been seen, a fresh red coat, a brass helmet with red plume dancing. A red arm went up, signaled the column to come on. Dorande sat back on the sea chest, thinking, "They caught him. Alive they will bring him to Bayne—to Bayne with his mouth of a fox."

She looked ahead. The lone dragoon who had signaled had cantered out of sight. Of Horton and the others there was no sign. The savannahs at the left crawled past. Trees closed about her, throwing the road into deep shadow. Not far ahead, she saw the end of the trees, broad fields lit with sunset red through which Bayne and his men rode.

Then from the woods three shots ripped out—one—two—three. Dorande's horse shied. One wheel struck a big rock and the cart tipped to the right. She tried to recover her balance, slipped with the cart as it overturned. As she fell, she caught a glimpse of ragged men pouring from the woods, leaning from big horses to slash right and left with heavy swords. The sea chest broke from its fastenings, pitched into her, knocking the breath from her body. Something banged against her head and her world melted in a blinding flash that sent her spinning into darkness.

Slowly her world returned. The sea chest lay across her legs. Her head, aching fiercely, was on a smooth rock. She tried to move but the weight across her legs pinned her. Suddenly she remembered the swift rush of men from the woods and lay very still, listening to hoarse voices from the right and left. From where she lay she could see nothing but the overturned cart. Then a head, topped by a broken cocked hat, peered over the side of the cart. She cried, "*A moi!* This chest—it crushes me."

The man stepped quickly to her, heaved up the chest and helped her to her feet. He was small and wiry, dressed only in his lamentable hat and ragged boots and breeches. Looking curiously at her, he asked, "You King's people?"

She leaned against the cart, hand to her throat. "No! And by what right do you interfere with my journey?"

The man smiled. "Not knowin' what your journey was, I couldn't say. You'd best talk to the captain."

She shook her head to dispel the ache that was slowly leaving her. "Your captain? Tell him to come to me at once."

The man smiled again. "He's right busy now. Better wait by the split oak till he's got time to talk to you."

Trembling with alarm and with mortification at having to obey this ragged gnome, Dorande moved past the cart and onto the road where she stopped as though she had walked into a wall. Bodies in green and red were scattered up and down the road. The survivors of the escort stood, sullen and weaponless, by a clump of bushes. But the men who guarded them, who scrambled over the carts, startled her even more than the sight of the dead. Some wore fragments of uniforms, some walked about in clothes that suggested European cities. Others, like her guide, were naked to the waist, while many wore only a breechclout, long leather leggings and moccasins. A few had fastened pads of moss to hip and shoulder against the chafing of rifle or cartridge box.

Her guide touched her elbow gently. "Yonder's the split oak, close to the fields. You'll have a morsel of quiet to yourself till the captain ain't busy."

She felt numbness fading as she walked to the tree. "I do not wish to wait."

"Don't nobody want to wait and the captain least of all. We aim to keep our feet busy. Hi! That's him! Listen at him."

A powerful voice roared from the woods, "Who saw him go?"

A man in sky-blue satin breeches and tattered hunting shirt called, "I did. Riding hard toward Cupboard Creek."

The big voice, closer now, shouted, "Then he'll have to double back through the fields or drown. Swamps block him. How's he mounted?"

"Tacky."

"Then bring me one! We'll fight this out on even terms!" The undergrowth crackled and a glossy, staglike black horse burst into the open. Its rider was tall, broad-shouldered in his white jacket faced with red. Dorande had a glimpse of strongly marked features, heavy black eyebrows and black hair under a black helmet with a white horsehair plume. He dropped to the ground, vaulted into the saddle of a weedy country horse and cantered past Dorande toward the fields to the left, his jutting nose and outthrust jaw sharp against the sky. "That's Captain, ma'am," said her escort.

Dorande turned on him. "Then call him back. I wish—"

"He's busy, like I said."

Dorande shrugged impatiently and looked toward the fields where the captain, giving easily to the uneven gait of his tacky, trotted on. Then he reined in, standing in the stirrups and scanning the far woods. Red showed among the trees and he grew tense. He roared, "Bayne! Captain Bayne!" and drew his sword.

The red vanished among the trees, reappeared. The captain shouted again, "You'll drown in those swamps, Bayne. Come out, and I'll meet you man to man, as I promised you when I was in the prison hulks!"

There was a strange, urgent menace to his voice that sent chills up Dorande's back. She pulled her blue cape about her and stepped out into the field where that voice was booming again. "Shall I send my men after you? How about your swordplay that you bragged of to unarmed prisoners of war?"

The undergrowth parted and Bayne shot out of the woods, his sword advanced. The captain gave a shrug of satisfaction and rode on to meet him. At a gallop the two men met, whirled, circled while their blades glinted. Red coat and white, black helmet and brass, swirled before Dorande's eyes and the air rang as cut and thrust were parried. Cheers broke out from the men who edged the woods. The captain was pressing Bayne hard, beating down his guard but never quite able to reach home. Nearer they circled until Dorande could hear the snort of the horses and the savage breathing of the men who fought. Suddenly Bayne whirled his mount in a beautiful arc and aimed a backhander at the black helmet. The cut was met by a stronger parry and Bayne's yell of rage rang through the woods. His blade had snapped and he was left with a short, jagged stump by the hilt. The captain lowered his point not ten yards from Dorande, panting, "You're my prisoner, Bayne."

Bayne's stooped shoulders slumped and he looked at his broken blade. Then he shrugged. "I yield. But I'd have had you except for this damned tin sword." He stepped his mount closer. "See how it snapped."

Dorande cried out in sudden warning. Surprised, the captain looked around, and in that flash of time Bayne lunged from the saddle and slashed his opponent's horse across the tendons with his jagged blade. The tacky screamed and its haunches buckled. Bayne spun his horse, and raced off down the road that led west to Nelson's Ferry and the Congaree. Hands to her cheeks, Dorande gasped, "I did that! He turned when I called to him."

The captain stepped clear of the fallen horse, drew a pistol and shot it neatly back of the ears. The animal quivered and lay still. The captain walked toward the oak where Dorande stood, surrounded by men who mounted in a storm of profanity. He held up his hand. "Let him go. Too much of a start. We're losing time. The sun's burning out." He strode forward, hard blue eyes narrowed under the vizor of his helmet.

Dorande put out her hand. "If you please, Captain." The eyes flicked toward her, lightened with quick interest, then hardened impersonally. Indignation swept over her again. "Captain! I wish to proceed!"

He barely glanced at her. "Sorry. I'll talk to you later," he said, and strode toward the prisoners.

She stamped her foot. "But I demand that he see me."

The wiry man shook his head. "Don't do to fool with him when he's wearing his bear-trap face. Later he'll talk fair to you. Better set on that moss. It's soft and they probably ain't many ticks in it."

Dorande bit her lip and leaned against the oak. Down the road, the captain was giving sharp orders to the prisoners. Then men of the band moved among them, slitting their boots, snipping buttons from their breeches and cutting their suspenders. There was another command and the prisoners, holding up their breeches as best they could, shuffled miserably to the east in their slashed boots. She watched them, half pitying. Then she said to her guard, "I do not see—there was a young cornet with them."

The guard, who was cleaning his sword with moss, looked toward her. "There was. He come after us and I hauled him off his horse 'cause we wanted his pretty coat and helmet for the captain to wear when he went out on the road for the convoy to look at us."

"Then he is safe?"

"Nope. Not very. He tried a little swordplay with the captain. There's safer things to do."

"He is dead?" She recalled Horton's eager, boyish face and

the round brown eyes. He had tried to be kind to her on the march. She said again, "Dead?" hoping for contradiction.

He nodded. "There's something kind of final about the captain and a sword."

Dorande sighed and watched the stir about her. The prisoners were now far away and the men of the ragged command were swiftly sorting out the horses of the convoy, emptying the carts and stacking them in a mass by the swamp. Some were making piles of salt beef and others swarmed about a cart, filling their pouches and cartridge boxes from its sacks. At the far edge of the woods, the green and red bodies were being laid in a neat line. She drew herself up. The captain was walking toward her, a man in a battered fur busby trying to keep pace with him. As he neared, Dorande heard his deep voice. ". . . and the only reason it worked was because Bayne's a damned poor cavalryman. If you'd been against Tarleton, we'd all be hanging from an oak right now. Your men were badly posted and broke out too soon. Never mind. It worked. See to the carts and tell Michau to have his men herd up the tackies we captured." The man in the busby nodded and went away. The captain halted before Dorande, touching his helmet. "I'm afraid we gave you a rather bad time, ma'am. My apologies. Women don't often travel in convoys and we had no way of knowing about you."

The sharp words that Dorande had prepared died away. There was something in that deep, strong voice that left her uncertain, even a little shaken. The level blue eyes looked straight into hers until her lids lowered. Then he smiled and his whole face changed. She threw her head back and returned his gaze, trying to keep from answering his smile. What was he? He spoke like an educated man. A gentleman brigand? There was no doubt about the brigand part and the knowledge stiffened her spine. She said coolly, "There is no need for apology. Kindly give me a cart and an escort I may trust. I do not wish to delay."

He smiled again. "I understand that. It may not be easy. Who are you and where are you going? Are you for the Crown? A British officer's wife, perhaps?"

She set her chin. "I do not care a stiver for the Crown or the Rebels. I am Dorande van Kortenaer, of the Dutch Republic. I go to my uncle, a French subject, on the Congaree."

He took off his helmet and ran his fingers through the fur band above the vizor. "You've come from Holland to go up the Congaree? You'll excuse my finding that rather odd."

"Find it as you please. I come from the Dutch island of St. Eusebius. That is all you need to know of me."

"A few more questions, if you don't mind, Miss van Kortenaer. Who is your uncle?"

Wearily she said, "Very well. He is Paul St. Aubin, a well-known merchant who came here two years ago from the Indies."

"I see. But what brings you to the Congaree in these times?"

She gave a wry smile. "I came for quiet, which was not to be found in St. Eusebius."

"To South Carolina for *quiet?*" He laughed shortly. "Let me know if you find any. Now about sending you along. I'm very much afraid that it can't be done."

"It must be done."

He said quickly, "It's not for lack of will. But the farther you go along the Congaree, the more gentlemen in red or green you find. We don't get along well with them."

"But you *can* send me with an escort under a flag of truce as far as the post at Nelson's Ferry."

He shook his head. "Flags of truce don't mean much these days. They're apt to lead to a gallows. In any event, I wouldn't dare send you. You've seen us, you've heard names mentioned. You could easily tell enough to bring a whole force down on us."

She said disdainfully, "You have my word that I tell nothing."

"That wouldn't help. Without knowing it, you could give them everything they'd need." He ran his finger along his strong jaw. "Here's the best I can do. I'll send you east a few miles to a house where some very good people will look after you. The name is Colclough—Ronald Colclough."

The choking memory of the morning swept over her. She said unsteadily, "Bayne hanged Mr. Colclough this morning. He burned the house."

He started. "Hanged! That murdering—Well, we'll let that pass, for the moment. Obviously you can't go there. And you can't go on to Nelson's Ferry alone. You'd be lost a dozen times. Nor can you stay right here, waiting for another convoy. There's only one course open."

"Indeed?" Dorande's black eyebrows arched. "And precisely what is that?"

"You'll have to come with us. For a while, at least."

"With *you?*" Her eyes darted at the motley men under the trees.

The captain smiled. "I agree that we don't look like palace

guards. But we represent as best we can the only symbol of the Army of the United States in South Carolina, so far as I know. May I present myself? I am Ross Pembroke, of Rhode Island, captain of Continental Dragoons, absent on command." He beckoned to a tall, slightly built man who seemed to walk on springs. "My senior lieutenant, Raoul Jaudon, of Charleston. Like me, he was captured at the siege of that city and, not liking the British prison hulks, escaped as I did. That was where we met Bayne. He was in charge of our hulk. The red-haired Scot wearing the French busby is Dougal McKinstry, junior lieutenant of our rather unofficial army. His history is like ours. The others consist of escaped prisoners, of men burned out of their farms or villages by the Crown. We are disheveled but reasonably honest. See here, Raoul, we've got a sidesaddle, haven't we?"

Jaudon nodded. "One of the boys was using it for lack of a better. Now he's got a dragoon's kit and won't need it."

"Have it put on a good horse, not a tacky. Miss van Kortenaer's coming with us."

As Jaudon strode off, Dorande drew a deep breath. "You persist in thinking that I go with you?" she asked indignantly.

Pembroke smiled again. "You've convinced me. Seriously, it's the only way. You must see that."

A cold chill settled over her. "And where do you propose to take me?"

"North across the Santee. Here's Jaudon with your horse. I hope you'll mount by yourself. I'd hate to have my men put you into the saddle, but I'd have to."

She said dully, "It seems that I have no choice."

"That's sensible of you."

"But it is late. I am tired. Now in a cart—"

"No. We go through the Santee swamps and a cart would bog down ten yards from here."

She clasped her hands. "No! Not through the swamps. I've seen them. We'd all be lost."

"I've men who know the country. You'll be safe. Now mount, please. I've waited longer than I should have. Our shots may have been heard." He touched his helmet and moved off.

Dorande looked at her horse, a gentle-eyed bay, and gathered her skirts. Her hand met a wide rip and her thoughts raced. She called, "Captain Pembroke! My sea chest."

He stopped, frowning. "What of it?"

"There—by those rocks!"

"Sorry. We've no way of carrying it."

"My clothes! This dress will tear in the swamps!"

"Can't be helped! Oh, the devil! Choose what you can carry rolled and strapped to your saddle. That's all!"

She knelt by the chest, opened it. There were capes and dresses of blue, of green, of yellow. There was an East India shawl with a feathery pattern. She found fine, lace-trimmed underwear, silk stockings and slippers. She thought, "This I *must* take—and this—"

Pembroke called sharply, "We want to start."

In desperation she spread out the shawl, rolled her stoutest clothes in it. Her guard, hovering close, caught up the bundle and lashed it to the pommel. Dorande bent over the chest again. There was the dress that her mother had designed and had made for her to wear to the Governor's Ball in Curaçao the coming winter. A slave girl had smuggled it to her in the jungles and she had taken it on to Havana, sewn in waterproof cloth along with matching stockings and slippers. Her fingers caressed the cloth, rich brown silk, shot with gold. She caught the rich stuff to her. She couldn't leave it. The shawl would hold no more. From the road, Pembroke called again and her fingers tightened about the dress. She would have to leave it, trailing out of the open chest with the rest of her wardrobe.

A big deerskin sack plopped on the ground beside her, its mouth puckered by rawhide strings. Who had dropped it? It might have been any one of the three men now moving toward the road. She called her thanks huskily, but they did not look back. Eagerly she crammed her things into it, made a loop of the drawstrings, slipped the bag about her neck and mounted, feeling almost cheerful at her salvage.

Pembroke called something from the road and flames began to lick through the dry wood of the captured carts.

The column started and Dorande followed, looking nervously ahead through the gathering dusk that was lit up by the carts. She was heading straight for the horrible swamps that edged the south bank of the Santee. In the lead, beyond the captured horses, a single guide rode, threading his way from hummock to hummock. Her own mount stepped daintily on, hoofs coming clear and sure out of squelchy ground. Right and left, greasy pools gleamed livid and she was sure that they stirred with unwholesome life.

Then she rode among cypresses, their branches heavy with moss and roots gleaming and sticky. She concentrated on the horse just ahead, fearful of being left behind or straying into some bog hole. The trail bent and she saw Pembroke's white coat ahead. The sight gave her odd comfort which she choked back indignantly. "I do *not* wish to see him again," she told herself. "I need only require that I am sheltered and fed. Just the same, it would be only polite of him to come back and see how I do!"

The trees grew thicker. She ducked low to avoid branches that slapped and flicked at her. Then there were no more trees, just the slow roll of the Santee and the procession heading for the swamps of the north bank. Her wiry guard rode up beside her and she asked, "How long do we ride?"

"Ample."

"We go to a town, then?" She clutched at the comforting bulk of the deerskin bag. "You know its name?"

"If we was goin' to a town and it had a name, I'd know it."

Her chin puckered. "What? You mean we stay in the swamps?"

"No swamps. We're goin' to a place out of the old times. Folks call it Chilyon's Castle."

He fell back a little and Dorande's horse moved through the shallow ford. Something, she could not make out what, had reassured her. Of course. The name. It brought a picture to her mind of thick stone walls, wide rooms and deep fireplaces. Chilyon's. Chilyon's Castle. There she would be safe under high towers where bright banners fluttered and men-at-arms patrolled the battlements. She could close her eyes and see it, high on a rocky bluff, towers and donjon and barbican and wide gate with armored horsemen riding into its shelter.

Her eyes grew heavy and she swayed in the saddle. Her guard steadied her. "Best stay awake, ma'am," he said. "You'd make an elegant meal for a 'gator if you tumbled and maybe a water moccasin or two'd want to say hello." She blinked and sat upright. The northern swamps were near. Once across them, Chilyon's Castle must lie close.

II • Chilyon's Castle

Ross Pembroke rode on through the night behind the captured horses. The swamp growth was thick and a heavy mist rose, evil and clinging, from rank pools and streams. His coat was molded to him in a sticky pulp and the trailing plume of his helmet was sodden with the touch of the mist. High beyond the treetops a sickly moon shone, filling the marshy world with an eerie shimmer that clung to the weeping falls of Spanish moss.

He stirred impatiently in the saddle. There was little for him to do as the column could only follow the guide, Jim Nesmith, through the unhealthy gleam of the night. Fatigue was heavy on him, bone-deep across his shoulders and along his legs, a cumulative weariness that had begun with that first march of the Rhode Island Army to the siege of Boston in 1775. Each rolling month had contributed. Long Island, the British flanking movement and the miraculous escape across the East River in the boats of Glover's Marbleheaders; the retreat up Manhattan, through the Jerseys, through Pennsylvania. There was scarcely a major action of the Continental Line that he had not seen, from the smoky chaos about the stone houses of Germantown to the echoing thickets of Freeman's Farm where Burgoyne's red and blue files had crumbled away under a torrent of musketry.

Perhaps he had seen too much, first as an officer of the Rhode Island Line and then with the Continental Dragoons. Fatigue dulled the honest satisfaction of victory and poulticed the sting of defeat with apathy. He had shrugged away the Franco-American failure at Savannah and accepted his capture by Scottish infantry just before Lincoln's surrender at Charleston with resignation that was close to indifference. Perhaps his escape was due more to the foul conditions of captivity than to an urge to return to action. Why did he keep up the fight, leader of this partisan band that had begun with five escapees below the Georgia border and, gathering recruits, had rolled north across three great rivers? Perhaps it was a mere mechanical resumption of the only life he had known since 1775.

The swamp mists, heavy with rot, filled his lungs and he felt a sudden, keen longing for the clean, sharp air of Rhode Island. There the yellow, fanlighted house that looked from Mount Hope Point to the islands of Narragansett Bay would be basking in thin moonlight, its windows dark. In the library, moonbeams would be striking on his father's thick Bible, touching the illuminated parchment strip that marked the old man's place. Sister Judith, plump and blond, would be sleeping in the east chamber, across from sister Cora. In the broad west room, one or two cats would be tight-curled at his father's feet in the carved four-poster, knowing that their master would not stir until the sun touched the gray houses of Prudence Island, across Bristol Sound. Or was his picture true? He had had no word of his family since late 1779. The old house might be a heap of charred timbers in the brisk fall night. His father might be dead, his sisters married or seeking safety in Boston or Worcester.

He tried to fix his mind on the present, but vivid pictures flooded it. A winter dawn along the marshes by Popasquash Point, fowling piece under his arm and his dog Hardy circling on a scent. A cool June noon, with sun lying warm on the bricks of Brown College on its hill above Providence, and his father helping his sisters from the chaise on Ross's Graduation Day. Marching with the Kentish Guards, proud of the new uniform and trying to appear stern while black-haired Sally Hopkins waved from the balcony of her father's house, and other neighbors . . .

Raoul trotted up, an unreal figure in the milky haze. "I've been thinking about that girl, Ross."

Ross, recalled abruptly to the present, grunted, "You and the rest of the column. What about her?"

"Maybe she'd better ride up here with us."

"No. The less I see of her the better. If I'd talked ten seconds longer to her, I'd have escorted her to Nelson's Ferry myself. Hell and death! What are we going to do with her?"

"Maybe you ought to have sent her back with the dragoons," said Raoul.

"With them? She'd have been raped by the first man who got his breath back. She'd be in a swamp now with her throat cut."

"Reckon so," said Raoul. "Think she's really got an uncle up the Congaree? I only heard the tail end of what she was telling you."

"Probably she has. Ever hear the name? It's Paul St Aubin."

"St. Aubin," Raoul repeated. "Can't quite place it, but it keeps buzzing in my head. There's something about him—something unpleasant, but just what I'm blasted if I can remember. None of our business, though. We've got to find some way of passing her along."

"Yes," said Ross, frowning. "And there's another thing that bothers me. When she gets to him, she's going to be fizzing like a bomb with a live fuse. I guess her people are pretty important down in the Islands. Traders, I guess, not government officials, but she's used to being obeyed. To her, we're banditti and she'll probably march straight to Lord Rawdon and devil him until he sets the whole Royal army after us, just to keep her quiet."

Raoul said grimly, "We could do enough damage to make it worth while, if Rawdon ever caught up with us."

Ross laid a hand on his shoulder. "The first thing you've got to do is find that wife of yours. After that, you can challenge Cornwallis himself. Any idea where to look for her?"

Raoul's shoulders slumped and he shook his head. "Haven't heard from her since before Charleston fell. She may be held as hostage. She may have gotten away and found friends in the interior or even in North Carolina—that is, if Tarleton and Wemyss have left any of our friends alive." He shook himself. "No. Janet must be all right. I'll find her. Let's get back to that girl. She's concerned about getting lost, down there at the tail of the column."

"Then send her up the line. She can ride just behind the tackies. Hi! Who's that coming toward us?"

A wavering figure rode out of the mist. "It's me—Joe Frierson. Nesmith sent me back. He's spotted a fire near Chilyon's Castle. We're getting close."

"Does Jim know of anyone being around these parts?"

"No. That's why he sent me back. He wants to halt till he finds out about that fire."

Ross clucked to his mount. "He can halt. I'll go up with you and see what's happening. Raoul, take charge till I come back. Send word for Miss van Kortenaer to move up."

Ross rode up on a tongue of solid land, Frierson explaining, "Short cut. The rest'll keep to the swamps. Beats me how Jim knows this trail. Five feet right or left and we'd have been belly deep."

They found Nesmith waiting by a myrtle thicket. There was no need to point. Off to the north a bright, pulsing spot showed. Now and then it vanished, to reappear strong as ever. "Folks passing between us and it," observed Nesmith.

Ross leaned his arms on his pommel. "That fire might be a bad sign for us."

"Sure could tickle our ribs. Swamp trail curves toward it."

Ross frowned, then said quickly, "Frierson, hit back and keep the column halted till you hear from me. Want to look at that fire with me, Jim?"

"Don't mind if I do. You'd mind if I didn't. We'll be riding mean land in the dark."

It seemed to Ross that they were riding into a dense black wall, for the moon had gone back of clouds, but Nesmith's horse went steadily ahead. There were steep pitches of turf, sharp climbs and abrupt turns so that the fire showed to the right, to the left, sometimes almost in the rear. But each time the course straightened, there was the fire, dead ahead.

A voice sounded in the darkness, a dry, melancholy voice with a hint of a stutter. "Pass, friend," it said.

Nesmith checked so sharply that Ross cannoned into him. Ross whipped out a pistol, but Nesmith dismounted, chuckling, "Burn me, Moses! If it ain't Peter Horry."

A tall, gangling man moved nearer. "That you, Jim?" he asked as though Nesmith's presence were the most natural thing in the world. "Who's with you?"

"Soldier. Some boys are waiting below with some truck we took off an upcountry convoy. All right to bring 'em in?"

"I won't stop you," said the tall man sadly.

Nesmith mounted. "I'll get 'em. Look after my soldier and see he don't get lost in the dark." He rode away into the black night.

Ross felt a wave of suspicion. Nesmith had been with him since they crossed the Georgia border and seemed trustworthy. Yet the appearance of Horry was almost too pat. He passaged his horse away from the man.

"Better put that pistol away," said Horry. "If the boys by the fire are all right, it's not needed. If they aren't, it won't help."

Pistol still out, Ross said, "How do I know what 'all right' means to you?"

More doleful than ever, the other said, "My name ought to tell you. We're a big family, but so far's I know, no Horry's declared for the King. As a rule, we declare against him, sort of emphatic."

Ross thought of the Carolinians whom he had met. "Do you know George Horry Bonneau?" he asked.

"George's part cousin and part nephew to me. Don't know which he's more of."

Ross put away his pistol, dismounting. "I knew him in the

prison hulks. I remember his telling about his family. Horry. Of course. I ought to have known. I'm Ross Pembroke, late of General Lincoln's staff."

"You were in the hulks and got out?" asked Horry, as though commiserating. "Well, some do and some don't. Come up to the fire. It'll be some time before our boys get here."

As they walked on, Ross said, "How could you recognize Nesmith in the dark?"

Horry chuckled. "I saw your horses against the sky, so I knew you had to be friends. Far as I know there isn't a King's man with a mount like yours. They say even Cornwallis rides a tacky. Must be all good horses favor the Colonies, because they like to hang around where we are. We keep them in swamps that no Britisher knows and where no Tory'd dare come."

As they neared the fire, a dozen men, dressed and equipped much like those who followed Ross, looked up. Horry called, "All right, boys. This is Ross Pembroke, just out of the Carolina hulks."

Ross dismounted. A weedy, undersized man, whose face was thin and drawn under a battered infantry cap, stood close by. Ross tossed him the reins. "Mind looking after my horse?" he asked.

The man took the bridle. "Don't mind."

Ross looked more closely at him, saw a silver crescent on the cap plate. "Been with the 2nd South Carolina?"

"Some," said the man as he led the horse away, walking with an odd gait that was half spraddle and half limp as though an old injury had bent his anklebones outward. Ross watched him uncertainly. "He knows how to look after a horse, I suppose?" he said to Horry.

Horry's voice lost something of its melancholy. "I suppose he does. Sit by the fire. We've only got sweet potatoes, but you're welcome to a share."

"Thanks," said Ross. "We're loaded with stuff we took from a convoy and we'll issue anything your men need."

Horry sat by the fire, taking off a cocked hat that was too small for him. His face was broad and marked with down-running lines that matched his sad, stuttering voice. "Where are you trending from here?" he asked, settling into a tangle of long arms and legs.

"Just following out a plan we made after we got out of the prison hulks."

"Now I'd like to hear about that plan." The lines of Horry's face sagged lower.

Ross flicked bits of bark into the fire. "It sounds simple enough. So far it's been simple. Jaudon and I decided, as soon as we got clear, that just being out of the hulks wasn't enough. We decided to work north. Jaudon's South Carolina, and he's looking, first of all, for his wife. When he finds her, then he'll get into the fight again. I hope he'll keep on north with me, after that."

"North's a mighty big place. Couldn't you sort of point to the slice of it that you're aiming for?"

Ross shrugged. "I wish I could. Anyway, it's the slice where Washington's army is. I want to serve with the dragoons again. In particular, I want to serve under a Virginian I knew in the Jerseys. His name's Lee—Light Horse Harry Lee, they call him."

Horry glanced at him curiously. "So just the two of you started from clear down in Georgia?"

Ross nodded. "Just the two of us, at first. But right away we ran into other men who'd escaped or who'd belonged to units that had been broken up or just fallen to pieces. And it seemed that each man we met knew someone else who thought the way we did. When we had enough men, we headed north. We picked up horses here and there from Whig plantations. Some people had arms hidden and turned them over to us. We were lucky enough to strike a British convoy or two and got plenty of equipment and ammunition and rations from them."

Other men came closer to the fire and Ross saw the silver crescent of the little horse holder hovering diffidently in the background. Horry hugged his knees. "That's as good a piece of work as I've heard of. You started with nothing and then kneaded sort of an army out of it. Figure on all the boys going clear through with you?"

"Most of them, I hope. A few have dropped out already, but I expected that. I knew that all they wanted was to get near their homes. As for the rest—well, I've got no way of *making* them come with me. They picked me to lead them, I suppose, because I'd seen more service than the rest. But they could depose me tomorrow if they wanted to."

"M'm," said Horry thoughtfully. "You've mapped out a long road. I haven't heard just where the main army is, but I reckon it's clear up near the Jerseys. Now that seems a powerful long way to go for a fight when you could find ample right here."

"No," said Ross. "As far as I can make out, it's all over down here. There's no organized force in the field and the

British hold every major post in a big arc from Ninety-six to Georgetown."

Horry's big head sagged. "They sure do."

"There's another thing. Your people down here seem to have given up. Cornwallis has about as many Tory regiments as British. Then there's something else that I wouldn't have believed if I hadn't seen it in the Charleston papers. Congress has given up the states south of Virginia. We've lost two armies here in less than a year and Congress'll never risk a third. You've had some wonderful partisan leaders down here. Let me see, I've heard of Sumter and Pickens and—oh yes—Marion, Francis Marion. Where are they now, for example?"

"Where—where indeed?" echoed Horry sepulchrally.

"You see my point? The fight's going on. But not here. It's going to be won. But not here. That's why my intention's for Virginia and the north. As I see it, my reasoning's true."

The man with the silver crescent came closer. "Part of it *was* true. Now it isn't," he said in a tight voice.

Ross turned to Horry. "Does he know what he's talking about?" he asked in a low tone.

The lines on Horry's face deepened. "He's kind of apt to. He's Francis Marion."

"Good God!" exclaimed Ross.

Horry made room for Marion. "This is Ross Pembroke from Rhode Island, Francis. You've met his horse."

Ross tingled with embarrassment. He had taken Francis Marion for a hostler, had carelessly tossed him the reins! Yet why not? This frail, undersized man *could* not be the partisan leader whom British and Tories dreaded. He remembered having heard British officers curse him, had heard whispers that a man bringing Marion, dead or alive, to any British post would collect more gold sovereigns than most men saw in a lifetime. He got to his feet quickly and Marion held out a small hand, a boy's hand, saying, "Let me know what I can do for you."

Ross stammered his excuses. "Had no idea—please overlook—"

Marion smiled and Ross was struck with the warmth that lighted up the gaunt, almost wasted face. "Your horse needed to be taken. I was nearest." He stepped back, sat on a stump behind Horry, who was gazing mournfully into the fire.

Still shaken by his error, Ross said doggedly, "You hold that I'm wrong, Colonel Marion. I'd be glad to know why."

Marion pulled a tattered cloak about him. "Tell him, Peter."

Horry twisted his arms about his knees. "Well, let's take your points, one by one. First, you say the war's over down here." He talked on in his sad voice with its hint of a stammer. The war was very close to lost. It always had been. True, the British controlled the major posts and ports. But men were rising inside and outside the great arc. There was Marion, as Ross could see, deep in supposedly British territory. In the north, Sumter was stirring. Beyond the mountains, John Sevier and Isaac Shelby were gathering men. Bratton and Brandon were astir, and in the Williamsburg district John James of the Lake was rallying the patriots.

Ross listened closely, but his eyes were on Marion. Yes, the colonel was frail and undersized. His face, lined and swarthy, could be called ugly. But the steady black eyes suggested fierce but controlled fires, steadfast purpose and, above all, command.

Horry's voice rolled on. Yes, the upcountry people had been for the King, or at best neutral to the patriots. Upland and lowland, many people had grown discouraged and made the best terms they could with the Crown. Now it was different. The Crown had tried to force everyone into the Royal units, or be held traitor with life and property forfeited, regardless of previous commitments. And worse, British and Tory forces under Tarleton and Wemyss and Bloody Bill Cunningham were ranging the whole state, burning, pillaging, slaughtering, making little distinction between Rebel and Tory. Families had been burned out from the Enoree to the Salkehatchie and beyond. Tarleton had turned his troops loose on men who had tried to surrender, as in the massacre of Sumter's men at LeNud's, or of Buford's up in the Waxhaws. Men had come to see that the protection hinging on an oath of allegiance meant nothing, and were flocking to Sevier and Pickens and Sumter.

Horry hunched his knees closer. Ross had mentioned Tory regiments. There were many of them, but their men came from Connecticut and New York and New Jersey. Others, like the Volunteers of Ireland, had been recruited on the Philadelphia waterfront. The only South Carolina units were Browne's and Innes's, now that Lisle's whole command had gone over to Pickens. No, the war which always was and always would be almost lost was really beginning. Post by post, the British would be harried till they fell back down the Santee, down to Dorchester and Monck's Corner and to Charleston itself.

Horry stopped abruptly.

Ross said, "But you've been cut adrift by Congress. Don't forget that."

Without looking from the fire, Marion said, "No. Not adrift."

"But that Resolution," urged Ross.

Marion glanced at Horry, who took up the story again. "Yes, we saw that Resolution. Kind of strong, wasn't it? And it ought to have been, seeing it was written right in Miles Brewton's house in Charleston. No, sir! Nothing like that ever slid out of a goosequill in Philadelphia. We've got ways of knowing."

"Then we've got a chance!" exclaimed Ross.

"Sure," agreed Horry. "Always had."

From the edge of the fire a man called, "Cade Logan's bringing someone in."

Ross jumped up. "That ought to be Jim Nesmith and the rest."

Hoofs drummed closer through the night and Nesmith rode up, hatless and white of face. He panted hoarsely, "Freneau has run off with all the pack horses and some of your men."

Ross braced himself, then shouted, "Ran where?"

"God knows. A few got away with Jaudon and McKinstry, but most lit off with the pack horses and the spare tackies. Jaudon's on his way up here."

"I didn't hear any shots," snapped Ross.

"Happened too quick. Freneau and Case were the leaders. They ran the horses off quick and then set an ambush when the rest of us came up. We couldn't hit 'em. It'd have been murder—for us."

Ross hunched his shoulders, then said in a flat voice, "Nothing we can do. We can't run them down in the swamps."

"Not with Freneau leading, we can't. And that ain't all. They got the gal with 'em."

"Girl?" asked Marion quickly.

"Yes, a gal. Realest goddam gal I ever seen, too."

Marion rose. "Shall we get her, boys? Show hands."

Ross stared as hands shot up in the half-light. Marion called, "Peter, choose ten men. That's enough for what you've got to do."

Horry rose. "Wouldn't mind a bit, Francis, if you'd sort of point me in the right direction."

"I'll send a guide with you," said Marion.

"Me?" echoed Nesmith. "How'll I know where Freneau'll head in?"

"He won't keep his old course, so he'll have to swing south."

"South's a hell of a big place," grumbled Nesmith.

"Half a mile back you passed a big white stone," said Marion.

"I marked it."

"Break through the brush at its right to solid ground. Keep east two miles. Then wait."

"What the hell for?" asked Nesmith. "The Angel Gabriel?"

"For Freneau," snapped Marion. "His course will curve him right back to you."

"Maybe he'll lie up a day and play with the gal."

Horry shook his head. "Put yourself in his place. He'll keep going till sunup, making for some place he knows. He won't stop."

"You ain't seen that gal," protested Nesmith. "Most would tarry in a burnin' house with her."

Marion turned away. "Get her," he said.

Ross said, "I'm going with you."

As the detail filed out, Ross pushed up beside Horry. "What chance have we got of catching Freneau? My God, what that girl must be going through. She'd had enough for one day without adding this. Do you really think we'll find her?"

"You heard Francis say to wait until Freneau dropped into our laps. He'll drop. Better trot now. Nesmith's getting ahead of us."

Far off to the right, Dorande heard the sound of splashes and the crackle of bushes as Freneau and his men faded away through the night. Her horse stood in a pool of water between two trees whose skeleton branches reached menacingly at her. A few feet away, her guard lay dead, head and shoulders under water. Beyond him lay the man whom Freneau had shot for insisting that she be dragged along.

She passed her fingers over her eyes as horror crept over her. From the sodden ground and dark-glinting water, whorls and spirals of mist rose with a rank smell of decay. She drew an uneven breath and called, "Captain Pembroke! *Ohé,* Captain Pembroke!" The swamp stifled her voice as though the ghost-trees about her were too sodden to return an echo. Horror turned to sharp panic which she fought back. Where were the others? Somehow, the shifty Freneau had managed to lose the rear of the column, to let it blunder on, unaware in the darkness that the pack horses were no longer in the lead.

The first hint of danger had come when a man had ridden up and thrown a damp arm about her. Freneau had wheeled, cursed the unknown rider, saying that the loaded horses were worth a hundred women. Then a pistol shot had cracked, followed by the sound of many hoofs beating swiftly away in the night, leaving her in a haunted morass with two dead men at her feet.

She began to tremble, and gave a faint, whimpering sound which she tried to stifle by biting her wrist. That log, there at the edge of the dead pool to the left! The pool was not dead. Its surface broke in oily ripples as the log floated slowly forward, and a heavy musky smell rose through the swamp reek. Earlier, the unclean swamp life had been frightened away by the passage of many men and horses. But now —the live log drifted nearer.

Her mount whinnied in sudden terror and plunged forward. Dorande, thrown half out of the saddle, clung to its neck, straining to regain her seat as the log moved faster. She was back in the saddle, bent low as the horse lunged on, bursting through bushes, caroming off slimy trunks.

She set her teeth and let the reins hang loose. Wherever the horse went, she would go, rather than set foot in the swamp. Once or twice she heard the hoofs thud on solid ground, but the next few strides brought with them the suck and splash of the evil swamp. Branches whipped at her hands and face. Ankle, knee and thigh were bruised. But the horse kept on, galloping where the ground was firm, fighting on through the mire. Once it struggled nearly shoulder deep and rank water churned about Dorande's feet and she turned sick with dread as the swamp reached for her. Then with a great heave the horse moved forward, rising a little higher, sinking back, rising, and at last standing fetlock-deep in mud.

Dorande, panting, looked about her, dreading to see more· log-like bodies rippling toward her. The horse threw back its head and started once more. The trees were sparser now and vague light showed a hint of white skin through ragged cloth above her knee. What did it matter? She was alone in a swamp that spread to the ends of the world and back. In another world, men watched from the high towers of Chilyon's Castle. But that had nothing to do with the dark and fetid evils crowding around her.

Something soft bumped her knees and she threw out her hand, fingers closing on smooth deerskin. The dress and the slippers! She clutched the bag tighter, as if it were a talisman that would lead her from the haunted swamps into a bright, dry world.

She sniffed the air. There was deep blackness all about, but it was dry and sweeter. She checked her mount and sat listening. Her heart beat hard and fast as though it would shake her breasts and shoulders. She could hear nothing. She gave the horse its head and knew that its hoofs bit into honest turf. She was on a slope where boulders loomed vaguely. Deep relief swept over her. Rocks and dry ground! Rocks? Her eyes, accustomed to the night, caught movement ahead. As she swerved away, a man called, "That you, Jake? Find her?"

Dorande made out a tall man just ahead. She tried to steady her voice. "Stay where you are or I shoot!"

There was a whistle of surprise. "By God, it *must* be her!"

"I tell you, I shoot," she called again.

The man spoke soothingly. "You're safe. Some of the boys are out looking for you. How'd you get away from Freneau?"

"You knew about me?" Her hand was raised as though it held a pistol.

"Sure. Nesmith and a soldier named Pembroke rode up here. Then they heard Freneau's lit and figured Freneau'd take you, too. The boys went to change his mind."

"That soldier—he is here?"

"No. Went off with the rest to argue some with Freneau."

Dorande checked an odd feeling of pleasure by telling herself that Pembroke would have been after the pack horses, not a girl. She kept her hand up. "You say 'with the rest.' Who are they?"

"Marion's men, and you must be tired holding your hand up like that, being as there's nothing in it."

Her hand fell to the pommel. Marion! She had heard a Francis Marion cursed by British and Tories on the way to the Santee. A sly, crafty bandit chief, they had told her. What sort of country had she come to? Why hadn't St. Aubin's letter to Havana warned her?

The man, keeping his distance, spoke again. "Better come talk to the colonel."

"The colonel?"

"Uh-huh. Colonel Marion. He's kind of fretted about you."

She laughed shortly. "No doubt, since he knows nothing of me. Where am I?"

" 'Bout half a holler from Chilyon's Castle. I'll walk ahead. Your horse'll follow right enough."

Dorande struggled against wild laughter. The ride across the Santee and its swamps! Now an unknown man in the dark said she was near Chilyon's Castle! There was nothing but the open night ahead and the half-seen man. Suddenly she took comfort from the very thought of the Castle. Any moment she might see its high walls and turrets rising through the night before her.

She saw a faint glow of a fire and her horse stepped cautiously through a gap in crumbling, earthen mounds, topped by rotting stockades that began nowhere and ended nowhere. The light was brighter and she rode onto a stretch of level ground where men were pitching wood onto fires. She pulled up sharply. "The Castle! I demand to be taken to Chilyon's Castle."

The man looked back over his shoulder. "This is it, just where old Rupert Chilyon built it, fifty years ago, for the Indian trade."

The pictured fortress vanished and she looked at the level ground rimmed by useless earthworks and at the ragged men, much like those who had captured her. Her guide shouted, "She rode right up the hill out the swamp. Reckon her horse must have smelled ours and made tracks to 'em."

Dorande could only sit with the ruins of her mental picture, one hand clutching the deerskin bag for such solace as it might give. A small man came quickly toward her with a swaying limp. "I'm Colonel Francis Marion," he said in a tight voice as though little given to speaking. "Are you all right?"

"Quite, thank you," said Dorande wearily. She looked down at the slight man with his dented cap, faded red coat and little, rusty sword. A colonel! How could *he* ever help her on the road to the Congaree? Her eyebrows arched as she surveyed him.

"You're lucky to have come through the swamp," said Marion. "Tell us how we can serve you." The blaze leaped higher and Dorande made out a silver crescent and the words "Liberty or Death" on the cap's plate. Then she noted the dark face, the piercing black eyes. It was a face that could be hard in anger but now, to her surprise, she read genuine concern for herself. Her horse turned and her eye caught white flesh showing through her torn skirt. She said, blushing, "First I wish—I mean—my clothes—I came through the swamp."

Marion caught up a cloak and a blanket from the ground and led her mount to the deep shadow of the earthworks, where he handed her the bundle. "You'll find me by the fire," he said, and walked quickly away.

Dorande's aching knees nearly gave way as she dropped to the ground and draped the old blanket, kilt-like, about her hips. Her lips quivered as she saw the torn blue of her skirt hanging in festoons. She looped these up as best she could and threw the large cloak about her, tucking the deerskin bag under it.

The men about the fire vanished discreetly, leaving her alone with the little colonel, who waved her to a stump. "Sit here, ma'am. Are you hungry?"

She was suddenly aware of a great faintness. "At—at noon I ate."

Marion raked two sweet potatoes out of the ashes and laid them, flanked by a wooden spoon, on a slab of bark. "We have nothing else," he said, handing her the crude plate.

No butter, no salt. Her throat tightened at the first taste. She couldn't eat. Yet she must eat. She plied her spoon as bravely as she could. All at once she found that the potato skins were empty. As she put aside the bark, Marion smiled down at her. "Once more—what may we do for you?"

She looked at him in surprise. "You do not even ask who I am?"

"You've been in trouble. That's enough."

Dorande found herself telling about her weary flight from St. Eusebius to Havana and Georgetown, of the arrangements that had been made for her to wait with her uncle until her parents could come for her.

"Could have waited in Havana," observed Marion.

She spread her small hands. "There was fever, and I knew no one but my father's bankers. Up the Congaree is my mother's brother. And more, my father thought the chance better of their shipping to Charleston than Havana."

"I see. Now you want to go to your uncle, Paul St. Aubin, you say."

"You will send me?" asked Dorande, her confidence growing.

"I can send you to his plantation. But he's not there."

"You know him, then?"

"I've not met him."

Her eyes widened. "How, then, can you say, here in the swamps, that he's absent?"

"I've ways of knowing. He's in Georgia."

"Send me there, Colonel."

Marion's eyes were somber. "You wouldn't like where he is. But he'll come back to the Congaree. In the meantime, I can send you to kin of mine. I'll get word to St. Aubin's servants, and if everything is all right, you can go on to his plantation."

Dorande straightened. "And why should not everything be all right?"

"Things happen in Carolina. You may have noticed it."

"Ah, this war! I do not wish to hear about it."

Marion smiled grimly. "That's how I've felt since '75. But the war wants to be heard about. Now my suggestion? Does it suit you?"

She shrugged. "What else may I hope for?"

"Anything better that's in my power."

"And where are your kin?"

"In the High Hills of Santee." He rose quickly. "You're tried. Sleep on what I told you and we'll talk again in the morning."

Dorande looked with sudden apprehension about the camp. "I sleep? Here?"

"There's high ground beyond those trees. We rigged a lean-to when we heard you might be coming in. You'll be in a hollow, out of eyeshot. There's a fire lit and a spring close by. You'll be safe as in a castle."

She said gravely, "I haven't thanked you for what you do for me. You said I was lucky. I agree."

He shook his head. "If you were only lucky, you'd still be in the swamps. Luck met courage in you, and here you are. I wish you good night." He bowed, his cap tucked under his arm.

Later, Dorande lay on a bed of pine boughs, her clothes drying by the embers. She felt relaxed and safe. Her eyelids fluttered and sank. In her mind she saw the silvered plate above the keen black eyes. The image blurred, spreading the silver until it became full armor. The walls of the lean-to slowly funneled into high towers, stretched on and on in thick walls where bright banners flew. Safe behind the battlements of Chilyon's Castle, Dorande van Kortenaer slept, her cheek pillowed on the deerskin bag.

Ross Pembroke, bare to the waist and his white jacket over his arm, walked at dawn through the crumbling works of Rupert Chilyon's old trading post, the stir of the wakening camp in his ears. He surveyed himself ruefully. His trouser knees were split and there were sinister dark stains on his jacket, the freshest reminding him that Freneau no longer lived. The whole affair had not gone too badly. Most of the horses now switched their tails off to the right. Twelve of his original twenty-five men had reported with Jaudon. And the girl! She must have stumbled by rare good fortune up to Chilyon's.

There was high ground ahead of him and he ran toward it in search of a spring, his shaving kit in his hand. A hoarse voice bellowed at him and he saw a man, with most of the thrums missing from his hunting shirt, waving at him. Ross called shortly, "I'm just going to shave." He moved nearer the crest, could make out a clump of oaks, the brown of a tent.

The guard puffed up to him. "No higher. Marion's orders."

"Why not?" asked Ross.

"Don't know. Just orders."

Over the crest, a girl's voice called, "Oh, please! No!" Startled, Ross saw Dorande, bright hair falling over the cloak that muffled her, skimming toward the tent. Her bare feet twinkled as she ran and a towel flapped over one arm. Before Ross could mutter an apology, she had reached the tent, where she paused, smiled at him over her shoulder, a small hand fluttering in a wave. Then she was gone. The guard scraped his stubby chin. "Maybe *that's* why. Think likely it was me she waved at? Gals always did favor me."

"Must have been to you. There's a spring up there?"

"She was comin' from it. There's another beyond the horses."

At the second spring, Ross washed and shaved. As he hunched into his coat, he tried to recapture the image of the impish smile that the girl had tossed to him. He grumbled, "No shave, my clothes in rags. I must have looked like a Weekapaug scarecrow to her. Ten to one she didn't recognize me." He walked on past groups of men grooming horses, tending fires or shaking out blankets. Then he saw Marion bent over a bark plate by the earthworks. The colonel looked up as Ross approached. "Join me, Captain. Horry told me you'd turned all the pack horses over to us. No need. Just give us twenty-four hours' rations."

Ross took a plate heaped with dried beef and a mug that Marion handed him. "They're yours, I think. Your men recaptured them."

"I've no claim. I thank you, though."

Ross sat down, sniffing the steam from the hot beef. Then he raised his mug, noting gratefully that the contents were deeply amber. "Your health, Colonel." He sipped, then spluttered. "Good God! It tastes like vinegar."

"It *is* vinegar," said Marion. "I incline to it."

Ross set the mug carefully aside. "Do you mind telling me why we found you waiting for us at Chilyon's?"

"Just happened. I'm apt to happen in a lot of places."

"I see, Colonel. Next, can you tell me why so many left me? They weren't all in Freneau's plan."

"It happens." Marion sipped his vinegar and water. "I never count my men. No use. Some come along because they're going my way. Others for what they can pick up, for safety or for spying on me. When they get what they want, they melt."

"So a lot of men just used me for a convoy."

"Likely," said Marion, mug in hand. "I should tell you that I made bold to issue rations from your stock to Miss van Kortenaer."

"Made bold? She gets her share as long as she's with us."

"She's not with you. I'm sending her to kin of mine, if she wants to go."

Ross stiffened. "*You're* sending her? Damn it, she was in the convoy that *I* captured."

"You waived claim to the horses. Do you put her below them?"

"N-no," said Ross, remembering the smile and the wave.

"She can go with you if she wants, Captain. She'll be easier where I say."

Ross shrugged. "You know the country. I don't."

"The High Hills of Santee. Northwest from here. South from Camden, on the Wateree."

"Hold on!" protested Ross. "Camden's in British territory."

"So's Chilyon's. Haven't seen any British here, though."

Ross said reluctantly, "I suppose your way's best."

"Some would say so. You'll have to go way north of Virginia to find the main army. What would you do with her when you got there? Ask General Washington for an escort to take her back to the Congaree?"

"Hardly. But I do feel responsible for her."

Marion stifled a smile. "Naturally."

"Just the same, north is my aim, whether the army's in Pennsylvania or the Jerseys. That's where the fighting will be. I'll recruit men as I go. Maybe some of yours would join me."

"Under no oath to me," observed Marion, tossing his bark plate into the fire.

"Then you don't care if I talk to them?"

"You'd get none. And I reckon that the Carolinians who came with you will stay with me."

Ross flushed. "They all know me pretty well by now. What makes you think they'd leave me?"

Marion pushed back his skullcap. "I've a wonderful recruiting officer. The enemy."

"I realize that. From what Horry said, things must be very bad, but—"

Marion's dark face showed relief as Peter Horry ambled

up to the fire. "Tell Pembroke more about what's been happening, Peter," he said with a sigh.

"Happening?" Horry folded his long body in sections and looked dolefully at the fire. "Let's hold a quizzing glass up to the Pee Dee country. It's nice, up there. Or it was. Then Wemyss of the 63rd got tired of seeing it so nice and cut a path seventy miles long and fifteen wide. You won't find much in it now. Just burned houses. Bodies hanging to trees. All the sheep dead. All the looms smashed. Sheep and looms mean food and clothes. A lot of heads of families are dead. Women and children are still there, and winter's coming." His mock-melancholy had dropped completely from him. "And that's just one part of the state."

Ross stared into the embers. "Is it as bad in other parts?"

"Worse in some, not much better in others. In Charleston, the British seized over thirty of our leaders, men on parole like Chris Gadsden, Alex Moultrie and Ed Rutledge. They're all in a dungeon at St. Augustine in the Floridas."

"I see," said Ross slowly. "It's worse than anything I've known, even in the Jerseys."

Marion spoke tersely. "You've served there?"

"About everywhere from the siege of Boston to Chilyon's Castle."

"Continental commission?" asked Marion.

"Rhode Island, then Continental. I came down here to join Lincoln's staff after the siege of Savannah. Officially, I'm on command from the 3rd Continental Dragoons." He pushed back his helmet. "I thought I'd seen about everything, but this is a new war, a bad war. What the devil are those people going to do? No houses, no sheep, no looms and winter coming. Who did you say did all that? Wemyss? I think I've heard the name."

"Might have," said Marion. "Major Wemyss of His Majesty's 63rd, but heading a vicious lot of Tories. He's like Colonel Tarleton of Cornwallis's cavalry. Maybe worse. He burns and kills and pillages for the joy of it, it seems. You see now why most of your Carolinians, having a free choice, will stay with me?"

"Of course."

"Then how about you and your route north?"

"I'll get there somehow. People are on the move. I'll always be able to find a few who are heading in my direction and travel with them."

Marion glanced at Horry, who shook his head. "You wouldn't get ten miles that way, not as things are now. You wouldn't know where to go."

"It may take time, but I can do it," said Ross stubbornly.

"No," said Marion. "You'd make one stage. Maybe two. That's all. The best thing for you to do is stay with us. We've been down here recruiting and soon we'll move to our base. You can wait there until things are quieter. Then we'll find some way of heading you at least as far as Virginia."

"Guess you're right," said Ross reluctantly. "Yes, it's the only way, if things are as you say. At least, while we're waiting, I might be able to do some work for you."

Marion looked dubious. "There's work to be done, but—"

Ross's eyes snapped. "But what? I've served since '75. I know infantry and cavalry. I could even make a fair fist as a gunner."

"Yes," said Marion. "You know *your* kind of war. Not ours."

"War's war and armies are armies."

Marion sat back. "Tell him about partisan war, Peter."

Horry wagged his big head. "It's the only kind we can fight, unless a regular army's sent down here. Then we'd still be partisans operating with it in our own way. Here's the difference between our war and yours. A regular army wants to kill enemies, wants to take towns and forts and hold them. You agree? Now a partisan *never* holds ground. Not if he knows his trade. He always avoids open battle unless he has big odds on his side, in time or in numbers. Usually, he strikes, gets away, and the getting away is as important as the striking."

"But that's what I did when I hit my convoy," argued Ross. "I realize that there's a lot more to learn, but I can learn it."

"*Could* you? That's Francis's point. Look. You hit convoys on your line of march, convoys that were between you and where you were going. Could you have broken up your command into little groups, hidden in the swamps and then attacked? Could you do that again and again? Could you live in a given area, with two or three different bases, all quite close together, and strike and get away—strike and get away? With the enemy knowing roughly where your lairs were? Why, you'd have to forget everything you'd learned in the army. Isn't that so, Francis?"

Marion nodded. "Ask him about the carts."

"Yes, the carts," Horry pursued. "Why did you burn them?"

"Because I couldn't take them through the swamps," answered Ross.

"And why did you take the pack horses?"

Ross gave an irritated laugh. "Because I *could* take them."

Marion, listening intently, shook his head as Horry pointed a gaunt finger at Ross. "You burned the carts for the wrong reason. And you should have scattered or shot the tackies so they could not be used again by the enemy. If you'd kept on, you might have wrecked one more convoy, but soon after you'd have been run down *because* you'd have been so weighted with your captures you couldn't have avoided it."

"That's all very well," protested Ross. "But in the Jerseys—"

Horry cut in. "Up there you had a fixed force to fall back on. A real partisan has only the swamps and his wits. Once Francis took two cannon with him. They weighted us down and now they're at the bottom of the Little Pee Dee. We'll never march with guns again. No, with the best intent in the world, your instincts and training would trip you up, get a lot of your men killed."

Ross turned to Marion, but the colonel had risen, a warm smile lighting his face. Dorande van Kortenaer was walking gracefully toward the log, a fat deerskin bag dangling from her hand. No trace of her night in the swamps showed in her poise, her face or her clothes. Ross muttered, "Well I'll be damned!"

Dorande acknowledged the three bows and sat on the log which Horry carefully dusted for her. She smiled at him and then at Marion. "You sent me much breakfast, Colonel. I hope your men did not go without, and that you were not put to much trouble."

"The trouble was yours," said Marion.

"I do not understand."

Horry interposed. "Francis means if we hadn't gone looking for you, we wouldn't have the rations from the pack horses. And if you hadn't been in trouble, we wouldn't have gone looking for you."

Her smooth forehead wrinkled. "But you have *étapes*—depots that send you food?"

"Haven't heard about them," said Marion.

"And if you had not found the horses?" asked Dorande, still puzzled.

"We had a few potatoes."

"And when they were gone?"

"We'd have tried to find more."

Her black eyes were very big. "You expect nothing better?"

Horry stirred his long limbs. "We've been expecting better since '75. Someday we'll get it. But we've lived worse than this. After Gates was beaten at Camden, Francis and I thought we'd like to take a look at North Carolina. It seemed advisable, all of a sudden. I had an empty pistol and Francis had a rusty horse-fleam. We needed pockets the way a Scotchman needs knee buckles." Dorande looked puzzled and Horry went on, "Scots wear kilts and have bare knees. Anyway we got to North Carolina and—"

Ross watched Dorande as the major talked on. She was obviously unable to make out the slight, shabby Marion and the sad-faced Horry. Their courtesy and consideration she could probably have placed accurately in a different setting, but in this starving wilderness camp her past experience was useless. He saw her dark eyes go from Marion's face to his worn leather breeches, his rusty little sword, his charred leather skullcap.

When Horry paused, she asked, "And for many years you do this?"

"Have to. Or quit," said Marion.

Her head went back and Ross sensed that she was seeing only rags and rust. "It is against all law to rebel against your king. What do you fight for? Riches?"

Marion shook his head as Horry answered, "We *had* riches. We were the most prosperous colony. A lot gave up what they had because they didn't like being misgoverned by a king three thousand miles away. I don't know if we'll get back all we gave up when we win. Haven't thought much about it. We'll have our freedom, though. I *have* thought about that."

Dorande's white hand swept toward the camp. "But with just this, you cannot fight a kingdom, whether it's right or wrong!"

Marion looked gravely at her. "You told me your father is Dutch. His people fought a Spanish king for years, I've read. Often they had less than we have now. They won. We'll win."

She rested her chin on her fist. "You live like this, just because you believe you are right?"

"That's about it," said Horry.

"Yet you could be in your homes, if you stopped. In your homes and at peace."

Marion smiled grimly. "We wouldn't have peace inside us."

Ross glanced at Dorande and saw respect that was almost awe come into her eyes. "You are at war, yet you stop to take thought for me. When I saw Captain Pembroke's men, I thought them mere marauders. I thought the same of you. I expected talk of a ransom. Forgive me."

"Natural enough," said Marion.

"No. It was that I was stupid. I thought I had a grievance against all of you. Instead, I find myself in your debt."

"No debt," said Marion quietly. "But we want to be in yours."

"You? In my debt? How can that be?"

Marion straightened up. "Made up your mind about going to my kin in the High Hills of Santee?"

"Yes. I go gladly."

Marion coughed apologetically. "Remember, this part is only if you want to. When you get to my cousins, tell them that I want word passed to a man they know about. The word is that all the young men of the district are to come east and meet me. They'll know where. Better add, too, to let it be known that I've been recruiting from the Pee Dee to the Santee."

She looked at him, wonder in her eyes. "But that is so simple. There is no more?"

"Not as far as you're concerned. But before you decide to pass on this word, you ought to know that the men who meet me will be mounted and armed."

"So, taking your message, I concern myself with your war?"

"Some," said Marion.

Dorande's eyes fell. "This is important to you?"

Horry stirred. "Francis and I don't count. It's important to a lot of people, not just us."

Marion nodded. "It means that a lot of homes won't be burned, that a lot of people won't freeze or starve. It means a lot of men won't hang from a tree in their own dooryard. I'd call it quite important."

Dorande's mind filled with the memory of the burning Colclough house and the figure dangling from the tree. She drew a deep breath. "Yes. I take your message. Do I start soon?"

"Thank you. At once."

Ross started. "Good Lord, Colonel, she ought to rest up at least another day!"

Dorande smiled at him. "But I am quite rested. I have even packed my clothes. And Colonel, I haven't thanked you for sending me that man who had been *couturier*, lady's tailor, in Charleston. He made clever repairs."

Marion nodded at Horry. "He's married. He thought of him. Then if you're ready, I'll call your guide."

Ross got up quickly. "Don't waste one of your men. I'll go." He felt a glow of pleasure as Dorande said, "But of course! The captain will escort me, with no trouble to you."

Marion shook his head at Ross. "You don't know the way."

"You can give me a map, though. That's easy enough."

"No," said Horry slowly, crossing his long legs. "Her guide won't go by any map. He knows the right houses to go to and what to say to the right people. Also, to people who aren't right."

Dorande spoke softly, standing close to Ross. "The captain is a good swordsman."

"Don't need swords," said Marion.

Horry untangled his long limbs. "Especially when they're hitched to a uniform like that, topped by a French helmet. You'd last about two miles. No telling what would happen to the little girl."

Ross looked down at Dorande. "Do you feel safe with a strange guide?"

"If the colonel says I am safe. Thank you for your concern about me. Now, Colonel, I fetch my baggage?"

"Fetched," said Marion, nodding toward a spare, dark man who was leading two fine-limbed horses, one of them fitted with a sidesaddle. "That's your guide. Never makes a mistake."

"And you send word to my uncle, Monsieur Paul St. Aubin?"

"Man started last night."

"Last night?" echoed Dorande. "But you did not know until now that I would go to your High Hills of Santee!"

"No," agreed Horry. "But wherever you went, we thought your uncle ought to know that you were safe. We'll start another man out to tell your uncle or his people where you are. Don't reckon you'll tarry long in the High Hills."

Care touched her dark eyes. "No harm will come to you from what you do for me?"

"None," answered Marion.

"Then thank you for all you have done. I repeat your message." She solemnly checked off the points on her fingers. "Now I forget it until I see the right man. Then I forget it for always." She curtseyed and turned to her mount. Ross stepped forward, held out his hands. Her foot rested lightly in his cradled palms, then she swung into the saddle, pulling a long-vizored poke bonnet over the kerchief that bound her hair. She smiled down at the three men, turned her horse to follow her guide.

Horry observed, "That's a plucky girl."

"Yes," said Marion.

Ross glumly watched the horses start off, thinking with a shrug, "Let her go. She's got nothing to do with the war or—" He looked up quickly. Dorande had swung her mount sideways, calling, "Captain Pembroke! I had forgotten—"

She bent from the saddle as he ran to her. "I had forgotten to speak, but not forgotten what you did for me. I was trouble to you as well as to Colonel Marion. You could have left me across the Santee. When I was lost, you looked for me. No, I do not forget."

Ross looked up into her earnest black eyes, stammering, "Ought to have been able to do more."

She pursed her soft lips. "You did what was possible. Good fortune to you." She shook her reins and her horse started again. She looked quickly back over her shoulder. "And I regret that Colonel Marion could not spare you." She smiled and was gone, trotting hard after the guide.

Ross started slowly back past men who were rolling blankets, saddling horses or stamping out the embers of their fires. Horry called to him, "Your horse wants to see you. We start in five minutes and he's coming with us."

Ross saddled and mounted, then joined Horry and Marion at the head of the column that had formed quickly. As the troop rode out, Ross wondered how far Dorande had gone on the western trail. If her destination was near Camden, she might reach it in another twenty-four hours. He settled his helmet with a sharp slap. How long would it take Marion to find a way to send him north? It might be weeks, even months. In that case—well, the High Hills of Santee could not be so very far from the little colonel's mysterious base. He began to whistle softly to himself.

III • Snow Island

Never, in all the years that he had followed the armies of the Colonies, had Ross Pembroke known such a march. The thirty-odd men followed no visible trail for long, threw out no flankers, maintained no advance guard. Marion rode on some twenty yards ahead, his head turning right and left in alert motions as though he were questioning each stretch of swamp, each tangled thicket, each grassy savannah. He rarely checked his pace, but sometimes stood in his stirrups, face to the breeze that came down from the northwest, bringing with it the scents of the distant upcountry, the tang of the high waters of the Pacolet, the Broad, and the Wateree. Now he trotted along a sandy road that threaded through sighing pines, the others clattering after him. Again, he swung to the southwest, his horse breasting through undergrowth that looked impassable, only to yield, crackling, to the thrust of the horses. Or, cantering at the edge of a savannah, he slanted up a ridge where live oaks slapped and tore at the men who followed him.

Ross, riding at the head by Peter Horry, lost all sense of direction as Marion's route veered about the whole circle of the compass. He gave up trying to orient himself and turned his attention to this odd command. From time to time he dropped back to the rear, then rode slowly forward, watching the men whom he passed. It was impossible to strike a balance, to discover a type. He saw homespun and fine cloth, bright sabers and rusted. New carbines hung in leather buckets to set off pitted fowling pieces or long rifles. There were fine-drawn, sensitive faces, and rough tangled beards below hard eyes.

With each cast to the rear, the whole column seemed thicker and longer to Ross. When he rejoined Horry in the van, he said, "You must have put in a lot of work, getting all these people moving. I just saw eight more come in from that side road."

Horry shook his head. "Haven't had much time. Let me see. It was three days ago that Francis and I came down here to spread the word."

"Three days only?" exclaimed Ross. "Where did you come from?"

Horry turned sad eyes on him. "From the place where we started before we got down here. Yes, Francis dropped a word here and there, same as he's doing sending that little girl to the High Hills."

"Where are we heading for now?"

Horry pointed to Marion. "He's the only one who knows. We just follow."

"But suppose something happened to him?"

"To *him?*" Horry's voice was heavy with mournful surprise. "It doesn't. Just to other people. Francis has never been surprised, never been ambushed. He just rides along and smells out the land and people. I don't know how he does it. Maybe he understands horse-talk and his mare tells him. Night or day, sun, moon, stars or rain, he never misses."

Ross eyed the frail man riding on ahead. "He'd be worth a whole cavalry corps to a regular field army."

"Yes," said Horry. "Of course, I'm prejudiced. To me, Francis is the greatest man I've ever run into. Known him all my life. In fact, our families—we're all Huguenot French, you now—sailed from La Rochelle in the same boat, along with the Postells and some others. You ought to have known Francis in the old days. Never talked much, but he had a real wit. Now he rarely has time to use it. The war's everything to him and he's given up everything for it."

"Did he have a big plantation?"

"Middling, middling. He could have had one of the best in the state, because whatever he touches works. but Francis's father didn't leave much and had a big family. Then the wars began to come along. First the Indian wars and now this. Francis hates wars and fighting, don't mistake that. But when he believes in a thing, like our cause, he goes for it baldheaded. People began crowding rank on him without his asking it or really wanting it."

"I can understand that," said Ross. "Don't you worry about him though? Looks so damn wispy. One day he'll just blow away with the wind."

"Now that's kindly in you to be concerned about him," said Horry sadly. Then he laughed. "Don't let that slim, wiry figure fool you, as it has so many others. Give him a pint of vinegar and he'll work, ride and fight you and me into the ground. He'll wear out bigger and stronger men than either of us. Yes, Francis puzzles a lot of people. He won't retaliate against Tory burnings and hangings. He's never made a move to avenge the hanging of his own nephew Gabriel. He says that when the war's over, all of us have got to live together again and he's not going to do a thing to keep old hatreds alive. When he fights, he's always in the thick of things. And yet—" Horry dropped his voice—"he won't carry pistols. I saw you looking at that little sword of his. I tell you, it's rusted into the scabbard."

"My God," exclaimed Ross. "Then he's really fighting unarmed!"

"Exactly! And why? Well, for one thing he knows he isn't built to manage a sword and if he's got one that he can't use, then he won't be tempted to go hacking in. But more important, he knows that his biggest value is leadership. If he gets mixed up in hand-to-hand work, he'll lose touch. Oh, the boys know that, all right. They try to keep him in the rear and if they can't do that, they cover him. There—he's pulling up, ahead there, and signaling."

Marion had halted, hand raised. He called, "Bridge! Blankets!"

"Blankets?" asked Ross, puzzled. No one answered his question. The whole command had dismounted and was busy with its girths and saddles. As he watched, men folded their saddle blankets and laid them over the timbered bridge that spanned the stream where Marion had halted. Ross nodded in comprehension. The stream was too deep to ford and the bridge was the only possible crossing. Hostile ears, up stream or down, could have picked up the hollow drum, drum, drum of hoofs on the old planks. Now all sound was muffled and unreal and Ross, watching the column cross, was oddly reminded of the Boston stage coming into Providence over the dead carpet of a blizzard. He looked at Marion with increased respect. This was a trick worth learning.

Beyond the bridge, Marion rode straight through rough, wooded country, threading through swamps, scaling low ridges, cutting across streams that looked like the headwaters of big rivers. Ross could only make out that the column, instead of twisting and turning, was now traveling a direct line. Crossing a dune-like tract where pines rose high, Ross pricked up his ears. Where did that whistle come from? He heard it again, a high, singing note that ended in a quavering trill. "What was that?" he asked Horry.

The latter sighed. "Sounded kind of like a whistle."

"But where did it come from?"

"The trees, I reckon. Birds are partial to them down here. Aren't they in Rhode Island?"

Ross shrugged. The way continued straight as ever. The sun dipped and pools of shadow formed in the hollows. From time to time the strange whistle sounded, seeming to come from any point of the compass. Near sundown Ross looked on open country with water glinting in the distance where two broad rivers flowed. He pointed them out to Horry. "Do you know those streams?"

Horry nodded vaguely. "That's Lynch's Creek joining the Pee Dee. We're home."

"Home?"

"Much as we've got. That's Snow Island in the forks of the rivers. Swamp and river on four sides. Plenty of grazing. Big friendly places nearby where we can get supplies—if there are any. We can hit down to Georgetown, up to the Cheraws or over to Camden."

Camden, above the High Hills of Santee! Ross wondered if Dorande van Kortenaer had reached Marion's relatives, if she had delivered his message. She might already be setting out for her uncle on the Congaree. More likely, though, she'd have to wait and during that time Marion might have word to send her. In that case—

The whistles again. He was sure this time that they came from the trees in front. Then he saw Marion throw back his head and repeat the sound that was caught up and echoed from the hidden lands beyond the trees. Ross frowned at Horry. "That's your recognition signal, isn't it? You might have told me when we first heard it."

"Why now I might have," said Horry from depths of self-reproach. "Just the same, now that you've been wondering about it, you'll be able to sort it out from any bird call you hear, unless birds whistle like that in Rhode Island. No one's told me they don't."

"I'll know it all right. But who was doing it back there?"

"You didn't guess? That was when we met the first of the scouts from the island. There's a screen of men guarding it in a big circle. How far they range depends on where danger's apt to come from. One of the boys, maybe riding or maybe up a tree, saw us and whistled. Francis answered, else the alarm would have been given and in a half hour you couldn't have found a footprint or horse combing on Snow Island. It's Francis's way of fortifying and it seems to me a lot simpler than setting out trenches and trundling cannon. I'd a lot rather just whistle than dab around with a spade."

"I see—a phantom fortress."

"Gets pretty real at times," Horry said. "Here we are."

They were among the trees where man scrambled down, calling to the riders who wound on through shallow swamps, across clear streams and finally along a ford that slanted to the island. Marion headed his mount at a sandy trough that sloped down through bushes. Ross, behind Horry, rode up the gap in the undergrowth and found himself in a broad, grassy glade that swarmed with men. Marion dismounted by a tall, soldierly-looking man with sketchy braid on his blue coat. "How many, Hugh?" asked the colonel.

"Nearly two hundred, here, or on the way."

"There'll be more," said Marion as his horse was led away. "What orders for those who are here?"

"Feed them. Sleep them. Put them to work. Send me Tom Elliot with pens and paper." Marion walked off toward a great oak with his odd, limping gait.

The others dismounted. The tall men shouted a few commands while Peter Horry, leaning against his horse, surveyed him sadly. Then he said, "Haven't they been able to hang you yet, Hugh?"

The other showed white teeth in a smile and his gray eyes twinkled. "Better luck next time, Peter. What have you been doing to disgrace the family?"

Peter Horry moaned softly. "Couldn't find a thing that suited. Hugh, this is Ross Pembroke, a Continental from Rhode Island. He and I went looking for a little girl in a swamp, but she got away from us."

Hugh Horry whistled. "From *you?* She must have run like a deer."

"Oh, it turned out all right. She curved right back to Chilyon's Castle. My brother Hugh, Pembroke, is the brains of the family. I'm the beauty."

Other men came up and Ross's head swam with names as they were introduced. There were Postells and Jameses, Vanderhorsts, a brace of Conyers, more Jameses, Alstons. Hugh Horry observed, "A lot of people coming in, Peter. We never had more than seventy at a time, but now—"

A clerical-looking man nearby nodded gravely. "A great outpouring of the spirit."

A fever-wasted trapper spat appreciatively. "Sure is. Every son of a bitch and his brother's here."

The minister looked at him in mild disapproval. Peter turned to his brother. "Got an outpouring of rations to go along with the spirit?"

"Kettle's on. Join us, Pembroke. We've plenty, for once."

Hugh's kettle simmered close by the bushes that screened Lynch's Creek. "Beef and potatoes," said Hugh. "The beef's so lean there's not much nourishment in it, but I rather enjoy chewing it, seeing that it's the first beef on the island in nearly a month. Marion bring any salt? We're badly off for that." He filled and distributed wooden bowls.

Peter, chewing solemnly, shook his head. "Captured some salt that was going to the post at Nelson's Ferry, but Francis found some good Whig families who needed it more than we did, so he gave it to them."

Hugh sighed. "It's not so bad, now the hot weather's ebbing, but some of the boys still suffer from the lack. Hot weather and no salt make a bad combination. Look at that." He pointed to two hogs, who, standing on their hind legs, were greedily licking the sweat-soaked coat of a picketed horse which, in turn, licked another. Hugh Horry shrugged. "Well, we'll manage somehow. You staying with us, Mr. Pembroke?"

Ross took the bowl that Hugh had filled. "Looks as though I've got to, at least until Marion finds some way to pass me north to the main army." He frowned. "Just the same, I wish he'd give me some work to do while I'm here."

Peter Horry glanced at his brother. "What do you think, Hugh? Our friend's had long Continental service, infantry and dragoons."

Hugh looked doubtful. "Not right away, at least. You see, Mr. Pembroke, you're trained to work with an actual field force, and that's what we can't manage down here—yet. We've just got a few people who act as magnets. Men come to them for a given job, then they scatter till the next call. They have to. They've got to get back to their homes, guard their families, see to their crops and guard their homes against British and Tory raiders. Times are ruthless."

"Just the same," urged Ross, "if you kept at least part of those men in the field as a regular force, they'd be far more valuable than treble their number coming and going at will."

"How can we?" asked Peter. "Look, nearly all our leaders are in British hands. The only authority that exists is vested in Governor Rutledge. He's actually the government. There's no organization back of him. He can't requisition effectively either for supplies or munitions. We live on voluntary gifts and what we can capture from the British or the Tories. You can't keep a force in the field under those conditions. Just a few of us help hold the framework together under Marion and we do that because he *is* Marion and people trust him. Without him, all resistance would collapse from the coast to

Camden. It's been mighty close to doing that more than once as it is."

"I see your problem," said Ross. "But what are you accomplishing? It seems to me you're just prolonging the war. I say that with all respect for your hanging on."

"Wars," said Peter oracularly, "don't get lost by prolonging. They get lost by ending them too soon."

"You see," cut in Hugh, "the British and the Tories are yelling that it *is* over. The Crown's made all sorts of promises to people—protection, land, slaves and so on. A lot who'd fought earlier believed the promises. Then they found that not only did they get nothing, but the Crown expected them to take arms against those who stood firm with us. So, whenever we raid a British post or a convoy, whenever we break up a lot of Tories mustering for military service under the Crown, we show the whole state that the war isn't over. Not only that, but a lot of Tories somehow get converted and join us."

"Yes," said Ross slowly. "It's worth while. It's damned well worth while. Only—what's ahead?"

"Just this," said Peter. "We'll get stronger and stronger. We'll pen the British in their posts until they find it too costly to hold anything but Charleston. Then we'll take care of those Tories who've been burning and murdering. Also, we'll see to some of our own people who've been doing the same." He glanced over his shoulder. "There's Francis, over there by the big oak, beckoning to you."

Ross found Marion seated under a vast oak where a slight, curly-haired man wrote by candlelight. The colonel's voice came to him. ". . . and on August 15th, attacked Port's Ferry. 20th, Nelson's Plantation. Raided Kingstree the 27th. Struck the Black Mingo September 20th and the same day broke up a Tory muster at Tarcote's." He looked up at Ross's approach, then dismissed his secretary with a few words. Ross saluted. "Something happened, sir?" he asked.

Marion nodded. "Something. Word from Governor Rutledge up in North Carolina. He's commissioned me brigadier general and—"

"That's fine, sir."

The other looked surprised. "Rank? Not important. The big thing is that what I do now's official. Had no status before. Now I'm organizing on a brigade basis—at least, on paper. The men will probably come and go as they did before. Here are my first appointments." He handed Ross a sheet of paper.

Ross tilted it to the light. Peter Horry was made colonel of

Marion's cavalry, Hugh Horry of the mounted infantry, the brigade seemingly having no room for foot soldiers. Many of the other names he thought that he had heard on arriving at the island, but he couldn't place them.

He handed the sheet back to Marion. "That's a very compact unit, sir. Don't forget, I'll be glad to do what I can while I'm waiting."

"That's what I wanted to see you about. I don't feel that I can give you a command with men like mine in a war like this, as I told you at Chilyon's. But you *can* do this. I've got parties out now, taking the saws from every sawmill they can find."

"Sawmills?" exclaimed Ross. "What's that got to do with me?"

"A lot. I'll have them hammered into sabers. Sabers don't need powder and ball and I'm often very short of both. You'll teach my men how to use them. You'll give them confidence in their blades. Then they won't go home when they report here and find I've no ammunition for them. Will you do that for us?"

"Of course—so long as I'm here. I'd much rather command a troop than act as drillmaster, but if that's where you need me, I'll do my best."

"Thank you," said Marion. He rose from the crooked root of the oak and began to pace up and down. "Of course, *if* a real field army was ever sent down here again, you'd be more than valuable—assuming that you had kept your eyes open all the time you were with us. You could explain the regular force to me. You could tell its commander what we were trying to do and why." He stopped and looked thoughtfully at Ross. "What chance is there of such a force coming here, in your opinion?"

Ross shook his head. "None. Congress has lost two armies in this theater. They won't risk a third. Besides, who could command it? They've got plenty of good combat generals up north, but a man coming here would have to understand combat and supply and training and diplomacy and a hundred other things."

"That's what I figured," said Marion. "Now find Peter Horry and work out a plan for your saber instruction."

As Ross rose he asked diffidently, "Had any word from the High Hills?"

"Don't need word to know she got there all right. May be different when she reaches the Congarée. I've arranged so she can get word to safe people if need be. I wish her well. I also wish she had a different uncle."

As Ross walked down the island, he felt an odd uneasiness about Dorande van Kortenaer. Why was Marion concerned about the Congaree? Why would she have need to reach "safe people"? And what was wrong about that uncle? Raoul Jaudon, too, had seemed to have heard unpleasant reports about him. He tried to shrug off the question.

The widow Cantey, small and sparrowlike, cupped her elbows in her hands and shook her white head. For more than a week, the pale-haired girl with the dark eyes had lain there in the great bed racked by what seemed to be swamp fever. Lately, Mrs. Cantey had not been so sure. The fever was there, but accompanied by the effects of what must have been great fatigue and shock. She reached out a veined hand and touched the flushed face that lay on the pillow. The skin was hot and dry and the lids did not stir. At least, today there had been no return of the delirium that had seized the girl almost on arrival. The guide, sent by the widow's strange cousin-by-marriage, Francis Marion, said nothing about her, save that she was to be cared for. And there was the very odd message to be sent on from Marion to certain people. Mrs. Cantey had asked few questions, judging it better to know little about Francis Marion, even up here in the peace of the High Hills of Santee.

For days, the girl had tossed and turned, eyes sometimes staring, sometimes tight shut. She had cried out in a French that was differently accented from the widow's Geneva French. She had called in English and sometimes in a tongue which the widow took to be Low German. Night and day, the cries had come, bringing her or her brother, Emil Rusillon, running in alarm. No coherent story could be built from her words. She cried out about Negroes and burning houses, of girls leaping into flames. There were terrors which the widow guessed to be newer, fever pictures based on swamps and the dark, and fears that could not be named. It all reminded her of stories of the old days when the Yemassees swooped through Carolina over sixty years ago. And where had the girl come from? How had she crossed Francis Marion's trail? Mrs. Cantey sighed and left the room.

Late in the day, she looked in again. The girl still slept. Mrs. Cantey came nearer, saw that her lips were moving, as though delirium were returning. But the girl's face was calm. Bending closer, she caught the words—"le petit colonel—bien gentil—" That would be her cousin, Colonel Marion. Then she caught the word "noir," and feared that horrible pictures wherein Negroes and death were mixed might be returning. No, there was a ghost of a smile *"—le capitaine—le capitaine noir—"* The dark captain? Soneone who rode so mysteriously with the little colonel, no doubt. She touched the hand that lay outside the sheets and soft fingers curled about hers. The voice from the pillow was low. *"Ah! C'est toi, maman."* The girl slept on, dreaming of her mother.

Softly, Mrs. Cantey left the room to stand on the little veranda with the valley of the Wateree at her feet. The slanting sun was painting the river with new colors that darkened to the touch of the north wind. From the swamp pastures below, a small herd of cattle wound slowly toward the house, lowing as they scented the barns beyond. Hoofs clopped and a thick-set man, gray hair neat under a broad-brimmed hat, rode into sight. A diminutive Negro took his horse and he walked stiffly to the veranda of the little house. *"Ça va, ma soeur?"* he asked, inclining his head toward Dorande's room.

She smiled at her brother. "She sleeps, and quietly."

He said *"Bon!"* explosively and clumped into the house, returning with an oblong wooden box which he placed, with an almost ritual gesture, on a table on the grass. Brother and sister seated themselves beside it, folded their hands and watched the western panorama of swamp, river, plain and woods. When the sun was half hidden, Rusillon lifted the lid of the box, showing a glass plate under which brass wheels and brass cylinder gleamed. *"Maintenant, c'est l'heure,"* he announced, touching a spring. The music box began to tinkle out a *ranz des vaches,* an ancient tune of the Alpine herders, as brother and sister peacefully watched the slow ebb of the day.

A week later, Dorande lay back in a long chair on the little veranda. The fever had left her pale and worn, but her face was beginning to fill out. Only that morning, too, she had noticed that her green dress, carefully mended by Mrs. Cantey, no longer hung slack about her, but felt tight where it was supposed to be tight. Now she reached into the deerskin bag that hung on her chair. On pretext of mending, she secured from Mrs. Cantey a few skeins of bright silk which she was secretly working into a square of white Chinese silk, included by chance that day beyond the Santee. She had finished one crimson hibiscus and now, with soft green, was filling in the leaves of the second. She worked busily, one ear cocked toward the house, ready to hide her work at the least sound. They had been good to her, Mrs. Cantey and her brother Emil, though her presence must have strained the little household. She knew, from chance heard words that nearly all the slaves had run away in the troubled times, that the best fields were neglected and the herd woefully shrunk through requisitions by the Crown which paid in paper scrip of dubious value.

Her eyes roved away to the valley of the Wateree. The house was perched on a west-running spur of the High Hills, commanding a superb view from which she could already pick out landmarks. To the north, that thick growth of waving green cane showed the course of Little Rafting Creek. West, and edging the Wateree, was Gum Swamp, an expanse of feathery treetops broken by vivid caney stretches and wide pools. The nearby slopes were checkered with wheat and cotton fields and along the main ridge, the roof of a great house showed against the eastern sky.

She felt peaceful and secure. If only she could know that friends on St. Eusebius had survived and found a similar peace! She shivered as she thought of the island. Up to the time of her fever, she had built up, she thought, a hard protective shield about herself to fight off those memories. She had been headstrong, even imperious, feeling that if she softened in any way, her whole fabric would crack and the nightmare of St. Eusebius would claim her. She told herself that she had been coldly supercilious to that major at Georgetown, to the dead Cornet Horton. She felt uncomfortable as she recalled how she had spoken to Captain Pembroke after the terrifying end of the march of the convoy. She had been downright arrogant. "As if I had been Queen of France or Anne, mother of William V, Stadholder of the Netherlands," she thought. But she had to be, she assured herself in extenuation, else the long train of tragedy and hardship might have broken her.

She finished a second hibiscus leaf, then tucked the silk into her bag. The sinking sun told her that soon host and hostess would appear and they must not see the embroidery until it was finished. She folded her hands and savored the utter stillness of the day, let the gold and red of sunset sink into her with the soft greens and grays and browns of the High Hills of Santee. A scarlet tanager showed against the laurel bushes, poised on a branch and then sailed off down the valley like a flying spark. "This is peace," she thought.

She sat up. Across the Wateree on the road that led to Ancrum's Ferry, a regularly spaced procession of red dots trailed north. British dragoons! She turned her head away. She never wanted to see another helmet, another saber. And yet— where was Colonel Marion with his rusty saber, and dark-haired Pembroke with his white-plumed helmet? In the midst of their war, they had taken care of her. The captain was going at least as far as Virginia, he had said. Virginia—

She looked up with a smile as Mrs. Cantey, black shawl about her shoulders, stepped from the house. She raised black-mitted hands in surprise. "You have color today! What were you dreaming of? Some yellow-haired Dutch boy in Curaçao?" She sat down by Dorande.

"I only wondered—how far is Virginia?"

"Very far, no doubt. I have not been there."

Dorande leaned back, absently watching the Cantey herd wind up from the valley below. Soon she would hear hoofs as her host rode in from the fields. Then she saw him, tossing his reins to a Negro. He beamed on Dorande, touching his cheek to his sister's, glanced at the setting sun and presently emerged from the house, carrying the music box. Dorande smiled in sympathy. Every evening it had been so. When the sun dropped to the horizon, Rusillon would say, *"Maintenant, c'est l'heure,"* and the box would tinkle out a song that had sprung from some high, Alpine pasture. Now, as the simple air greeted the sunset, Dorande felt an odd burning back of her eyes. She did not want to leave these kindly people who had cared for her. She visualized a procession of days in the High Hills of Santee that would always end with a glowing sunset and a *ranz des vaches.* Surely she could wait here until her parents arrived.

The box stopped with a whir and Rusillon jumped up, staring down the road. Far below a light, covered coach rocked toward the house, a liveried Negro on the box and another riding the nigh leader. Mrs. Cantey exclaimed, "But who—" Then she settled back to await the arrival of the coach that was turning up the circular drive of the house. It ground to a halt. The coachman skipped from the box, let down a pair of steps, intoning, "Mr. Paul St. Aubin!" Dorande and her hosts stood waiting, as the door was flung open.

Dorande put her hand to her throat. The thin man in blue satin and peach-colored waistcoat was a strange caricature of her mother. His eyes were like hers, bright and black, but they moved covertly as though in the habit of looking at people and things from the side instead of directly. His mouth, too, recalled her mother, but the well-shaped lips seemed always in uneasy motion.

For an instant he surveyed Dorande with cold appraisal. Then his whole expression changed and he became less of a caricature. Sweeping off his hat, Paul St. Aubin flung out both arms. *"Ciel!* And can this be the little girl whom I saw in Curaçao so long ago? The image of my adored sister! Almost

do I bless the blacks of St. Eusebius for sending you to me."
He kissed her on both cheeks. "And now, do me the honor
to present me to these good people."

Dorande winced at the bland condescension of the words
braves gens.

"*Mon oncle,* my friends Madame Cantey and Monsieur
Rusillon."

Madame Cantey dropped a curtsey while her brother
bowed, saying, "No doubt, Monsieur, you have family matters to discuss. The house is at your service. May I hope that
you will honor us at dinner?"

St. Aubin smiled negligently. "Thank you, but I am pressed
for time. I shall speak with my niece out here." Brother and
sister withdrew to the house and St. Aubin turned to Dorande.
"There is much, my niece, that I do not understand about
your being here. Nor do I see how word of your presence
reached me. But that may wait."

Dorande thought of the silent, keen-faced Marion, of the
men who starved to follow him, of the white-plumed captain.
Their aims and plans were no concern of hers, of course, but
all of those people had been kind to her. She said carefully, "I
fear that you would find all that of little interest, *mon oncle.*"

He glanced keenly at her and she was disconcerted by the
cold appraisal in his eyes. Then blandness returned and he
said indulgently, "No doubt matters seem unimportant to
you. But I have friends whom your account, which I trust
that you will render, will interest greatly. Now for the present, I regret that I must leave you with these worthy people
for a little time longer. For my part, I go on to Camden,
thence west to Ninety-six and beyond, where I have affairs
to attend to. Those completed, I arrive here once more and
you shall accompany me to my estate, Mon Plaisir, on the
Congaree."

Dorande hesitated. Her father's letters had been explicit.
She was to stay with Paul St. Aubin, her mother's brother.
And yet her uncle's oblique glances, his effusiveness which
overlay a core of hard calculation, disconcerted her. She said
slowly, "But—that may be long. It is better perhaps that I
wait here until my parents arrive. Thus I should be no care
to you."

The indulgent smile returned. "Ah, very well I understand,
ma nièce. I am virtually a stranger to you. And you feel grati-
tude to these worthy souls who have sheltered you. Don't be
afraid. You will not find life dull at Mon Plaisir. I entertain
much, particularly English officers and officials, some of
whom are *de la noblesse.*"

There was a rattle inside the carriage and a sharp voice called in English, "Paul! You know I don't like to travel after dark. Say what you must and be done!"

Dorande saw a strikingly pretty face, petulant and frowning, under masses of dark hair. St. Aubin started, then scuttled to the carriage where he spoke earnestly, almost pleadingly with the girl. She vanished from the window with a flounce and St. Aubin returned to Dorande, looking almost sheepish. He coughed, waving toward the carriage. "The daughter of a most wealthy planter. I escort her to Camden at his request. He is greatly esteemed by Lord Rawdon, who commands the troops there and whom I am happy to count a friend." He coughed again as he found Dorande's black eyes studying him speculatively. He went on, hurriedly. "Ha! H'm! Yes. The daughter of a good friend." He turned away, strolled a few paces along the grass, surveying the grounds and the houses. "A pretty property. Who is the owner?"

"The owner? I believe they share equally, brother and sister," answered Dorande, puzzled.

"They speak well of the English King?"

"Of the King? Why, neither for nor against. They are good, quiet people who ask only to end their days peacefully in the High Hills of Santee."

St. Aubin narrowed his eyes. "Neither for—nor against? Now I find that *most* interesting, *ma nièce*. Yes, a pretty property."

"I should be happy to stay on it, *mon oncle*," said Dorande in a low voice.

St. Aubin inclined his head. "Your wish does you honor. But that would be against your father's wishes. Who may say when he and my sister can find passage for Charleston, with the French and English fleets astir through the West Indies? It is at Mon Plaisir that he expects to find you. It is arranged, as you well know." He stepped closer. "And a word in your ear. These good folk are all very well. But their world is not for you. I, Paul St. Aubin, am moving surely into higher circles, higher and higher, and you shall come with me, as shall your father and my sister, your mother. After all, what is a van Kortenaer? A colonial trader, like a St. Aubin—a St. Aubin of the past."

Dorande flushed. "My father—" she began.

St. Aubin held up his hand. "A respected name, which I shall help him to make eminent. Look what I have done. I, a Frenchman, one of an enemy nation, have achieved an excellent standing with the *milords*, with the English of rank and family here. I have done them favors that they will not forget.

In the old days, when Fortune refused to smile on me, I am quite aware that your father held me in little esteem. In no way shall I ever bear that against him." He smiled. "When we shall meet him in Charleston, you and I, he will find that my good friend, Colonel Balfour, who commands there, will furnish me with an escort of honor at the wharves. It will be a pleasure to see the expression on the face of Syvert van Kortenaer. Now I take my leave. You will have word of me from time to time and will be ready when next I call." He bowed, entered the coach, from which a sharp, scolding voice sounded, and the wheels ground on down the drive.

Dorande stood watching it. Then she sighed and walked slowly into the house.

The next afternoon she wandered along the slope that led down to Gum Swamp and the Wateree. The day was warm and bright, but a north wind brought a foretaste of the brief Carolina winter. She breathed in the clean dry air as though to brace herself against the thought that before too many days had passed, she would have to say good-by to Madame Cantey and her brother and go with her uncle to the Congaree. She tried to reason away her growing dislike of that move. After all, Paul St. Aubin *was* her mother's own brother. With whom else should she stay? It was utterly natural, especially since her father had suggested it. And yet she could not help recalling the odd expression of people when they learned her destination. There was the cavalry major at Georgetown, and the civilian official at LeNud's Ferry on the Santee. At Chilyon's Castle, Colonel Marion's eyes had hardened at the mention of her uncle. It was strange, too, that the little partisan leader had known where St. Aubin was, had known he was not then on the Congaree. Her frown deepened as she remembered the shrill, black-haired girl in the coach. "Daughter of a good friend, *allez!*" she thought. "She addressed him as Paul and ordered him about like a lackey."

She turned up the hill as she saw Madame Cantey come out of the house and set the music box on the table against her brother's return. The widow smiled as Dorande joined her. "You look thoughtful, *ma petite*. You worry about your parents, perhaps?"

Dorande's fingers touched the smooth top of the music box. "Only that they may be long in coming here. And in a week, a fortnight, my uncle returns. Madame Cantey, I was asking myself what would happen should I say, 'No, *mon oncle*, I wish to remain here in the High Hills of Santee.' "

Madame Cantey spoke quickly. "It would not do. We have made inquiries of the most discreet. Your uncle has gained power among the English and if he really wishes you to go to Mon Plaisir, that power he will use. Of that we have been assured. He may even come with soldiers." She sighed. "*Mon enfant*, I fear that you have no choice."

Dorande's black eyes snapped. "He would not dare!"

"*Au contraire*," said the widow simply. "As I say we have been assured—" She stopped, looking at the road from the Wateree. Then she said quietly, "You would be well advised to go into the house—to my room on the second floor."

"To the house? But why?"

Mrs. Cantey pointed down the road. Just beginning the long climb, a column of cavalry stirred up yellow dust. The men wore green jackets and low, black caps. In the van rode a man in a red jacket and shiny brass helmet. Dorande said, "And I should leave you alone to face them?"

"They will only wish to buy cattle and hay, giving bits of paper for them."

"So you will need me to make record of what they take."

Mrs. Cantey sniffed. "Of course, a *jeune fille* like you could hardly guess the effect on a man of your hair and face, not to mention your figure, which speaks for itself. These men are Tories, by their green jackets, hard men, sweepings of the north and central states. That one Englishman will not be able to control them. Run along. I've dealt with such *partes* before."

Reluctantly Dorande went to Mrs. Cantey's room and stood back of the worn curtains where she could safely watch. The troop had reached Mrs. Cantey and the British officer, a big, competent-looking man with a lieutenant's knot, dismounted with a courteous touch to his helmet. The Tory officer, who stayed glowering in the saddle, was short and heavy, with a thick, protruding lip that set his face in a sullen scowl. She heard the Englishman saying "—we only need a statement of the number of your cattle and how many you'd sell to the army, if necessary."

"Are all these men necessary to count a few beeves, sir?"

"Not at all," laughed the dragoon. "We're also patrolling down to the Congaree."

Mrs. Cantey shrugged. "As to the cattle, it is my brother who concerns himself with them. He is not here."

"No trouble about that. We'll come back this way in a few days. Just ask him to have a list ready for me to take to Camden. In the meantime, we'd be monstrous obliged if you could find a cold joint and a peacher of brandy for myself and Lieutenant Kroysing here. We'll pay, of course. Lord Rawdon's most particular about that."

"Officers on His Majesty's service are welcome. There can be no talk of pay. My servant will set a table at once." She went briskly into the house.

The Englishman called, "Come on, Kroysing! Food!"

Kroysing dismounted, growling, "How about liquor?"

"I ordered a peacher or two of brandy."

"That'll do for a start." The two passed into the house and out of Dorande's sight. She left the window and sat in a deep chair covered with a bright India print, idly picking up a book from a table. It was Horace Walpole's *Castle of Otranto*. She skimmed through a few pages, but its shivery superficial atmosphere failed to hold her. Downstairs she could hear Mrs. Cantey speaking to a servant. A horse neighed in the distance. There was no sound from the troopers. She looked cautiously out of the window. A few men held their horses below the drive, but where were the others? Movement down the valley caught her eye. The red-brown cattle were milling about in a field and green men were among them, heading them toward the road. The herd moved faster and faster. Heedless of Mrs. Cantey's warning, she sped down the corridor to the back stairs. "Madame! They drive off the cattle! All of them!" There was no answer. She skimmed down the steps, and through the kitchen window saw the widow by the barn, tugging at the halter shank of a horse that troops were leading away. She called again. Chairs scraped in the dining room and a thick voice shouted, "Who the blazing hell's that?"

Eyes snapping, Dorande tore open the door and stepped into the room. The two men had pushed back from the table that was littered with dishes and bottles. The Englishman rose unsteadily. "Your servant, ma'am. Lieutenant Manningtree, 17th Dragoons." With an unsteady hand he indicated the other. "Lieutenant Kroysing. Pennsylvania. Loyal as the devil."

Dorande clenched her fists. "Your men drive off the cattle! They take horse from the stable! Stop them at once!"

Swaying on his feet, Manningtree said, "Can't have that, Kroysing. Hospitality. Fed us. Gave us dashed good wine and brandy."

Kroysing, more sober than the other, looked under lowered brows at Dorande. "Who are you?" he growled.

"That is no matter. Order your men to stop."

Manningtree urged, "Go along, like a good fellow."

"You're always saying you're senior," sneered Kroysing. "*You* tell 'em."

"Won't listen to me. Your men. Provincials. *I* hold His Majesty's commission."

Kroysing laughed shortly. "Heard you say that before. All right. You're senior. You take the old woman. The girl's mine." He darted past Dorande and slammed the door. Pale and trembling, Dorande cried, "Open that door!"

Kroysing nodded grimly. "We're going through it. You and me."

Manningtree stumbled across the room, pistol in his hand. "Christ blast you, Kroysing! Get away from her!"

Kroysing laughed scornfully. "Put that barker away. How long would you last with my Irish boys out there if you shot me? They'd report in Camden that a Whig winged you from a swamp." He opened the door, jerked his head at Dorande. "Get along."

Her voice died in her throat and her knees went numb. She managed to form the words, "Keep away! My uncle, Paul St. Aubin, he will hear of this!"

Kroysing flushed, took a step toward her. Then he spat on the floor and turned aaay. "God spit me! *Another* of the Frogeater's nieces. Wait a minute! Prove you know him."

Manningtree, eyes wide, wove toward her. "Look! You were in Bayne's convoy when the blasted rebels upset it? That so?"

"Yes. From Georgetown."

" 's true, Kroysing. Better not touch her. St. Aubin's niece, sure enough. Lord Rawdon knows about her. By God, you'd hang, I tell you."

Mrs. Cantey suddenly appeared in the doorway and caught Dorande in her arms. "Why did you come down? Why—"

Kroysing said roughly, "You anything to St. Aubin? God knows *you're* not one of his regular nieces!"

"I am nothing to him, but he shall know that you take our stock—unless your men let them alone."

Kroysing sat down heavily, scowling and gnawing his thumb. "He'll hear, right enough. That's the trouble. He'll holler for his share."

Manningtree bowed unsteadily. "It'll be right as rain, ma'am. You've taken the oath, of course?"

"Why should I, who surely am not a soldier, take an oath?"

"Oh, must take it, you know. Sir Henry's most particular. You're for the King or against him. Can't have any shallyshil —I mean shilly-shallying about it. Hi, Kroysing! Where you going?"

The Tory lurched from the room without answering. Manningtree smiled apologetically. "Provincial. Rough block. So you're St. Aubin's niece? Ho! St. Aubin, loveliest villain of the plain! See? I'm a scholar." He burst into laughter as Kroysing returned, a book under his arm. "Look at Kroysing. Got a book. Bet a sov he can't read it. Ho!"

Kroysing held the black-bound book under Manningtree's nose. "I can read enough to know what *this* is. Are you sober enough to?"

Manningtree blinked at the riffled pages. "Stab me, if it isn't a prayer book!"

"What kind? Not Church of England, is it? Not for a God damn. It's a meetinghouse book."

Manningtree nodded vaguely. "Meetinghouse. 'Course. Call 'em White-meetners down here."

Kroysing shook him roughly. "You've served in the North?"

The other squared his shoulders in drunken dignity. "Everywhere. New England. New York. Jerseys. Pennsylvania. Ever tell you what happened to me at White Plains?" Swaying, he explained confidentially to the women, "Near New York."

Kroysing shook him again. "Blast White Plains. Who were the damnedest, rottenest Whigs? Were they Church of England?"

Eyes closing, Manningtree mumbled, "Meetinghouse people. Fought dashed hard. Killed a lot of my friends. Old Derby Starr of the 23rd, he was—"

Kroysing splashed brandy into a glass. "Drink this. Now what would Colonel Tarleton say to a book like this? What would he say about people who owned it?"

Manningtree gulped the brandy. "He'd call them God damn seditioners."

Kroysing shoved a paper at him. "Here's an order, all writ out pretty. You know what Tarleton'd want. Sign it." He had to wrap the other's fingers about the pencil and guide his hand as he signed. Then he stowed the paper in his coat. Manningtree muttered, "Good old Tarleton," and his head thumped on the table. Kroysing sneered and rumpled the brown hair. "Try to drink *me* under the table, would you? You jolter-headed bastard." He turned to the women. "Get out before my men come. Go back of the barn." He made a rough gesture toward the door as he shouted, "Mulhern! Riordan! Casey! Lug this superior swine out of here and tie him to his horse."

Dorande faced him. "Soon I see my uncle. I tell him—"

Kroysing smiled sourly. "What's done is by Manningtree's order. Got it in writing." He looked hard at Dorande. "Let me know when your uncle's tired of you."

"You!" blazed Dorande. Mrs. Cantey tugged her through the door.

"Run," she panted. "It is wiser."

Dorande picked up her skirts and scurried after her, stopping on a hillock back of the barn. Trembling with anger and mortification, she sat on a rock, her fists clenched. Sounds drifted up from the house, shouts, the clop of hoofs. They died away and she drew an unsteady breath. "They are gone."

Mrs. Cantey sat erect and impassive. Then her eyes filled and tears slid down her wrinkled cheeks. Dorande took her hands gently. "It is over. We go to the house. I shall tend you and you shall have a tisane and then sleep. When you wake, it will be as though they had not come."

Mrs. Cantey murmured brokenly, "It is of Emil that I think. What will he find when he returns?"

Dorande held her hands tighter. "He will find you sleeping. I shall sit by the music box with him."

Dorande was the first to smell the smoke. She sprang up, sped around the barn and then stopped, covering her face with her hands. From every shattered window, sharp flames licked, curled, climbed toward the shingled roof. Slowly she lowered her hands and stood frozen. Kroysing, a carbine in his hand, ran coughing from the front door and started toward the end of the drive where his troop waited. As he passed the table on the lawn, he abruptly swung up the butt of his carbine, brought it smashing down on the music box, which burst in a shower of wood and brass. Then a thick pall of smoke gushed from the house, rolled over the grass to hide the wreckage on the table and the running Kroysing.

Dorande gave a low, choking sob and fell to her knees, her eyes smarting as though the tart smoke were closing about her. A light breeze sprang up and the smoke cleared to a yellowish haze. Through it she saw the sun touching the far horizon, slanting across the calm valley of the Wateree. On the grass, by the table, the spiny roller of the music box blinked cheerfully. Then the smoke thickened.

Dorande got numbly to her feet and moved away from the growing heat. She thought, "I must tell her. But how can I?" Mrs. Cantey spoke from the haze behind her. "I would have spared you seeing what they did. I called to you back by the barn."

Dorande led her gently away from the smoke. "Spare me? Then you knew what they would do?"

Mrs. Cantey nodded. "When the Englishman grew drunk, I knew what would happen. There will be no need to search the ashes. What little we had that was worth taking is gone."

She raised her head. "But the land remains and the Wateree with its sunsets."

Dorande's lips quivered. "That canaille smashed the music box. I saw. It was so needless."

Mrs. Cantey's face set. Then she said sadly, "Ah, it is Emil who will miss it. It came from Geneva, twenty-five years ago." She patted Dorande's hands. "Now we must think of you. We shall live in the barn where there is plenty of room—now." Her breath caught as she thought of the empty stalls. "We shall make you comfortable until Monsieur St. Aubin shall come."

Dorande said quickly, "Yes! Until then, I stay and help you. I— Ah! Here is something else for us to do."

Emil Rusillon, his face a mask of woe, stood before them, eyes watering from the smoke. Like a hurt child he mumbled, "Look, *ma soeur*. Not even this did they spare." He opened a soot-grimed hand to show, bent and twisted, a single, notched brass wheel. "Not even this. Ah, it is *le bon Dieu* who must sorrow deeply when His people turn to beasts." With an effort he drew himself erect. "*N'importe*. We build again, on this spot." He dug his heel into the good earth. "And you, Mademoiselle, keep a high heart. What roof we have shall be yours. And see—" His other hand moved from behind his back. "This I find in the road, dropped by a trooper." He held out the deerskin bag.

Dorande's breath went out in a long, tremulous "O-o-oh. And you thought to bring it to me!" She took the bag in her arms, seeing Rusillon through a mist. In tragedy, he sought to comfort her as, just before, he had seemed almost to be comforting God for the wickedness of His people.

Rusillon continued, "Now, when the flames have died down, let us walk around the foundations and plan for the rebuilding. *Ma soeur,* I have always felt that your room was too small, and I shall value your advice on where the kitchen shall be. Courage! What are a few boards, a cow or two, a horse? *Enfin*, do not *we* remain?"

Dorande tried to answer him, but her throat closed on her words. Surely the good God of Emil Rusillon could not be feeling completely sad.

IV • The Swamp Fox

As November trailed its warm colors through the swamps that edged Snow Island, Ross felt an increasing sense of restlessness. His days were full enough, and he realized that what he did was useful as Marion's men responded to his saber instruction. The glades rattled as his pupils hacked at each other with hickory sticks. Later, the ring of steel was heard as blunted swords replaced wooden staves. Despite this activity, the world and the war seemed to stand still for him. Each night patrols went out at sundown. In twenty-four or forty-eight hours they returned, having snapped up the rear of a British column on the Georgetown road or scattered a levy of Tories marching to join Cornwallis across the North Carolina border.

Ross watched these groups with growing envy. At least, they were doing something, even if that doing seemed to him random and futile so far as the course of the war was concerned. There was no immediate hope of his being passed on into territory whence he could push on to Washington's main army. He even thought of attempting to join the defeated and discredited Horatio Gates in North Carolina, but all reports indicated that that little army was crumbling away through inertia, disease and desertion. No useful purpose could be served by going there.

Yet, through his growing discontent, he found fascination in the swamp world of Francis Marion. Ross saw groups of women ride onto the island under guard. Their bodies looked grotesquely swollen and their gait was slowed to an awkward waddle as they made for the tent that Marion had pitched for them. Later they emerged, wondrously slimmer and with their arms loaded with homespun petticoats which were at once cut up and remade into shirts and breeches. Many of these women had ridden far, wearing the cloth intended for

Marion's men to avoid confiscation at British posts or by Tory raiders.

There were days of famine, days of relative plenty. Twice the garrison was reduced to a small pot of boiled rice per man. Each time, as the last grain of rice was eaten, haggard, wary-eyed men drove cattle onto the island, and cursed their pack horses loaded with more rice or potatoes. There was even one memorable day when the garrison feasted on rice *and* potatoes.

So November wore on and loneliness gnawed at Ross. All those who had come up from Georgia with him had either scattered to their homes or joined Marion. Even Raoul Jaudon, his closest friend, was off to the northwest watching the British, one link in a long chain of observers who, by means of secret relay stations, kept Marion posted on enemy doings. And Raoul never reported in person to Snow Island, but devoted whatever spare time was allotted to him to an unending search for his wife Janet. Ross's mind often turned to the memory of Dorande van Kortenaer. He hoped that some of Marion's couriers might bring word from the High Hills of Santee, but they all seemed to be working farther north, ranging up from Camden to the point where the Wateree became the Catawba. The chances of making his way to the main army seemed remote as ever and Ross even considered the possibility of gaining the coast, whence small craft might take him even as far as Chesapeake Bay.

At last, on a crisp night when the moon sailed high over leafless trees and laid bright bars across the Pee Dee, Marion sent for him. He found the slight brigadier and Peter Horry sitting by a fire under Marion's great oak. As Ross reported, Marion said tersely, "Tell him the news, Peter."

Horry pushed his hat onto the back of his head. "Why, it's about Cornwallis. There he was, up in North Carolina, happy as a cuckoo in a high-holder's nest. Then last month—or so we just heard—he tried to shove his left wing south and west. Seems that Campbell and Sevier and Shelby caught that wing at a place called King's Mountain and sort of abolished it, in a nice way."

Marion said quietly, "His whole left wing. Gone. Finished off by partisans—not regular troops. You said, back at Chilyon's, that partisans just prolonged the war."

Ross sat beside Horry, frowning. "I admit that's important—very important, for the moment. But where are those partisans now? Scattered to their homes?" He glanced at Marion, who nodded. "Well, then, what happens? The British control the sea and the roads leading inland from the coast.

They'll just ship in more men to replace the King's Mountain lot and things will be just as they were."

"Militarily, yes," said Marion. "From the standpoint of morale, no. And we've got a war of morale down here, not a textbook war. That news'll hearten every patriot and discourage every Tory. Now I've got some work for you, if you want to try it." He settled back, glanced at Horry. "Tell him, Peter."

Horry cracked his knuckles and frowned at the fire. "There's a place called Prevost's Plantation across the Black Mingo. About thirty Tories and twenty men of the 71st Scots are there, with loaded carts. Francis wants you to take thirty of my cavalry and persuade the Scots and the Tories to go back to Georgetown. The house is on high ground. It's stone, with a peel around it and plenty of cover nearby."

Ross started. "What? You're sending thirty men against fifty, covered by a stockaded stone house?"

Marion rose. "We're used to thirty against a hundred. Hit them, break them and come home. Start in ten minutes. Guides are waiting for you."

Ross ran off to see to his equipment, his mind buzzing with excitement. The mission seemed complicated but he was sure that he had faced worse in the past. Marion was obviously testing him in assigning him this command. He smiled to himself as he mounted. He would do his best to show the brigadier that formal training, if it were sound, could be successfully turned to this partisan war which the latter felt was so specialized.

Grimly satisfied, Ross stood by the sallyport before Prevost's stone house. Down by the Black Mingo, a detail of his men was gathering weapons from the dead Tories. Another group guarded green-jacketed prisoners. Within the stockade he could hear cheering as the British colors were hauled down. By the casemates that flanked the stockade, the crews of the two brass grasshoppers were shuffling sullenly into line. Jacques Jenneret, his senior lieutenant, grinned as he passed him. "Looking at your work and finding it good?" he asked.

"It'll do," said Ross. His plan, heavy with hazard, had worked like a watch. From dense cover, he had sent Jenneret with ten men riding past the stockade. As he had hoped, a horde of mounted Tories had rushed whooping in pursuit. At a safe distance from the fort, ten more riders had struck the pursuers from the flank, charging and wheeling to charge again in a tight, compact body while the first group suddenly halted its flight to charge in turn. This had drawn out the

Scots of the garrison, and as they formed, foolishly, outside the stockade, Ross himself had swept down on them with his remaining men from the rear and crumpled the whole line before a cartridge could be bitten. Beyond a few minor wounds his thirty men were unharmed.

He glanced over to the left where the Scots, sullen in their plaid trews, watched his men stack the captured arms. Ross called, "Paul McCord, bring me the Scots' captain."

McCord, lithe and easy in a hunting shirt and homespun breeches, guided a bony, ginger-haired man to Ross. The Scot's face was bleeding where the pommel of Ross's saber had slammed in the first wild onslaught. Ross smiled at him. "Not badly hurt, I hope, Captain?"

"Nae, but I'm sair affrontit that the Seventy-fairst should be cowped by sich gangrel bodies," he answered glumly, eying the unmilitary men about him.

"Fortunes of war, sir. Now I'm afraid you'll have to hurry. Your men may take what rations they can carry. Then you'll start at once for Georgetown. All horses and carts to stay here."

The Scot frowned. "Ye make gey hard terms, mon."

"There are no terms. That's simply what you're going to do. Where's that Tory officer? He'll be under your orders?"

"Dod aye, he wull," said the Scot grimly.

McCord shook his head and spoke with the accent of his Scottish forebears. "Dod aye, he winna." The burr faded out. "He's dead by the Black Mingo, trying to cross blades with Will Yarborough."

When the prisoners had gone, Ross made a quick survey of the post. The salt, grain, beef and homespun would be parceled out among the men, and the carts burned at once. He would take the underfed tackies, which Marion would then distribute to burned-out families. As he walked about the enclosure, he began to study, almost unconsciously, the siting of the casemates, the solidity of the house, the line of the stockade. A thoughtful frown appeared on his forehead and he sat on an abandoned drum, eyes narrowing. Then he pulled out paper, a flattened bullet and began to write. When he had finished, he ran his eye over the second sheet. "—and for these reasons I propose to resite the casemates, strengthen the stockade and loophole the house. There is plenty of water. The post could be held against at least a battalion, supported by a light field piece." He signed the letter and called for a man to take it to Marion.

The sun was low when the courier returned, stifling a grin as he handed over a sheet of folded cartridge paper. Ross opened it, staring in chagrin at the single line of writing. "Pitch the cannon into the Black Mingo. Come home." The signature—Fran. Marion—ending in an involved curlicue, was unmistakably firm. Disappointment flattened Ross's voice as he called, "All right. Run the guns into the river. Saddle up. We're starting back."

It was close to midnight when Ross sighed the dark mass of Snow Island and heard the shrill whistles. As he crossed the ford, he saw fires everywhere, scented a bustle that suggested immediate further action. The brigadier was by the great oak, small hands folded on the rusty sword hilt. He nodded to Ross. "You did very well. Excellent work—up to the last."

Ross shook his head impatiently. "I must say, sir, that I still think I was right."

"That's what I was afraid of," said Marion.

"But look here, sir," Ross persisted. "Prevost's is a fort in itself. It'd make a wonderful rallying point, a strong, permanent one." He dug the ferrule of his scabbard into the ground. "I'm not saying you're wrong, sir. But consider this. You told me that Sevier's men 'had scattered after King's Mountain. Suppose that they'd had some place like Prevost's to rally on, to refit, to start out again."

Marion shook his head. "You're right—in terms of *your* war. Not mine. I can see that it's hard for you to realize that the men who come to me, to Sumter, to Brandon or Sevier *aren't* soldiers, as you understand the term. They're our personal followers, if you like. We send for them. They come *if* they can or if they want to. There's no organization in the state to give any of us more authority over them than that."

"But it would take so few men to hold Prevost's," urged Ross.

"No doubt. But assuming that I could always be sure of having, say, fifty men there, and that I could keep them supplied, they'd be out of *my* war. Half that number can do real service in cutting off convoys and breaking up Tory formations."

"Then what good do our raids do?"

"A lot. And as I said, you did this well. Those Scots of the 71st have got to be re-equipped from head to foot, also rearmed. That will take time. The Tories you scattered will vanish to their homes. They'll be very slow to answer another King's recruiting officer. Some of them may even come to us."

"We could have done all that and *still* held Prevost's, sir."

Marion looked keenly at him. "You still think you're right?" Then he smiled, laid a hand on Ross's shoulder. "I'm glad you do. You know your own war. You're learning ours. The time *may* come when this state will see both kinds of war going on at the same time. Then you'll be very valuable."

Peter Horry ambled up through the gloom. "We can move in ten minutes, Francis," he said as he nodded to Ross.

"Listen for my whistle in eight," said Marion. He turned to Ross as Peter slipped away. "Tired?" he asked.

"Tolerably," answered Ross.

"Too much to see more action?"

"More action?" Ross was alert at once. "I'm ready now."

"Good," said Marion. "We're gambling. You know of Colonel Tarleton? Of course you do. He's been convalescing from fever in Charleston. Cornwallis has recalled him. He's moving west along the Santee with one troop of the 17th Dragoons. It'll be a close-run thing, but we're going to try to ambush him and his troop. I want Tarleton, Bloody Tarleton, alive. You'll ride with Peter's cavalry. If we spring the trap, Tarleton's your concern, your only concern. You understand?"

Ross felt a chill that was half apprehension and half excitement. "Perfectly. You want him, alive and unhurt."

"Exactly. He's said to be a good swordsman. Can you manage him?"

"I think so. French swordplay is better than British and I learned from a French *maître d'armes*."

"Then that's settled. You've five minutes to find a fresh horse." Marion tucked his sword under his arm and limped off past the line of fires.

Under a chilling drizzle Marion's command struck south toward the headwaters of the Black Mingo, toward the Black River, toward the flat stretches of the Santee banks by Nelson's Ferry. Ross rode up the column, past Hugh Horry's mounted infantry, each man balancing musket or rifle across his saddlebow, past Peter Horry's cavalry with its rude but deadly sabers hammered from sawmill blades. From each left arm, a splash of white cloth showed dimly, a precaution against straggling.

At the head of the cavalry, Ross swung in beside Peter Horry, who pointed through the wet night. Twenty yards ahead Francis Marion rode alone, a great patch of white between his shoulders.

"Do you know the trail he's following?" asked Ross.

Horry wagged his head. "The only trail we've got is the print of his horse's hoofs. He makes his own trails. All I know about this one is that it'll be rough and fast. Make up your mind that any riding you've ever done before will seem like a mild little canter along the Charleston Battery compared to this."

Ross settled himself in the saddle. "I can guess what it'll be like. I've followed Light Horse Harry Lee in the Jerseys."

Horry gave an ominous chuckle. "But you've never followed Francis when he was spoiling bad to get somewhere and meet someone."

Rain fell harder, changing the drum of hoofs to a squelchy plopping. The white patch on Marion's back turned to a dull gray, became barely distinguishable. Mile after wet mile was left behind as the route led unerringly through swamp, over ridge, across sodden savannah. Ross's head grew heavy. It became a physical effort to keep his lids apart. Arms and legs filled with darting needle-pains and the drenched uniform chafed him. He dozed fitfully in the saddle, wrenching himself back to consciousness when his mount stumbled. Each time that he roused himself, he was dimly aware of Marion, always pushing on in the lead, erect and alert in the saddle, his head turning from side to side as though questioning each new breeze or drift of rain.

Ross's eyes smarted with fatigue. He could no longer keep them open, but rode on, neither fully asleep nor fully awake. He forgot the purpose of the ride, forgot his own particular business with Tarleton. There was a sensation of light behind his closed lids and he touched them with numb fingers, expecting to find them sore and swollen. His eyes opened.

The column had halted in a live-oak grove through which the first rays of a watery dawn struggled. Marion was talking earnestly with two men in homespun who leaned against spent horses and answered him wearily. Then the two men, bridles over their arms, moved off through the trees.

"What now?" mumbled Ross to Peter Horry, feeling vaguely pleased as he noted that the latter looked quite as worn as he himself felt.

Horry painfully detached his long frame from the saddle and stood, sag-kneed, by his horse. "That's now," he said, nodding toward Marion, who was beckoning to the pair.

Ross's feet and legs stung as he slid to the ground. "Bet it's a halt," he grumbled. "He's been setting the pace and he'll be worse off than we are." Then he swore in exasperation under his breath as Marion hopped from the saddle like a cricket and came to meet them. His eyes were clear as ever and his aquiline face, though very serious, was calm. As Ross and Peter stood before him, panting, Marion spoke in his tight, unhurried voice. "Missed him."

"Gone?" croaked Peter.

"We had bad information," said Marion. "He started earlier than we were told. A day's march ahead."

Ross leaned against his horse, too weary to feel anything except relief at the thought that the return to Snow Island would be at an easier pace. He forced himself to look at Marion. The brigadier seemed to be breathing normally. The small hand that raised a water bottle to his lips was steady. Ross winced as he caught the reek of vinegar.

Marion calmly corked the bottle and went on. "A day's march. We'll rest two hours. Then we start."

"For Snow Island?" asked Ross.

Marion looked surprised. "For Tarleton. Only one route he can take. It's through country I don't know. I've sent for guides. We'll cut overland and head him off."

Astonishment cleared the last cloud of fatigue from Ross's brain. "Two hours' rest?"

Marion nodded. "No more. And we've got to hit a better pace. Only covered forty miles in the night. Tell your troop commanders and your brother, Peter. The attack orders will stand."

"My God, what's he made of?" marveled Ross as he and Peter walked stiffly toward the waiting men who had thrown themselves from the saddles into the wet grass.

"I warned you," said Peter. "He's part rawhide and part vinegar, wrapped around the biggest heart on the continent."

"How does he know where Tarleton's gone?"

"Only one way he's likely to go. Cross the Santee at Nelson's, then hit up the east bank of the Wateree, intending for Camden. It wouldn't stagger me much if Francis spoiled that intention." He rubbed his thighs, groaning. "I'm sorry for Tarleton. I'm sorry for a lot of people. Just think of the hundreds of folks who have to spend their nights in a stuffy house, lying asleep on a frowzy bed, smothered by blankets, while we breathe in this lovely swamp air."

"My heart bleeds for them," grunted Ross.

When he had unsaddled and rubbed down his horse, he got his shaving kit from the saddlebags and lathered himself at a pool. Long ago he had found out that cold water and a shave were even more restorative than sleep. As the razor slid along cheeks and chin, his mind ran over the plan of attack, a plan that was typically Marion's. When Tarleton's troop was sighted, half of Horry's cavalry would show itself, invite pursuit and lead the enemy onto the muzzles of Hugh Horry's men, who, dismounted, would fire from ambush. Then the rest of Peter's troopers would charge the shaken dragoons from the flank. This surprise should even the odds between

Marion's scant seventy men and Tarleton's possible hundred. As to his own role, Ross felt no uneasiness about the first part. Tarleton's known impetuosity would place him in the thick of things. As for the second part, the disarming and capture—Ross shrugged. The fortunes of war would see to that. He stowed away his kit and settled himself for such sleep as was possible.

Through a day that alternated mistlike showers with stretches of dank, breathless sun, the column wound on. Ross rode in a trance, his senses aware of his surroundings but his weary brain not taking them in, beyond the fact that the course lay generally west and trending north. At the rare halts, he dropped from his horse and stretched on the ground, helmet over his eyes, while Marion, seemingly unwearied, waited patiently for his command to take the rest that he himself did not need.

Late in the afternoon the way seemed to be heading more and more to the north, a guide in a wide straw hat riding beside Marion. The false energy of overfatigue seized Ross and he began to feel tireless, his mind and senses abnormally alert. It suddenly occurred to him that the day's march must be swinging close to the High Hills of Santee and he thought of Dorande van Kortenaer. Was she still secure in the uplands, or had she been passed along into the care of her equivocal uncle on the Congaree? He asked Peter about the terrain and felt keen disappointment on learning that the Hills and the line of march were now slanting away from each other.

Later, in inky darkness, there was an unexpected halt. Ross heard Marion call for Peter Horry, who trotted away toward the dim square of white that still marked the brigadier's shoulders. Ross fretted and fidgeted. He tried to lie down on the ground that sloped away to the north, but tension and fatigue set his skin tingling and prickling, forbidding any thought of rest. Suddenly he started forward, hearing his name. He found Marion and Horry well ahead of the halting point, staring north toward a dull glow on the near horizon. As he joined them, he heard Horry say uneasily, "I tell you, Francis, I don't like it."

Marion spoke quietly. "Nor I. But that's because I don't know what it's about." He pointed to the glow as Ross reported. "See that?"

"Can't miss it from here, sir. It's hidden from the trail down there. What is it?"

"Don't know. I sent the guide ahead fifteen minutes ago. He hasn't come back. I've never been up this way before. Peter says you've got a good feel for country. Think you could get close to whatever it is, find out about it and get back here?"

Once, in the early fighting in the Jerseys, Ross had led a party of stragglers through a night blizzard off the feature-less flats up to the heights about Morristown without map, compass or previous reconnaissance. But here in South Caro-lina, where tree, grass and swamp were utterly alien—His jaw tightened. "Thanks for the chance, sir. I'll try it."

"Good luck," said Marion. "And thank you."

Ross stood motionless for an instant, trying to gauge the approximate distance that he must cover, then gave up the attempt. In the deceptive night, the blaze might be one mile away or five. He decided to gamble on the lesser distance, slipped off his spurs, attached his saber to the saddle and slipped two short-barreled pistols into his jacket. "Tired of riding?" asked Horry sardonically as he took Ross's reins.

"A long time ago. Besides, if that fire's close and means bad news, I don't want that beast whinnying while I'm trying to take cover."

As he started off he heard Marion mutter to Horry, "*That's* sound scouting." Hurrying on through the dark, he found that the brief phrase gave him real pleasure, even something more than pleasure. It was almost comparable to the night when the Virginian Harry Lee had complimented him on his first coup against mounted Hessians.

The trail led up along a gradual slope, spotted with clumps of trees. A vague moon had sailed through the clouds and he watched his course carefully, taking advantage of all possible cover as he worked from clump to clump. All at once his feet went out from under him and he slithered into a deep lane, possibly an old Indian trail that led on toward the glow that still hung, no closer, no farther, on the horizon.

He kept to the hollow way, making as little noise as possible. Suddenly he stopped, his nostrils filled with the reek of burn-ing wood. The wind, shifting slowly, brought with it the crackle of blazing timbers. Whatever the fire might mean, it was even closer than he had figured as a possible minimum. He slipped up the bank and into the undergrowth that snapped to his progress.

Cautiously he pushed forward, twice taking advantage of tunnel-like paths made by fox or rabbit. The ground dipped, rose again, and as he topped the rise stealthily, harsh light flared in his face.

He dropped to the ground, staring out over a long, level stretch. Not far away to his right, a big, deep-porched house burned furiously, the flames and smoke rolling toward him with the shifting wind. He wondered for an instant why the blaze had not been more apparent from the halting place, then realized that earlier there had been little wind and that mists had blanketed sight and sound.

His eyes grew accustomed to the vivid glare and all at once he forgot about the house. Over the empty level stretch, men moved, men in red jackets, in brass helmets with floating red plumes. Then there were more men in red with leather skullcaps. There were men in Tory green. They were all moving methodically, carrying furniture from the lower floor of the house and stacking it on a blazing bonfire, running with torches to sheds and outhouses, leading off horses and cattle. Ross drew in his breath sharply. He estimated the force at between one hundred and fifty and two hundred, more than double the strength that lay below with Marion. The wind freshened and from a distant, confused huddle, metal glinted and his ear caught the stamp of waiting horses and the clink of trace chains. Field pieces! Two at least, he reckoned.

He raised himself to his hands and knees. He had found out everything that Marion wanted to know, and the sooner the ragged handful slipped out of possible reach of the force about the burning house, the better.

He dropped flat again. A tall, slender man, immaculately uniformed, was striding toward the nearest bonfire that was topped by a mahogany table. He had an easy, gliding gait that told of lithe strength. By the burning mass he stopped, took off his helmet that, in addition to the regulation red plume, had a great plaque of glossy fur or feathers. Ross could not tell which, rising from the base of the vizor. The man shouted in a clear, commanding voice to a sergeant who was superintending the conflagration, "Rot your guts, where are those blasted spades?"

The sergeant stiffened to attention, replied inaudibly. The officer's voice blared out, "I said 'at once'! They only buried the blasted swine yesterday. Dig up his grave over there. There's not a crumb of treasure in the house and those Rebel bastards probably buried it with him. Move, now, or you'll lose your sergeant's knot and the drummers'll trice you up for a flogging."

The sergeant and his party left at a double and the officer leisurely prodded the fire, tossing a couple of leather-bound books onto the blaze. Another voice called from the darkness and Ross stiffened with quick recognition, not only of the name it called but of the voice itself. "Colonel Tarleton!"

The voice came closer and Ross instinctively slipped out a pistol as Captain Bayne stood in stoop-shouldered obsequiousness before Tarleton. Tarleton snapped, "Well, Bayne?"

"That peasant who came in, sir—" began Bayne.

"Never mind him. Has that wench talked?"

"Not yet, sir. My men, sir—well, they began to act ugly when I tried—ah—other methods."

Tarleton settled his helmet and looked coldly at Bayne. "I see. Influenced by your men. That's why you're assigned to command Provincials, not His Majesty's Dragoons." He jerked his head to one side. "Go back there. See that she talks."

Ross, still fingering his pistol, saw Bayne wince, then rally himself. "She'll talk, sir. But this peasant—I think you ought to hear his story. Sir, I know my duty. I wouldn't have left the wench if it hadn't been important."

Tarleton jerked his head again. "Get back to your work. Send the damned oaf here, under guard."

Bayne slumped away out of sight and Ross stowed his pistol again, his hand shaking. He could have shot Bayne easily, perhaps Tarleton as well, and then slipped off through the night. Yet he knew that if the opportunity had repeated itself, his finger would never have tightened on the trigger. Such work belonged neither in his war nor in Marion's.

He sank deeper into the bushes, ready for a quick retreat, as he watched Tarleton strolling slowly away from the fire. The colonel's bearing, his every movement, showed Ross that he would be as dangerous an opponent as he had ever faced. Suddenly he started to his knees, eyes wide in alarm. Two troopers were escorting a man in homespun up to Tarleton. Even without the wide straw hat, Ross would have recognized him as the guide who had ridden with Marion, the guide whom the brigadier had sent on to investigate the fire.

The man was talking rapidly to Tarleton, pointing off through the night toward the spot where Marion lay hidden. Tarleton's attitude changed swiftly from arrogance to keen, military interest. At last he patted the straw-hatted man on the shoulder. Then he stepped back and his voice ran out triumphantly. "Trumpet-major! Sound 'To Horse'!" Then he shook his fist in the air, yelling, "The devil spit me! I've got that God damn Swamp Fox in the hollow of my hand!"

Ross backed away quickly, knowing that any sound he made would be drowned in the tumult of shouts and bugle calls. He must get to Marion at once with the news that he had found Tarleton, not accompanied by a mere troop of cavalry, but with Tarleton's entire Legion, which must have been sent down from Camden to meet him.

Heedless of noise, careless of the tumbles that he took through the undergrowth, Ross plunged on. Thorns tore at him, branches slapped across his face, roots tripped him, but he only ran the harder. Picking himself up after a hard toss, he leaned against a tree for an instant to catch his breath. Through the pounding in his ears, he heard another sound, whipped out both pistols.

Off to the left, something, someone was thrashing on desperately, keeping roughly to the same course that he was following. The sounds came nearer and he crouched, one pistol raised, the other on his knees. A dark shape showed through the trees and bushes, seemed to be slanting closer to him.

He lowered his pistol, incredulous. The figure was a woman's, quite tall. In the eerie light he made out masses of dark hair falling over a bramble-snagged cloak. He started up, called softly to her, but she struggled to increase her gait. All at once she stumbled, caught herself, faced him, her back against a tree. Ross did not move. He called again, as softly as he could, "Steady! You're all right!"

Palms against the rough bark, she threw back her head and her voice came brokenly to him. "I won't talk! You can't make me!"

Still not moving, Ross said quietly, "You don't have to. You're safe. I'm a captain, Continentals. Attached to General Marion. He's not far from here." He took a few steps forward. In the dim light he could see that she was young and probably pretty. In the same level tone he said, "Tarleton had you? And Bayne? They tried to make you talk?"

Her knees buckled and she started to slip to the ground. Ross caught her elbows gently, kept her from falling. "It's all right. Francis Marion will look after you."

Her voice was still shaky, still dark with unbelief as she said, "That's true? Marion's near by?"

"Very near. I'll take you to him."

For an instant he thought that she was going to fall again, but she rallied, drew a deep breath. "Give me just a minute. I —I'm a little shaken. They—Captain Bayne—the others— wanted me to tell them things. They twisted my arms. They bent my fingers back." Her head went up proudly. "I didn't tell them anything."

Ross nodded gravely. "I'm sure of that. How did you get away?"

"Captain Bayne's men—they hate him—and when he went to find Colonel Tarleton, they let me go. They said what they were doing wasn't soldier's work and they were going to desert." She shook herself and Ross saw that she was trying to force a smile. "I didn't mean to take so long. Shall we find Francis Marion now?"

Ross pointed to the old sunken trail off to the right. "We'll go that way. It's how I came here. Sure you're all right? Then better follow just behind me. It's narrow and I'll warn you of any rough going."

He helped her onto the trail and started downhill. Over his shoulder he said, "What were they trying to make you tell?"

"So many things. Mostly where my husband was. I—I couldn't have told them that even if I'd been willing to." Ross heard her breath catch. "I—don't know. They had his name on some kind of a list."

Ross tried to make his voice reassuring. "We'll find him for you."

"He's all right. Oh, I'm sure he's all right. You see, he was captured before Charleston fell. I know that much, at least."

Ross started. "Captured? So was I. What's his name? Maybe I've seen him."

"It's Jaudon—Raoul Jaudon."

Ross stopped abruptly, turning to stare at the tall girl. "Jaudon? Raoul?" He leaned against the sloping bank of the trail. "Well, if that isn't the—" He drew a deep breath. "No—I guess it was pretty much inevitable. If you'd just gone a little east into the Williamsburg area, you'd have been bound to get word of him. He's well and riding relay for Marion right now. He escaped from the prison hulks just before I did and we met in Georgia and decided to come north together. Yes, Mrs. Jaudon, I guess you'll see your husband pretty soon."

Her hands reached toward him through the dark. "Raoul! You're sure?" he turned away from Ross, her head bowed.

Ross scuffed his boot against the bank. "Oh, he's all right. He's been hunting you. It's—do you want to stop longer and get your breath?"

She said eagerly, "No! No! Let's find Marion."

As they pushed steadily on, Janet Jaudon told her story in broken sentences. She had lived with cousins near the North Carolina border. They had been burned out. She had gone to friends to the west. Tarleton's men had come. Again and again she had moved, just ahead of raiders. "—so when that dreadful Dunlap came into our area last month, old General Richardson's niece—she's a cousin of mine—told me to join them. The poor old general was very ill from what they'd done to him while he was a prisoner of war." Her voice broke as she hurried on. "He died last night and they buried him in the family plot. Then Tarleton came before any of us could move."

"I know," said Ross grimly, remembering Tarleton yelling for spades to "dig up the old swine" in hope of treasure in the grave. He stopped, shrilling out the whistle that he had learned on Snow Island.

It was answered not far off, followed by Marion's level tones. "What did you find?"

Ross took Janet's hand and led her on. "Raoul's wife, for one thing. Tarleton and his whole Legion for another. He was very busy burning the Richardson place—*and* talking to your strawhatted guide."

"Guide?" said Marion sharply. Then he turned to Janet and his voice changed. "I'm very glad you came to us. You'll forgive me for a moment?" He seated Janet on a stump where Horry spread a cloak, then he faced Ross. "Go on about the guide."

"He was telling Tarleton things that seemed to interest him. Also, he kept pointing in this direction."

"What makes you think the whole Legion's there?"

"Three things," answered Ross. "One, field pieces wouldn't be sent out with one troop of cavalry. Two, there were a lot of sergeant's knots. Three, there were also Tory regulars, not local levies."

Marion stood silent for a moment. Then he said, "That guide! He—never mind him now. You've had experience against British cavalry. Got an idea what he'll do?"

"Yes," said Ross. "Tarleton's a hell-for-leather sort and he had his buglers blowing their lungs out sounding 'To Horse.' I heard him yelling that he had you in the palm of his hand. But he won't move in the dark."

"Why not?"

"He wouldn't dare send his dragoons down here over such rough country at night. They're not trained for such work. Also, he'll be afraid of an ambush. Even if he did want to send them after us, he'd have to weigh the chance that you'd slip around him and hit his artillery and infantry while he was gone." Ross grinned to himself in the dark. "I hear you've been known to do such things."

"Yes," said Marion slowly. "That's about what he'd *have* to figure. His infantry'd be useless and his guns are chained to the road."

"Exactly. But he'll be after you at the first light, thinking that you don't know his strength."

"Which I do, thanks to you," said Marion.

"Well," said Ross, "we've missed our chance at Tarleton. But at least we've plenty of time to get back to Snow."

"Ample," said Marion. "Now I want a word with Mrs. Jaudon." He stepped over to the stump and spoke for some time with Janet Jaudon, Peter Horry joining in from time to time. Ross leaned against a tree, suddenly lightheaded with fatigue that settled over him. Marion would pull back a few miles, allow time for a good sleep and then start for Snow Island on the Pee Dee. He thought blissfully of lying down, of pulling a blanket over him and plunging into a fathomless sleep.

He caught himself with a jerk as his knees started to buckle. Marion and the two Horrys were talking by the stump. There was no sign of Janet Jaudon. Then he saw other figures moving up through the gloom, troop commanders like John James of the Lake, the giant Conyers, John Postell.

Marion called to him and he came over, stiff-kneed, still relishing secretly the thought of a few hours' sleep. Marion faced the group about him, then spoke tersely. "Tarleton's Legion's close by. Ross Pembroke found it. We've made a plan." He stepped back a pace. "Tell 'em, Peter."

Peter, his stutter barely perceptible, rapped out a few short sentences, his mock-melancholy gone. "Light fires and keep them going. The main command falls back two miles. One troop—that's yours, John Postell—stays close by the fires. Francis will be with you. So will I."

"And Ross Pembroke," put in Marion.

"Of course. Is that all clear?"

"How long do we wait by the fires?" asked Postell.

"Until the patrols that Tarleton sends out at dawn get a good look at us. Then we fall back on the main body under my brother Hugh. Fall back slowly."

Someone muttered, "All clear."

Marion said, "Any questions?"

"Yes," said Ross. "Where's Raoul's wife?"

"Safe," said Marion. "I sent her on with a guard to people who'll look after her. We'll pick her up on the way home."

By the line of small fires, Ross dropped to the ground beside Peter Horry. "I'm not criticizing, but what's the good of letting Tarleton see us? We can't hit. He's more than two to one against us."

Horry sighed. "Now Tarleton, he's been in a Charleston hospital and Francis thinks he really needs some fresh air. So we're going to take him on a long, long ride and show him some of the most beautiful swamps in South Carolina. You see, he'll never quite catch up with us and he'll never quite lose sight of us—until Francis thinks the Legion's gone just far enough. Then we'll vanish."

"That's all right," said Ross. "But Tarleton's said to be a damn fine cavalry leader. Suppose he catches up with us."

Horry looked pained in the firelight. "Catch up with Francis when he doesn't want to get caught up with? No, my mind won't stretch far enough to figure on that. Of course, there's one thing, Ross. You can forget about your job of taking Tarleton."

"That can wait," said Ross. "But maybe I'll get a chance at one man I saw by Richardson's—Captain Bayne."

"I've heard you mention him," said Horry dryly. "Seems to me you don't like him too well. But he can't be important enough so you'd stop a war just to fracas with him."

Ross was silent for a moment. Then he said, "Bayne's the kind of officer who's always spared from his regiment for jobs no one else wants. He was in charge of the prison hulk where I was penned in Charleston Harbor. I could tell you plenty about him. He had several of us tied up, hand and foot, then struck us in the face, with his fist. And not just once. There were a lot more tricks, but you can take that as a sample. That's why I don't like Bayne."

"Yes," said Horry, rubbing his long chin. "I can see. If that had happened to me, I don't say that I wouldn't be downright cross." He stirred his long legs. "Maybe it's my eyes, Ross, but it seems to me things are getting a little lighter."

Black faded slowly into gray. At a command from Marion, Postell's troop mounted, drew back a little from the fires. Ross, sitting his horse on the far right of the line, was the first to detect movement among the trees in front. At first it suggested waving branches. Then there was a muted gleam of metal. One crouching man stood out clearly, his head moving right and left as he advanced, bent-kneed. There were more men, then behind them a hint of scarlet and a misty sheen of brass that told of dragoons riding slowly down the sunken lane. Suddenly an infantryman yelled, fired his piece and Ross heard a bullet sing high overhead. The dragoons began shouting, "Hoy! Hoy!" like fox hunters.

Marion raised his arm, dropped it, and Postell's troop filed away at a sharp trot, Ross, Peter Horry and Marion bringing up the rear. Ross looked back over his shoulder. The dragoons had halted and the infantry, Pennsylvania Tories by their green jackets and black skullcaps, were nosing about the fires. He slackened his gait a little. There was no need to hurry. The infantry would hold their ground, the dragoons would wait until the main body of Tarleton's cavalry caught up with them. Then they would push ahead, hard and fast, leaving the foot soldiers to follow in their wake. As to Tarleton's little cannon, they were probably on their way back to Camden under light escort.

It was quite light when the troop overtook Hugh Horry and the rest of the little force in an open space where south winds brought up a reek that told of Santee swamps not far away. The whole command halted, relaxed but alert until brass and waving red horsehair told of the nearness of the pursuit.

Ross rode on like an automaton through the day, exhausted to the point where he no longer felt hunger or fatigue. The ride began to assume a distinct pattern as Marion, tireless and ranging now in the van, now in the rear guard, issued his terse commands. Fast through wood and swamp. Halt in the open. On again at the first hint of scarlet and brass.

If the open space were wide, the leading dragoons were allowed to close in to fifty yards, whooping and waving their sabers, before the rear guard melted away. If it were narrow, two or three men only were left in sight, ready mounted.

Sometimes Marion would ride close by Ross, asking quickly, "Forget what you learned with us and tell me what you'd do in Tarleton's place." Ross's answer would be greeted with a nod and an abrupt command. Sometimes with two or three privates, sometimes with Peter Horry or John James of the Lake, Ross lingered to the last instant before plunging into the deep woods once more, waving derisively at the dragoons who labored along on their weedy tackies in the wake of Marion's long-limbed, powerful horses. Sometimes he went on to the main body with orders from Marion for another troop to relieve the current rear guard.

Late in the afternoon, Ross sensed a new pattern. Conyer's troop, the best mounted of the whole command, took the rear in a glade that was swamp-fringed to the north. When the dragoons broke cover once more, Marion led Conyer's men straight into the swamp. Ross gasped as the horses splashed and floundred among tussocks and evil, slimy pools, expecting his mount to bog down shoulder-deep any instant. But the sight of Marion, riding on ahead, gave him new confidence and he let his horse follow the brigadier's.

Then he saw that Marion's big sorrel was swinging in a wide circle that seemed to cut back on the route they had traveled. The rest of the command had gone straight on, avoiding the swamp. Through the poison of fatigue, Ross felt a chill sweep over him. A bare thirty men, headed by

Marion, were curving back on a line that must bring them across the path of the dragoons and the following infantry.

Snakes slid away into the muck, terrified by the splashing progress. An alligator plopped into a deep pool in a string of hissing bubbles. Ross was barely aware of the noisome swamp life, heedless of the evil beards of Spanish moss that trailed across his face. He was intent only on following the sorrel.

There was firm ground under the hoofs of the troop. Marion dropped lightly to the ground, calling, "Dismount! Hatchets!"

Stiffly, Ross alighted with the rest, saw the men deftly hacking away branches of dark cypress, bringing them quickly to a spot where Marion was pointing, then weaving them into a rough screen that blended in with the swamp. Ross on creaky legs joined Marion, then stumbled in surprise.

Through the cypress screen he looked out on level ground not thirty yards away, ground that was scored and chopped by the passage of hoofs. Marion held up his hand in warning and the rest of the troop melted back into the deeper swamp.

The line of hoof marks cut east and west across the level, emerging from thick woods on the right and vanishing in thick woods on the left. Marion had cut a wide circle through forest and swamp to bring him far back on the trail which his whole command had covered earlier.

Then a continual slow, hollow drumming caught Ross's ear. A horse whinnied, a saddle creaked, bit chains jangled and a dragoon sergeant rode out from the right. His tacky was lathered with sweat, his scarlet jacket was black under the arms and across the shoulders. Sweat poured from under his helmet and sunken eyes moved in a mask of fear and exhaustion. So they came, one by one, the dragoons of Tarleton's command. Men slumped in the saddles, most of them too spent to watch to the right and left. Ross touched Marion's elbow, pointing to a dragoon who must have abandoned a foundered horse back on the trail and now trotted forlornly on, clinging to the stirrup leather of a comrade. Marion nodded impatiently, a finger to his tight-pressed lips.

A high, ringing voice sounded just out of sight and Ross crouched lower behind the screen. Brisk hoofs clopped and Tarleton, his reckless, handsome face furious, burst into sight, lashing with a crop at the flanks of the floundering tackies. "Hell, guts and molasses! Ride that horse! Call yourself a trooper, do you? Blasted clumsy cowherd! What d'you mean, letting your mount get into such a state? Silence! God stiffen you, you'll get a lesson when we halt! Sergeant! Get his name! And you! Yes, you, you cross-eyed bastard! That's the third mount you've foundered in a month!" Then Tarleton passed out of sight.

The last trooper was followed by a sweat-drenched officer, who swayed in the saddle with fatigue. With a start, Ross recognized Bayne, who rode on, spiritless, his chin sagging on his collar. For an instant, Ross almost felt pity for him, realizing that Tarleton's sharp, bullying tongue must have sapped Bayne as much as fatigue. Then he remembered the hulks and drew out his pistol. A shot would be safe enough, for the infantry must be far in the rear. Also, it would be an act of mercy to shoot the wretched tacky through the head, leaving Bayne to struggle along on foot.

Marion's hand, surprising in its springlike strength, dropped on Ross's wrist. Ross recovered himself, nodded and restored his pistol. Then Marion stepped back from the screen, limped over to the waiting troop. "Carbines!" he called. The men unslung their short weapons. Marion called again, "Right half-troop! Fire, then reload." The carbine shots rang out. Marion turned to the left half, nodded. Again the trunks gave back the echo of the volley. Marion remounted. "Thank you, gentlemen," he said and headed his sorrel into the swamp.

Ross followed him, lost in frank admiration and equally frank wonder. Like a deep-sea sailor, Marion had steered a course that brought him exactly where he wanted to be, guided by no known landmarks. The cypress screen, blending so perfectly with the swamp background, was an ingenious device which he must have used time and again, to judge from the deftness with which Conyers men cut and rigged it. From its shelter, he had shrewdly appraised the condition of the pursuing force for future reference and plans. Then by his two well-spaced volleys, he had created a disturbance which must force Tarleton to detach at least a portion of his weary troopers to investigate and which surely would bring the unseen infantry ahead at the double, further sapping their strength.

The party rejoined the main body as night fell. But night brought no rest. Instead, the whole command moved in an arc to the south, lit fires, doubled back on their original trail and then struck north so that at sunrise, Ross and Peter Horry looked from a low hill into a sodden valley where Tarleton's men had made a wretched camp. Then two troops were sent down to show themselves and the game of the day before went on until at last Marion halted in an endless, swampy tract that Peter Horry identified at Benbow's Ferry, not far above Kingstree on the Black River.

"Orders, sir?" asked Ross of Marion, noting that the

mounted infantrymen had left their horses and were cunningly placing themselves behind fallen logs and rocks that capped a slight rise beyond the ferry.

Marion shook his head. "I'm letting Tarleton give orders now."

Ross smiled grimly through a stiff mask of fatigue. "If he can find you, he'll attack if he has to charge by himself."

"That's the order I want him to give."

The command sank out of sight in the position that Marion had chosen. Ross surveyed the only possible approach for Tarleton, the fine field of fire, saw that three fine exits through deep swamps lay in the rear and his admiration of Marion grew even deeper. He thought, "Lord, how we could have used him when Burgoyne was coming down the Hudson! He's miles above *this* work."

Men at the far left of the line began to shout and point. Ross, aching in every joint, ran toward the spot. A single figure in Tory green was struggling on through foul bog land, struggling on toward the position. Muskets and rifles covered him as a few men ran down the slope and seized him, dragging him back with them. Someone began to yell, "Tory bastard! Hang him! Who's got a rope? Hang the son of a bitch!"

Marion materialized from nowhere, his eyes cold and his mouth set in hard lines. "Throw away that rope. Anyone who hurts that man answers to me! *Bring* him here. Don't drag him!"

The man, his green uniform in rags, stood dripping and panting before Marion as Ross came up. In broken sentences he told his story, wiping mud from his face with a ragged sleeve from time to time. Two days ago he had deserted from Tarleton's infantry and had followed Marion's command as best he could, watching hoofprints. Tarleton's command, he said, was in a pitiful state. Half the dragoons were dismounted, the rest labored on on spent horses that could barely raise a trot. The Legion infantry was as badly off. There had been many desertions, many stragglers. Tarleton's rage increased with each mile, a rage that he vented on his whole command, regardless of rank. So ran the gist of the man's tale.

"Where is Tarleton now?" asked Marion.

"Started back for Camden, sir," said the Tory. Then he began to grin. "The night I bust away he'd lost your trace. I never seen nothin' like it. He sat himself on the ground and begun to hammer the grass with his pistol butt, cursin' you an' cursin' us. Looked plain daft, God damn if he ain't. Then he gets to his feet and begins hollerin' that he's got word from

Cornwallis to high-tail home to Camden. Some of the boys began to laugh right out, seein' no couriers'd come in since we left the Wateree. He ain't heard the laughin' at first, and he shakes his fist at the swamps and says 'To hell with the God damn Swamp Fox. He ain't worth powder an' ball. I'll go north and catch Sumter, a real, fightin' gamecock.' The boys began laughin' louder and Tarleton gives orders for floggin'. That's when I lit."

Marion looked keenly at him. "Gone?"

The man nodded. Marion drew a deep breath. "Take care of this man, Peter. We spend the night here. Anyone can sleep who wants to."

Ross spread his blankets beside Peter Horry's under a live oak. As he settled himself, he looked toward the fading west. Marion stood, one foot on a log, staring out over swamp and wasteland as though his knee eye could pick up the rear of Tarleton's spent force. Ross shook his head. In the space of a very few days, Marion had led Cornwallis's finest cavalry commander on a zigzag chase from near the Wateree clear across the state to the head of navigation on the Black River. That chase had ruined Cornwallis's best cavalry for weeks to come, had worn away trained Tory infantry. In accomplishing this, Marion had lost not a man and had expended from his scanty store of ammunition nothing but the few rounds fired far, far away by the cypress screen. "The Swamp Fox." Thus Tarleton had christened Marion in Ross's hearing. That christening was one deed of Tarleton's that Ross could applaud. Francis Marion, the Swamp Fox! If only his talents could be employed in some decisive theater of war.

V • The Ironmaster

The next day, accompanied by two riflemen, Ross took the trail that led north and east across the confluents of the Black Mingo to Snow Island. The rest of the command, already shrinking as men drifted away to their homes, would follow later. In the meantime, Ross was charged with seeing to such couriers as might have come to the island, forwarding their messages if they seemed important and also making sure that rations, previously arranged for, were available for the men on their arrival.

Not long ago, Ross would have looked upon the intervening thirty miles as formidable. Now he rode along easily, setting his own pace, barely conscious of the distance. Some day he would take his proper place with the Continental Dragoons, whose officers he would astonish with terse accounts of what it was like to ride with Francis Marion.

As the miles flowed by under his horse's hoofs, he found himself rising in the saddle from time to time, scanning the terrain for landmarks. It was odd, but he was eager to reach Snow Island, not merely as a journey's end, but because, having been out with Snow Island men, that strip of glade and grove and swamp had somehow become a part of him. He felt unexpected pleasure when he heard the first of the whistles, put pride into his answer.

Then one of the lesser fords splashed to the passage of him and his companions. He heard shouts of welcome, met queries and profane badinage. Suddenly he saw a tall man walking dejectedly toward him and sprang from his horse crying, "Raoul! Where the devil did you drop from?"

Raoul rallied a little as Ross slapped his back. Then he sat dispiritedly on a log. "From the northwest. No news of Janet —anywhere." He passed his hands over his face. "God, but I'm tired. I couldn't lift my foot as high as a stirrup."

Ross shook his head. "That's too bad, Raoul. But I'm afraid

93

you've got to start out right away. Marion wants to see you. You can pick him up near Benbow's Ferry."

Raoul's shoulders sagged still more. "Wants *me?* That's all right, if it's essential. But couldn't you send someone else? What does he want anyway?"

"No," said Ross. "It's *got* to be you. You see, he wants to introduce you to a most charming young lady whose first name is Janet, so you'd better—"

Raoul stared at Ross, incredulous. He sprang from the log, shook Ross violently, slapped him hard across the shoulders. The next instant he was racing off, shouting for a fresh horse. Ross watched him, smiling to himself in sympathy. Then he consulted with the few men left on the island. There was little for him to do. No news had come in during the absence of the main command. Rations had arrived and had been safely stowed. Without orders, kettles had been placed on fires so that food would be ready when Marion's men rode across the ford.

Ross ate a little cold beef and rice, his eyes roving over the island, marking each remembered point as though recognizing an old friend. A few women moved among the trees toward the south end and Ross wondered if they had been bringing more homespun for Marion's men. Two of the women were moving toward him, half seen through the branches. One seemed young and slim, the other was bent and limping.

He dropped his plate, staring south. Then he slowly rose. One of the women threw back the hood of her cloak, showing masses of light blond hair. Even at that distance, he thought that he could make out black eyebrows and eyes. He kicked his plate aside and ran toward them, calling, "Dorande!"

The blond girl started, then flew over the ground toward him, crying, "Ah, *le capitaine noir!*" Her small hands were held out and Ross caught them eagerly. "Dorande! I thought you'd be on the Congaree!" He beamed at her as her hands held his tightly.

Dorande spoke hurriedly, her eyes on his. "I ask for you when I first come here. No one would tell me of you, nor of the little colonel. Where have you been?"

"You asked for me, did you?" said Ross. "I'm flattered. I've been—" he hesitated, remembering Marion's dislike of talk about projects past or present—"oh, I've just been out for a ride."

Dorande dropped his hands and her eyes widened. "You go for a *ride?*" Her voice was incredulous. "At this time?

Don't you—*Voyez!* You are here now. You must take some men. You must come with me. As many men as you can find."

The smile faded from Ross's face as he read impatience and even disapproval in her dark eyes. Then he shook his head. "I can't send men out without General Marion's orders!"

Disappointment clouded her face and her fingers worked nervously along the edge of her cloak. "It is necessary? Then find the colonel—the general. At once. You must. Where is he?"

Again caution checked Ross's words. He said slowly, "Oh, off somewhere. He'll be here before too long."

Dorande struck her hands together. "There are things that may not wait. Do you know what happens in the west? They burn the house of Marion's cousins where I stay. We take shelter with neighbors. More men come and burn *their* houses, the next and the next. I tell you, I see it all! I and others, we escape with guides who tell us they will take us to General Marion. We go through wood and through swamp. I see more burnings. I see old men and women and children in the woods and swamps with winter close. And you—" she stamped her foot—"*you* take the air on your horse and say you can do nothing!"

Flushing, Ross protested, "If you'll only wait! Marion himself—"

But Dorande had turned away and was running toward the other woman, who had fallen on the rough ground. "*Ah, la pauvre!* That knee again." Before Ross could move, Dorande had deftly helped the other to his feet and was moving off with her toward the women's tents, forbidden ground for men by Marion's strict orders. Ross kicked at a root. "I'll be—So all this time I've been taking a little genteel exercise, have I? Been twiddling my thumbs and yawning, have I?" He leaned against a tree, obstinately. "I'll settle that with her if I have to wait till sunup tomorrow. Guess I'm just a plain idiot. Thought for a minute she was glad to see *me*. Instead, she just wanted me to order out a brigade of cavalry for her. Just the same, I really can't blame her. She must have seen a good many bad things and from what I said she must have thought that I'd been just hanging around here and—" He moved wearily away from the tree as a whistle sounded from the far end of the island, a sign that someone was coming in. Any further talk with Dorande must wait until he had found out what the whistle meant.

There was nothing important at the upper ford, just the return of a single forager. But men kept coming to Ross with questions. Should the few cattle on the island be slaughtered against the return of Marion's men? Did he think the storage place for the little powder reserve dry enough? Who had the right to a canoe that had mysteriously drifted down Lynch's Creek, the man who first sighed it or the man who swam out and towed it ashore? He settled each problem as best he could, but night fell, deepened. The fires about the women's distant tents died away. There would be no more talk with Dorande until the morrow.

Ross was roused from a deep sleep by a growing crescendo of whistles, a swelling volume that could only mean that Marion's men were close to Snow Island. He threw off his blankets and jumped to his feet, surprised to find that dawn was creeping through the eastern trees. He clapped on his helmet, buckled his sword and ran to the main ford. He must have slept through the first signals, as the far bank was astir with men and horses. He heard Marion's voice, saw him set Ball, his big sorrel, down the slope and into the water. Two by two the remains of the command followed him. Suddenly Ross gave a shout, waving madly. Just behind Peter Horry's cavalry, Raoul and Janet rode side by side, their faces alight.

Raoul shouted and Janet returned Ross's wave. Then he forgot them both as he saw Dorande, fresh and eager, the first sun touching her bright hair. She stood on a bit of high ground not far off, her eyes on the little column and on its leader whose mount was just leaving the water. Ross left his post, tried to join her, but the steady-flowing column was between him and the high ground. He caught a glimpse of Marion reining in sharply, saw Dorande, hands clasped, talking eagerly to him. Then Marion dropped to the ground, motioned to Peter Horry and the three walked rapidly toward Marion's great oak in the center of the island. Ross made a gesture of disgust. He knew better than to go to the oak unsummoned. He turned away, was caught up by Raoul and Janet, who delightedly hailed him as responsible for their reunion. They led him away, each talking vivaciously, and Ross found that their infectious joy wiped away the chagrin of Dorande's last words to him. He listened to their story, but his eye kept straying to the distant oak where he could just make out Dorande's blond head between Marion's battered skullcap and Peter's cocked hat.

Under the oak, Dorande was talking earnestly. "—And then the next house they burn. Soldiers in green, soldiers in red."

Horry and Marion exchanged glances. The former said, "The Legion, on its way to meet Tarleton."

Dorande went on. "Others join them, neighbors of the people who shelter Madame Cantey and Monsieur Rusillon and myself. More come, not soldiers, and there are more burnings. I see it all."

Marion looked disturbed. "Just a minute. Do you mind telling us *how* you got here? Not many know about this island. Fewer are supposed to."

Dorande looked at him in surprise. "But it was simple. Some of us escape, friends of Madame and Monsieur. I say to them, 'This must stop. I will go to the cousin of Madame, who sent me here.' Men trusted me, sent me on first to one house, then others, where I found people who had ridden with you. I tell each my story, and—" she held out her hands— "*voilà*, here I am."

Horry muttered, "It's probably all right."

"Got to be," said Marion. He glanced at Dorande. "You weren't hurt by the Tories?"

"Ah, that is what is strange. But one man mentions the name of *Monsieur mon oncle*. They do not concern themselves with me after that."

"Lucky," said Marion. "Now tell me what I can do for you."

Dorande's eyes widened. "For me? But I wish nothing. It is for the people north in the High Hills of Santee. *Voyez, Monsieur le général*, what I saw was terrible. About the soldiers, I can do nothing. But the names of a dozen of those who came after them, who were worse than the lowest soldiers, ah, believe me, I can tell you of them. Take your men. Show those *vauriens* that it is not safe for them to molest the good folk of the High Hills. I will ride with you. I will take you to them. I will start with you, now."

Marion shook his head. "I'm sorry. It would only waste time, men and powder."

Dorande sprang to her feet. "You do not understand? Not even when I talk of your own cousin, of her brother? Then listen. The thumb of Madame Cantey they squeeze in the lock of a pistol, hoping that she will tell them of treasure. Monsieur Rusillon, they hang up by his wrists, they beat him with musket butts. Think on that, and give me your answer."

"No," said Marion.

Dorande clenched her fists. "But I say to you—"

Marion, face impassive, said, "Tell her, Peter."

Horry's voice was gentle. "I know it sounds callous. But

things like that are going on all over the state. Sometimes people on our side do them. Suppose we call up all our men, burn out the people you're talking about. We're just piling up more bitterness. And we're not fighting this war for revenge. That way, we'd beat ourselves. And we don't mean to be beaten."

"But Madame Cantey—of the family of the general!"

Horry shook his head. "People don't count. If we take our men out, it's to do something toward winning the war. It's not to raid people who've injured other people who *happen* to be kin." He lowered his voice. "There's not a man in this command who couldn't tell you of the same things happening to a father, a brother, a cousin. In a week we could spend our whole force in avenging just one of them."

Dorande, chin in hand, looked first at Marion, then at Horry. "I think I begin to see. This war of yours, you hold it bigger than any person. That is it?"

"Yes," said Marion.

Horry said earnestly, "If going to the north of the High Hills would shorten the war a day, we'd start now. But, my dear, as things are, we'd be going just because Francis's cousins suffered. That's not reason enough."

Dorande frowned, threw back her head. "It is I who am wrong. I did not understand, and I should have." She turned to Marion. "At least I may tell you that Madame Cantey and her brother are safe. Will you send me back to them?"

Marion looked keenly at her. "You're not afraid of the journey?"

"I? Who have lived through the revolt on St. Eusebius? No, I am not afraid."

"No, I don't reckon you are," said Horry. "We can spare a guide all right."

Marion studied the ground at his feet. Then he said slowly, "I think better not."

"But I cannot live on this island," cried Dorande. "And when my uncle returns from the west, he will look for me *chez* Madame Cantey."

"We can save him the trouble," said Marion. "I can pass you on south to the British post at Nelson's Ferry on the Santee. From there, the commandant will send you up the Congaree to your uncle's place."

"But Madame Cantey—" began Dorande.

"I like your concern for her," said Marion. "But I recommend my plan. You'll be safe up the Congaree."

"If you think it best, then I go," said Dorande quickly. A look of contrition came over her face. "I argue with you and do not thank you. This is twice that you take thought for me.

Believe me, I am grateful. Is there nothing I may do in return?"

"Perhaps," said Marion, eyes thoughtful. "I know safe people up the Congaree. Through them, I'm planning to send a young lady to those parts. She'll be watching and taking notes of all the troop movements that go west past the Congaree and north up the Wateree."

"But what have I to do with her?" asked Dorande.

"Only this. Make her your friend. That'll help her in her work. You see, if plans work, she'll live in the little cottage on your uncle's place."

"At my uncle's place? At Mon Plaisir? You know it, then?"

"Well," said Marion.

"But he has only just built it. How could you know it?"

Horry spoke up. "No, your uncle didn't build *that* place. It used to belong to—well, to a friend of Francis's and mine. He was denounced as a rebel and the property was seized for sale by the Commissioner of Sequestered Estates. Your uncle bought it."

Dorande's hands moved uneasily. "He bought your friend's estate?"

"No reason why he shouldn't have," said Horry. "It was for sale, after all."

"I suppose so," said Dorande, frowning. Then she looked at Marion. "And this young lady—but surely I will be her friend, if that pleases her."

"It will. She's the wife of one of our officers. Her name's Jaudon. He'd lost her for a long time. We found her on this last ride, thanks to Ross Pembroke."

Horry nodded appreciatively. "Got to thank Pembroke for a lot of things on that sally of ours."

Dorande's head went back and she flushed. "I hear last night that you played fox and geeze with Tarleton. And he— Captain Pembroke, he was with you?"

"Don't recall he missed a step," said Horry.

Dorande got to her feet, her flush deepening. "Then it is I who have an apology to make before I start for the Santee. When will that be?"

"Noon," said Marion. "I suggest you make your apology brief, if you think it's necessary. You'll have to get your things together and I want you to meet Madame Jaudon."

"*Soit!*" said Dorande. "But the apology comes first."

Peter Horry raised a warning finger. "When you make your apology, remember that it has nothing to do with Mrs. Jaudon."

Dorande nodded in comprehension. "*Entendu*. I speak of that matter to no one—ever."

A dozen matters had occupied Ross since he had left Raoul and Janet. Much of his time had been spent at the upper end of the island devising better means for storing food, arranging for new picket lines for the restless horses. When he was finally free, he hurried toward the center, craning his neck for a glimpse of Marion's oak. All at once he made a gesture of disappointment. None of the trio whom he had seen there earlier was about. He kept on, toward a lair that Peter Horry had scooped out for himself in a sandy bank. Peter *must* tell him where Dorande had gone. He was bound that he would justify himself in her eyes.

He dropped into a dry stream bed that masked most of the island from him, knowing that it was a short cut to Peter's den. Suddenly he heard a plop and a thick, soft brownish object fell at his feet. He heard a smothered gasp above him and saw Dorande staring down from a high rock at the deerskin bag which she had dropped. Ross called a greeting, caught up the bag that seemed stuffed to bursting and sprang up beside her.

He held out the bag uncertainly. "Look here! You're not leaving, are you? There's something I've got to say to you. I—"

Dorande reached for the bag. "And I to you. I did not know—" She gave a cry of dismay. She had caught the bag by the drawstring, which promptly snapped. A cascade of brown silk, shot with gold, spread over Ross's arms. A pair of slippers fell to the ground, silk stockings oozing from the toes, then a splash of fine linen whose lace edges were crumpled. Dorande cried out again and caught the bag from Ross, hastily cramming the gauzelike linen out of sight. Ross bent quickly as her fingers became entangled in filmier lingerie. When he had carefully retrieved the slippers and stockings, there was only brown silk to be seen. Dorande stowed the footgear away, her forehead wrinkled partly in annoyance, partly in embarrassment. Then a smile showed at the corners of her mouth. "Truly, it *was* awkward, wasn't it?"

"Of me," said Ross.

"*Du tout*. Of the bag. And—and—oh, it should not have happened. I had so carefully prepared a speech to you."

"To me? But I was going to—"

She held up a slim hand. "I was wrong, Ross Pembroke, last night. I was stupid. I thought you a *fainéant*, a do-nothing, who stayed behind while others fought. Now I hear the truth from the general and from Monsieur Horry. Believe me, I regret what I said and what I thought. I should have learned better from the past." She held her bag tighter as she looked gravely up at him. "Now—I am afraid that I must go."

"Go?" echoed Ross. "No! Not just yet. You must tell me—why I've not had a real word with you. I'd have found you before, only—I tell you, five minutes can't do any harm. Then later in the day—"

Dorande frowned, then seated herself on the flat rock, her bag beside her. "I could wish for more time," she said in a low voice.

Ross took off his helmet and sat beside her, the worn leather headdress with its metal crest between them. "Now tell me how long you'll be on Snow."

Dorande's eyes were on the ground. "A very little time more. An hour. Perhaps less. Monsieur Horry is seeing to my horse and my guides."

Ross started indignantly. "An *hour?* Or less? Look here, Dorande—I mean—Miss van Kortenaer—"

Unexpectedly she smiled at him as she flushed. "But I like it. 'Miss' makes me think of the French drawings of 'La Miss Anglaise' with long necks and long teeth." Her smile faded. "Yes, I go on the road to the Congaree, to my uncle. General Marion thinks it best."

"He wants you to go to your uncle?"

Dorande had picked up Ross's helmet and was absently stroking the trailing white plume as though she held a kitten. "He thinks it wise. That is different from wanting."

"But why?" Ross burst out.

"Because of General Marion's reasons. Do you not find that enough?"

"Do you want to go?"

Her eyes met his, then dropped. "Want to go? Surely no one may force me." Her voice was a whisper. "No—I do not wish to leave Snow Island."

He watched her fingers, now playing through the worn fur band over the vizor of his helmet, and he found an odd pleasure in the sight. "Confound it," he grumbled, "Marion's nearly always right, but in this case—" he paused, aware of dark eyes studying him—"but you were going to say something?"

She surveyed him gravely, head a little on one side. "Do you shave every day?"

He started. "Do I what?"

"I see many men who look like prickly pears. But you—even on the Santee, at Chilyon's Castle, you were smooth. And it is so here."

Between surprise and pleasure he answered, "Just a habit of mine. The other men are always humming me about it."

"I see. I just wondered."

"You just—well, you're not the only one able to wonder. I've always wondered how you managed to keep your hair just so. I've wondered how, living in the tropics, you have a complexion like a Rhode Island girl. And what makes your eyes dance when you're interested or excited and what makes your chin lift when you've made up your mind about something."

Her eyes sparkled. "Truly—you've wondered about all that?"

"Yes—and what would happen if—"

She got up quickly as someone called her name over the slow clop of advancing hoofs. Three grave-faced men who had not been on the ride to the Wateree appeared, leading a fourth horse with a sidesaddle. Dorande's forehead puckered. "I do not like this, Ross Pembroke. But this is *au revoir*."

"It's—it's—" Ross caught up the helmet from the rock where Dorande had laid it. "It's not even that. I'll get Marion's permission and ride at least the first stage with you—that is, if you permit it."

Her eyes lit up. "I should find that *épatant!*" she said.

"Then tell your guides to go slowly. I'll see you at the ford." He raised his hand to the brim of his helmet and ran off, scabbard tucked under his arm.

Ross found Marion seated under the great oak once more, crumbling bits of bark into a small fire. He nodded as Ross came up. "Did Gavin James find you?" he asked.

"No. Haven't seen him. I'm going part of the way with Miss van Kortenaer. I knew you'd say yes, but I just wanted your approval to make sure."

Marion, eyes still on the ground, shook his head. "I've got no real authority over you. Go if you like. But I'd sent for you to ride up into North Carolina. To Charlotte."

"To Charlotte? Where Gates and what's left of his army are?"

"Yes."

Ross swallowed hard. "You've got no real authority over me. But you know that as long as I'm with you, I'll never go against what you think best."

"Thank you," said Marion. "Yes, I know that."

"Then for this once, can't you send someone else? I've offered to ride the first stage with Miss van Kortenaer."

"You have?" said Marion.

"You've got thirty men who could ride the Charlotte trail blindfold. You'd have to send guides with me."

"I've fifty who could ride that trail. But this time, you're best fitted."

Ross sat down resignedly. "I'll go to Charlotte. What's to be done there?"

"You'll have to find out when you get there. But the time's come when that force, or what's left of it, has *got* to take us into account. It's got to stir, and let us know what it's doing, and what a force like ours can do along with it. Go to the commanding general. Tell him about us, about what we do and why. Tell him what we've found out about British and Tory strength. I've written and rewritten. And I've had no answer. Maybe I don't know how to talk to a professional soldier. But you do. And you know how to talk to one about us. That's why I've chosen you as the only man I've got who can do any good up there."

"I see," said Ross slowly. "I'll go. I'll do my best. But I don't know how receptive Gates will be."

Marion smiled. "That's for Gates to worry about, perhaps. Thank you for taking this job. Now for your first order. Get down to the ford as quickly as you can. Then come back to me."

Ross raced down the island toward the main ford. Marion would send Dorande down to Nelson's Ferry on the Santee, where the commander of the British post, Major Archibald McArthur of the 63rd, could be trusted to accept a flag of truce and pass her on to the Congaree. He found Horry close by the ford, watching the little troop file across. He turned abruptly as Ross came up, dropped a hand on his shoulder, saying, "I told her." Then he was gone.

Ross shouted and Dorande, at the head of the column, turned in her saddle in midstream. Her hand flew up, waving frantically as she called to him. The wind blew her words away and Ross waded out into the current. She called again and her voice came faint but clear. "Ross! We do not say your English 'good-by.' It is *au revoir*. I do not forget!"

Her horse was across the ford, lunging and scrambling up the far bank. He had a last glimpse of her blond head slipping away through the trees. Then he turned dejectedly and regained the bank. *Au revoir!* What hope was there of that? She would go to her unsavory uncle on the Congaree. Then her parents would come, and she would feel the deck of a ship under her little feet as the prow headed south toward the emerald-green islands of the far Caribbean Sea. And he? It was inconceivable that their paths might cross again. Utterly. It was somehow comforting, if foolish, to imagine some fantastic chain of circumstances that would give him once more the sight of that slim, rounded figure, those deep black eyes and the mass of blond hair above the dark brows. But, of course, fantastic. As he walked back to the great oak for Marion's final instructions, he found himself wondering if the Providence merchants had ever really explored the possibilities of trade with Curaçao, Surinam, and the island of St. Eusebius.

Three nights later, Ross and his lone guide scaled the rocky shelf of the uplands, that strange formation that zigzagged crazily southwest from the North Carolina border down to the Savannah River and Georgia. Finally, when a misty light lay over the uplands, the guide reined in, holding up his hand. Ross pulled up beside him on a low ridge facing west into the rain. "That's it. That's Charlotte," said the guide Buttrick, pointing.

Rolling fields stretched out before them, seamed with broken fences, a gutted house or two. On the near horizon, a few solid roofs showed, and the cupola of a courthouse. Dotting the fields, set down haphazard and following no plan or order, ramshackle huts of canvas and charred boards swayed to the wind and the rain. Offal and rubbish littered the spaces about the huts and a sour, heavy smell rode on the storm. The men who moved about the huts were ragged. A few had broken boots and most of them stumped about with their feet muffled in rags. Huddling close by a fire, four men squatted, their muskets held by the circle of their folded arms, their hands stuffed into their sleeves or under ragged coats. The muskets looked rusty, even at this distance.

Ross said, "Good God! It's worse than Valley Forge."

Buttrick nodded. "I'd hate to have to look at something it was better than. Where's Valley Forge?"

Ross smiled grimly. "About a mile and a half this side of the northeast corner of hell." He leaned on his pommel, studying this outpost of the Army of the United States. Of course, with men in such condition, it didn't really matter where the post was sited. The Rock of Quebec would have been highly vulnerable with such a garrison. But these scarecrows lay in their filth in a hollow field, their shivering guards in the very center. From the higher ground on any side, a handful of cavalry, mounted on tackies, could have swept the hollow clean. A company of riflemen could have moved in and surrounded those men without firing a shot. He thought, "Who in God's name put the camp there?"

"Who put that camp there?" He started, as a strong voice repeated his words almost identically. Bushes crackled nearby and a heavy-shouldered man, cloak blowing back to show a blue coat faced with white, rode into the open, a dozen officers at his heels. Ross stared harder. Whoever the man was, he had the saddlecloth of a major general. *Who?*

He swore under his breath and slapped his saddle. He had thought of Wayne, of Sullivan, of Muhlenberg, of St. Clair, when he and Marion had spoken of a successor to Gates, if one were to be appointed. Now one had been chosen, as was obvious from the starred saddlecloth, a new commander for the Southern theater, the last man in the world of whom Ross had thought, and yet far and away the most eligible. He had commanded divisions in hard action. He had served later as Quartermaster General to the whole army. "Damn me for a chuckle-headed bastard," fumed Ross, watching the cavalcade sweep through the camp. "The one man who knows, firsthand, how to fight troops and feed them and clothe them!" He nodded to Buttrick. "Come on. We're at the end of our ride. There's our commander for the South."

He set off through the camp at a sharp trot, unchallenged by picket or sentry. He overtook the group of officers, saw heads turn in surprise as he rode up the column. Someone called his name in astonishment, a big, heavy-set man in a dragoon's helmet. Cavalry for the army, Ross thought, as he acknowledged Colonel William Washington's shout. Other familiar faces—John Eager Howard from Maryland, Edward Carrington, the Virginia gunner, gigantic Dan Morgan whom Ross had first seen in the ringing thickets about Freeman's Farm on the Hudson, the Pole, Kosciusko, somehow managing to preserve his panache under a rain-sodden feathered fur cap.

The leading figure turned to the sound of hoofs and voices and Ross felt a sudden lift of spirit as he saw the jutting brows, the vivid blue eyes, the pure Grecian nose of an old neighbor. He pulled up beside the commander, saluting. "General Greene, sir. Captain Ross Pembroke, with word from General Marion."

The blue eyes narrowed for an instant, then a surprisingly warm smile spread over Geeene's florid face. "Well, well!" He held out a strong, scarred hand. "This will be good news on the east shore of Narragansett. Theophilus Pembroke's boy! Had a letter from Kitty at Philadelphia and she said your father hadn't given up hope. Here! Pull in beside me. Yes, your family's all well. Your sister Judith married young Minden at the College and Cora's—let me see—oh yes, she's to marry someone from Boston—invalided gunner I think—in the spring. Jove, this is lucky! I've a courier going north tomorrow and we'll both send word home. Your family'll know you're all right before the ice is out of the Pawtucket River or the Seekonk." He wheezed slightly as he spoke and Ross knew that Nathanael Greene's long battle with asthma was still being waged. "Last time I heard—but that can wait. Who sent you on here?"

"General Marion—General Francis Marion," said Ross.

Greene snapped his fingers. "This is sheer providence! I was told in Philadelphia that I must get in touch with Marion but no one seems to know where he is. Thomas Sumter's coming in within a day or so and I've had no trouble sending word to Pickens out in the west. But Marion! You've been with him? You can tell me about him?"

"That's what he wants, sir, although he didn't mention you by name. It's my guess that he had some hint there'd be a change in command and sent me to talk to whoever replaced Gates."

Greene stared at him. "How the devil could he have known, off down wherever he is? Confound it, I only got here a few days ago!"

Ross smiled. "Marion listens to the trees and the winds and the rivers. They seem to tell him a lot."

"That's what I heard. I found a letter he's written Gates, who'd never answered it, and I've been trying to frame a good reply. You'll help me with that. Let's get back to quarters. I've seen enough for today. My staff's been taking notes. We've a lot to do, getting things straightened out here."

"These will be your winter quarters?"

"Winter quarters!" snorted Greene. "I didn't leave West Point to supervise winter quarters down here. No! I'm taking the field. I've been promised reinforcements, but if they don't come, I'll do what I can with what I have."

The thirty-odd houses of Charlotte huddled forlornly in the cold rain and the streets were a slop of red mud. Despite the dreary setting, there was an air of purpose and activity that differed widely from the militia camp that Ross had first seen. The men and officers who rode or waded through the slush were ragged, but they carried themselves well. Whatever mission each was on, there was an air of definite aim. Greene indicated a platoon in worn hunting shirts that marched briskly away to the south. "Delaware Continentals. They and the Marylanders have got to be the nucleus of my force."

"Good commands," said Ross. "I remember them at Monmouth and Germantown."

They reined in before the courthouse, a plain wooden building set on high, brick pillars. Green turned to the officers who followed him. "I'd like your reports not later than noon, gentlemen. I'll be occupied with Captain Pembroke for at least an hour."

Ross followed him up the long steps, noting that Buttrick had found friends among the militiamen quartered under the courthouse, and would be taken care of. Greene walked rapidly past saluting aides and threw open the door of a small room at the right, where a stand of colors was flanked by a pair of captured British espontoons or pikes. "Sit down, Pembroke," said Greene. "Now start talking about Marion and keep on talking until I can see him sitting beside you there."

Ross grinned. "It would be just the same if he were, sir. He'd just say, 'Tell him, Pembroke.' He doesn't talk much. Maybe I'd better start with my first meeting with him. Then you'll see him as I saw him." Ross talked on about the slight, wiry, silent man, of his unshakable integrity, his resolution, the unbounded trust that he inspired in people. He told of the rallying of Marion's men for a given mission, of their scattering, of the fluidity of the organization, if it could be called one, with its small cadre of officers and men about whom the temporary force was built. He eagerly described the way in which Marion steered across country, his uncanny sense of what the enemy would do and what the enemy hoped that he would do. He found himself enthusiastically sketching the sudden shifts of base, moves known in advance to no one but Marion and goals known to him alone. He told of Snow Island in detail, of its ring of patrols and the whistles that marked arrival and departure, of their garrison swelling to two or even three hundred men, then shrinking to a mere dozen. Greene, tilted back in his chair, listened with his hands folded over his waistcoat and his eyes closed. When Ross had finished the tale of Snow Island, Greene nodded. "It sounds like Athelney."

"Like what?"

"Athelney. Alfred the Great's base against the Danes. It's at the junction of the Tone and Parret in Somersetshire."

Ross smiled to himself as he remembered that next to Henry Knox, Nathanael Greene was the leading military scholar of the American army. There had been a night at Valley Forge when, in a dripping hut, Ross had seen von Steuben and Lafayette stare in wonder as Knox, the Boston bookseller, and Greene, the Warwick ironmaster, discussed Wallenstein's siege of Straslund in 1628.

Eyes still closed, Greene said again, "Yes, Athelney. I like the sound of that base. I like his keeping on the move. What does he plan to do that I ought to know about?"

"He hasn't actually planned anything. What he'd like to do, with your approval, is to start operations against Cornwallis's lines of communications and posts. There's George-town, there's Nelson's Ferry on the Santee. There's Camden itself."

Greene opened his eyes slowly. There was nothing sleepy in that direct blue gaze. "He wants to capture them?"

"No, sir. I told you, that's not Marion's way." He smiled wryly as he remembered the reception of his own proposal to garrison Prevost's on the Black Mingo. "What he wants to do is to keep the roads and the posts under such pressure that Cornwallis will *have* to weaken his main force to protect his convoys and to secure his posts. Take Nelson's Ferry. That's been reinforced three times since October just because Marion moved in its general direction. He didn't even show himself."

Greene got up and walked across the room to the rain-smeared window. Like Marion, he limped noticeably, from an old knee injury. Ross remembered that that same limp nearly kept Nathanael Greene from enlisting in the Kentish Guards in '74. Somehow, the limp and the noticeable asth-matic wheeze transported Ross for the moment from North Carolina to Rhode Island. He could see Nathanael Greene and his brothers supervising the forging of an anchor while he himself and a few other half-grown boys peered in awe at the sparks that flew in the dark shed and tried to stop their ears against the crash of the hammers. Nathanael Greene, the ironmaster, a Quaker until he was read out of the congrega-tion, now, by common consent, the first soldier of America, next to Washington. He remembered, too, seeing Nathanael Greene leaving the little church at Newshoreham with pretty Kitty Littlefield on his arm. Now the ironmaster stood quietly in a North Carolina courthouse and listened to a tale of a Huguenot leader who planned to strike at His Majesty's troops along the Santee or the flat, swampy coast.

Greene turned from the window, rubbing his round chin, as he might have rubbed it at the successful forging of one of the famous Greene anchors. "That's interesting, Pembroke. I think that Francis Marion and I will get along. I'm going to give you a letter to take back to him. But that will contain generalities. I want you to carry back to him, in your head, as clear a picture of what *I'm* trying to do as the one you just gave me of *his* intent." He sat down again, leaning forward with his hands on his knees. "I'm not counting my reinforcements until they're here and boiling their kettles. I've got something under a thousand dependable troops. All in all, about two thousand. The best figures I can get show that Cornwallis has about thirty-two hundred—good, solid units. I figure that gives him, for all practical purposes, a strength of four to my one. Is that clear?"

"Quite," said Ross.

"I'm not going to stay here in North Carolina. General Kosciusko is going to make a survey for a camp in the Cheraws, just across the South Carolina line on the Pee Dee." He glanced at Ross. "Where's that in relation to Snow Island?"

"Oh, say sixty to seventy miles, a bit to the west of north of Snow. Marion will like that."

"I hope so. I also hope Cornwallis won't. It puts me nearer Charleston than he is himself—and Charleston's his most sensitive point." He shifted in his chair, crossed his hands behind his neck and looked thoughtfully at Ross. "You've been in pretty much since the start, haven't you?"

"I couldn't have been much closer to the start without serving at Concord and Lexington."

"I thought so. H'm. You've kept your eyes open. I can see that by what you chose to tell me about Marion and conditions here. Just run over the campaigns of this war in your mind. Can you remember any instances of a commander splitting his forces in the field?"

"Splitting his forces? Lord, yes. Washington did at Long Island. Burgoyne did when he sent Breymann and his Brunswickers into the Hampshire Grants—to Bennington, wasn't it? Oh yes, and then Howe scattered his Hessians so we could hit them at Trenton. Washington did it again in '78 when Lafayette was nearly caught at Barren Hill in the Jerseys." He laughed. "Experience is a great teacher, isn't it? Cornwallis did it again last fall when Ferguson was wiped out at King's Mountain." He wondered what had lain behind Greene's questions. Surely the ironmaster's brain, steeped in military lore, could have found a hundred examples.

"Ye-es," said Greene slowly. "You mentioned some good cases. Always ends fatally, doesn't it? That is, unless you're lucky, like Lafayette at Barren Hill."

"Bound to be fatal," said Ross.

"Bound to be." Greene looked absently out of the window, teetering back and forth in his chair. "Sure to be." The legs of his chair hit the floor with a smart rap. "But it's what I'm going to do."

Ross started. "You're *what!*"

"Yes. That's what you'll tell Marion. I think he'll approve. Of course, it's against all military logic."

Ross tried to visualize Marion's dark face when he heard of the plan. Suddenly he knew that Greene was right, knew in advance what Marion would say. War in the Carolinas was *not* logical, nor fought according to the books, as Marion had shown a dozen times over. He said, "I know Marion, sir. He'll approve."

"That's my hope." Greene began to limp up and down the room again. "Of course, I've got to justify this to the Congress, to Washington. I know Washington'll see that I *have* to fit strategy to local conditions which I can't change. By splitting my army into two parts, one to the east and one to the west of Winnsboro where Cornwallis is, I can feed them more easily. We'll draw our supplies from the very areas from which Cornwallis draws. Then, if he tries to hit the western force, he'll uncover the coast right down to Charleston. If he comes against me, he bares all the west from Ninety-six down to the Savannah. From our standpoint, having those two forces will make it easier for us to rally the people to us. They'll be able to establish small supply depots. But, for the moment, the most important point is this."

He stopped, facing Ross, and thrust his hands under the tails of his coat. "So far as I can reason, what Cornwallis wants to do is, first, to pacify, so far as he can, Georgia, South Carolina and North Carolina. I guess that he feels the first two states are about as he wants them, barring minor opposition, which he can overlook. He must be planning to refit and move into North Carolina in force, hoping to rally large numbers of Tories, under men like this Hector McNeil, to his colors.

"Then, of course, he'll move right on into Virginia, where he'll be close enough to work with Sir Henry Clinton's main army around New York. He'll reason, I'm sure, that they'll have little trouble then in catching Washington and our main army in a sort of military nutcracker. Perhaps he's right." His jaw tightened. "That is, if Cornwallis really does get into Virginia with his army intact and three pacified Southern states in his rear. We're going to see that that doesn't happen. Our first move has got to be to keep the war going and to stop his invasion. Now, think you can tell Marion all that?"

"Couldn't be clearer," said Ross.

"There are a few more things he'd better know," Greene went on. "Dan Morgan will command the western force, with the best troops I've got. I'm going to establish a Camp of Repose in the Cheraws and whip what's left of the army into shape. General Isaac Huger will command under me. Now I'm going to draft that letter to Marion. Come back at noon and we'll talk about Rhode Island over salt beef and corn bread."

"I'll be very glad to, sir. And about this letter to Marion—do I understand that I'm to report back to you after I've seen him and talked to him?"

Greene blew out his cheeks thoughtfully. "I'm going to keep my cavalry as strong as I can, and I'll need every experienced officer I can find. But—" he drummed his fingers slowly on the table—"you see, you've developed other skills down here. You've learned things that I don't know, that mighty few of us know. Sooner or later, I'll have to have you with me. But for the moment, I'm rather inclined to leave your assignment to Marion. He's going to play a pretty big part, along with Sumter and the others, in what we do." He smiled in dismissal. "Till noon, then."

Ross stood frowning in the rain outside the door, feeling definitely disappointed. It was only logical that he should return to Marion, tell him of Greene and the plans for the future. But then? He had hoped, even expected, to be assigned to command a troop, perhaps even a squadron of cavalry under William Washington. Then he shook off his somber thoughts as best he could. At least, the Southern theater had a commander in every sense of the word. That was the important point. His own immediate duty was to serve where that commander thought best.

A door opened along the courthouse gallery and William Washington stepped out, his light, springy step belying his air of comfortable stoutness that had deceived more than one British dragoon. His plump face lit up as he saw Ross. "Well! So it was you, after all. I thought I was seeing ghosts when you came past us. Where have you been? We all thought you were a prisoner!"

Ross shook hands, noting the shabbiness of Washington's white cavalry jacket, his mended boots. "I got away from the hulks with a few others," he explained. "Since then I've been with Marion."

"With Marion? In the swamps?" Washington stared. "Must have been mighty uncomfortable campaigning! Well, it's going to be different now." His round face glowed with satisfaction. "You know, I'd never noticed Greene much in the old days and I thought he'd found his proper billet when he was made Quartermaster General. Lord, I was wrong. At the end of his first day here, he knew more about the army and about Cornwallis than Gates had learned the whole time he was here. And how he can handle men! We saw him take command from Gates and you'd have thought, watching him, that Gates had won a big campaign and was being moved up to a higher post. It was a real lesson in courtesy and propriety. And his staff! Do you know about it? Then you better come and meet the members and the field commanders. Kosciusko's out hunting for spades and pickaxes and Greene just sent for Dan Morgan, but the others will be there. You probably know most of them from the old days, or at least you've seen them."

The room into which Washington led Ross was dim, and for a moment he could only make out a group of men in worn uniforms frowning up at him from sheaves of papers. Then the room seemed to brighten and he heard chairs scrape on the floor, heard his name called. It was a little like the first day of the fall term at college, when classmates, half forgotten during the long halt of summer, poured back to the brick college on the hill.

There was handsome John Howard of Maryland, whom he had first known in the useless fortifications that curved about Brooklyn in '76. Near the stone Chew house at Germantown in Pennsylvania, Howard had hastily bandaged Ross's shoulder, both of them eying the Skippack road uneasily, waiting for the onslaught of von Donop's Hessians. Beyond him was Edward Carrington, the Virginia gunner, who had brought up his grasshoppers at Monmouth under guard of Ross's dragoons, to hammer at von Knyphausen's flank. Across the table was another Virginian, Otho Williams, who had come to Boston in '75 as lieutenant in Cresap's rifle regiment.

It seemed utterly natural to Ross to meet so many familiar faces in the chill North Carolina rain. Those who had stayed on, through parching summers and bitter winters, while George Washington's army swelled, shrank, swelled only to shrink again, formed an odd freemasonry that had little to do with position or state of origin. The ties had been formed on the hills about Boston, had grown and strengthened on the killing march to Quebec, in the desperate retreat from Manhattan down through the Jerseys, in all the years when successive British commanders had won battles, but never campaigns. Those men who had only gone part way in that grueling march through time, those who had joined later, no matter how earnest, or how notable their services, were somehow unconsciously shut out of that inner group who had gone the whole distance. They might be welcome to the military mansion that George Washington held intact, but to one room they could not be admitted. Ross had noticed this, even on the prison hulks in Charleston Harbor. Someone was sure to say, "Do you remember that day outside Boston when we sighted the first of the siege train that old Henry Knox brought overland from Ticonderoga?" Or, "That was like the time when Johnny Laurens and that Frenchman, Chevalier du Plessis, tried to rush the Chew house singlehanded." Then the invisible door would close, made up of shared memories that might run as far back as the Concord-Lexington Road, or the steep glacis at Stoney Point where Anthony Wayne, head bleeding, was carried on the shoulders of the first wave of the attack.

William Washington was introducing the one stranger in that room, a tall, grave man, who stepped across to shake hands with an unmistakable cavalryman's stride. "Will Davie of South Carolina, Pembroke," said Washington. "He was at Long Island." Ross tried to keep the inevitable unspoken question out of his eyes as the biography stopped short at '76.

Davie met Ross's glance frankly. "I'm a case of mistaken judgment, maybe of lack of faith, Captain Pembroke. I went back to the college at Princeton in the Jerseys after Long Island, and took my degree. I thought the war was over, and went into law up here in North Carolina. I figured I was wrong when Lincoln came down here in '79 and so I did some cavalry work around Charleston. Then I came back up here and went into law again."

Howard said quietly, "He doesn't say, Pembroke, that he got wounded at Stono before he came back here."

Davie smiled gravely. "Maybe I would have come back, after the surrender. Anyhow, my first work took me into a hot Tory district and when I saw the way things were going and what the Tories were doing, I made up my mind right away that even if George Washington surrendered, the war couldn't be over for me. So I raised a couple of troops of cavalry and some mounted infantry and tried to make myself as objectionable as I could to anyone in green or red. I'd been hoping to get assigned now to Dan Morgan, but Greene's got other work for me."

Carrington muttered in Ross's ear, "Sold every damned

stick and acre and black that he owned to fit out those men."

Ross looked at Davie's steady eyes and firm mouth and chin. He felt that, somehow, that invisible door that he had just imagined would never quite close on William Davie. He said, "You were at the College of New Jersey, at Princeton? You must have been about Harry Lee's time."

"Lee? The one from Stratford in Virginia? Oh, I knew him, but he was a class or two ahead of me. He was always with James Madison and Aaron Burr. Funny about Lee. He belonged to the Cleosophic Society there, as Tory as Lord George Germain. He certainly changed afterwards."

Howard chuckled. "No doubt of that. It's like young Hardy when Grant's Highlanders came up Gowanus Creek at Brooklyn. Remember how Stirling—

Ross dropped into a chair and listened to the reminiscing, smiling to himself. The door had closed, but Davie was on the inside. He studied the group. They were all desperately tired. Coats and boots were patched. Caps, helmets and cocked hats had obviously seen hard service and would see more before they were replaced. Yet there was an air of efficiency and purpose about each man, no hint of fumbling or uncertainty. It would have been hard to pick a better set of men with the whole Army of the United States to choose from.

The talk swung from the past to the present. One or two seemed inclined to commiserate with Ross over wasting his talents with a partisan band. Ross, a little to his surprise, found himself bristling, coming almost angrily to Marion's defense. "If it weren't for Marion's men and others like them, you wouldn't have *any* war down here to use your professional talents on," he concluded. "Partisan? Maybe, but I know I've learned a lot from him and there isn't a man in this room who couldn't—if he would."

Carrington laughed and clapped Ross on the shoulder. "You've been with irregulars, with militia, too long, young man. Lord, don't you remember the militia we saw in the Jerseys? In New York? What were they worth? You know how much—or how little. You'll change your mind when you're back in regular service." He laughed again. "Militia! Yes, we've seen them."

Ross set his jaw. "Maybe. But you haven't seen Marion." Quick steps out on the gallery interrupted him and a huge form darkened the window as it passed.

Then the door banged open and Dan Morgan's booming voice filled the room. "All arranged, boys. Will, you'll handle my cavalry. John Howard, my infantry's yours."

Everyone jumped to his feet. "We're going out?" asked Howard eagerly.

The vast man stepped across the threshold, exuberant and bursting with energy in the fringed buckskins that he had made peculiarly his own uniform. "Going out! Yes, the Old Wagoner's going to crack his whip over Tarleton. I've sent word to Triplett and Tate. We're going to hit west of the Catawba and see what happens." He peered at Ross. "Who's that?"

Washington introduced Ross, saying, "He was with the Rhode Island infantry on your flank at Freeman's Farm in '77."

Morgan's laughter rang out. "Ho! I remember them, all right. I blew my turkey call and they came running. Under Varnum, weren't you? Better ride to the Catawba and the Pacolet with us and we'll show you some sport that'll be as good as any you saw on the Hudson." He waved a huge hand at Washington and Howard. "Be at my quarters at two sharp. We'll do some thinking." He waved again, slammed the door shut and glided away down the gallery.

Ross raised his eyebrows at Howard. "I'd say things were going to happen."

"Hope so," said Howard, frowning, and jerking his head at the vanishing Morgan. "You see, he's plagued by the rheumatics so badly that every move just about wrenches his heart out. He'll fight as long as he can stand up. After that—" he shrugged—"we can only hope there's someone else to take his place. Do you mind if we go on with our work? We're about through with these recommendations for Greene." He pushed a paper across to Davie. "We've agreed that we'd better move the militia in the eastern posts over here, where the cross is on the map. That leaves those irregular levies that came in last night and Ed thinks—"

Ross sat back listening, drawing new confidence from each idea that was presented across the table. He was suddenly reminded of the councils that he had attended on Snow Island and recognized in the present the sure purpose and ability that he had known there in the past. He recalled Greene's words. "I think Francis Marion and I will get along." So would the respective staffs and field commanders.

At noon, Ross left the staff room and joined Greene under the national colors and the captured trophies. The commander looked tired and a good deal of the freshness had gone out of his face. Nonetheless he smiled at Ross and waved him to a seat at the table where Spartan servings of salt beef, corn bread, potatoes and coffee were smoking in the chill room.

"Got a lot of work to get through before we can see where we are. Help yourself to that butter. General Huger sent it over this morning. Yes, a lot to do. Confound it, I never knew there could be so many snarls. A good deal of friction. X doesn't like Y and Y won't serve under Z. Then X, and Y, and Z are all sour because someone from the next parish wasn't appointed to this post."

General Greene talked on, laying down his knife and fork and staring out of the window that was streaked with a fresh burst of rain. He thought he could solve a good deal of that. He'd have the dissatisfied ones to dinner, pay them some attention and see if things couldn't be smoothed. There'd be trouble in collecting boats to float down to the Cheraws, boats that would serve as bridges across the numerous streams if a retreat seemed necessary at any time. But wagons! He couldn't expect Carrington and Davie to function without wagons and if he *had* to impress civilian vehicles, why he just had to, that was all.

Ross, concerned about the food that grew cold on the general's plate, tried to divert his mind to easier channels. "I was very much impressed, sir, with your staff," he said.

Greene brightened. "I couldn't be luckier! But, Jove, I've got to give them something to work with. We've *got* to build up a regular force here, or the nearest thing we can to one. I've been thinking over what you told me about Marion and matching it with what I've had from Sumter and Pickens. Without a regular force, the whole South's lost. And yet— the sort of force I'll have will be useless without partisans. And by the same token, they'll be useless without me. We've got to work and think and act as close as that!" He held up his right hand, the five fingers pressed together. "It comes down to this. We do *not* fight, except on our own terms, not on Cornwallis's terms. We move lighter than he does and we've got to be able to dictate on that point. If we keep to that rule, retreat, retreat, retreat if we have to, strike hard when we can—well, we won't win many battles, perhaps. *But*—" he smacked his hand on the table—"we'll win the campaign! There's lots to do first. I wonder why Sumter doesn't like Washington. Then there's—" He broke off, smiling at Ross. "But we were going to talk about Rhode Island, and we both want to send letters north about you. And for another thing, I've been wanting to hear how you've spent your time since you got out of the hulks."

Ross found himself telling about his escape, the slow gathering of a band in Georgia, the ride north, the attack on Bayne's convoy.

Greene nodded appreciatively as he explained how he had disposed his men, adding, "Hope the attack was worth while."

"It—it was an odd convoy," said Ross slowly. "You see, there was a girl in it." He told of Droande, of the night in the swamp, meeting Marion at Chilyon's Castle and of his sending Dorande to the High Hills of Santee.

Greene cocked an eye at him. "I'd say you didn't heartily approve of that last."

"What else was there to do?"

Greene smiled. "Not having been there, I couldn't say. Was she pretty?"

"Yes, I suppose she was. She—oh, the devil, yes. She was—is—damned pretty. Hair so blond you don't know if it's gold or silver, black eyebrows and black eyes and a way of cocking her chin up when she's determined about something." He rolled crumbs of corn bread between his fingers. "I told you she's French and Dutch and she speaks very good English—with an accent of course, a very fetching one."

"Did you ever hear what happened to her after she went off to join that uncle of hers—you said uncle, didn't you?" Greene was watching him sympathetically as he sipped his coffee. "I suppose not. Wars have a way of rolling people apart."

"And together," said Ross quickly. "She was burned out twice by Tories up in the High Hills of Santee and then what do you think she did? Found a guide and came across country to find Marion. She had an idea that he'd take his men and track down the burners, especially since her hosts were Marion's cousins."

"What? She came clear from the Wateree to Snow Island?"

Ross smiled crookedly. "I told you she was a very determined young lady—or little girl, as Peter Horry always calls her."

Greene snorted. "Determined! I'd give her Morgan's corps if she were here. What did Marion do?"

"He persuaded her that revenge on those Tories wasn't part of the bigger business and—well, she went away with an escort to the post at Nelson's Ferry. From there the British would send her on to her uncle."

Greene's eyebrows went up. "So you were at Snow Island when she came there?"

"Didn't I tell you that war sometimes brings people together instead of rolling them apart? It's happened once. It can happen again."

Greene sighed. "I hope so. I must say I'd like to meet that young lady. At least, she's closer than Rhode Island. I've not seen Kitty since Valley Forge. A long time, a very long time. You know, I had the command at West Point before I was ordered down here. Kitty had actually started from Providence to join me." His eyes were far away. "Yes, started. Washington's orders were urgent, but I tarried as long as I dared. I even rode east a little when I finally set out, hoping to meet her, because I'd had word that she was just about a day's journey away. Then I simply didn't dare go any farther. Poor Kitty. It must have been confoundedly sad for her, crossing the Hudson from Verplanck's and finding me gone."

There was a tap on the door and a sergeant, facings faded beyond recognition on his patched uniform, saluted, handed Greene some papers and withdrew smartly. Green ruffled through them. "Ah, this is good. A draft of a letter to Marion. I've told him about what I told you concerning co-operation between regulars and partisans. That part's all right. Now, you know him. I want you to look at my opening paragraph. He'll get his whole impression of me from it and I can't afford to give the slightest cause for offense. I phrased it as carefully as I could, basing it on the picture that you'd given me of him. I may be utterly wrong." He handed Ross a sheet.

Ross glanced at the superscription, "To Brigadier General Francis Marion," then began the first line.

"I have not the honor of your acquaintance, but am no stranger to your character and merit. Your services in lower South Carolina in awing the Tories and preventing the enemy from extending their limits have been very important. . . . I am fully sensible your service is hard and your suffering great, but how great the prize for which we contend. . . ." Ross felt that he could see Marion reading the letter under the great oak on Snow Island. Completely devoid of vanity, he would take "your services" to refer to his whole band and the recognition would touch him. Later he would go over the sheets with Peter Horry, then assemble his officers and say, "Tell them, Peter."

He handed the letter back to Greene. "Don't change a comma. He'll be in complete agreement."

Greene drew a sigh of relief. "Then that's all right. I'll have it fair-copied. When can you start back with it?"

Ross got up. "I'll find my guide and see what his ideas on travel are. I'll probably sleep through the afternoon and go back after sundown."

"Is your first stage a long one?"

"Not very."

"Good. When you wake, come back here for dinner. I'm

having General Huger, Kosciusko and McDowell, the King's Mountain one. Have a good sleep and dream about your little Dutch girl. And—by the way—who's this uncle of hers?"

"A Frenchman named St. Aubin, Paul St. Aubin."

Greene's eyes widened. "St. Aubin? Oh yes, to be sure. I just wondered."

As Ross left he heard him calling, "Bring me that letter from Governor Rutledge—you know, the one about Tory sympathizers and land confiscation."

On the long ride south from Charlotte, Ross had fretted with impatience. He was eager to deliver Greene's letter to Marion and to explain verbally all that he had seen and done. He was also quite as anxious to gain the brigadier's permission to start back as soon as possible and join his old colleagues in the campaign that Greene's army was about to open. Then, when the first whistles told of his approach to Snow Island, the road to the north dimmed in his mind. He saw scouts high in the trees, then sighted the upper ford where ragged, lean men waved and shouted to him, welcoming him to the hidden camp. Of course, this return was not quite like finding himself among his fellow veterans of the northern campaign. It couldn't be. And yet—

He found Marion, seated as usual under the great oak. The brigadier sprang to his feet, dismissed two or three officers who were with him, and limped forward, his hand held out. "This is fine, Ross. You didn't lose any time, I see."

Ross flushed with unexpected pleasure. It was the first time that Marion had used his Christian name. "Thank you, sir. My guide chose his trails well. I've a letter and messages for you from Charlotte."

Marion seated himself in the curve of a chairlike root, indicated a flat rock close by for Ross. "I want to listen. Then I'll read. What did you find up there?"

Ross plunged into an account of his meeting with Greene, of his talks with the general and his staff, Marion nodding in silent approval from time to time. When Ross had finished, Marion asked, "Know Greene?"

"I've known the family all my life. They live across the bay at Warwick."

"Is he ambitious? As a soldier, I mean."

Ross smiled. "You've answered your own question. Would an ambitious man accept this Southern command? Particularly a complete stranger like Greene?"

"Right. Is he set in his ways?"

"He's always been alive to new ideas. If you can show

him he's wrong, he'll change. I wish you could have heard him questioning me at dinner about your maneuvers against Tarleton. At first he thought the whole thing was a waste of time. Then he—well, Kosciusko was there and they both said it was mighty close to genius."

Marion made a deprecating gesture, then asked, "Anything else about Greene?"

"Only that he's always had a terrific temper, but it's so under control that few people have ever seen him lose it."

"How does he feel about us?"

"That's in the letter. He realizes that the kind of army he's likely to have, both in quantity and quality, won't get far unless it works with partisan commands."

"We won't get far without him. Now the letter, if you please."

Marion's face was impassive as he read. When he put the sheets away, he said, "That's courteous. I agree with his comments. We'll get along. Now this part about you. I appreciate his leaving the decision to me, for the moment."

"About me?" asked Ross, surprised. "Oh, yes, I remember now. I'm at your orders, sir."

Marion tapped the folded sheets on his knee. "I'd like you to stay here. A campaign's opening. We'll be in it. There's work for you, big work, now that a regular force is in the field."

"If that's your decision, sir," said Ross. Somehow, his disappointment at not joining Washington's dragoons or Greene's staff was not very keen, here under the trees of Snow Island.

Later, Peter Horry hailed him. "Been wondering how much more of Marion's time you'd waste. There's something I want to tell you about." He leaned back against a rock and stretched out his long legs. "People are funny. There's an old Quaker who ranges between here and the Santee. Now where most folks would be looking for peach brandy or killing someone or writing a sermon, this Quaker's always messing about with paints and colors. Some of his pictures are right pretty."

"What's that got to do with me? Does he want to paint my portrait?"

"No, I don't really think he does," answered Horry. "You see, he's sort of sensitive." He reached in his pocket and handed Ross a thick square of folded paper. "But he was here two nights ago and left this for you."

"For me? The old chuff doesn't know I exist!"

He carefully broke the seal and unfolded the paper by the firelight. "What in the name of—" he began, staring at the sheet. There was no writing, just a landscape, crudely but vividly done in crayon. There was a swampy river, a stockaded fort over which the British colors flew. Beyond the sallyport, a light coach with four horses faced west. In the left foreground, sketched in lightly but skillfully, was the figure of a girl. She was slight in her blue cape from whose thrown-back hood a cloud of golden hair escaped. Her dark eyes, barely indicated but unmistakable, seemed to be looking toward the north, away from fort and river and coach. The figure was crudely done, like the rest of the sketch, and yet the Quaker artist had somehow caught the very essence and being of Dorande van Kortenaer.

Ross's breath went in quickly as he stowed the sketch in a stiff leather case that he carried in his inside pocket. In the morning, when he was alone, he would study it more carefully. He had taken in the whole message. Thinking it might be unwise to write, Dorande had found this means of telling him that she had reached Nelson's Ferry safely, that she was about to take the road to the Congaree. And her dark eyes looked north toward distant Snow Island.

VI • Lee's Legion

The valley of the Congaree shimmered under a warm haze that turned the river into a strip of lazy silver. From the deep porch of Mon Plaisir, Dorande could see the wind trace ruffles on its surface as the stream slid south past the bluffs on its way to Howell's Ferry and on to its junction with the Wateree. At either corner of the broad façade, a Pride of India tree spread its leaves to the wind and the thick grass of the lawn rippled gently. The sun was bright and the air was soft, but to Dorande, bred in the tropics, neither sun nor air seemed to have any warmth and she drew her cloak of light blue silk about her.

She glanced at the trim little cottage that perched on the bluffs above the river. Soon her new friend, Janet Jaudon, would come up the path to the big house, swinging along lightly. Dorande smiled to herself. It had been easy to carry out Marion's wish—that she be a friend to the tall, dark-haired girl who seemed fully to reciprocate Dorande's instant liking. And Dorande had become quickly aware why the little brigadier had stationed Janet in the cottage overhanging the road along which British and Tory columns passed on their way west to Ninety-six or north to Camden and Winnsboro. How the matter had been arranged still puzzled her.

A day or so after her arrival at Mon Plaisir from Nelson's Ferry, Paul St. Aubin informed her that he had thought it wise to invite a well-vouched-for young lady to act as companion for his niece. "A young widow," St. Aubin had said, "and of a family of the most respectable. A widow, yes, whose husband fell fighting for the Crown." Conjecture as she might, Dorande could not guess the channels by which Marion had been able to bring Janet, with her spurious widow's weeds, to the favorable notice of Paul St. Aubin. That he had, further increased Dorande's opinion of the brigadier's powers.

122

There was a good deal about her uncle that puzzled her, too. In the first place, he had asked no questions concerning her wanderings, nor her unexpected arrival at Mon Plaisir, accepting her statement that other refugees had looked after her and helped her to the British post at Nelson's. But there was more than that. He seemed to have lost the hard, calculating manner that had disturbed her at Mrs. Cantey's. His flamboyance was discreetly toned down, his dress had become almost somber. While she had no idea of the purpose of his frequent absences, at least no women like his companion of the High Hills of Santee had appeared.

Guests came and went, but they were always men, officers of British or Tory formations, or lawyerlike civilians. With the officers, decent competent men for the most part, St. Aubin was a generous host, his bearing showing grave respect for the real combatants for the King. The civilians, on the other hand, seemed to defer to him, sat for long hours about his great table that was soon littered with deeds, with official documents. What little talk Dorande heard dealt with the legal denouncing of this rebel or that, of land grants to the west, to the north. Once or twice she caught references to the Cherokee Indians and Rebel settlements far to the west, though the connection between red savage and peaceful farmer escaped her.

Now voices came to her through the open windows of the dining room where her uncle entertained two passing officers, one a ginger-haired Scot of the 71st and the other a Boston-born major of Tory cavalry. She had sat at table through the long meal and heard talk of the war, that seemed so distant from the soft valley of the Congaree. Once or twice she checked a start as Marion's name was mentioned. She had excused herself with the appearance of the port.

Now the last rites of wine seemed ended. She heard the scrape of chairs, then voices growing louder. St. Aubin appeared on the terrace with his guests and Dorande turned to the trio with a smile. The officers, level-eyed courteous men, acknowledged her greeting pleasantly. It was obvious that they stood a little in awe of her uncle and for an instant Dorande felt almost proud of him, standing there between the two big soldiers. And yet she could not shake the feeling of distaste, now faint now strong, that she had known at her first sight of him.

The Tory turned to St. Aubin. "I suppose you've met the new Commissioner of Sequestered Estates who's come out from England, sir?"

St. Aubin's face showed grave appreciation. "Yes. He has

even honored me with a visit. A just man of a sobriety that I find surpassing."

Dorande checked an exclamation of surprise. A high official from England! She remembered his visit. A dour, morose man, with the stern joyless face of a *prédikant* of a Dutch country church. Did this official's puritanical garb, speech and habits account for the change in her uncle? She looked curiously at him. With eyes that were almost reverent, he was murmuring praise of the Commissioner's abstemiousness, his devotion to the Crown, his stern justice to all who were in any way tainted by treason.

The Scot, dangling his bonnet from a bony hand, coughed. "Aye, but he's a sanctimonious auld tattie-bogle, for a' that. His face minds me of my mither's ain sister, leaving the kirk of a wet Sawbath."

The Tory laughed. "Just the same, we need something like that to tone down those rake-hellies in Charleston." He bowed to Dorande as mounted orderlies led horses up the drive.

When the guests had gone, St. Aubin, the odor of piety still about him, inclined his head gravely to Dorande. "You improve each day, *ma nièce*. The impression which you produced today was excellent."

She raised her eyebrows. "But I merely sat there."

He smiled. "But you sat perfectly. Our guests will remember Mon Plaisir as a house presided over by a well-bred young lady possessing all that there is of the most decorous. Now I have news for you. You recall that I left the table to speak to a messenger? *Bon!* He brought, with other matters, a letter to you from—" he paused as though relishing the slight suspense—"from St. Eusebius."

Dorande went pale. "From Mother? That can't be. From Surinam, from Havana—"

He held up his hand. "There was also one for me, which I read hastily. Your parents are well. In the present disturbed state of the seas, they found it wiser to go to St. Eusebius, which is now tranquil. There they hope for better chances of passage here."

Dorande put out a hand which trembled a little. "The letter—"

"It is in your room, since I presumed that you would prefer to read it there than in the presence of our guests."

"In my room?" Dorande gathered her cape and skimmed lightly over the threshold.

St. Aubin clasped his hands behind him and paced slowly up and down the porch, wondering if he were quite wise in settling on the Congaree, rather than finding a plantation to the north, say in the neighborhood of Camden, on the direct route of the armies. No, for the time being, the Congaree was the spot for him. He could reach the British high command quit easily from Mon Plaisir and still keep an open channel to Charleston. As the armies pushed north, the Charleston functionaries would increase rapidly in importance. He was conveniently located at a halfway point. North lay Camden and Winnsboro. West lay Ninety-six and the frontier. East lay Charleston. South lay Fort Galphin and Augusta. He would stay, waiting on events.

Events. How long would it be before this new, this third American army could be brushed aside? He hoped that the rumors of winter quarters were true, for the American commander, whom the British called a Quaker blacksmith, had established a camp for prisoners of war. Up to now, those captured by the Rebels were either killed out of hand or given meaningless paroles. Now they would be confined. The question of exchange arose; say—a British major against an American. Through channels, a discreet man—and who more discreet than Paul St. Aubin—could exert influence, so that Major A, rather than Major B, would be the prisoner to be exchanged. Major A and his friends would undoubtedly pay well for his liberty. His mind traced out a careful chain of known Whigs and Tories, lukewarm or venial, through whom he could reach into the headquarters of this new Greene or down into Charleston itself.

Dorande sat by the window that looked out across the lawns to the Congaree and carefully dried her eyes. Her mother's letter that lay in her lap was bittersweet. Both parents were safe and peaceful on St. Eusebius, as St. Aubin had said, and the last sheet listed more of her friends as alive and well than she could have hoped. The ringleaders of the blacks had been duly hanged and slaves moved about the island in apparently unshatterable docility.

But when would her parents sail? When? Her mother wrote of privateers, some of whom preyed on enemy shipping, some boldly on any prize that looked worth while. Then there were men of war, mostly flying the British colors, and that was even worse, since the Stadholder of the Netherlands had finally declared war against Britain. Where could a neutral flag be found, especially now since war had frightened commerce from nearly every bay and harbor and roadstead?

Dorande read the letter again, but it held no hint of a hopeful answer to the "when." Weeks or months might pass before they could leave the island. Then there might be more weeks and months, waiting on another island for the next stage of the journey. At least, her mother and father were safe and ready to start north with the first chance that might offer.

There was a light tap outside. Dorande called *"Entrez!"* and Janet Jaudon slipped into the room, closing the door behind her. "Oh my dear, I just saw your uncle. That letter—he told me—no bad news, I hope." She drew a hassock beside Dorande's chair, slipped an arm about her shoulders.

Dorande sighed. "Not bad news entirely. They are safe, *papa et maman.*" Her hands tightened on the letter. "Oh, but when—when?"

"Sooner than you expect, I'm sure," said Janet gently.

Dorande felt sudden contrition. She was concerned with the mere passage of time, while Janet must face, day in and day out, constant, bitter anxiety about the husband whom she loved and the cause in which she believed. She smiled at Janet. "But soon, of course. And now, the waiting is easier since I have you by me. Now tell me how you spent your morning."

Janet rose and looked out of the window. "I was doing arithmetic."

"Arithmetic! You add two and two, and again two?" asked Dorande, puzzled.

Janet turned back to Dorande, dropping her voice. "Two hundred and two hundred, on and on. The men we've seen pass here. The men I've heard about, one way or another. Dorande, I'm worried. Twenty-three hundred of them under General Leslie, new men from New York. The Brigade of Guards. Von Bose's Hessians. The best the British have."

Dorande's eyes widened. The King's own Guards. Old, professional soldiers from Germany. She thought of the ragged underfed men of Snow Island, of the little brigadier, of Ross Pembroke in his worn white coat and dented helmet. "But General Marion must learn of this, Janet!"

Janet said calmly, "He will. By tomorrow."

"Of course," said Dorande quickly. "I had forgotten." She clasped her hands and leaned forward. "I could help you in this. I, too, can listen and watch. All this is nothing to my uncle, a foreigner like me, and hence would not be against him."

Janet shook her head. "It's like you to offer, my dear. But the less you really know, the better. This isn't your war. One day soon you'll leave the Carolinas. No. It could even lead you into real danger over something that doesn't concern you."

"But so much has been done for me," said Dorande.

Janet laughed. "You don't think you're doing anything in return? How about the Canteys and other burned-out families you've helped with the gold and jewels you brought here, sewn into your clothes? You've done enough, more than enough." Her voice dropped lower. "When next I send word to General Marion there would be plenty of room for an added line or two. I saw you and Captain Pembroke talking there on Snow Island. Would you like to write him?"

"But what have I to say to him?" asked Dorande, lowering her eyes.

Janet smiled at the ceiling. "Well, I saw you talking. Raoul and I think a lot of him."

Dorande said demurely. *"Oui. Il est charmant."*

"Then why not a word or two?"

Dorande sighed. "You yourself said just now that soon I leave the Carolinas. Who may say if I ever return?" Then she added as though to herself, *"Quand même,* I wonder what he does now. I would like to know."

Early in January, 1781, Marion left Snow Island with his usual lack of notice and with no word of where he was going or when he might return. Ross, left in charge of the camp, watched the few remaining men breaking up bales of green jackets, spoils of a recent raid to the west. The garments, intended for some Tory formation, would be dipped in kettles where oak galls simmered, a crude dye that would fade out the notorious color.

Rations were low and he had to limit himself and the others to a small pot of boiled rice per day. While dry sticks crackled under the kettles, a heavy-faced trapper, whom Ross had seen before, splashed across the ford and asked for food, saying he reckoned he'd set a while on Snow. Ross knew the man, sound enough, but incredibly stupid. What food there was would be better saved for a more valuable man. Shrugging, Ross handed him a pot of cold rice. "That'll have to do, Spencer. How'd you come down here?"

"This'll do elegant," said Spencer as he scooped up rice with his fingers. "I come down the Pee Dee."

"See anything?"

"I seen the Pee Dee."

"I mean, anything unusual?"

"The river ain't unusual. Been there some time." He

touched a green jacket with his foot. "Now I call that right pretty, that coat."

"It'll be prettier when it comes out of the dye pot."

"Could be. I seen maybe forty-fifty men come up the Pee Dee wearin' coats like that, and little black caps."

Ross spun about. "Coats like that? Where?"

"Up the river, like I said. 'Bout four hours ago."

"Sure they were like this?"

"They was green and, my, them fellers had pretty swords and guns!"

"Where were they heading?"

"I ain't asked, but if they kep' on, they'd most likely hit in here."

Ross exploded. "Why the hell didn't you tell me at once?"

"You ain't asked." Spencer ate imperturbably.

Ross shouted, "Gavin! Gavin James!"

James, his keen, sharp face alert, ran up. Ross spoke quickly. "Spencer ran into a Tory force up the Pee Dee, heading this way. Get all the horses off the island, all weapons and stores."

Gavin James nodded. "I'll clear the place in thirty minutes."

"Make it twenty. Take what men you have and cover the other side of the ford. You're in charge till I get back." Ross called, "McRae!" and a dark Ulsterman trotted up. "Did you hear what Spencer said?"

"Didn't miss."

"You and I are going to take a look at the Tories." Ross changed his helmet for a light-infantry cap, discarded his saber for a pair of short pistols. "Ready?" he asked. "Then you take the lead. We go by the north ford and on foot."

Progress was difficult, but McRae set out at a steady jog trot that soon had Ross panting. They slithered through swampy stretches, scrambled over rocks, skirted the edges of broad savannahs. It was lucky that the weather had turned unusually cold, driving alligators and water moccasins deep into the mud and keeping the rattlesnakes torpid in their caves.

By the edge of a deep thicket, McRae threw himself to the ground, pointing. Ross crept beside him. Through the roots of the brush he made out a level stretch with the Pee Dee in sluggish flow beyond it. At the far end, men in green were emerging cautiously from the woods, fanning out like skirmishers. Ross stared. There could be no mistaking the color of the jackets. He squinted, trying to identify the unit, but could not make out the facings of the jackets. He counted them. Twelve skirmishers only, but the woods behind them stirred with the passage of more men, hidden by the trees.

The skirmishers halted, a sergeant waved to the woods, and green jackets flooded out onto the flats, the men correcting their alignment as they came with a deftness that brought a whistle of admiration from Ross. He exchanged glances with McRae, who got to his knees. Ross nodded. "Double back and warn Gavin James. Tell him—Hi! Hold up!" He dragged McRae down, staring out across the flats.

Halfway between the thicket and the waiting infantry, the woods crashed and crackled. A single horseman burst into the open. He wore a bright brass helmet with a trailing white plume that seemed fine as silk. His green jacket was immaculate. His white leather breeches looked freshly pipe-clayed and his knee-length boots gave back the pale glitter of the January sun that had broken through a cloud film. The rider shouted, waved to his men and sent his black horse in a showy leap across a brook.

McRae nudged Ross. "Will I show myself and draw him into pistol range for you?"

But Ross had risen to his knees. McRae tried to drag him down, hissing a warning. Ross pushed him away and broke through the thicket shouting, "Major Lee! Oh, Harry Lee!" He waved his cap and ran on. "Major Lee. This way. Ross Pembroke, acting for General Marion!"

The rider checked his mount, spun about and then shot toward him, staring down from keen blue eyes. He pulled his black on its haunches, vaulted lightly to the ground and clapped Ross on the shoulder. "Damn my eyes if it isn't my old Rhode Island skull-splitter! What in blazing hell are you doing *here?*"

"Getting ready to lay an ambush for you. Those green coats fooled me. You've changed the cut since '79. Hello! What's this?" He touched Lee's epaulettes. "Lieutenant colonel? That's fine! Don't tell me *you're* with Nat Greene! I was up at Charlotte last month and he didn't speak of you."

Lee's broad, oval face glowed. "He couldn't have, because he didn't know. You ought to have seen his expression when I marched the Legion into camp. He gave us a day's rest up there in the Cheraws and then sent me down to look for a man named Marion, Francis Marion." He indicated the green men who had halted. "This is the advance of the infantry. The cavalry's following. Marion and I are going to clean out this part of the state."

Ross felt a sudden withdrawing. He had liked and admired Lee in the past, especially on those occasions, such as the attack on Paulus Hook, when he had accompanied the Legion as a volunteer. He would have liked nothing better than to serve under Lee—in a different war, in a different theater. But he felt uneasy when he thought of the Virginian's dashing flamboyance, his insistence on etiquette in the field and his love of show—and thought of the silent, reserved Marion with his dislike of display. Then, too, Lee was an officer of the Continental Line, Marion only a state brigadier. That point might loom unduly in Harry Lee's mind. It occurred to Ross that he might find himself cast in the role of buffer between the two.

Lee talked on and Ross felt again the charm of his manner and the warmth of his smile. "Well! I never expected to see you waving like a windmill in the middle of a Carolina meadow! My God, what's happened to you? You're thin as a rail. And that cap! That leather shirt! Those boots!" He settled his helmet on his carefully powdered head. "You said you were with Marion? Then better take me right to him."

Ross grinned. "I would, only I don't know where he is."

"Damn and blast! Doesn't *any*one know where he is? Yesterday I ran into two scouts who said they were his, but they couldn't tell me anything. How the devil am I going to find him?"

"It's more likely that he'll find you, rather than your finding him. I'll send McRae, here, back to Snow Island to get things ready for you. I'll guide you in."

"Fine!" cried Lee. He blew a silver whistle and two helmeted cornets rode out of the woods.

"Better dismount all riders. We'll travel rough until we sight Snow Island," warned Ross.

"As you say," said Lee. "You and I'll take the lead." He blew his whistle again. The infantry formed into column with a precision that drew a mutter of applause from Ross. The Virginian chuckled. "Like them, eh? They can charge like grenadiers and scatter like rangers. They can wallow in a swamp or put on a drill that'd satisfy Frederick of Prussia." He signaled with his arm and the column started with a sure, easy swing, flankers out and alert. They were beautifully trained and equipped, as Harry Lee's men always were. What would the ragged men of Snow Island think of them? Or they of the Island garrison?"

Lee clapped him on the shoulder. "Good, aren't they? But wait till you see the Legion cavalry."

Walking beside Lee, Ross shook his head. "I'm afraid you won't find anything like them, at least for show, where we're going. We've been living off the country, using makeshift clothes and weapons."

Lee broke in, "Don't forget I was at Valley Forge. I know what an army in rags can do. I admit I've got a weakness for show and polish. But I know show and polish are no damned good until you've got a real soldier to apply them to. And maybe it's not so important then. Now tell me about Marion's command. Is it South Carolina line?"

Ross shook his head. "I don't know just what you would call them. I suppose it's best just to call them Marion's Men. It's a rating that'd suit them."

Lee said resignedly, "Well, if that's what we've got, we'll just have to make the best of it."

Ross kept to a narrow trail that hugged the right bank of the Pee Dee, looking for a landmark that would swing him toward Snow Island. Then from the treetops he caught the high-pitched whistle of Marion's men. Lee looked about him in wonder. "What the devil's that? Where does it come from?"

Ross smiled. "It's the equivalent of 'Turn out the guard!' on Snow Island." He led the column across a narrow arm of the river, then found himself at the north ford with the island stretching out before him. On the far bank a frail man stood alone, leaning on a rusty sword and watching the stream. Lee indicated the figure. "Good God! Is *that* supposed to be a guard?"

Ross repressed a start of indignation, then answered shortly, "You might call him that. Follow me closely now. There's a shoal where the water's less than ankle-deep."

Marion limped to the edge of the water and Ross saluted, saying formally, "General Marion, this is Colonel Henry Lee. He and his Legion are under General Greene's orders to report to you."

Lee raised his hand to his helmet, saying in a puzzled voice, "Servant, sir."

Marion inclined his head. "We'll be glad of any aid or advice that you can give us, Colonel. Let's talk."

As Marion led the way to the old oak, Ross watched Lee, who seemed puzzled and a little discouraged by the swarms of unsoldierly looking men on the island. In dozens they clustered about the ford, watching the infantry of the Legion cross over.

Peach brandy was produced as well as vinegar and water for Marion. The general raised his mug. "Your health, Colonel Lee."

"Yours, sir." Lee drank, then set down his mug. "I'll be frank with you, General. When Greene sent me down here, I didn't like it worth a damn."

"Few would," observed Marion, sipping his vinegar.

"I don't even know why he sent *me*," said Lee. "The real action'll be up north. But down here—" He drank again, leaving the sentence unfinished. Ross saw his eyes straying off toward Marion's men. It was natural that Lee should look at them in terms of militia bodies that had come into other camps, used up supplies and drifted off in time of need. Ross also had the impression that Lee was weighing his own long experience and Continental rank against Marion's partisan life and his local commission from a governor in exile.

Ross started to speak, with an idea of leading the conversation into channels that would reassure the Virginian, but Marion broke in. "Your strength, Colonel?"

"One hundred cavalry, one hundred eighty-two foot."

"Down here," said Marion, as though echoing Lee's earlier words. "Yes. Quiet. Little glory. There are things to be done, though. When will your cavalry be here?"

"Say—an hour and a half, two hours."

"Then, if it's agreeable to you, we'll make a plan. I recommend that we capture the Georgetown garrison." Marion spoke casually, as though suggesting a mere tour of Snow Island.

Lee looked surprised. "Georgetown? On the coast?"

"Yes. Starting at sundown."

Lee pursed up his lips. "That's—yes! By Jove, we'll do it. Sundown's the best time to start if you want surprise. Let's think this out, in detail. What day seems best to you?"

Marion's eyebrows went up. "Day? Why, *this* day."

Lee got to his feet, flushing. "But my men won't have had more than three hours' rest."

"Nearer one," said Marion, reaching for the vinegar.

"Damn me if that's—that's—" He smacked his fist into his palm. "If your men can do it, my troopers can. But how about my infantry? They can't keep up with mounted men."

"I'll show you," said Marion, leading the way to the Pee Dee shore of the island.

The afternoon had begun to fade, but the river had come to sudden life. Out of hidden tributaries, from deep-scooped holes in the banks, from black-rimmed swamps, from under driftwood stacks, a weird flotilla was making its way to Snow Island. There were flimsy canoes and heavy-beamed boats from the days of the indigo trade. There were high-powered bateaux and whaleboats with the mark of the Royal Navy on their planks. Some were poled by lean, bearded men, riding easily with the current. One canoe had a gray-haired woman at the bow paddle and a gangling boy at the stern. A heavy-set girl handled the pole of a long scow and snapped terse orders as two boys in the bow leaped ashore and guided the prow toward the bank where other craft rocked to the gentle current. Lee stared, feet apart and hands on his hips. "What in the name of the Eternal!" he gasped.

Marion said, "Scouts picked up your trace two days ago. I had my people scour the country for boats. Thought we might need them."

"Need them? What are you going to do? Challenge the Royal Navy?"

"Not this time." Marion pointed to the stream. "Infantry. Float down the Pee Dee. Cavalry overland. Meet at George-town."

Lee still stared at the rocking boats. Then he whipped off his helmet, flourished it in the air, clapped it back on his head. He held out his hand and Marion took it, looking mildly surprised. Lee, his voice shaking a little with excitement, cried, "General, my Legion and I'll be proud to follow where you lead. We're under your orders. Damn resting! I'll start my cavalry the instant they cross the ford. Tonight! And here I've been, worrying for fear my men would just rot in swamps down here."

"Thank you," said Marion. "Sundown."

Later Ross stood by the north ford with Peter Horry, watching the Legion cavalry ride onto Snow Island. By four and by four they came, brass helmets glinting and white plumes a-flutter about their shoulders. The horses were sound and trim, pommel and cantle held neatly rolled blankets and the forage nets were well filled. Then faces began to separate from the anonymity of the ranks. Some of them recognized him, greeted him with surprised shouts or jovial obscenities.

Horry eyed them with professional approval. "Look right pretty, don't they?"

"Lee's men always look that way, though they don't mind getting messed up in a fight."

Horry nodded equably. "Now I don't mind having them with us. I don't mind having Lee, either. Of course, I don't know much about his kind of fighting, but I do hold he talks about it downright sumptuously."

"Don't let that fool you, Peter. He means it. He loves war for its own sake. It wouldn't surprise me, when this is over, if he took service with the Sultan of Turkey or the Czar of Russia. You find people like that now and then." He smiled reminiscently. "As a matter of fact, the best work he ever did for the army didn't have anything to do with fighting, so he just laughs at it. It was important though."

"Like me, always hiding my brightest laurels. Only I've hidden them so well I can't even find them for myself." .

"No one lets Lee forget about this. He saved the army from starvation at Valley Forge. There was an unusually early run of shad up the Schuylkill. I've never seen fish so thick. They were almost crowding each other onto the banks. Lee took one look at the river and then rode his dragoons right into the stream and kept them milling their horses about. That turned the shad and by the time the fish had gotten straightened out, we'd forked enough on shore to feed us for a year."

Horry was impressed. "That's soldiering. Now if I were you, I'd tell that to Francis. It's the sort of thing he likes to know about men he works with." He pulled out a bulbous silver watch. "Nearing four. Francis wants us back by the oak."

Under the great tree, a battered skullcap and a shiny brass helmet were bent over an outspread map. Horry nodded at them. "I wouldn't go so far's to say they were matched for size, but they make a good span." He raised his voice. "You about ready to listen, Francis?"

Marion looked up, then glanced at Lee. The Virginian stepped forward, rigidly at attention, shouting, "Legion officers! Report!"

From the Legion camp, from the trim picket lines where troopers were busily grooming their mounts, helmeted men came running, holding sabers and sabre-taches clear of the ground. Ten paces from Lee, they halted, dressed and the senior, Major Rudulph, saluted. Lee returned the salute meticulously, then snapped, "At ease!" Ross felt himself involuntarily answering to the commands. This was more military formality than he had seen since his capture outside Charleston. Marion said something in a low tone to Lee, who shook his head vigorously. An inaudible argument followed, Lee interrupting it to call "Rest!" to his officers.

The officers broke formation like schoolboys, and Ross suddenly found himself overwhelmed. Major John Rudulph and the others crowded about him, slapping his shoulders, deluging him with questions. It was like his reception in the chill courthouse at Charlotte. There were the Virginians Eggleston, Winston and Handy; Power and Manning, the Pennsylvanians; Middleton from South Carolina and Lovell from Massachusetts, the saturnine Frenchman, Ferdinand O'Neal.

Then there were strangers to be introduced like Patrick Carnes who had served with the Pulaski Legion, the surgeon, Dr. Alexander Skinner, Captain Michael Rudulph and Peter Johnson.

The torrent of questions and comments died abruptly as Lee shouted, "Your attention, gentlemen, if you please. Just draw up closer here. General Marion wants to avoid a formal presentation and I agree with him. I'll just say this about him. We're under his command. You won't have to be with him long to be proud to serve under him. I know that I am." He turned to Marion, who stood silently, hands behind his back. "I'll just name my officers for you, General, so you'll know who's going to do what. This is Major John Rudulph—"

As each name was called, Marion inclined his head, his keen eyes taking in every detail of feature and bearing. When Lee had finished the list Marion's face broke into a quick, warm smile. "There's work to do. I'm glad that you're the ones to do it with me."

Lee handed Marion a map. "Now for the details, General."

Marion stepped back. "Tell them, Colonel Lee."

Lee stared. "I? It's rather irregular, you being senior to me."

"Seniority waived," said Marion.

Lee's voice, its earlier flamboyance replaced by confident authority, swept over the semicircle of officers, as he outlined the dual attack by land and water that would strike the Georgetown garrison in a dawn surprise. The pick of the Legion would move with the pick of Marion's men.

When he had finished, a low mutter of astonishment rippled over the listeners. Rudulph said slowly, "Then we embark at sundown tomorrow? That's pretty soon."

Lee flung up his arm. "No! Sundown *tonight!* General Marion will set the pace for those of us who go overland. If any officer feels that he is unable to match that pace, I shall be most happy to receive his resignation here and now."

A grim smile broke over Rudulph's weather-beaten face. "*That's* campaigning. No resignations, sir."

"Then take your posts, gentlemen. Assembly sounds in half an hour."

Dusk was creeping down the tunnel of trees, blanketing the river and muffling the sounds of Snow Island, when Ross joined Rudulph by the sandy point. Ninety picked men of the Legion were grouped close by. Rudulph scowled at the empty stream. "Where are those God damn boats?" he asked sharply.

Ross, remembering that Rudulph was irritable and profane in waiting, quiet and deadly in action, spoke soothingly. "You fell in five minutes before the time Marion set. He works closer to the dot than a Swiss watch. He never—ah!"

In the gloom upstream a ripple sounded, the ghost of a splash. Ripple and splash were repeated, fainter and fainter, until they were lost in the dimness of the Pee Dee. Down the river, looming larger and larger, came canoe, scow and cargo boat, handled by young powerful men who had replaced the old men, the women and boys who had ferried the craft to the island. Ross laughed. "There's your five minutes, Rudulph."

"Damn me for a sad bastard," muttered Rudulph, staring at the approaching flotilla. Then he signaled the nearest lieutenant. File by file the picked men tramped to the water's edge, took their places in the boats with a faint rustle of stripped-down equipment. Ross and Rudulph entered the leading canoe, which shoved off silently into the current. The amphibious arm of the expedition was launched.

The raid on Georgetown had been a qualified success. The two wings, one by land and one by water, had met at the little town, smoothly and on schedule. Due to the stupidity or treachery of a guide, the water force had taken a route which led it among the guard posts beyond the barracks. The alarm had been given. The troops had barricaded themselves in stone buildings and had answered all summons to surrender with musketry. A few of the garrison had been killed as they ran for shelter. The British commander of the post had been snapped up by the wing of the advance headed by Ross. His Tory second-in-command had been killed by one of Marion's men in revenge for an unforgiven flogging.

When Marion and Lee rode in with the mounted troops, they had found Ross and Rudulph maintaining a close blockade of the garrison, but unable to do more owing to lack of artillery or scaling ladders. Lee, eager and impetuous, had urged throwing the Legion infantry against the stone houses, a plan that Marion rejected in view of certain heavy casualties.

Still, the raid had accomplished many things. It would paralyze the Georgetown area for some time. No troops would move north from it against Greene in the Cheraws. The garrison would receive reinforcements that otherwise might be sent to Cornwallis at Winnsboro. Horsemen, needed to strengthen Tarleton's command, would be wasted on needless patrols to guard the base against a second raid that Marion *might* make.

At the first halt beyond Georgetown, a courier from the north had ridden into the swamp with news that set the whole command cheering. Up in the northwest of the state, Dan Morgan, the Old Wagoner, had waited for Tarleton at a place called the Cowpens. Tarleton's command had been riddled with rifle fire, ridden down by Washington's cavalry. Once again, as at King's Mountain, Cornwallis had lost his left wing.

Three days later, the combined forces of Marion and Lee, joined by those of both commands who had been left at Snow Island, headed mysteriously south beyond the Sampit River. Ross caught up with Lee at the head of the Legion cavalry and the Virginian grimaced as he indicated Marion, riding far in the van, tight-lipped and silent. "Why the devil didn't you tell me he wasn't human? When I first saw him, I thought we'd have to carry him on a litter. I don't mind telling you I need a litter a damn sight more than he does. Doesn't he *ever* eat or sleep?"

"You'll get used to him, if you live," answered Ross.

Lee pursed his full lips. "I'd stay alive just to learn from him. I thought I was at least middling seasoned, but he keeps me thinking, '*There's* something I could have used at Brandywine or near Paramus.' Well, I'm going to have plenty of time to watch him." He glanced at Ross. "You've heard where we're going?"

"Only that we're following Marion," said Ross.

Lee leaned toward Ross. "For the moment we're keeping it pretty close, but you certainly ought to know, shuttling between me and him." His voice dropped lower. "We're going to the north bank of the Santee. We're going to take Fort Watson."

Fatigue left Ross as the scope of the operation filled his mind, dazzled him. The war in the Carolinas was becoming truly national. This would be no mere raid to scatter a few Tories or destroy a dozen carts. Marion and Lee together would strike at the artery, the main road from the coast to Cornwallis. The blow might even fall just when the garrisons of that road were sending men east to guard against another stroke at Georgetown. Other strong companies, intended for Cornwallis, would be immobilized. Loads of precious supplies would be captured, or penned up indefinitely in some halfway fort. Cornwallis, already watching both Greene and Morgan, would now have to look to his rear, might even be forced to detach men to guard the Santee posts.

Later in the day, Marion sent for Ross. "Column halts in five minutes," Marion said tersely. "Sending ahead a detail of twenty dragoons, one lieutenant, one cornet, one guide. You go with them. In command."

"The guide has instructions?" asked Ross.

"In full. Follow him."

When the dragoon detail formed during the halt, Ross smiled to himself. Not so long ago he would have been horrified at the idea of setting out ahead of the main body with virtually no orders. Now he knew that the guide would take the party where it was supposed to go, that someone would materialize with instructions for the next stage. He read astonishment in the eyes of the ruddy-faced lieutenant of the detail, a Virginian named William Winston with whom he had ridden a few miles on the march from Georgetown. "You mean we just follow that guide? Nothing more than that?" Winston asked incredulously.

"That's more than we usually know," said Ross. "You take the lead behind the guide. I'll keep to the rear, watching for stragglers."

"The Legion doesn't straggle," said Winston stiffly.

"It better not. In this country, a man out of line is a man lost."

He pulled up by the trail where it rose from a swamp and watched the troopers ride by. He felt his confidence mounting. After all, these were *his* sort of troops, trained, disciplined cavalrymen. He was sure that he could bring the best of the type of war that he knew to support the type that he had learned from Marion. The dragoons were excellent material.

Ross drew up on the bank and watched the competent looking lot, a mixture of eager, fresh-faced boys and lean, hard men who had ridden with Bland's dragoons. There was even a scarred, grizzled sergeant who had long ago deserted from von Riedesel's Brunswick cavalry to take service with the armies of the New World. They were all well mounted and well turned out. All, that is, save for the last rider, who was putting a big-boned black at the slope ahead of him. His jacket, originally green, was stained and faded until it had the unhealthy iridescence of slime on a pool. The sleeves were too short and the shoulder seams gaped. His breeches were the color of dead leaves and his helmet was swathed in a shabby canvas *couvre-casque*. Ross stared at the man in wonder, marveled still more as he saw a draggled cornet's knot on one shoulder. The presence of such a tatterdemalion among Lee's men sent a sudden dart of suspicion through Ross's mind. Could the man be a Tory who had sifted to the Black River along with the "new-laid Whigs"? Suspicion was replaced by incredulity as the shabby figure, sweeping off the lamentable helmet, bowed low in the saddle to Ross and spoke with a strong French accent. "May I be permitted? Philippe-Georges de la Piconnerie de Chanzy, on command from the *regiment de Gâtinais,* and at your service."

Ross bit his lip. The man was obviously no Tory. But what sort of Frenchman was he? He had known keen, rapier-like Frenchmen of the type of Fleury or Armand. Also, he had seen others, swaggering into camp and demanding command of a division at least, on the strength of peacetime European service on the Continent. This cornet could have no pretensions to high rank and hence could be no LaRoche Fermoy. Nor did he suggest the Fleury of Stony Point.

The cornet still held his helmet poised and bent slightly from the waist as though to repeat his salute. With carefully concealed mockery, Ross bowed to the pommel. "And I am Ross Pembroke, late of Rhode Island and on command from the Continental Dragoons. At *your* service."

The Frenchman's hands flew in the air. "Ah! Of the Rhode Island! But I know it as well as my own Nouart in the Ardennes. I have eaten your clam-chowder" (he made one word of it) "and of your lobsters with their great claws. Your Newport, your Providence. Such pretty girls. Tell me, *mon ami,* are the girls of the Carolinas as *sympathique?*"

Ross shrugged. "That's a matter of opinion, I suppose."

"Ah, I believe you, it is a matter of opinion. My brother, Auguste-Philibert-Adrien, who commands a squadron in the hussars of Bercheny, where there are many Germans, tells me that across the Rhine they say, 'One man's owl is another man's nightingale.' I find that most true. The girl of the Rhode Island, the girl of the Carolinas—owl or nightingale? Who shall say?"

He talked on, explaining himself volubly. His father, it seemed, had been unable to procure for him a commission in the cavalry, and the son had to be content with infantry. Only recently, through the influence of Rochambeau, had he been detached or placed "on command" with Lee's cavalry. "Ah, you may believe me, it was something, that day at headquarters when our Rochambeau stirred himself for me. All your great ones I saw. I even had the shake-hands from your Washington, a favor which I owe again to our Rochambeau, who has some consideration for me, since he is connected by marriage with my Aunt Frédégonde."

Ross set his teeth and listened in spite of himself. The man was impossible. A phrase which he had read somewhere— could it have been in Fielding?—ran through his head—"a pert, railing fribble." The acid characterization, save for its connotation of foppishness, seemed to fit de Chanzy perfectly. And yet—a frown showed on Ross's forehead as he studied the cornet.

He was quite tall for a Frenchman and sat his horse with long-legged skill. In contrast to his shabby, almost slovenly clothes, his weapons, so far as Ross could see, were faultlessly cared for. The pistol butts that showed in his holsters were worn but well polished. His saber would have passed the most rigid inspection. Its hilt was clear and well forward, ready for instant use. The leather of the cartridge boxes about his waist was supple with carefully applied oil. His hands seemed unusually strong and deft. When the fingers shifted on the reins, they moved surely with no fumbling or rustling of leather.

De Chanzy leaned suddenly forward in the saddle and touched the croup of the horse just ahead with his crop. The rider, who had been dropping back slowly, perhaps with the idea of resting and then catching up with the column at his leisure, turned a startled face about. The cornet said crisply, "Perhaps you prefer their company to ours? It is not a choice which I recommend." Ross saw the crop point toward a dusky backwater that showed just to the left of the trail. The water showed arrowlike markings where snakes swam. More were coiled on a log that slanted up onto the land. The trooper started, gathered his horse and closed up on the files ahead.

Ross's eyes narrowed in surprised approval. The trooper's attempt to straggle had been firmly checked and yet in such a way that the man would feel no resentment. Was his first impression of the cornet a wrong one? He rode beside him through the depending night, asking questions from time to time, listening carefully. As the miles rolled slowly by under the hoofs of the troop, Ross felt a growing conviction that he *had* been wrong. De Chanzy was young, in a strange country, a strange army and in a very strange part of that country and army. Overanxiety was probably responsible for that first burst of rather florid volubility. Now the cornet spoke earnestly of the motives that had brought him to America, of his immersion in the liberal current that was sweeping France, of his devotion to the writers who headed that liberalism, of Condorcet, of Diderot and Voltaire and Rousseau.

It was quite an undertaking, Ross reflected, for a young Frenchman, seemingly unmoved by thought of gain or glory, to fight in an alien war for a nation whose very right to exist many people disputed. It would have been easy for him, since his family apparently was quite influential, to transfer to a regiment marked for home service, or to have left the army altogether. Yet de Chanzy looked upon his presence in the New World as something so logical as hardly to be worthy of comment. Caught up in the flood of liberal thought, sincerely believing in it, it would have been unnatural, in his eyes, to be anywhere else or to do anything else.

His judgment of men interested Ross keenly. He saw through the thin veneer of Light Horse Harry Lee's flamboyance, shrewdly appreciating the Virginian's unusual abilities as a cavalry leader, his integrity and his devotion to a cause that many thought hopeless. He shook his head in wonder over Marion. "Ah, *mon cher,* as yet I have seen little of him, but that little has told me much. Here in the Carolinas, he *is* the war. He is the banner, as well as the leader of his men. You agree?"

"Yes. Here in the east, at least. But don't forget, he's only one of a great many. There's Sumter and Pickens and Lacey and Hardin, just to mention a few."

De Chanzy was unconvinced. "No doubt they do well. But it is my conviction that were your Marion removed, the whole Southern war would tumble down, like a log pile in the Jura when the key log is taken out. Marion. Surely the name is French."

"Lots of French around here," said Ross, smoothing his saddle blanket. "Most of them came after the Revocation of the Edict of Nantes. They're Huguenots, French Protestants or whatever you like to call them."

"Ah, and Milord Cornwallis may well wish that the ship that brought them here had never made port," laughed de Chanzy. "*Ciel.* It grows so dark, so dark like black. With your permission I go up the column to be sure my little devils keep order."

Riding alone in the rear, Ross tried to sense the general direction of the column, but a thin overcast hid the stars and he had only a vague impression that the guide was making right-angle turns or wide, sweeping curves. There was a long halt on the shoulder of a low ridge over which the roof of a big house showed. Torches flared in a field whose southern edge was screened by a hickory grove. Silent Negroes hurried among the weary troopers with pails of coffee, hot and strong, with chunks of corn bread and slabs of salt beef.

The night wound on interminably. Ross shuttled between Winston at the head and de Chanzy in the rear. In between, the double file of helmets rocked and nodded as their owners dozed, swayed, caught themselves, dozed again. At last Ross caught a hint of light along the sky in a totally unexpected quarter. He had been sure that the course, for the last half hour, had been southeast and here was day slowly breaking to the left rear. The light grew stronger and he could make out the old, rutted road over which the column wound, heavy growths of hickory and live oak on either hand. Underfoot, the ground seemed dry and firm. With day coming on, they must be close to whatever mysterious destination Marion had set for them.

"Are we nearly there?" he asked the guide.

"Some'd say so," was the answer.

"You'll burst a blood vessel one day, chattering like that," said Ross. "The road looks clear ahead. Any reason why I shouldn't ride on a bit?"

"Ain't heard of none. That don't mean there ain't none."

Ross trotted on, keeping well to the center of the grassy track. Woods were still thick on both sides, the treetops faintly touched by the dawn. There was nothing to distinguish the road from a dozen others that he had ridden, and yet there was something that seemed oddly familiar to him. He tried to analyze the feeling and finally put it down to the smell of early morning in the woods.

The trees thinned suddenly. Ross pulled his horse onto its haunches and dropped to the ground, his hand covering the animal's nostrils. He stared ahead, flattening himself into the undergrowth. Beyond the last trees, a line of rough, grassy mounds showed, topped by a sagging palisade, the very same stretch of works that he had seen months ago when he had ridden into Chilyon's Castle with Peter Horry after their vain quest for Dorande. Under a tree that had sprouted out of the works, a man was outlined against the paling sky. Broad silver buckles winked as he moved his feet. His stockings were of white silk and his breeches were cherry colored below a glossy blue coat. A low branch hid most of his head, but Ross guessed that it was topped by a fine-napped beaver. As he watched, the man gestured with a gold-topped stick as though directing workers inside the old castle. Then, suddenly, he dropped from view.

Ross crouched lower, still holding the horse's nostrils, easing his fingers from time to time to allow the animal to breathe. Could some wandering band of Tories, even of British, have occupied Chilyon's Castle for an overnight rest? And yet those clothes! They could have belonged to someone from the Confiscation Office, to an *agent provocateur* who lined his pockets by stirring up the Whigs and then selling their plans to the Crown. He might even be an Indian agent, guiding a band of the dreaded Cherokees against the lowland settlements.

The man reappeared outside the works and Ross almost dropped the pistol that he had drawn. Then he vaulted into the saddle, sent his horse up the slope, shouting, "Raoul! What in the devil's name!"

Raoul Jaudon turned quickly, threw his hands in the air, then shook Ross by the shoulders as the latter dropped to the ground. "Ross! In the name of the Goose Creek men, what are you doing here? I heard you'd gone with Washington and Morgan. What are you up to? Going to raid the Santee posts by yourself?" He slapped Ross's back. "Good to see you, damned if it isn't. But I'd expected Lee's dragoons."

"Don't look so blasted disappointed. I'm a pretty good dragoon myself, Raoul. There are twenty dragoons with two good officers coming up the trail right now. I'm supposed to be in command and Marion said I'd get word about what we were to do when I got where I was going."

Raoul blew out his cheeks. "Fine. I didn't feel easy about the job when I first heard of it, but I ought to have known that Marion wouldn't have sent Lee's men without including someone who knew our kind of fighting—and theirs." He turned and shouted to the stockade. "Sandy! Dragoons coming up the track. Get out ahead and meet them. Bring them in through the east sallyport." He linked his arm with Ross's. "Come on in through here. It won't take long to show what you're supposed to do."

The interior of Chilyon's Castle was empty, save for a few men who were piling oat sacks in an old shelter. To the left was the low ridge behind which Dorande had slept that first night. Closer, he thought he could see the scars of the fire where he had talked with her and Marion and Peter Horry. He touched the empty cartridge box on his left hip. Inside, wrapped in oiled paper, was the old Quaker's sketch of a fair-haired girl looking out on the fort at Nelson's Ferry. He shook his head. At that very moment she might be on the wharves of Charleston, or on the deck of a schooner heading south for St. Eusebius.

Raoul's voice broke into his thoughts. "Let's set up headquarters on this log and get on with the war."

Ross shook his head again, eying the dragoons who were riding through the old sallyport. For the moment, past and future did not count. There was only the present, and the present was the war. He sat beside Raoul, stretching out his booted legs. "You've put on weight, Raoul. Relay riding seems to agree with you."

"Never felt better in my life," said Raoul. "As a matter of fact, though, I'm dead—officially. Poor Janet. I hope she doesn't know how damnably becoming widow's weeds are to her." He drew out a sheet of paper. "Now, here's your job. I think you can follow this map. Here we are, at Chilyon's Castle, north of the Santee and east of the Wateree. Are you oriented?"

"Got it," said Ross, frowning at the spidery lines. A few miles to the south the Santee flowed, with Nelson's Ferry a little to the southwest of the Castle. Running his eyes west, he made out Fort Watson on the north bank, with the notation "Stockade on an old Indian Mound" beside it. West again, and Fort Motte on the south bank, just above the junction of the Wateree and the Congaree. The Congaree! He snapped his finger nervously against the paper. "Look here—St. Aubin's place—isn't that—"

Raoul cut in quickly. "No, it isn't on this map. It's got nothing to do with it. But *this* has. See McCord's Ferry? On the Congaree?" Ross nodded silently, limited his vision to the plainly marked ferry. Raoul went on. "All right. That's your objective. There are a good many boats there. Some of them quite big. Colonel Watson, from his fort, has had people collecting them there. We don't want him to use them, either for stores or men. You and your dragoons are going to go there, burn them or stave them in, and then head for Fort Watson where Marion and Lee will be attacking. At McCord's Ferry, you'll find thirty to forty cavalry. They may give you a little trouble."

Ross, his mind now completely absorbed in military matters, rubbed his chin. "What sort of troops?"

"New York and Pennsylvania Tories with a few convalescents from the British 17th Dragoons. How do you plan on handling them?"

"Get them into the open and charge," said Ross without hesitation.

"What are Lee's horses like?"

"A cross between deer and elephants."

"They'll do then. You ought to bowl over the enemy tackies without any trouble. The boats are on the south bank."

Ross slowly folded the map and stowed it away. "I'll go over this with Winston and de Chanzy before we start."

"And be sure and tell them that McCord's is as far as you go. For you, that's where the Congaree ends."

"You said that before," said Ross shortly.

Raoul smoothed his white stockings. "You think a lot about Dorande, don't you?"

"You know confounded well I do—even if I've only seen her a couple of times."

"War times count double. Just the same, don't forget this. She's about the first attractive girl you've seen in a long time. Moreover, she's foreign, and brought up far differently than either of us. The war's about the only real common ground you two have between you—barring the fact that you're both rather far from repulsive. I know that she is and Janet says that you are. *But,* when this war's over, Dorande'll go back to the Indies and her Dutch island. Maybe she'll go before that. Then where will you be? Just now she's *not* at McCord's, and that's all that matters to you."

"I know it. And don't exaggerate the amount of concern I have about her. She's fascinating, I find her uncommonly attractive, but—"

"But don't *you* exaggerate your damn New England indifference. You've talked to Janet about Dorande and a woman's mighty smart about such things." He rose. "I've got to go now. Let your men rest a little, but be sure to start them within the hour."

"You're going? I thought you'd stay on with us."

Raoul shrugged. "In this macaroni suit? No. About the time you started for Georgetown, I got word from Marion to be here at Chilyon's with that map and the instructions for the dragoons. Also rations. I must say you haven't kept me waiting long."

"Come along with us anyway. You can report back to Marion at Fort Watson with us."

Raoul said quietly, "I'm going south from here. Into Georgia. Marion's orders."

"Into *Georgia?*" Ross's voice rose in surprise.

"Yes. There are things there that want finding out. There are people to see." He stopped abruptly, his jaw setting.

It was obvious to Ross that Raoul would say no more about his mission. It was equally obvious that he neither liked it nor would turn from it. Suddenly his own battered helmet and frayed uniform seemed like protective armor. He himself would wear it only over sure, known paths, far from the misty, fear-haunted course which lay before Raoul.

When Raoul had ridden away through a sallyport, Ross turned with a sigh to the dragoons who were busily filling their fodder sacks from the store of oats. Their horses stood waiting, girths loosened and bits slipped from their mouths. They looked fresh enough, as did their masters, but he wished that he could allow a good two hours of rest. That was not to be thought of, however, if the party were to reach McCord's Ferry at the most favorable time for attack.

He looked about for the other officers. Winston was standing off to the left, talking with the old Brunswicker sergeant, Kuhn, but he could not see de Chanzy's faded, out-at-the-elbows uniform. He signaled to Winston, then shouted, "De Chanzy! Where the devil's de Chanzy?"

A voice at his elbow answered calmly, "A question which I often pose to myself."

Ross turned quickly, exclaiming, "Well, I'll be damned."

The shapeless canvas *couvre-casque* had been stripped from the Frenchman's helmet, showing a full, creamy white plume, glittering leather and a thick band of glossy black fur above the vizor. The jacket was not only richly green and immaculate, but fine green silk showed on the revers, the cuffs, the lining. The spotless white breeches were loaded with high-running whorls and arabesques of gold braid.

Still staring, Ross said, "Did you find a tailor along with the oat sacks they left?"

De Chanzy shrugged. "On the march, my old rags do not too badly. Now, we go to make an attack. I wear all this to do honor to your war."

Ross looked at the Frenchman with renewed respect. "Thank you," he said gravely as Winston clanked up. "Now, gentlemen, here's our mission. The British have collected boats at McCord's Ferry. Marion wants them smahed. He and Lee will be moving on Fort Watson. Smashed boats will mean no reinforcements for the fort." He spread out Raoul's map. "Here's our route."

VII • Mon Plaisir

Ross had swung his dragoons a little to the southwest of McCord's Ferry, which lay just beyond a low ridge. A golden light, filtering down through a hickory grove, caught up the sleek leather of the dragoons' helmets, glinted on well-kept blades. As Ross surveyed the weather-beaten faces before him, he realized that few detailed orders were needed. The party would ride up through the trees in double file, then, at the crest, would swing into line and crash down onto the ferry with the sinking sun at their backs. It would be a wild, straight charge since de Chanzy's reconnaissance had established the absence of the most rudimentary posts or pickets. Ross felt deep confidence. The dragoons could be counted on to take care of routine matters mechanically. They would space themselves properly as they formed from column into line. Just before the moment of contact, they would open in the center to allow him to drop back among them without command. Anything beyond routine they would meet competently as it developed.

Two by two they threaded up the slope among the trees, carbine buckets creaking and metal chinking softly. All at once, Ross was on the crest and in the open. Right and left behind him the dragoons were fanning out, Winston on the right flank, de Chanzy on the left. A low cry escaped Ross, was echoed along the line. It was even better than de Chanzy had reported. The ground sloped smoothly north with the bright river at its far edge. Close by the bank, in front of some flimsy huts and sheds, the thirty-odd men of the garrison were sitting, their horses at sloppy attention, sabers sheathed. A man in red was languidly going through the ceremony of hauling down the colors to mark the official close of another dull day along the Congaree.

Ross stood in his stirrups, glanced over his shoulder, signaling the charge. The roar of hoofs was in his ears as the dragoons closed about him, pelting down the slope in a solid wall.

147

There was clear grass ahead of him. Then the grass was gone and his horse was rearing and lashing out in a tangle of red coats, buckskins, green coats and hoofs. Sabers were glinting, but not a blow was struck. The big, powerful mounts of the dragoons bowled over and through the terrified garrison. The weedy country-bred horses sprawled in a whirl of kicking legs, sank to their haunches or, bits in their teeth, raced wildly away toward the river where the dragoons, in compact squads, caught their dangling reins.

Ross rode clear of the melee, circled, shouting for the dragoons to rally for a second charge. There was nothing to charge. The few men who remained mounted were penned by Winston's wing. The others, weapons on the ground, were huddling in bewildered panic by the largest shed. Off by the river, de Chanzy, saber in his teeth, bent from the saddle to drag a cursing ensign of British infantry along by the collar.

Ross sheathed his saber. "All right! Bring him here. Winston! See to the boats. Quick, now! De Chanzy, detail the prison guard and set out your videttes. Any men you don't need, send to Winston!"

He had barely finished his orders before horse holders were told off, guards were posted and a swarm of dismounted dragoons raced off to the dark line of boats drawn up on the bank. Winston found sledges, mauls and axes neatly stacked in a shed and hastily passed them out. Kuhn, the scarred Brunswicker, shouted in guttural triumph as he rolled out a barrel of tar, unearthed bales of tow. Fires began to crackle under the nearest boats, while axe, sledge and maul crashed into thwart and bottom.

Ross turned to the British ensign, a fattish young man with bulbous eyes set in a puffy face. Before Ross could speak, the ensign panted furiously, "I will *not* answer any questions."

"That's lucky," said Ross shortly. "I'm not going to ask any." His eye lit on a British farrier sergeant in his somber black uniform. "You, go among your mates. Find out if anyone's too badly hurt to march. Corporal Farr, watch him."

Down by the river, planks screeched as heavy crowbars ripped them from their frames. Clouds of black smoke from the tar and tow hung heavy over the boats that Winston had marked as too strong to batter to pieces. Ross made a rapid tour of the bank. When he came back to the shed, the farrier sulkily reported that two men had been killed by heavy falls. There were painful sprains and bruises but none sufficiently serious to prevent marching. Ross ran his eye quickly over the prisoners, a strange mixture of fever-wasted British cavalry, Tories in green jackets with red facings, Tories in buckskins and country cloth. The ensign stepped angrily away from the dragoon who covered him with a short carbine. "Sir, I demand to know—"

Ross cut in, "Later. Now form your men up in a column of twos, ready to march at once."

"But this is an outrage. I haven't had my dinner. I'll make a complaint."

"You'll make any complaint you please to your commandant at Nelson's Ferry. We'll take you part way there. The rest is up to you," Ross answered shortly, his eyes on the most western of de Chanzy's videttes, silhouetted against the sunset.

The ensign wilted. "B-but good God, man, how—how'll I ever be able to explain—look here—be a good chap. Give me a letter saying—you know—overwhelming numbers—fought hard—all that sort of thing."

Ross stood in his stirrups, staring west. The vidette was slowly turning his horse, his eyes apparently fixed on the road that led on up the Congaree. Without glancing at the ensign, he snapped, "Be ready to move. Hurry it up!" and started at a trot toward de Chanzy, who was cantering down the western slope toward him. The Frenchman looked inquiringly at him. Ross said, "Form the prisoner guard up the slope heading into the grove. If I give the word, start them back east at once. We'll catch up with you."

De Chanzy nodded calmly. *"Parfaitement,"* he said, and rode toward the sheds, shouting orders.

Ross kept on. The vidette, still looking west, was passaging his horse slowly and expertly down the slope, ready to whirl to the river at a gallop if necessary. "What do you see?" called Ross.

The dragoon pointed at the road that coiled lazily west along the Congaree. Dust plumbed high and thin into the sunset. That meant cavalry, not infantry. There were three distinct plumes that Ross estimated at twenty men each.

The dragoon muttered, "Coming this way, slow."

Ross jerked his thumb at the sinister rolls of smoke from the ferry. "Wait till they sight that. Then they'll speed up. Report to de Chanzy. Tell him to pull in all his videttes and start the prisoners along the east road."

The vidette saluted and galloped off. Ross took a final look at the dust plumes, then raced back to the bank where sledges pounded and men coughed in the tar smoke. Winston grinned at him through a black mask, teeth flashing white. "Just five barges left."

Ross leaned from the saddle. "Visitors coming. Cavalry." Winston started. "Sure it's cavalry?"

"Dust clouds are too high and thin for infantry. Keep on

with your work, but hurry it all you can. I'll be up by the trees where we started our charge. I can see the west road and not be seen. When I lift my helmet, pitch everything into the river that can possibly be used again, mount and get out quick. De Chanzy's started already with the prisoners. I'll get as good a look as I can at our visitors."

Winston nodded and Ross took his post, well screened by the trees at the crest. He had a clear view of nearly a mile of road. Over a low fold of ground he could make out part of the leading dust cloud, saw riders emerge from it as the wind freshened. The two leaders wore red coats, probably British officers holding provincial commissions. The others, who trailed after them, seemed much like the garrison of the ferry, men in faded red coats, men in Tory green or homespun, the latter groups predominating. Ross guessed that they had come over from Ninety-six or even from The Long Canes.

The officers in red seemed to be talking earnestly to each other, pointing at the smoke that still rolled high. He wondered why they didn't send out a patrol to investigate. Probably they figured that the ferry garrison was heating tar to calk the carefully collected boats. He glanced directly down at the river, saw Winston shading his eyes and staring anxiously up at him. Ross kept his hands folded on his pommel and looked back at the road. One of the red officers had signaled and a squad of mixed red and green broke off from the column, joined the leaders and then trotted sharply toward the ferry.

Ross stood in his stirrups and waved his helmet, the white crest brushing his cheek. The dragoons boiled into increased activity. Horses were brought to the bank, men shoved half-demolished barges into the current, tossing burning tar and tow into them. All at once the river edge was clear. Winston's men mounted, swung quickly off and up the slope toward Ross, who dropped farther back among the trees.

He was just in time. The patrol appeared suddenly among the sheds, the men shouting and pointing at the wreckage that drifted downstream. Then one of them caught sight of the vanishing Legion jackets and whooped like a fox hunger. Ross chuckled excitedly. The enemy had a hasty glimpse of men in green jackets riding away, and they could make what they wanted of it. The jackets, with their deceptive color, might be worn by other Tories, setting out in pursuit of a Rebel band that had somehow managed to wreck the post. He was sure that, as these men had obviously come from the west, they would be ignorant of the Legion's presence in the South, let alone of its green jackets. He himself they could not have seen, since irregularities in the ground covered him.

A signal must have been passed from the patrol, for the rest of the column, some fifty men, as Ross reckoned, appeared among the sheds at a smart trot, the tackies laboring along bravely under their heavy riders. The scouts talked briefly with the officers, who sat their horses rigidly, staring ahead. Then the taller of the two raised his arm and the whole command started up the slope, the leading column in skirmish order, the rest following in column.

Ross, keeping his cover, fell back on the right flank of the advance, his military instinct telling him that it would be valuable to know who these men were, in what exact strength, where they were going and when. Much of this he could deduce from their equipment and the amount of rations carried.

Now in the right rear, as the command entered the hickory grove, Ross studied them. They carried spare rations and their fodder nets were filled. Therefore, they were bound for some point well beyond McCord's. Their arms were a weird assortment and, while all the men rode well, they kept sloppy formation. Obviously a scratch lot of Tories, some local and others from out of the state, with a sprinkling of British convalescents or men returning from command or detached service. If their officers were at all competent, they would not follow Winston far, even if the identity of his command were discovered. The Legionnaires, incomparably better mounted, could merely walk away from pursuit or, if pressed at all, turn and ride down these tacky-mounted men without a blade being drawn.

He followed a smooth-sided ravine that led away south, remembering that farther back he had noted great stretches of open fields bordered with woods. From those woods he ought to be able to get another flank view of the enemy from closer quarters and perhaps gather their destination from some indication. He himself would be well on his way to overtaking Winston and de Chanzy. If he were seen he would have no trouble. In open field or thick wood he could maintain a tantalizing distance from any small number of pursuers and possibly take a prisoner for information purposes.

Ten minutes' riding brought him among wide-spaced oaks where underbrush had been carefully cleared. Down a lane of trunks that spread toward the river he saw motion, heard a clatter of voices. The newcomers had given up their pursuit and were streaming back toward McCord's. Ross faded to a safer distance among the trees, frowning. He wanted very much to see just what they would do when they reached the ferry. If they scattered to the sheds, it might mean that they were to stay in garrison. If they bivouacked, dawn would see them on their way again. If they left at once, then it might be well to hang on their flank and find out if they kept on east along the Santee or turned north up the Wateree.

It was worth the delay and the slight risk, he decided. He swung back west, keeping as close to the left flank as he dared. Even if the drum of his horse's hoofs were heard, that could rouse little suspicion. Such an ill-disciplined lot would be accustomed to the sound of stragglers trying to catch up to the main body.

There was marshy ground ahead of him, then he saw a firm, level stretch south of it. He set his mount at a gallop, passed the end of the marsh, turned sharply north. The horse took the turn easily, its body slanting inward and its powerful haunches driving.

There was a ripping, crackling sound, a hideous lurch. The sunset world spun about Ross, gave him a terrific jolt on the right shoulder, bowled him crazily along the ground. Trees, fading sky, grass, more trees whirled before his eyes, steadied, faded out completely.

Through a thick haze he blundered to his hands and knees, tried dizzily to get to his feet while the realization of his plight seeped through his aching head. When his horse had banked for that last sharp turn, the right stirrup leather had snapped and he had been hurled to the ground like the rawest recruit. He had probably lain stunned for a minute or two for there was no sign of his horse. Now he was weaponless save for his saber, dismounted in enemy territory.

He stood panting as his head slowly cleared. In the dimming light he could make out scattered spots where hoofs had torn up the turf, but the ground was too hard to show any continuous pattern that he might follow. The clearest prints seemed to lead toward the woods at the north. He shrugged. At least, it was a chance. He unbuckled his spurs, stowed them in his pockets and, catching up scabbard and sabretache, walked swiftly toward the trees.

All at once he muttered, "Got it!" and began to run toward the thrashing sounds among the trees. The remaining stirrup, the dangling reins, perhaps a broken girth had halted his horse there in the woods. He laughed to himself as he caught a muffled snort, the beginning of a whinny. There was no need for precaution. The enemy force must be far distant now. He pushed on toward the sounds that had first caught his ear.

A lazy voice said, "Up with your hands, my lad, and tell us who the devil you are."

Breast deep in bushes, Ross stopped, hands held high and eyes suddenly narrowed in alarm. Something within him prompted insistently, "Don't panic!" as he studied the pair in the clearing beyond the bushes. A tall, fair-haired captain, red-coated and with a British light-infantry cap set rakishly over his right eye, sat a shaggy tacky while he covered Ross with a double-barreled pistol. His companion, in the same uniform, stood with his bridle over his arm while he coolly hammered a light over a short-stemmed pipe, eyes owlish on Ross.

Hand still high, Ross suddenly decided on the offensive. "Have you got a Loyalist body hereabouts?" he asked, trying to keep his tones firm and yet reasonably polite.

The mounted officer grinned boyishly, but his pistol was steady. "Wouldn't you just like to know?"

Ross took a step forward. "Yes. And if you have I want to see your muster rolls."

The other officer, a lieutenant, still drawing on his pipe, said pleasantly, "Would you, now! And by what right?"

"I was bringing twenty-two men up from Dreadnaught. They rode away from me this noon, heading north. I got on their trail, but my stirrup leather broke and I lost my horse. I enlisted those men. They're for Camden. If they've joined you for extra bounty, then you can't hold them."

The captain shook his head. "We've got no new men. Where did you say you were from?"

The lieutenant, pipe now comfortably alight, mounted, saying through the pipestem, "He means Fort Galphin. Dreadnaught's what some of the Loyals call it. I fancy he's all right. His lot dress up in anything they can find."

The captain nodded. "Oh, Galphin, of course. On the Georgia border. How's old McTavish?"

"Who?" asked Ross.

"McTavish. The commandant."

Ross felt confidence returning. "He must be doing fine if he was man enough to oust Tom Browne from command there."

The officers exchanged glances. The pipe smoker spat and said, "That's right. Browne, the bloody, butchering bastard. Now, sir, you might oblige us with your name and rank and service."

The answer had been forming in Ross's mind for some minutes. He said readily, "Ralph Potter, commissioned captain by Browne. Up north I served with Loyalists under Burgoyne. Down here, I've been with Dunlap and Coffin. I started upstate with Lisle until I found out he was really taking his men to join the Rebels. I got away and went to the Savannah and Dreadnaught."

Both officers looked satisfied. The captain sighed. "If you've just come up from the Savannah, I don't suppose you know about anything happening on the river a little while ago."

Ross felt increasingly easy. He said, "May I drop my hands? Thanks. No, I haven't heard of anything."

The lieutenant puffed at his pipe. "Some damned scoundrels wrecked all the boats at a ferry over there and nobbled the garrison. Whoever did it cleared out just in time, but we sighted them. Blast me if I didn't think they were Loyals. Helmets, green jackets and all."

Ross looked wise. "Ah, that'd be Hardcastle and his gang. They've a lair somewhere and raid both sides. Marvelous horses, the best of equipment." He wagged his head knowingly. "A lot of people would like to know who supports them, but Hardcastle's a slyer fox than that damned Marion or Sumter."

The captain looked blank. "Never heard of any of them. We're fresh from the Barbados." He gathered his reins. "Well, see here now. I'm Captain Dickson Abbott assigned to the 63rd and this is Lieutenant Milne Carst, also of ours. Can't have you fossicking about the woods all night. Better come along with us and have a drink. Maybe we can fit you out with a tacky. We're bound for Camden, and you can come with us if you like."

Ross acknowledged both introduction and invitation. "Kind of you, gentlemen. But I'm bound to find that animal of mine. I know he's in the woods somewhere."

"Can't be. We'd have seen or heard any beast ahead of us." Abbott reached down and patted Ross's shoulder. "Really, I insist. Must come along with us. Someone will find your horse."

Ross made a quick decision. He would go with the pair, trusting to his own wits to keep him out of trouble and to get him a mount. By the next morning, he could rejoin Winston or even the main body under Marion and Lee. The risk seemed fairly small to him—for wartime. His escorts were too new to the Carolinas to possess much dangerous knowledge. For a short time, at least, he would be sponsored by them and apt to meet no one who might ask awkward questions.

"I'm much in your debt, gentlemen," he said, swinging up behind the lieutenant, who rode the stouter horse.

The trail that they followed ran well inland from the river and the sheds by the ford. The Englishmen talked as they rode and Ross listened as best he could. The two were anxious to reach Camden where they hoped for orders to push on past Winnsboro and overtake Cornwallis. The British commander, they said, was straining to catch Morgan before he could make a junction with Greene, who was thought to be moving his main force west from the Cheraws. They were certain that if Cornwallis caught Morgan alone he would easily avenge the two left-wing defeats of King's Mountain and the Cowpens. All this was interesting but by no means vital. Marion and Lee undoubtedly knew far more than these two men.

The Captain shouted, " 'Ware gate!" and whipped his tacky into a gallop, heading at a low white frame that showed dimly. He took the jump easily. The lieutenant whooped and started after him, Ross dropping to the ground lest the overloaded horse peck at the top bar and throw both his riders.

When he caught up to them, he felt gravel under his feet and smelled fresh turned earth through the thickening gloom, indicating a well-tended garden. At the far end he made out the bulk of a big house, with lights bright in its windows and throwing high pillars into bold relief. Abbott dismounted, calling, "Come along, Carst, Potter. King's people here, Potter." Ross clanked up the broad steps after them. A white-covered table stood by the open door, its clustered candles shining down on an array of bottles, platters of cold meat, a flattish bowl where bright-colored fish swam. Four British officers, a sleek, rather somberly dressed civilian, turned inquiringly as Abbott hailed. "Got clean away. Blasted if I know who they were or why. Smart piece of work, though. Got the whole confounded garrison and clapper-clawed every last boat into matchwood. My friend Potter here says they're a lot of New World Robin Hoods." He rattled off the names and ranks of the other officers.

Ross acknowledged the introductions, his eye taking in the green facings of the 63rd, the blue of the 23rd, denoting a chance-gathered lot returning from command to go north to Cornwallis.

The civilian, who had stepped indoors for an instant, returned with a murmured apology to his guest. Abbott waved to him. "And, by all means, our loyal host and valued friend, Mr. Paul St. Aubin," he proclaimed, anglicizing the name into "Auburn."

Ross and St. Aubin bowed profoundly. Ross said, "I have been anxious to meet Mr. St. Aubin, whose beliefs override the bonds of nationality. His name is well known in the South."

St. Aubin made a suave gesture. "I see that monsieur realizes that devotion to the monarchical principle permits me, a humble French subject, to hold that our royal government acts wrongly in this war, and to govern myself accordingly."

Ross made a perfunctory response, while his face felt like

a rigid mask. His mind repeated incessantly, "St. Aubin—St. Aubin—St. Aubin." Dorande might be somewhere in the big house! He had had no idea that the Frenchman's property lay so close to McCord's. From an upper window one could easily have seen the smoke, perhaps the burning itself, might even have made out his own distinctive white coat moving among the green jackets of the Legion. He had a sudden impulse to raise his voice, to step close to the open front door, but caution held him back.

Other redcoats moved toward him, asking questions whose answers required all his wits. A red-faced major of the 23rd, in particlar, seemed far less ready to accept his story than Abbott and Carst had been. Fortunately his memory just served well enough. Yes, he remembered very clearly the bridge of boats between Ticonderoga and Independence. No, it was not the Rhetz regiment which had been left behind as garrison, but most of the Hesse-Hanau grenadiers.

Abbott broke into the stream of questions. "See here, young Potter hasn't had a drink yet and I'd promised him one, ten, a dozen."

A lieutenant of the 23rd handed Ross a glass of brandy. "There's a drink and here's a toast! Gentlemen, the King!"

Even St. Aubin glanced at Ross as the toast was proposed. Ross deliberately raised his glass, then moved it in a wide circle over the bowl where the fish glinted. "The King," he said, holding his face as impassive as he could.

The major flushed angrily, but two or three pairs of eyes met Ross's in quick understanding. Other glasses, some boldly, some furtively, were passed over the tank as their holders drank to "The King—over the water"—to the exiled Stuart Pretender and not to Hanoverian George III.

Ross felt the tight band about his chest relax a little. His gesture, whether approved or disapproved, had sealed his acceptance as a Tory. Once again he blessed his memory for retaining the odd ritual which he had seen captive British officers perform after Burgoyne's surrender at Saratoga, more than three years ago.

Tension slightly relieved, Ross found that he was extremely hungry and secured from the table a thick slice of pink, tender ham enclosed between two pieces of bread, white and fine-textured. He stepped away from the table, glancing with forced casualness into the hall. There were Negro voices somewhere in the rear but he could make out no other sign of life.

The officers about the table seemed ready to take their leave. "Must be getting on. Decent of you to feed us, St. Auburn." . . . "Be sure and commend me to my Lord Cornwallis when you write him." . . . "Have a cousin, ensign in the 71st. Wounded you know. I'd be uncommon grateful, St. Auburn, if you'd drop a word to Colonel Balfour or the Sequestration Office. Chap deserves a good billet where he can pick up something for himself."

The voices faded from Ross's ears. There, hanging to the newelpost, was a big, deerskin bag. He had seen it on the night march through the swamps after the wreck of Bayne's convoy. He had seen it again on Snow Island, indiscreetly spilling out delicate lingerie as he handed it to Dorande. He edged into the hall itself. To the rear, light shone from an open door that slanted inward. He nearly dropped his glass. Across the smooth surface of that door a shadow moved, vanished, disappeared, then showed again. There was no mistaking that fine profile, that slim, graceful figure, black against the white wood.

The shadow was gone but Ross heard Janet Jaudon's soft voice. "But my dear! You mustn't sell *that!* Wasn't it a present from your mother? I thought so. And besides—the Stinsons are Tories, utterly rabid Tories." Janet! what the devil was *she* doing at St. Aubin's?

Then the reply sent Ross's heart racing as the well-remembered tones reached him. "I know only that they were burned out, that they have no home, no cattle. This stone, it is a small one, but out of it may be built a house, a barn with cows and sheep in it."

Ross heard a ghost of a sigh from Janet. "Remember what happened when you helped the McQuillans. They were so grateful that they burned out the McNullas by way of thanking you."

"*Ça ce peut!* But among the Stinsons are a grandmother and a sick baby."

Ross set his glass on a small table. The lighted doorway was not really so far down the hall. There could be no danger in — A red arm reached from the porch, tugged at his insistently. Ross made an impatient gesture, then recovered himself as he saw Carst, half amused, half irritated. "Damn my wig, Potter. I've been shouting my lights out. What the devil's the matter with you? We're going to catch up with the column and find you one of these damned camels that the natives call horses. Come along!"

Ross took a last look at the door. The light had gone out and there was no sound from the rear of the house. Resignedly he let Carst lead him to the table. "Here he is, Abbott. He'll come along with us. 'Fraid that beast of mine won't carry the two of us very far, but Potter can hang onto a saddle strap and we'll take him in tow."

St. Aubin stepped forward blandly. "But there is no need of that, I assure you. See, you good fellows, I shall escort you from my estate, as is only right. Thus I may go on to your column with you, followed by my servant who shall lead here the horse that you provide for our good friend, the captain." He bowed to Ross, who noted St. Aubin's eyes had nothing to do with his smile. "You, monsieur, would surely find it more *commode* to await your horse here, than to run, *ventre à terre*, between your comrades. Ah, but I insist. I shall not be long. In the meantime, house and slaves are yours to command."

Ross had to fight to keep elation from his voice. He managed to say, "Good of you, but really—longer ride for you—"

Abbott clapped Ross on the shoulder. "Capital idea, St. Auburn's. You'll have no trouble picking up our scent. I'll leave a corporal at the point where we turn north. We're heading up the west bank of the Wateree. Night march and nailing fine weather for it."

Ross forced another show of hesitation, but St. Aubin, bowing again, purred, "It is a favor that you do me, in waiting. On my return, I shall ask for five little minutes of your time to tell you of an idea that may profit both of us."

Ross acknowledged his bow. "Your debtor, sir."

"*A bientôt,*" murmured St. Aubin.

When the last hoofs had pattered out of hearing, Ross strode quickly into the house. The servants had extinguished the lights and the hall lay before him, a dim tunnel. He brushed against a spinet set in a recess under the stairs, moved forward more cautiously, wondering if he dared risk calling. Suddenly he knew that there was movement in the dark ahead of him. He caught a whiff of delicate scent, the rustle of silk. His hands went out quickly and he cried softly, "Dorande!"

The girl was closer than he thought and his arms encircled slim shoulders, shawl covered. Two hands fell on his epaulettes, tightened there. Then Janet Jaudon's voice, low and tense, came to him. "Ross Pembroke! What on earth are you doing *here?* Here, of all places."

Shocked by his mistake, Ross could only stammer, "Dorande. Where's Dorande?"

"Never mind. She's safe. But you—"

"Never safer, Janet. For the moment, I'm an accepted Tory. St. Aubin's getting me a horse."

Janet's low laugh was unsteady with relief. "At least, I'm flattered that you mistook me for Dorande, even in the dark." She gave him a little hug, then stepped back. "It's good to see you, Ross. And Raoul?"

"Well, when I last saw him, which was not many hours ago at Chilyon's Castle."

"Did he know you were coming here?"

"Of course not, or else he would have sent a message by me. In fact, he ordered me not to go beyond McCord's."

Janet bustled about the hall, lighting the candles. "It's lucky you disobeyed orders. There's a message for you here. It's already gone on to—what was his name?—oh, Winston. If you'd been separated from him and not come here, you wouldn't have found him where you expected."

Ross shrugged ruefully, turning his helmet in his hands. "Can't the war wait—just a little?"

"Have you ever known it too?" asked Janet. "Just a minute and I'll get the details for you." She slipped through another door.

Ross paced restlessly up and down, worrying at the fastenings of his sword. He was sure that St. Aubin would need a good hour to return with a spare tacky. But Janet's message! Would it send him out into the night at once, with no chance to see Dorande? If the matter were of high importance, he knew that she would let nothing stand in the way of its execution. Five minutes only!

There was a soft gasp behind him. He turned, incredulous. In the doorway to his left, Dorande stood, wide-eyed, lips slightly parted in surprise. Light fell on her blond hair, her dark eyes, her slim figure in peacock-blue silk. He stepped toward her, hands out. She gave a low cry and caught them. The war, men in red jackets, the house of St. Aubin, were banished from the world. She said unsteadily, "I am glad, Ross Pembroke. Janet only told me that someone waited in the hall."

Ross could only stare down at her. His clasp tightened, drawing her nearer. Her eyes were half closed and he murmured, "Ah, Dorande!"

She gave a start, freed her hands and stepped back. "Yes, I am glad you are come. Now listen well. This is the news which Janet wishes you to receive. It is all that there is of the most serious. The Legion—all the Legion of Lee—goes north to join General Greene. It is ordered that you go with it."

Long habit focused Ross's mind on the news and he tried swiftly to evaluate it. The Legion had been sent south to work with Marion. Now it was recalled in haste. He glanced at Dorande, trying to think of her only as a source of military information that concerned him. But a smile kept twitching at the corners of his mouth. Standing there so straight and grave, she looked like a good little girl reciting her catechism.

Dorande went on, closing her eyes from time to time in an effort of memory. Morgan was falling back on a northeasterly course under command of Greene in person. The main army, under Isaac Huger, was marching northwest, hoping to form a junction. "But this Cornwallis," said Dorande earnestly, "he is not like the other good, comfortable British generals, who are slaves to their baggage. No. Milord Cornwallis, he burns his wagons, his very tents, much of his stores. He pushes hard after your Morgan. And Tarleton pushes harder than all, he being *mal vu* since his defeat at Cowpens and wishing greatly to redeem himself. This much I tell you. You, a soldier, will know better than I its significance."

Its significance was glaring. Let Cornwallis catch and demolish Morgan's picked corps, the half-trained men marching northwest from the Cheraws would be easily disposed of. The loss of this, the third army to be sent to the Carolinas, would seal the fate of the South, if not the whole country. Yes, the Legion was needed. Hard, fast-marching infantry, skilled cavalry, would be vital to Morgan's safety, would form a screen between the pursuit and the main body of the pursued. Every trained cavalryman would be needed. In that case—

He asked abruptly, "You know the route of the Legion?"

"Only that they go east of the High Hills of Santee. But I send a black to guide you. You may trust him. He is nephew to that Antigua of Monsieur Harleston who takes word to the Whigs on the coast. I find him now."

"There's no hurry. I can't start until your uncle gets here. I want to talk to you, Dorande. I want—"

A defensive mask set over her face. "But you have the message."

"Blast the message. I—there's a lot that I want to tell you. I want to tell you that your hair looks like spun gold in the candlelight, and how your blue silk sets off your white throat. Did you ever know, Dorande, that your eyes turn up at the corners distractingly when you smile? That little points of light dance in them?"

She put her hands to her cheeks. "Oh, please!"

"And you've hardly said that you were glad to see me. You—" He stopped short, listening. "Who's out there, beyond the big window?"

Dorande glided to the sill, eyes wide. Then she said, "But there is no one. I can see well."

Ross was relieved. "Must be the wind in the shrubs. But as I was saying—"

Dorande shook her head. "I must find the slave, Tobias. Then I come back. You wait?"

Ross laughed. "I'll try to."

"So. Then I hurry myself." The door swung and she was gone.

Ross leaned on the newelpost by the deerskin bag, his mind a happy blur. He glanced toward the window again. If only he could rid himself of the impression that, for an instant, someone had been there, listening and hostile. But Dorande had said that there was no one.

He raised his head and swore under his breath. A horse—two horses—out in the night. Could St. Aubin have returned so soon? He stepped quickly to the room to the right of the hall, where one candle burned. Spurred boots clicked up the steps and onto the porch, paused, then came into the hall.

Ross looked up politely, then sprang back. From the threshold Captain Bayne glared at him in cold triumph, his stooped shoulders twitching in excitement. His foxlike eyes, however, were cold and steady. Ross's hand moved to the hilt of his saber, but Bayne whipped out a pistol and covered him.

Ross's hands flew high above his head and Bayne nodded in cold satisfaction. "Just keep them there—if you want to live, Pembroke." He moved close, unhooked Ross's saber and sent it clattering along the floor. "There! That's better. Now, what are you doing here?"

"Try and guess," said Ross, studying his captor, watching for the least chance to grapple and disarm him.

Bayne's smile twisted across his face. "Not worth while. Not of the least importance. I'm on my way from Ninety-six to Camden, Pembroke. How'd you like to go there with me? A very good friend of mine is Provost and I think he'd like to see you. He'd like to hear that you're an escaped prisoner. That when a prisoner, you struck one of His Majesty's officers. How'd you like that, Pembroke? How'd you like to see the hulks again?"

Still watching him closely, Ross answered, "Not very much, Bayne."

Bayne's smile twisted again. "I daresay you're right. And you know me. I'm kindhearted as a child. I think—I think I won't take you to the Provost. In fact, I won't even take you prisoner. Instead, I'll leave you right here and good old St. Aubin will know what to do with you. Oh, don't look hopeful. You'll have no chance to get away. And as I'm in a little hurry, we'll make sure—this way." He raised his pistol, leveled it at Ross's head, then slowly let the muzzle sink. "In the shoulder? Too easy. The guts? You'd make a devil of a mess on the floor. The knee? Ah, that's it. A nice lump of lead under the kneecap. Maybe you won't lose your leg, if they get you to a good surgeon in time. Maybe."

The muzzle dropped and dropped with agonizing slowness. Sweat stood out on Ross's forehead and his knees were weak. With an effort he straightened himself and laughed. "What have you been doing with that barker, Bayne? Twisting women's thumbs in the lock? You may be a good soldier, but you forgot to set your flint."

For an instant, Bayne's small eyes flickered down to the lock of his pistol. In that flash of time Ross took a gliding step forward and swung his fist as hard as he could. He felt Bayne's head snap back as the blow landed just at the hinge of the jaw. Bayne's feet flew up. Head, shoulders, heels, struck the floor in three distinct thuds. He twitched and lay still. Ross caught up the pistol, its flint in perfect condition, and moved quietly to the door, recovering his sword as he went. He was sure that he had heard two horses on the drive outside. He looked out cautiously, saw a bored trooper standing with his back to the house, two bridles over his arm. It was obvious he had overheard nothing.

Ross, still trembling in the relief of his escape from Bayne, took a long stride onto the veranda, jammed the muzzle of the pistol into the man's back. There was a gasp of surprise and fright and the trooper's hands went high. Ross reached around and disarmed him, wondering how he could dispose of him. It was one thing to knock Bayne unconscious, another to club a stupid lout into insensibility merely because he was in the way. Then he remembered seeing a heavy-doored closet just beyond the spinet. He jabbed the pistol closer, gave a short order and marched the trooper into the house, his prisoner walking with high-kneed steps and crooked fingers. The key was on the outside. Ross flung the door open, shoved the man inside. "Just keep quiet in there and you'll not be hurt," snapped Ross as he slammed the door and turned the key, which he slipped into his pocket.

He heard a gasp of surprise behind him, turned to see Dorande, who must have come in through the rear of the house. *"Mais que fais-tu là?"* she cried.

Ross raised a warning finger, whispered quickly the story of Bayne's arrival. Dorande listened, frowning. "But I do not understand. You take his pistol from him? And where is this Captain Bayne now?"

"In that room, where I hope he'll stay for a long time. I —I had to be a little rough with him. His orderly's locked in that closet."

"That closet? But he will hear us."

"I think not. And what if he did?"

Dorande twisted her hands. "You do not see, no? He hear us talk, perhaps. And why, one will ask, do I, niece of Monsieur St. Aubin, talk in amity with rebels? Oh, Ross Pembroke, this may harm—"

Ross turned quickly as he saw her eyes go wide, staring past him toward the room where Bayne lay. The captain had at least partially come out of his stupor and swayed in the entrance on hands and knees, blinking stupidly.

Dorande murmured distractedly, "He has seen us. *Nom de Dieu, que faire?*"

Suddenly a frightening change came over her face. Her eyes blazed and her teeth were bared in rage. *"Non! Non! Jamais! Jamais de la vie!* You are vile, you insult! That I go with you to your *va-nu-pieds* camp? Go! Now! At home, my blacks would whip you from the house! Go! This instant!" Her little fists drummed on Ross's chest and he caught an intense whisper. *"Act! Act!* Seize me! He watches, but does nothing!" Her voice went up again. *"Poltron! Goujat!"*

Ross caught her tightly to him and began backing down the hall. Dorande kicked and struggled, set her teeth in the cloth of his sleeve. To the left, Bayne was reeling to his feet, apparently still half-conscious. Ross dragged Dorande on with one arm, the other holding the pistol that covered Bayne. He held Dorande closer, felt her body tight against his. He laughed roughly. "You'll thank me for this tomorrow, my lady. Bayne, stay where you are. Remember to tell the Provost about this when you see him." Dorande squirmed and writhed more violently as they reached the porch, wrenching one hand free and striking at him. By the steps she nearly broke away, then fell to her knees, Ross keeping hold of one slim wrist.

The horses were close by the steps. Still clinging to her wrist, Ross straddled Bayne's mount, then bent and caught Dorande in his arms, swinging her to the saddle in front of him. Her face was pressed against his shoulder and he could feel her heart beating through the thin silk that covered her breast. As he gathered the reins, looping them through those of the trooper's tacky, he felt Dorande's breath on his cheek, heard her murmur, "Well done, Ross Pembroke."

As Ross swung the horses out toward the drive, he took a last look at the house. Bayne, sag-kneed, was standing in the doorway, weaving drunkenly. Dorande, her feet hanging over the high side of the horse, gave a long, tremulous sigh and settled herself. "You are very deft, Ross Pembroke," she whispered. "You have carried away many young girls?"

"Not a *great* many," said Ross, shifting his right arm to form a cradle for her back and shoulders. "Are you comfortable?"

"Oh, a little, I think. Now, this will be better." She blinked her arms about Ross's neck and dropped her head on his shoulder. "No. Take the path to the right. That way we do not meet those who may ride up from the river. Then we wait till we hear horses. You put me down and I run, run, run. Such a story I have to tell. Very nearly has a great devil of a Rebel carried me off on his saddle, like a chevalier-errant of the old times! Ah, I do believe, Ross Pembroke, that our little comedy was a success."

Ross felt the cling of her soft body, the pressure of her arms, the softness of her hair against his cheek. "Suppose, Dorande, that I should tell you that this is not comedy, but very real?"

"Perhaps I should be angry."

"Angry, with me?"

"I think. But not for supposing."

"I find it pleasant to think about."

"That no one may forbid."

"And you?"

"Who knows my thoughts? But at least—I do not say to put me down, here, at once, do I?"

"You could say that only into deaf ears."

"I ask when it is necessary." She gave a sigh and her arms tightened still more about his neck. "Ah, Ross Pembroke, you are going far away, very far away and into cruel places. Believe me, I wish you well."

"Any place I go is easier than doing what you've chosen to do, Dorande. I wish—I wish we could ride on and on, like this. Does it make you angry when I say that?"

Her head stirred on his shoulder, and he saw the white blur of her face in the darkness. He bent, gathering her closer, knew that her cheek glided along his, that her lips lifted to his, clung to him as her arms clung. The two horses clopped docilely along over springy turf.

A little later, Dorande gave a soft, breathless, little laugh. "Once more, you have shaved yourself." Her fingers strayed along the line of his jaw. "Was it that that first made me notice you? I think perhaps. And yet you frightened me. You looked a warrior so terrible. You've new fur on your helmet. I remember holding it on my knee and stroking it, at Snow Island."

"I remember seeing you. I liked your doing it, though it made me a little jealous, perhaps."

"Jealous? Of a helmet! *Que c'est drôle!* Tell me why?"

"This," said Ross, "is the best reason I can think of," and gently lifted her head again.

She laughed low. "I do not understand. Tell me again. I am not clever."

Suddenly she gave a start. "We have ridden so far. No, no! This is the place. Tobias waits over there, under the big magnolia. Ah, Ross Pembroke, I could wish that I had forgotten to give you the message, which takes you so far."

She gave a wriggle and dropped to the ground, clutching at her skirts that billowed up. Ross swung down behind her. "But Dorande, our time is our own. Let St. Aubin ride home and stable his horses if he wants. He doesn't mean anything to us!"

"He is clever. You do not know how clever. We must act and act again, I tell you." She raised one hand. "Listen! On the drive! Horses come! No, Ross Pembroke, please! Now we play the final act." Her hands flew to her hair, moved deftly and a cascade of tresses tumbled about her shoulders, slid halfway to her waist. Then her fingers were at her throat. There was a ripping sound and a white shoulder, the hint of a slanting breast, in the dimness. She caught the torn cloth close about her and before Ross could move slipped her free arm about his neck, bent his head to hers. Then she was gone, racing along a path that led toward the drive. Her voice carried a depth of rage and desperation. "*A moi! A moi!* Here! Ah, *le ravisseur! Au secours!* Help me!"

Far off on the drive, Ross heard angry exclamations, the dying beat of Dorande's feet. From the magnolia the sleepy Tobias glided, swung into the saddle of the trooper's tacky. Ross mounted mechanically and sat motionless, listening to the noises in the distance. Quietly Tobias reached out a hand, caught Ross's bridle and started the horses through the darkness toward the east. Ross let the reins hang limp, his head turning and turning as the last sounds of life faded away in the rear.

VIII • North to the Dan

Flogged on by the February storms that lashed down with sleet, with rain and again with sleet, the Southern Army reeled desperately on across North Carolina, heading for the Virginia border and the crossing of the Dan. To the west, moving roughly parallel, Cornwallis drove his exhausted men in pursuit. He marched without wagons, without tents. He marched without rest and without mercy, and the old-timers of the American flankguard who remembered the indolent, lackadaisical Howe, the pleasure-loving Burgoyne and the cautious, almost apathetic Clinton, marveled while they cursed the extraordinary British energy. Always when a deft maneuver, a sharp fight, seemed to promise at least a temporary respite from the eternal pressure, American videttes rode in reporting that O'Hara's mounted infantry or Tarleton's Legion were within sight, were within musket shot or even saber stroke.

To the east, the main body of Greene's command, a scant thirteen hundred miserably equipped and half-trained troops, slogged on and on. Between them and Cornwallis ranged a mere handful, seven hundred men who screened Greene's starving, weary force, hid his true direction from hostile eyes, kept Cornwallis off balance, forced him into false moves that wasted time and miles. The seven hundred were the pick of the army. Greene had given the command to Dan Morgan, but the Old Wagoner had cracked his whip for the last time and, riddled with rheumatics, had dragged his huge body home to Virginia. In his place the Marylander Otho Holland Williams took charge and with him were Kirkwood of Delaware and Campbell of Virginia. William Washington rode with his cavalry and always at the point where the British were closest the troopers and foot soldiers of Light Horse Harry Lee fought, fell back, circled, attacked, fell back again.

The roads were thick rivers of mud by day, rivers where the lightest wagons bogged axle-deep and horses floundered.

By night they froze into miniature mountain ranges, iron hard, that ripped boots to pieces and lacerated pasterns and fetlocks. But none of these picked men, the Light Corps, fell out, none straggled. Seasoned campaigners, they knew as well as Otho Williams what had to be done if the Southern Army were to live, to fight again. At all costs, Cornwallis must not be allowed to get ahead, to slip to the east between them and Greene. One meal a day they ate, with only six hours' rest. Half the Corps was on night duty, so a given man slept only six hours in each forty-eight, slept and took his post again.

The Corps kept perilously close to Cornwallis, alarmingly far from Greene and the main body. The Corps might be trapped, might be wiped out. Militarily, that did not matter. It was only important that Greene reach the Dan, cross it into Virginia, where he could call for reinforcements and supplies from von Steuben's camp. As the freezing, drenching days went by, it became obvious to all ranks that, so far, the Corps was succeeding. Cornwallis mistook it for the advance, not the flank, and deduced that Greene would cross by the upper fords of the Dan. Meanwhile the main army strained on toward Boyd's and Irwin's ferries, far below the fords, a destination that Cornwallis doubly discounted, being sure that no boats were available for such crossing. No spies, no scouts brought him word that Carrington had swiftly and secretly combed the river for anything that would float. No one told him that, as he made his decision to press for the upper fords, boats were drawn up in dark lines on the south bank of the Dan.

It was killing work, the hardest soldiering, perhaps, that Ross had ever known, riding in the farthest fringe of the Light Corps. Days blurred into nights and nights melted into days with nothing to mack the passage of time save the monotonous alternation of heavy gray sky and sullen black sky. There were miles of riding when not the least flicker of hostile movements rewarded the unending tense watch. There were stretches of quiet, dripping woods that suddenly erupted waves of the haggard enemy. He rallied dragoons and knots of Legion infantry in a field where shouting Welshmen of the 23rd, converted to mounted infantry, dropped from their horses and swept forward, bayonets aslant, to be crumpled and shattered as Lee's dragoons smashed in among them and the Legion infantry followed hard on the pounding cavalry. Twice, with Marion's tactics in mind, he led yelling Tories of Tarleton's Legion into ambush, then turned on them with his silent, furious troopers. By a stream that flowed across the Dan he rode in a wild melee where privates suddenly took command of platoons and majors and captains fought like simple soldiers, riding knee to knee with the other green jackets. Behind them, the Legion infantry, a handful at a time, were ferried across to the safety of the north bank in a pair of leaky barges. When the last man was on the far shore, Lee in person led a whirlwind of troopers against the enemy, scattered the attack, disengaged with rare skill and then waited on the south bank until the last trooper had swum his horse across.

Little detail stayed in Ross's weary brain. His chief impression was of bone-deep, aching weariness that dulled his mind and unsteadied his hand, of raw, biting cold and sodden clothes, of endless hunger ache. With de Chanzy, who always radiated a sort of desperate infectious gaiety, he fumbled among the knapsacks of the British and Tory dead. The packs were mostly empty, but de Chanzy found a true prize, an oak-hard slab of smoked alligator meat, probably taken from some smokehouse far down in South Carolina. Hiding the treasure, which was usually fed only to dogs, under their cloaks, they built a fire, managed to cook the strong-flavored meat and ate it to the last shred, de Chanzy delicately cutting up his share with a silver knife and fork which he kept in a leather case.

Near mid-February, most of the Light Corps suddenly realized that Otho Williams had changed his plans and was striking northeast for the Dan, probably reasoning that Greene and Huger had been able to cross the Dan into Virginia. This knowledge reached few of the Legion, for Cornwallis, too, had slanted east and was moving up the Corps road, closer and closer to the rear guard. Throughout a whole day the Legion fought to disengage, strove to beat back the advance and yet not to commit itself to an action that would pin it down. Lee was everywhere, an irrepressible, hard-fighting figure, managing somehow to give forth a kind of radiance that fatigue, hunger and danger could not dispel. His men seemed to multiply themselves. Ross, riding in the van, found himself with the Rudulph brothers, with the Frenchman O'Neal, with Johnston, with Winston or de Chanzy.

A messenger came from Willliams, giving the new route and suggesting a short cut to the Legion and the rest of the rear guard. There was a last wild charge, a skillful withdrawal that turned into a forced march. When it seemed safe to call a halt and rest the men, Ross dismounted and shared a soggy slab of corn bread with de Chanzy and a sergeant of Delaware Continentals who had in some way been caught up by the Legion. De Chanzy was about to bite eagerly into the moldy mass when he straightened and dropped the bread, staring south. Then he snatched up a trumpet that an exhausted boy bugler clutched in his sleep, and sounded "Troopers—mount!"

Ross swore wearily, climbed into the saddle. There would be no rest. The cavalry of Tarleton's Legion, the bright helmets and red coats of the 17th Dragoons were in sight, riding hard. Lee's men formed quickly and their colonel passed along their front, head turning from the steady ranks to the pursuit which swept nearer and nearer. He paused by Ross, shaking his head regretfully. "No fight. We've outfought them before. Now we'll outride them."

Half an hour later, Ross looked back from a ridge where the road to Boyd's Ferry on the Dan spread its greasy length. Tarleton's men were slowing up, then halting. The Legion horses had carried Lee's men out of danger. Ross laughed as he saw Tories and dragoons astride their blown tackies, shaking their fists and shouting furious curses. De Chanzy clapped him on the shoulder. "Now all is well, *mon vieux*. Presently we canter up and raise our sabers in salute to our Greene. I assure you this double march, it will be noted as classic. It becomes history. You and I, who have ridden in it, we too become history."

Ross shrugged. "People can write what they damn please about it and none of us will be able to say if they're right or wrong. We've all been so scuppered that people can say we've been marching across the moon or fighting against Frederick of Prussia. Maybe we have been. I don't know. Lord, this has been worse than the retreat across New Jersey. Hope to God there's a Trenton or a Princeton at the end of all this, as there was then."

De Chanzy wiped his sleeve across his forehead. "At the end of this, *mon ami*, is the Dan, warm food, hours to sleep and not to march. Tell me, like a good fellow, are the girls of the Virginia pretty?"

Ross frowned. "We're close to the Dan, but don't try to make engagements with Virginia girls—just yet." He looked back over his shoulder. Slowly, but inexorably, Tarleton's men were coming on through the fading light. Behind them Ross caught the dull wink of bayonets as Cornwallis's seasoned troops followed fast—the 7th, the Guards, von Bose's Hessians, the quick-stepping Jaegers. "You see, we don't even know that Greene's actually *across* the Dan. *If* he's still to the south of it—well, in that case I think that you and I have fought our last battle."

Dusk fell, deepened into night. Ross and de Chanzy rode

in silence on the flank of Winston's troop, their ears filled with the squelch of hoofs, the creak of wet leather and the muted clink of steel. Ross suddenly straightened in the saddle, exclaimed, "God above! Look!"

Far ahead, spreading to the right and to the left, fires glowed, fires laid out in regular lines and groups. Through a blur of fatigue, Ross thought that he could make out companies, regiments and brigades. Something must have gone wrong, gone very wrong. De Chanzy muttered, "Ah, *les pauvres! Les pauvres!* It is we who have failed. We gave them too little time to cross the Dan, which is still far." He straightened himself. "*Mon ami,* our course is plain. We must turn back, we must strike and strike yet again, we must keep Milord Cornwallis from those fires. Will you do me the honor of riding at my left when we charge?" He reached into his saddlebags, drew out a broad strip of green silk and expertly knotted it, cravat-like, about his throat. "This, you conceive, is scarcely *tenue de fantaisie,* but it must serve."

Ross touched the spare cartridge box at his waist. Under the cover, still in its oiled silk, lay the old Quaker's sketch of Dorande at Nelson's Ferry. In a few minutes, orders would come down to countermarch and form line of battle. He wondered in what form she would get news of the last desperate fight that would occur so soon. No doubt she would only hear the British or, worse, the Tory version. Greene's shambling, ignorant rabble wrecked for all time by the King's people. Such reports would tell how the Rebels ran like sheep—

He touched de Chanzy's shoulder. "Better get ready. I hear some damned courier coming down the column." He gave a sudden triumphant shout. "Listen to that, de Chanzy. Hear that cheering? They know, up there, that we're all going to turn and fight and, by God, they're cheering the news!"

The hoofs came closer as though carried along by the shouts of the men in the ranks. Suddenly de Chanzy was pounding Ross's back, waving his helmet in the air and roaring at the top of his lungs. The courier was shouting that Greene *had* crossed the Dan, that he had left those fires burning to light the march of Williams's Corps. Not a man of the main force, not a crumb of its equipment was south of the river, not a man! The rider cantered past, shouting his news while his voice crackled and rasped with weariness. Up and down the weary ranks of the Light Corps, the cheers rolled and thundered. Forgotten were the killing hours of the march north. Forgotten were the forty fighting miles that the Legion had covered that very day. The army, the Southern Army was safe.

Ross, his throat aching, looked back over his shoulder through the gloom. Far to the rear, new fires sprang up, spread. The cheers of the Light Corps, wind-borne, had carried their own message to the hard-riding enemy and that message had been understood. Pursuit was useless, and Englishman and Tory dispiritedly halted to light their campfires for the night.

Then from the ranks, Ross caught a sour murmur. "Just the same, we're right where we started from. There's not a patriot force left in South Carolina and there won't be in North Carolina when we cross into Virginia. What the hell's been the good of this?"

Ross smiled to himself. No patriot force in South Carolina? The grumbler was wrong, utterly and completely wrong. Had he never heard of Marion, of Pickens, of Sumter? Something struck him between the shoulders and he sat up with a jerk.

De Chanzy was laughing at him, supporting him with one arm. "If you sleep in the saddle, *mon ami*, at least link your arm with mine. *Parbleu!* You very nearly fell among the hoofs."

Ross mumbled, "Thanks. Wide awake," and promptly slept again. De Chanzy held him firmly, humming to himself and wondering how he could repair his uniform against the day when Greene himself should inspect the Legion on Virginia soil.

Through days of cold rain, Greene rested his men as best he could, regrouped his scattered units, argued vainly with militia leaders whose men, their short-term enlistments expired, were melting away to their homes. Through his scouts, he watched Cornwallis, noting that few fresh troops reached him, that supplies were scanty among the British and Tories. Such intelligence brought a smile to Greene's worn face. Somewhere, far to the south, a diminutive brigadier with dark, aquiline features was probing the sensitive points along Cornwallis's line of communications. That the probings were successful was evidenced by Cornwallis's lack of replacements, rations and powder.

Then Greene gathered his army for a move south across the Dan. The initiative was now in his hands. He would fight Cornwallis when he pleased, on ground of his own choosing.

In advance of the main force the Legion moved south of the Dan, supported by Andrew Pickens with his militia riflemen and by Oldham with his Marylanders. The mission was to harry Cornwallis's depots and posts, to strike Tarleton if possible and to break up reported Tory musters in the neighborhood of the Haw and the Deep.

The rains had ended and Ross rode in the van beside Lee and his Massachusetts adjutant, Lovell, grateful for the sun that softened the crisp air. While Lee and Lovell argued over Legion matters, Ross looked back down the column and felt a deepening confidence in the future. There was the Legion cavalry, trim and workmanlike under John Rudulph. Behind the last sweeping white crest came the bayonet twinkle of the Legion infantry, swinging along with a veteran stride. Somewhere beyond them was Oldham with his Marylanders, flanked by Pickens's militia. Ross had inspected the militia before the dawn start and thought he had never seen better troops, many of them being time-expired Continentals who had joined up for the emergency. They were not uniformed, but by Pickens's orders each man wore a sprig of green in his hat.

Despite that confidence, inspired by this picked might that marched on west of the Haw toward the Alamance, Ross felt as though he and the whole column were walking on thin black ice that gave a little with each step. Scouts and country people had reported that Tarleton lay encamped a few miles ahead, that his horses were unsaddled and no rigid guard kept. That might be so, yet it didn't seem like Tarleton, as Ross knew him. Would the thick timber through which they were now riding suddenly burst out in flame and smoke, echo to the rattle of musketry? Would the thin glare ice break at the next step—the next?

With a word to Lee, Ross dropped back past Eggleston's troops, past Johnston's, to Winston's, where de Chanzy hailed him. "All goes well là-haut?" called the Frenchman.

Ross frowned. "It goes—so far. Damn it, one minute I think we could storm the Rock of Quebec and the next I'm wondering if the road's going to blow up under our feet. It's early afternoon but where—and how—will we be by night?"

"Ah, well I know your feelings," said de Chanzy. "Me, I am sure that a whole legion of invisible mice parade their cold, pink feet up and down my back. Holà! We halt? Diable, I do not like this. And here gallops our good Lovell."

The adjutant, his face red and eyes blazing, reined in by Ross. "No time for explanations," he panted. "Just do as I say. Give me your sword. Oh, damn it, hurry. All hell may bust loose on us. That's it. Now—yes, by Jove, turn that coat of yours inside out so the red facings don't show. Fine! Now you're coming up to the head of the column with me. You're one of Washington's dragoons. Come on. You'll get the why's later."

Puzzled and disturbed, Ross followed the adjutant on past the leading troop and found Lee, one leg crossed over his pommel, talking earnestly with two plainly dressed men who balanced long rifles across their saddles. As Ross rode up with Lovell, Lee glanced casually at him, saying, "Oh, so that's the prisoner? I'll talk to him in a few minutes." He turned to the others. "Yes. That's just what I want. One of you ride ahead quickly and give those orders to Colonel Pyle. The other can go on to the rear of my cavalry and come on with us."

The taller of the two men asked Lee to repeat his commands while Ross listened in utter disbelief that slowly faded to certainty. Pyle was a well-known Tory and these two were marching to join him, to take the field against Greene. Blundering on the road, they had mistaken the handsome Lee for the handsome Tarleton, whom they obviously had never seen, and, equally, had mistaken Lee's men for Tarleton's green-coated Legion of Tories. Still, there were only two of them and Ross wondered why Lee bothered to talk with them, why he didn't merely disarm them and send them to the rear.

The tall Tory saluted Lee and cantered out of sight. The other was escorted down the column by two troopers. When they were out of sight, Lee's calm composure vanished. "Listen to this, Lovell, and then take the word to each troop commander, to Pickens and Oldham. Pyle's up the road with four hundred mounted rifles, on the way to join Tarleton. Tarleton's moved on past the Alamance since we last had news of him, so our chance of surprise is gone."

Understanding came in a flash to Ross. Pyle would hear that the Tory Legion was down the road, that they had with them a prisoner from Washington's white-jacketed troopers. As Lee paused, Ross's mind worked on. The safest and best move was a quick countermarch, since those four hundred men under Pyle would strengthen Tarleton beyond any hope of a successful attack by Lee's men. Ross froze with astonishment as Lee went on, his firm mouth biting out each word.

"Be sure you get all this, Lovell, I've sent word to Pyle, who thinks I'm Tarleton, that I'll go ahead of him, looking his men over as we pass. Pyle's to draw up on the *right* hand side of the road, in double line facing us as we pass. I'll ride clear up to him, the Legion cavalry and infantry following close. Remember that—*close!* So, when I reach Pyle, we'll overlap his line head and foot."

Lovell jerked his head in frowning concentration. Ross exclaimed involuntarily, "My God! We're going to ride up that whole damn line?"

Lee glanced impatiently at him. "It's the only way out, I tell you. Listen closely, Lovell. Pickens and Oldham, with some of their men in Continental uniform, have *got* to keep out of sight. *Got* to. Let them fan out right and left through the woods. I don't want to see a single man of either command on the road. And Pyle's men just mustn't—or we're done. Clear so far?"

"All clear," said Lovell while Ross looked on incredulously.

"Now, when I reach Pyle, I'm going to shake hands with him. *Then*—I tell him who we are, show him that he's covered top to bottom. He'll have his choice of disarming and disbanding his men at *once*—or—" He paused significantly. "But I've heard about Pyle. He's said to be a decent, level-headed sort of chap. He'll give them orders to lay down arms. I know that I would in his place. Now off with you and make sure that each man knows what's to be done."

Pyle's men were at the right of the road, raggedly drawn up facing the oncoming Legion. Ross, weaponless, rode between de Chanzy and a trooper, intense apprehension cutting at him. The black ice, he felt, was growing thinner and thinner. The Tories in their country clothes with white tabs in their hats were cheering their supposed comrades, their sabers sheathed and their rifles and muskets lying easily across their saddles. It couldn't last. Someone, just a single man, would recognize the trick, the Legion would be taken in the flank and crumpled up like a corn husk.

He eyed the green-jacketed troopers. They were not answering the cheers. Their hard, hot eyes saw only hated Tories, there within sword's reach. Far up the column, Lee rode slowly, as though weighing and appraising this new formation. At the far end of the Tory line Colonel Pyle, a tall, fine-looking man, sat his horse, obviously impatient to greet the famous Tarleton, to hear some words of praise of the men whom Pyle had rallied.

At Ross's right, de Chanzy was equally ill at ease, seemed to feel the strange shrinking sensation that drew chin down into stock, elbows against sides.

Then out of the corner of his eye, Ross saw quick movement at the left end of the Tory force. A rifle barrel glinted, a shot rang out. As though an invisible spring had been tripped, the Legionnaires pivoted as one man. Swords rasped out, horses, stung by the spur, reared and lashed out and a green wave reaching from head to foot of the Tory line engulfed, swept away, pounded down, slashed at Pyle's command.

Over the furious yells and curses, Ross heard Lee roaring, "No! No!" The melee reached a violent crescendo. Suddenly it was all over. The field beyond the road was covered with flying men, most of them streaming blood from saber slashes. Others lay, either still or writhing, at the edge of the grass, two yards in, five, ten, twenty yards in, while the Legion cavalry sat their horses, staring after the fugitives, reddened swords hanging loosely by their sides.

Ross, who had instinctively swung away from Pyle's men at the first shot, found himself jostled and shoved on down the road by men who still stared, horror-stricken, at their own work. He worked his way clear, dropped to the ground close by the far end of Pyle's line. The Tory colonel lay face down, his coat a mass of bloody rags. Someone jostled Ross and he snapped a question at a stranger in green. It was not a stranger. Harry Lee's face was a ghastly white, his mouth hung open and he looked vacantly at Ross through sleepwalker's eyes. Panting heavily he mumbled over and over, "What happened? Oh, my God, what happened?"

Ross caught him by the shoulder as he staggered. "Colonel Lee!" he shouted. "Do you hear me? Listen! *They* fired! They fired first. I saw it."

Head swaying, Lee croaked hoarsely, "The order to charge. God Almighty, who gave the order to charge?"

Someone justled past Ross and he recognized young Eggleston, commanding the rear troop. His saber was drawn but unstained. He shouted furiously to Lee, "Sir, I request permission to place my whole troop under arrest. Flagrant disobedience of orders."

Lee caught at the last word. "Orders?" His eyes cleared a little and something of his normal calm returned to him. "Did you give that order, Eggleston?"

Ross again shook Lee. "Sir, there *was* no order. I can vouch for that. The troopers heard the shot. Being old soldiers, they reacted at once."

Lee passed his hands over his eyes. "But I was shaking hands with Pyle. I was just going to give him his instructions to surrender. I was shaking hands with him."

Lovell spoke quietly. "The command is waiting for orders, sir."

Responsibility threw a mask over Lee's face, stiffened back and shoulders. "To all troop commanders, prepare to camp at the left of the road. My compliments to Colonel Pickens and Captain Oldham. I'll be obliged if they will report to me at once. Send Surgeons Skinner and Irvine to see to Pyle's wounded. Prepare a count of the killed."

"Ninety-two Tories killed, sir," said Lovell. "Most of those who ran were wounded. Our loss—one horse wounded." He saluted and rode off to distribute Lee's orders.

De Chanzy dropped beside Ross, saluted Lee, who looked questioningly at him. "The shot, *mon colonel*," said de Chanzy. "I myself saw that Pyle's men noted our militia in the woods, thus ending our little farce. Pyle's men fired and then—what would you?"

Lee paced slowly up and down, striking his hands together, eyes on the ground. Then he straightened up. "Thank you, Cornet. What's done is done. The responsibility is mine." As though to himself he muttered, "My responsibility. And Pyle was shaking my hand!"

While surgeons and volunteers moved among the wounded of Pyle's command, the Legion and its auxiliaries went into camp farther along the road. Guards were posted, infantry and cavalry patrols moved down over the fields or through the woods. Ross, still sick and shaken, tried to lose himself in the bustle of the camp where every man worked furiously as though to sweep away the memory of what he had seen and done. On a rock at the edge of the field, Lee sat, silent and motionless, his head in his hands.

Ross groomed his horse, a tall, powerful black, until the animal's coat shone. There was relief in sweeping the stiff brush over haunch and withers, an odd satisfaction and a touch of forgetfulness of the immediate past as his mount leaned his weight against the grooming kit, sighing with satisfaction. When he stopped and straightened up, the horror swept back over him, showing him again the eyes of a helpless Tory as a dragoon thrust at him, a pair of bleeding wrists crossed over a screaming face.

An arm dropped on Ross's shoulder and he looked up dully at de Chanzy, lips compressed in a pale face. The Frenchman said gently, "*Mon ami*, I agree that it was *affreux*, but you must apply logic. Our Lee had no choice but to attempt his plan. It was excellent, as I pointed out to the good Sergeant Kuhn, who agreed. That matters did not turn out too pleasantly, ah, that was decided by chance, and by the first Tory who fired, seeing Oldham's men. To fire thus was only natural. Equally natural was what followed."

Ross flared. "God damn it, was it natural to cut down helpless men?"

"But who of our troopers could know them helpless, having fired? Tell me, would you have moved differently than did our Lee? If so, how?"

Ross scratched his nose on the back of his currycomb. "N-no. I've got to admit I'd have done the same, only—well, I couldn't have thought through the chances the way he did."

"*Mais précisément*. Of one hundred chances, Lee had ninety-nine of winning a bloodless victory. So let us follow logic and see what is gained. First—our Lovell tells me that Pyle's command is the first organized group to come to the aid of Milord Cornwallis. The first, I say, and that in the face of our retreat to the Virginia, which, as you conceive, must have looked a rout to the simple countrymen. Second, the fate of this, the first group, will not encourage others to fly to arms in defense of the King. Lastly, we may now move against this species of Tarleton, knowing that he will not be reinforced. All this is something, I think."

"Guess you're right," said Ross. He stepped back and surveyed his black. "How do you think the mare looks?"

"*Mais pimpante.* You have named her?"

Ross frowned. "I only got her after I lost that gray that Lee gave me when I rejoined. I'll call her—I'll—yes! She's Mon Plaisir."

"But a name of that sort, it belongs to a chalet, a villa!" protested de Chanzy.

"Exactly," said Ross. "It does. But also to my horse. Mon Plaisir de la Congaree." He wondered if Dorande would ever see those sleek shoulders, those small, pointed ears.

"But that is too long."

"Too long? Don't have to use all of it all the time. Does anyone call you Philippe-Georges de la Piconnerie de Chanzy?"

"Rarely, I confess. I hear men say 'that Frenchman' or even 'that damn Frogeater.' More recently, I note I become 'Phil,' American fashion, which does not displease me."

"All right. We'll shorten this young lady to 'Ree.'"

De Chanzy shrugged. "You are irrepressible, *mon vieux*. I dispute with you no more. Now come with me to my saddlebags. I have some brandy in my *sauve-vie*."

Ross smiled as he stowed his grooming kit, remembering the phrase "pert, railing fribble" that he had first applied to the Frenchman. He knew that de Chanzy, shocked as he himself was, had first reasoned out the day's events to him and later become absorbed in the horse with the sole aim of diverting his mind from tragedy.

The next dawn, a dragoon patrol escorted into camp a full three hundred long-striding men under Colonel William Preston. Far off in the mountains of western Virginia, they had had word of Greene's retreat to the Dan and had tramped the weary miles clear to the Haw in North Carolina. They had not known the purpose of Greene's move, did not know that he had safely crossed the river and now was preparing to enter North Carolina again. A patriot army was in trouble, they thought, and they had set out to help as they could.

Ross, watching them with de Chanzy, observed, "Another gain you didn't mention, Phil. If Pyle hadn't been broken up and Tarleton been scared into moving on, those boys would be dead as Pyle's by now."

The two moved closer to the willow clump where Lee was talking with Preston, a big man with a sword hanging from an embroidered baldric that contrasted oddly with his rusty black coat. Preston was saying, "No, my boys don't give three hollers for British infantry, on horse or afoot. They know we're as good as they are. But sabers—now that's different. I got to admit that sabers make us mighty creepy. Seems like always when we've got men in the field, down comes British cavalry, cutting and slashing. Always British or Tory."

Lee, still looking white and sick, suddenly brightened. He gave a short laugh. "Always British, eh? We'll fix that. Rudulph, John Rudulph! Mount every trooper in camp! Parade 'em past Colonel Preston's men. Then do it again. Keep 'em at it until every mountain man's seen the Legion dragoons. Right away. The command is 'Carry saber!' "

Round and round the field the green dragoons rode, their white crests tossing and their blades bright in the new sun. Ross saw the mountain men stare, draw nearer, pointing. He caught a hushed exclamation. "Mean them fellers is *our'n?* By chops, I'm tarryin'!"

That night the whole command fell in. The Legion, Pickens's men, Oldham's and Preston's. Ross watched them forming on the road and felt a return of that same confidence that he had known before the massacre of Pyle's command. He muttered, as he mounted Ree, "What's happened has happened. Let's get on with the war!"

Far to the south, beyond the Dan, beyond the Deep, the Yadkin, the Catawba, dusk lay softly along the valley of the Congaree. Dorande leaned against a pillar of the porch, a wrap of green silk about her slim shoulders. From an open window her uncle's voice, sharp and exasperated, came to her. She knew that he was expostulating to one of the Tory members of the Friday family from Friday's Ferry upriver. What would he think, she wondered, if he knew how often she had talked with the Whig Fridays? A half smile touched her soft lips as St. Aubin's voice rose higher. "And in January it is James Postell at Wadboo, where royal stores were burned. Then, you conceive, it is John Postell at Monck's Corner, the very gates of Charleston. Next we find Marion and that *âme damnée* of his, Pierre—no, *Peter*—Horry at the mill of Monsieur Singleton and again at Wyboo Swamp. English soldiers die, Loyalists die. Thousands and thousands of pounds sterling vanish in smoke of burning stores. Worse, people who were loyal now begin to question themselves. Many trail after *ce sacré* Marion like *les moutons de Panurge*. And you do nothing, you others! You think Marion a second Bayard, that he possesses the horn of Roland? *Va!* I grow weary of all this. Have you no one clever enough to raise a great number of people, take them to this species of Marion and then lead him and his scum into a trap? No! I tell you, you are sapless as a rotten apple of Normandy!"

There was a grumbling response, then silence as the two apparently moved into another room. Dorande shrugged. St. Aubin's list was not complete. And that very night there would be more to add to it. That very night the drolly grave Peter Horry would find a mound of unguarded stores east of Nelson's Ferry. Beyond Chilyon's Castle a gathering of Tories would be dispersed by John James of the Lake. And the news had been sent from Mon Plaisir.

These thoughts flowed along the top of her mind. Her eyes were on the north, straining as though she could see past the great tumbling rivers. The latest reports told her that Greene was nearing the Virginia border. *Et le capitaine noir?* She explained carefully to herself, "It is that I admire him. I like him. A good man, stanch and devoted. And there the end of the matter lies. What if I did kiss him? It was *tout à fait en camarade*. It was! A lonely boy who rides off to fight. What would you? Do you give him the shake-hands? That would be stupid!" Her lips quivered. "Oh, Ross Pembroke, where are you? No—it was not—I do not think it was quite *en camarade*."

She sighed and looked down through the darkness at Janet's cottage. No lights showed and word had come to the house that Janet had a touch of swamp fever. Actually, Dorande knew that Raoul had crept up from the river after sundown, that he would leave long before dawn. She stepped away from the pillar. Someone was coming up the path from the cottage.

It couldn't be Janet. Yet—Dorande sprang lightly to the turf and ran to meet the gliding figure that stopped suddenly, shielded from the house by a thick magnolia. Janet's voice came to her, low and eager. "It's all right, dear. I've left everything locked and Raoul won't make a sound. But I just had to tell you. Five days ago, our army crossed the Dan into Virginia. Raoul brought the news down. They're safe, safe!"

Dorande threw her arms about Janet. "But I find this *épatant*. Many will be happy for it."

"So many. I just had to tell you. Now I must run back." She gathered her skirts and skimmed away.

Dorande returned to the porch, her thoughts somber again. The army was safe in Virginia. The whole army? Did a tall, dark man in a white jacket stand on the north bank of the Dan and laugh in mockery at Milord Cornwallis? A light glowed from the house and she held her left hand to it. The ring on her little finger had been carved in a far-off time somewhere along the South American coast to represent openwork basketry. Now, woven through the gold mesh were two white strands that might have come from some island loom—or from the horsehair crest of a helmet.

She put her hand quickly behind her as St. Aubin stepped silently into sight. "You find the evening agreeable, Dorande?" he asked.

"It does well enough. Tell me, is there no word from Charleston?"

"None that you do not know. The fleets disturb the peace of the Caribbean. My sister and her husband will not find it easy, as I warned you earlier, to take passage for the Carolinas."

Dorande sighed, her eyes looking down the dark valley of the Congaree. "*Mon oncle*, the blacks talk of trouble along the Santee. The Rebels raid and burn. You are not alarmed for Mon Plaisir?"

In the darkness St. Aubin permitted himself the luxury of a smile. "I? Alarmed? No, I do not think the rabble will strike here. No doubt they have their reasons. Now I have a favor to ask of you. Not far below the ferry of Monsieur McCord there lives a widow of the utmost respectability. Her name is Motte, Madame Rebecca Motte, born Brewton, a family much honored here. She is, I am told, of the Rebel persuasion, but holds those views *bien paisiblement*. It would be pleasant, I think, were you and our good Madame Jaudon to call on her."

Dorande checked a slight start. She had never met Mrs. Motte but messages that had to do with the accumulation of stores, with the movements and thoughts of men, had passed between Mon Plaisir and the widow's house. She said idly, "And it is to divert me and Janet that you suggest this?"

"Why else? She has, I am told, recently completed a fine new house which she would be pleased to show you. And, for my part, I should be interested in what you tell me of it, such matters as the number and size of her rooms, their furnishings, the source of water, the number of acres. It is agreeable to know such details of one's neighbors. Likewise, it is possible that she would help you in your charities toward destitute families, for I know that you make no distinction between Whig and Tory, an attitude which does you much credit."

Dorande inclined her head obediently. "Very good, *mon oncle*. If you will be sufficiently good as to command the carriage tomorrow morning, Madame Janet and I will do what you wish." She reflected that such a call, sanctioned by her uncle, might prove very valuable, for she was well aware how wrong was her uncle's estimate of the mildness of Mrs. Motte's views. Also, it would distract her own thoughts from the weary army north of the Dan. Or wherever it might be. News traveled so slowly—

IX • The Tide Rolls South

Late in February, Greene's main army poured south across the Dan behind the screen of the Legion and the light troops. Off to the east, centered about Hillsboro, Cornwallis stirred, made frantic appeals for Loyalist recruits and started after Greene.

Ross, riding with the Legion, saw the Light Corps under Otho Williams take up its old post between the main army and the enemy, saw the retreat to the Dan unfold itself like a blurred copy of an old canvas. Far in advance of Greene, Williams sparred and maneuvered. On the farthest fringes of the Light Corps, the Legion dragoons and Washington's white-coated horsemen charged, fell back, struck, scattered, re-formed, charged again. Ross felt as though some spell had moved him back in time and space. There were the same bloody scuffles that were forgotten before they were fairly ended, the same wild rushes after vanishing redcoats, the same frantic rallies when Tarleton's horsemen appeared in unexpected strength and in unexpected places. Back and forth the main bodies marched behind their fast-moving screens of light troops and horsemen, like two skilled mounted swordsmen who circled, turned, wheeled, cut, thrust, parried, always breaking off from any final commitment.

The Legion cavalry rode through swamp, through field, over sharp-edged hills. They slept when they could, ate when they were lucky. As in the west, wherever they rode by squad or platoon or squadron, wherever danger was sharpest, they found their colonel, gay and glowing once more, never tiring, fertile in ruse and expedient, hard in attack and stubborn in defense.

Ross stayed with Winston's troop, urging on the exhausted men, doing without sleep to help some trooper with a mount that seemed about to founder. Winston, gaunt and weary, always cool and quiet, handled his command like a machine.

182

De Chanzy was in the van of each attack, the last man to fall back in retreat, seemingly oblivious of a wrenched knee that had swollen to twice its normal size. As he rode or limped along on foot he smiled to himself, humming his own version of an old French war song, *"Tarleton s'en va t'en guerre, miroton, miroton, mirotaine"*—At the dawn of the century, he told Ross, French troops had sung that air, deriding Marlborough—or Malbroche as they called him—but it was far older than that. Rather earlier, French troops had sung it as they marched to the Crusades, Palestine, the Low Countries. And now it had reached the hills of North Carolina. The song had traveled far.

Through fatigue-blurred eyes, Ross became aware, as March rolled on, of more and more troops on the roads, troops that did not belong to the Light Corps. About the hills where Reedy Fork and Troublesome Creek rose to tumble on to the Haw, the main army was concentrating. Across Reedy Fork, Winston's men circled over cleared ground, combed through thick woods, looked up from their saddles to stare at a wilderness courthouse. Ross noted it down as a landmark—Guilford Courthouse. East or south from it, he didn't have to ride far to sight Tarleton's videttes. Close to the north and west, he knew that Greene's tattered men were camped.

De Chanzy observed with a shrug, "Ah, *le pot bouille*. Our Greene, *mon vieux*, is about to stir us into that pot like so many leeks and carrots. For some days I have noted the bubbles rising in the pot, as has Sergeant Kuhn. *Ouf!* I am weary. *Fatigué à en crever!*" He glanced curiously at Ross. "And you have been at this little game how long?"

"I told you. Since '75."

De Chanzy sighed. "Then at least I may hope to survive one more year. But, *diable*, I fear that our Greene prepares very hot water for us."

So the two armies feinted and maneuvered through space and time, until they finally passed into the gap between darkness and dawn of March fifteenth. Night still lay thick along the road that led south and west from Guilford Courthouse to distant Salisbury. It wrapped the three troops of Legion dragoons in a mantle of anonymity, reduced the Legion infantry and Campbell's riflemen, moving right and left of the road, to a mass of crackling sound that had no form or body.

Ross, riding with Lee and de Chanzy, close by the head of Armstrong's troops, could only be sure of the existence of Armstrong's leading files. The commands of Eggleston and

Rudulph might be crowding close in the rear, might have dropped back beyond reach of eye or ear. De Chanzy worked his shoulders under his green cape. "*Diable!* It is like the day we ride to meet Pyle. Mouse feet perform squadron evolutions along my spine."

Ross grunted in reply. He felt as though black Ree were stepping among eggshells whose breaking would be fatal. Lee, erect and alert in the saddle, kept peering ahead. "God blast it, Ross! Could Heard have taken the wrong road? We ought by now—" Something white shimmered far down the road, swelled toward them. A cautious voice called, "Who's there?"

Lee stood in his stirrups. "That you, Heard?"

The shape materialized into Captain Heard of Washington's cavalry, four white-coated dragoons behind him. Heard was panting with excitement. "Flushed 'em, by the Eternal, we flushed 'em."

"Scouts?"

"Whole God damn British Army. Cornwallis must have rolled them out without breakfast. Tarleton's in the lead. I got close enough to recognize his men. Light troops following."

"Sure it's not just a reconnaissance?"

"Positive. I heard wheels."

Lee nodded quickly. "Get on back and report to Greene. Tell him I'm going ahead and engage."

Heard saluted and slipped off with his dragoons clattering after him. Lovell, the adjutant, rode up, awake and unobtrusively competent. Lee went on, "There you are, Billy. Action ahead. Warn the infantry and Campbell's men. Where's that bugler?" A small shape on a pony edged in between Ross and de Chanzy, Eggleston and Rudulph close behind him. Lee reached out and patted the boy's shoulder. "Good boy, Tommy. Stay close to me. Eggleston, Rudulph—we're going to try to pull Tarleton along with us. The usual plan. When we sight, rear troop countermarches, hits for the rear at a gallop and into the fields. Re-form in open order. Center troop, the same as soon as Rudulph is clear. Armstrong, you stand fast until Eggleston's clear. The infantry have their orders by now. Off with you. Ross, stay with Armstrong. Your knee bother you, de Chanzy?"

The Frenchman, wincing as Ross's horse jostled him, answered smoothly, "But not in the smallest, *mon colonel*."

"Then stay by me. We'll set a slow pace until we sight them."

The intense black of the wood road began to lift as the

troops clopped on. The infantry had obviously been told whether to halt or fall back as Ross could neither see nor hear them. The veil lifted and lifted.

Ross froze in the saddle. There was a twinkle of bright steel far down the road through the thinning gloom. He caught the swish of badly kept leather, the clink and clatter of weapons. There they were, troop after troop of Tarleton's Legion, just entering a stretch where the road narrowed between high banks. Behind the last of the Tory riders, Ross made out open fields, sensed that infantry moved through them in the wake of the cavalry.

Tarleton's men were coming on slowly, even negligently. Then someone shouted, "Hoy! Forr'd there, forr'd!" In the distance, sabers rasped out. Ross checked Ree, drew his saber and made sure that both pistols were secure in their holsters. He glanced at Armstrong, whose teeth were clamped down over his lower lip. Then Armstrong's arm flew up in the signal to halt. In the rear, Lee barked, "Now, Tommy, countermarch! Gallop!"

The bugle blared out and Ross heard a shifting and pounding as Rudulph's troop, then Eggleston's, wheeled and raced to the rear. There was a stir among the Tories. Someone yelled, "Yeeeaah! Bastards is runnin'." There was another voice, high and insistent, that Ross had heard often on the retreat to the Dan. Tarleton was yelling. "God blast you, charge! Wet those sabers! Get in! Hoy! Tear 'em, tear 'em!"

Ross's whole body contracted as Armstrong made a quick signal. His troop started at a walk, broke to a trot, then into a pounding gallop, the big Virginia horses beating away the few hundred yards that separated the two bodies.

Ross felt Ree rear under him, saw her black hoofs lash out. There was a tacky down, another. Armstrong was ahead of him, then behind him. Troopers closed in, were left behind, forged ahead. The din thickened. Eggleston burst into sight from nowhere; Rudulph's men were coming up fast. From the rear, Lee must have seen something to bring them back to the charge in column.

The woods ended. A British bugle was blasting "Retire by troops!" and the open field, dim with dawn mist, was covered with scattered groups of Tarleton's horsemen, racing back to a second wooded patch, their infantry, in good order, conforming to their move at the double.

Lee's bugler sounded "Trot," then "Walk," and the three troops re-formed expertly from the disorder of their success. Lee jingled up beside Ross and Armstrong, grinning fiercely. "By Jove, that'll teach Tarleton to charge Virginia horses on tackies. Fine work, Armstrong. Capital. Their whole lead section was ridden down. We've got most of them as prisoners and Lovell's questioning them. Come on. I want to see the rest of this. We've got to know who's there, how many he has and what he intends." De Chanzy, pale and riding with his left knee well away from the saddle, cantered up. Lee called, "Sir, you're a cavalryman!" He turned to Ross. "Damned if he didn't see what your charge was going to do before I did. *He* gave Tommy the order to bring up Eggleston and Rudulph. Yes, sir. You're a cavalryman!"

They rode on across the open field, then cautiously through the woods. Ross remembered that beyond there were more clearings, a Quaker meetinghouse. They were past the trees and into the open. The dragoons reined in quickly, without word of command. Ross straightened up, threw back his head while de Chanzy muttered, "Ah, *ça*. Yes, now the pot boils."

Through the uncertain light, coming slowly toward them, was the main British army, Tarleton's light troops, now reformed, well in advance. Ross glanced back over his shoulder toward the woods they had just left. Bushes swayed to the movement of many men. He could just make out the skullcaps of the Legion infantry, the civilian hats, green-sprigged, of Campbell's men.

He felt a touch on his shoulder, turned to find Lee's hand there. Without looking at Ross, Lee said, "You know the British regiments pretty well, don't you?"

"Could pass a fair test on them, I think," answered Ross.

"All right. I'm going to engage the advance with my infantry. Tarleton won't dare charge again, but we'll keep the dragoons where he can see them. I'll break off if and when the main body moves on us. Then the infantry'll cover the dragoons, and hit right back to Greene. He's at the courthouse, not more than four miles off. When we pull out, I want you to stay here as long as you dare. Take a good look at everything, then report to Greene. You know what he'll be asking you."

Ross nodded. "Sure. What regiments. Their strength. How they handle themselves. Also, how soon they can cover those four miles and how much your action delays them."

"Perfect. Stay as long as you want. You can outride anything they've got. Just make sure no one slips around ahead of you."

"Can I keep de Chanzy?"

Lee threw an arm about the Frenchman. "Think I'm going to let you have my little fighting cock? No, sir. He's going to stay right with me. Tommy! Sound 'By sections, to the right!' then, 'Right by trooper.' "

The dragoons wheeled off to the right and the infantry emerged from the woods. Ross turned his attention to the enemy van, that was advancing steadily. There was green infantry on the left, red on the right, with Tarleton's cavalry in the center and rear. Among his green dragoons, patches of red showed where details of the British 17th rode.

Ross cupped his hands about his eyes, stared at the oncoming skirmishers. De Chanzy jogged his elbow. "The gentlemen in green? More Tories, one might say, I think."

Ross studied the green infantry. They might be the foot soldiers of Tarleton's Legion. But there was something odd, something increasingly familiar about their silver-fronted skullcaps. And the facings of their jackets were almost plum color. All at once he remembered a wild struggle in a patch of woods near Breymann's redoubt along the Hudson. Silver caps and purplish facings worn by men who carried short, rifled carbines and knew woodcraft. He called to Lee, "Recognize those chuffs? Hessian Jaegers."

Lee nodded quickly. "Right. They'll have to be handled carefully. Can you make out the red boys?"

Ross looked again. British light infantry, which was always formidable. The regiment? He suddenly gave a long, low whistle. "The light infantry of the Guards! Lord Cornwallis is certainly paying us a compliment."

Lee cast a wistful glance at his own infantry, at Campbell's men. Ross knew he was wishing that the main British force were far distant, that he dared throw his men at the picked Guards and Jaegers. Then Lee relaxed with a sigh and settled himself to watch the distance shrink and shirnk between the two bodies.

Musketry began to rattle along from both sides, the Legion firing from formation and Campbell's Marylanders throwing themselves flat or sheltering behind trees. The Jaegers were disregarding the infantry ahead of them and sending slow volleys toward the dargoons. The shots snarled high and keen, cutting leaves and twigs from the trees. Ross remembered the tendency of both Hessians and British to aim too high. He also guessed that the Jaegers were using British cartridges which carried too much powder for the weight of the bullet and increased the margin of error.

Lee's cavalry was gone, filing away north through the woods. Out in the field the light troops, Guards and Jaegers, were halting to fire, advancing, halting. Ross drew closer to the woods, marking a path up which he could make his escape to the north when the time came. The halts, the grudging advances of the enemy light troops, had lessened the distance between them and the main body. The light from the climbing sun had scattered the last mists and Ross could distinguish color even among the rearmost of Cornwallis's regiments. He drew a glass from his saddlebags and studied the array. Little by little the facings of the uniforms told him their story. A full battalion of Guards, another. The blue facings of the 23rd, the red-on-red of the 33rd. Then a heavy mass of men in white-piped cocked hats and blue coats with yellow cuffs and facings. He laughed shortly. Old friends, those Hessians of von Bose. They had landed on Long Island in that hot, far-off August of 1776. Von Dittforth had commanded them, then Max von Westerhagen. The 71st Scots with their white facings, their flat bonnets, caught up with a plume. Far on the left, more light infantry, drawn from each regiment, and beyond, the high bearskins of the Grenadiers of the Guard.

Some of the formations looked lopsided as though the long pursuit and subsequent maneuvering had taken their toll in stragglers and casualties. But their spirit, so far as his trained eye could tell, was good. Unless there had been changes lately, the commanders were of high quality—Webster, O'Hara and Leslie. If von Westerhagen were with the Hessians, they would be slow, cautious but tenacious.

He head a whistle blow over by the Legion infantry. The men, with Campbell's, were falling back into the woods. It was time for him to go.

Clear of the retiring infantry, he cut a wide circle to the west, remembering from his explorations with de Chanzy that this would bring him out on the low hill just south of the Reedy Fork Road and the courthouse itself. Later he heard voices from the woods to the right and swung down toward them, knowing that Greene's men must be there. He shouted as he saw some of Washington's dragoons waiting among thin trees, rode on until he found their colonel, his face deceptively placid and eyes alert. Washington acknowledged his salute, calling, "Any sign of them?"

Ross laughed. "Plenty of signs and plenty of them. I'm looking for General Greene."

"Keep on along the line. Can't miss him. He was posting Eaton's men last I heard of him, across the Salisbury Road."

Ross kept on, past Kirkwood's Delaware Continentals, past Lynch's Virginians. In answer to his questions, men pointed east toward the main road. Then he found a twisting rail fence with a clearing just in front of it. Lying along it were the men of Butler's North Carolina militia. Startled eyes looked up at him, eyes that were unsteady and white about the sockets. Ross felt suddenly cold. Raw militia, and in the very front line. That was bad. Deeper, among the trees, were groups of seasoned riflemen, who leaned on their weapons, watching the militia. That was worse. It was obvious that they had been stationed there to shoot down any militiamen who tried to run. More and more militia. The cold feeling grew as Ross noted their shaky hands, their quick, shifting eyes.

Suddenly all heads turned east to the sound of hoofbeats. Nathanael Greene rode into the open, a few aides following him. He looked plump and cheerful, except that his jutting brows were knotted tight. He sighted Ross, called out to him as though to a chance-met friend on a peaceful ride. "Glad to see you, Pembroke! Lee sent word you had something to tell me." He reined in, smoothing out the spotless white lapels of his blue coat. "Just a moment, please. I want to speak to our Carolina friends here."

Greene dropped to the ground and Ross saw the white-socketed eyes turn toward him, apprehensive and a little resentful of his loops of gold braid, his polished boots. Greene took off his hat with a natural gesture and leaned on the fence. Ross saw something of the tenseness leave the militia. Greene spoke easily. "Not a great deal for you to do, boys. The British and the Tories will be coming down that road before very long. Give them two volleys—" he held up two fingers—"that's all. Make sure they're aimed. Take your time. When you've loosed the second, why just go back through the woods—any way you please. You'll find Stevens's Virginians in there and Lawson's men. Go right through them. They're expecting you." He smiled suddenly. "Doesn't sound like much, does it? Just two rounds per man. I know you'll do it. Thank you, boys."

He calmly mounted his horse, raising his hand in acknowledgment of the cheers that welled up from behind the fence so unexpectedly. Ross stared in wonder. Greene, with those few, easy words, had utterly transformed those militiamen who, a moment before, were ready to panic at the rustle of a rabbit. Greene touched his arm. "Now then, Pembroke, as one Rhode Islander to another, what's Cornwallis got to show us?"

Ross, riding beside the ex-ironmaster, detailed what he had seen, concluding, "It's my opinion, sir, that they'll be some time in reaching your first line. They've about four miles to cover. Most of it's through woods. Lee shook them badly and they'll be feeling their way along, fearing an ambush."

Greene glanced up at the clear morning sky. "H'm. That'd bring them here about noon, seeing that Cornwallis is driving them. If it were Howe or Clinton, I'd say sundown. Guards, Jaegers, Hessians and British line." He smiled. "What's happened to the British idea of 'conquering the Americas with Americans'?" The easy assurance had gone from his face, and he slapped his holster. "Hold! If we can only *hold!* That's all we've got to do. Damn victory! This isn't for the newspapers and gazettes! We must stand firm and do all the damage to Cornwallis that we can, the maximum. What we need is *success,* not victory. Victory could ruin us. Success—which means heavy losses for Cornwallis—will save us."

"I don't follow, sir," said Ross, frowning.

"What?" asked Greene sharply. "You don't see it? Look here. I can throw everything I've got at Cornwallis and stand a fine chance of a whopping military victory—that'll leave us with no army down here. But if I hold him at arm's length, pound him without committing myself, why, then my army's still intact. He's frightfully damaged, miles and miles from his nearest base and from any hope of reinforcement. At the end of the day, I don't care if I fall back and let him have the battlefield. He's welcome to it, so long as my army's a working unit. He can sit among his dead and wounded and write the most flowery dispatches that were ever penned. Tomorrow, Pembroke, what's he going to do tomorrow—with *his* victory and *our* success. He won't dare follow me. He won't dare fall back into South Carolina for reasons of morale; it'd be an open admission of defeat. No. All he can do is to limp off to Wilmington on the coast or up into Virginia where we've plenty of people waiting for him.

"Now I want you to ride for the high ground near the courthouse. Williams and Huger are there with their Continentals. Tell them what you've told me. I'll send you to Lee with orders later." As he rode off, he called back, "Might like to know that our friend Marion's raising the devil with supplies and reinforcements down on the Santee."

Ross followed the path that Greene had indicated. Off to the right, among more woods and clearings, he saw Stevens's Virginians in good order. Then, in the open, he mounted a slope, riding among the Virginia regulars of Greene and Hewes, among Gunby's men and Ford's. Even in their fragments of uniforms, eked out with homespun and buckskin, they looked hard and competent, kneeling or lying on the ground but retaining their formations. Ross reported to

Williams and Huger, who listened attentively, eyes on the patches of woodland and cornfield, on the narrow avenue of approach through the trees down which the British advance must come.

His report rendered, there was nothing for Ross to do but wait for Greene. He dismounted, studying the land about him. Behind the hill and just across the Reedy Fork Road was the rambling courthouse with its thick-throated chimney. In the western woods he made out horses and transport wagons, well placed for a quick move in the event of disaster. East of the courthouse a wide clearing spread flat and smooth, then ended abruptly in a wall of trees. To the southeast, about midway between his post and the woods where Stevens and Lawson waited, was a partially cleared hill. Ross made careful note of it and its approaches. It would make a fine rallying point if the first and second lines gave way.

As his eyes began to interpret vague movements within the wood lots or caught waiting men in the open, Greene's dispositions became spread out before him like a map. On the left of the American line, Lee's dragoons were drawn up in fairly open country. Ahead of them, and flanking the left of the militia along the rail fences of the first line, were Campbell's rifles and the Legion infantry. On the right, they were duplicated by Lynch's men. Any troops crossing those cornfields toward the fences would have to face not only the militia fire, but also the enfilade blasts of the flankers. In the rear of Lynch, Washington's white-coated troopers were maneuvering smartly into position in a toss of plumes and glitter of polished steel. The second line Ross could barely make out. They were well posted, however, and could easily fall back up the hill to the shelter of the Continentals and Captain Singleton's two grasshoppers. There was a rumble and a clatter down in the lowlands. From a thick patch of woods, two more pieces trundled out, moved south down the Salisbury Road, went into position between Butler's and Eaton's militia along the rail fence, a good half mile from the hill. Ross frowned, disturbed by two things. First, Greene had placed every available man in line. There were no reserves. Second, once action was joined, the commander on the hill would see little detail, owing to woods and smoke. He thought of Baum's position at Bennington, where the Brunswick colonel held his main body on a slope so steep that he could not see his attackers until they were on him, John Stark in the van. He turned away. Greene knew what he was about and there was no need for a captain of cavalry to worry.

The morning wore on under a cloudless sky. Greene and his staff returned to the hill, stood quietly watching the narrow avenue through the trees. Close to one o'clock, scanty rations of salt beef and corn bread were issued. Ross ate the tough meat as he leaned against Ree, who was munching her oats quietly. In the midst of a bite, he dropped his hand, staring south. Singleton's gunners, in the heart of the first line, sprang into activity about their brass pieces. Far beyond them, color stained the wood road, flowed on, became clearer and clearer.

The color rolled on, sifted through the woods, spilled along the road. Ross recognized the blue and red of the Royal Artillery as two light pieces were trundled forward, facing Singleton's guns. A dead hush hung over the windless day. Ross heard the creak of wheels off beyond the courthouse, the neigh of a horse. One of Gunby's men blew his nose loudly, a startling sound in the universal calm.

Beyond the first line, Cornwallis's men came on, moved to their stations. Ross got out his glass. On the British left he made out the Scots of the 71st, the blue and yellow of the von Bose regiment, east of the road. West, through the trees, he saw the blue facings of the 23rd, the red-on-red of the 33rd, with the silver caps of the Jaegers behind them. The Guards, the grenadiers and the light infantry companies were probably deployed in support of the Jaegers, the Scots and the Hessians. There was no sign of Tarleton's dragoons and Tories who must be waiting far down the road, cavalry being useless in the early stages of a battle in such terrain.

Singleton's first shot echoed flatly through the windless air, was answered from the British lines. The exchange of salvos went on for half an hour, neither side doing any damage that Ross could see. He looked at the British right. The Hessians and Scots, when the moment came, would be thrown against Lee's men and Campbell's on the American left. There was no motion among the red coats or the blue. Ross studied the ground to the east of the hill, searching for the best route to follow when Greene should send him to Lee. It would probably be simplest to drop down the north slope of the hill, ride past the courthouse, over the eastern clearing, and then circle down to Lee and the left wing. He turned to look at the north contour, saw slow, steady motion in the woods and on the western reaches of the Reedy Fork Road. Wagons were pulling out, with much cracking of whips, backing and jockeying. Ross called in a low tone to Gunby, who stood near him, leaning on his sword and studying the British dispositions with a practiced eye. "Know anything about that?" asked Ross, jerking his head toward the wagons.

Gunby, lips compressed, said curtly, "No concern of mine," and returned to his study of the terrain.

Ross was dissatisfied. Could Greene have scented disaster already and started his precious trains to safety? It didn't seem like the old ironmaster, somehow, this hint of timidity and lack of confidence. He heard his name called, saw Greene beckoning to him and ran to join him, bridle over his arm.

"Look here, Pembroke," said Greene. "Lee knows what to do just as well as I do. I've no special orders, so you might as well scurry over to him now. Better take this path that goes north and—" He turned to point, then his arm dropped by his side and his heavy shoulder heaved with anger. "Hell and death! Those wagons! They were not to move without my express order. Get over there as quick as you can, right up to the head of the column, and turn those muttonheads back. Use force if you have to."

Ross mounted Ree and sent her skittering down the slope to the Reedy Fork Road, then turned her head west. The move was much further advanced than he had supposed. He galloped past team after team, shouting at the drivers to halt and turn back. At once, a dangerous jam formed on the road, but there was no time to see to it. The foremost wagons must be checked.

When the head of the column was sighted, Ross pulled Ree back on her haunches. The thudding of Singleton's guns and those of the British was swallowed up in a ripping burst of musketry. Smoke rose high in the direction of Guilford Courthouse, a sign that the real action had begun. He started to swing about, then realized that, for the moment, the battle had nothing to do with him. At all costs the wagons must be brought under Greene's hand again.

The task seemed hopeless, interminable, as teamsters swore and argued with him. It was obvious to him that some daring spy, British or Tory, had worked to the rear of the American Army and given the order to withdraw. At last, the sound of the distant battle ringing in his ears, Ross managed to get the last wagon turned about and on its way to its original station. His mission was over and he was free to join Lee in the fighting.

Cutting to the rear of the hill where he had left Greene, he found there was nothing to see against the skyline save billowing smoke. Huger and Williams must have moved their men down the slope, possibly thrown them into action. Ross kept on, skirting the front of the courthouse, then riding straight across the wide clearing that he had noted during the morning. As he pressed on, he kept turning his head to the south where the choking smoke rose, but there was nothing to tell him of the progress of the fight.

He plunged into a wood lane that led south and east. Unless it took some odd turn, it should bring him into the rear of Lee's position. Spent balls began to whine, catlike, over his head. He could hear shouts above the rattle of small arms, the occasional thud of a light field piece far to the west. There was movement among the thinning trees. Close by, a harsh voice snapped *"Achtung!"* and Ross halted, bending low in the saddle.

Ahead of him were blue uniforms, heavy men in white-piped hats. Beyond them he made out the flat bonnets of the Scots!

At the touch of the reins, Ree swung in a half circle, went racing back along the path. Lee must be cut off from the main body. There was no other explanation. All the Legion and Campbell's men must be on the low hill that he had noted to the south of the courthouse, Scots and Hessians all about them.

Clear of danger for the moment, he stopped, listening. Firing from the high ground was steady and well sustained. He deduced that von Bose's men, having tasted the disciplined volleys of the Legion and Campbell's deadly rifles, were in no mood to push closer. The Scots seemed to be drifting to the west as though in answer to some order.

Ross rode on. There was nothing he could do so far as Lee was concerned. His best course would be to seek the hill south of the Reedy Fork Road where he had left Greene. At a smart trot, he retraced his course, veering always to the west, but careful lest he blunder among red coats or blue. He kept on the path, ears alert, slackening his pace as he came to the courthouse clearing.

He pulled Ree up so short that he pitched forward in the saddle, a shout of alarm and horror escaping him. There, to his left, was the east shoulder of the hill, covered with a broken drift of men. Greene's first line must have gone, his second. The third and strongest was nowhere in sight and frightened refugees poured over the position where earlier Ross had talked with Greene and Gunby. And driving steadily ahead in magnificent formation moved the British grenadiers, shoulder to shoulder with His Majesty's Foot Guards.

It was all over. Ross bent lower as though a fist had been

driven into his stomach and his mouth was dry. The Guards and the bearskins of the grenadiers pounded on, bayonets steadily aslant. Then from the west there was a pounding of hoofs, a flutter of white crests, a blur of white jackets. Two troops of Washington's dragoons roared down on the rear of the attackers, sabers flashing and their great horses throwing themselves forward in vast bounds.

The red ranks crumpled, scattered, were torn apart and their formation lost. Ross whipped out his saber and spurred Ree toward the hill. A dip in the ground hid the turmoil for an instant. When he topped it, the dragoons, red swords held high, were riding clear of the infantry, who instinctively formed in small circles, bayonets out. Washington's men swept off in a wide arc, scattered by the impetus of their charge. A bugle blared and they rallied.

Ross took his place beside a lean-faced captain whose eyes looked hot and sunken under the vizor of his helmet. He stared blankly at Ross, repeating woodenly, "Grenadiers and Guards! Rode right through 'em."

Ross nodded. "I saw it. Beautiful."

The captain shook himself. "Can do it again. Ride by my left. We'll cover each other when we go in again." He glanced toward a stocky major who was holding up his hand, watching the last troopers resume their places. By his side a bugler waited, instrument to his lips.

Ross braced himself. Off on the hill, grenadiers and Guards were straightening out their ranks, shifting this way and that. Ross figured they were trying to form a square of four bristling walls to receive the charge. He shot a look at the major, whose hand was still raised, the bugler watching him.

All at once, deep-toned drums began to beat out of sight beyond the grenadiers. The major stood in his stirrups and yelled "Hold it!" and spun his horse about. The drums were louder, their tempo rising as they beat out the double. From a welter of smoke Ross saw solid companies, spotted here and there with the blue and red of Maryland, crash into the left flank of the British column.

It was no place for cavalry. With the dragoons, Ross could only sit and watch. Slowly at first, then faster and faster, the British fell back, fighting hard. More drums beat; the red and blue of the 23rd, the red-on-red of the 33rd, swung in to support, found hard-fighting Virginians on their flanks. There was a movement of stalemate, then the backward movement set in once more.

By Ross's side, the dragoon captain watched, motionless, his mouth agape. All at once he caught Ross by the collar, whinnying, "Look-look-look! By their guns! Cornwallis himself! We'll get the guns! By God, we'll get *him!*"

The rout moved faster and faster and Ross stared, fascinated. There was no doubt about it. The tide would sweep over the guns, engulf Cornwallis, clearly visible over there with his staff. The war in the South was over! Was over! Ross found that he was standing in his stirrups, yelling the words again and again. No power on earth could untangle that milling mass that shot, stabbed, cursed in their southward flow. Ross waved his helmet wildly. "It's over," he yelled again. "By God, Cornwallis *can't* use his artillery. He'd mow down his own men."

As Ross spoke, he saw Cornwallis survey the tumult as coolly as though reviewing troops in a barrack yard. Then he spoke to a tall officer in artillery blue and red. The officer shook his head. Cornwallis spoke again.

Ross suddenlly slumped in the saddle. The two field pieces were firing grape indiscriminately on friend and foe. He saw a knot of Guardsmen swept away by the first blast, saw the next strike among sweating Virginians. Step by step, firing steadily, the American pursuit broke off, disentangled itself from Guardsman and grenadier, withdrew sullenly among thick trees where grape rapped against the trunks with a sinister, hollow sound. Cornwallis had shot down his own men, who were probably doomed anyway, to save his army.

An hour later, through gathering dusk, Greene calmly withdrew his men, unit by unit, while the Virginia line, under heavy fire, stood unyielding to cover the withdrawal. From the courthouse hill, Ross looked back on the torn field, then at Greene, who sat his horse, motionless, as torn companies of Marylanders cheered him. Washington and Williams were urging him to throw the freshest troops, the virtually unused cavalry, against the shattered British. Ross smiled grimly as Greene kept shaking his head. The victory—if possession of the field meant that—might lie with Cornwallis. But success rode on the torn banners of Greene's army, intact though battered, as it withdrew to the north and the shelter of Troublesome Creek.

Ross overtook the Legion on the night road, splashing over the shallow ford of Reedy Fork. He rode past the infantry, exhausted, but pushing on with a strength-conserving stride that marked them as veterans. They seemed to have suffered little, to judge from the solid mass of skullcaps that flowed on through the dark. Then he saw the toss of white, heard the jingle of bits and knew that he was among the dragoons. Rudulph's troop was bringing up the rear and he questioned its commander. Rudulph answered sharply, "Sure he's here. Everyone's here. Never had a chance to charge. You don't lose men when they spend a whole afternoon leaning against their horses and scratching themselves."

Ross kept on until he heard Winston's pleasant voice near the head of the column. The Virginian laughed. "Where the devil were you during the action, Ross? Rolling dice with the headquarters drummers?"

"I might just as well have been. Seen Phil de Chanzy?"

"Lee was using him as a galloper. You'll probably find him up yonder."

There was no mistaking Light Horse Harry Lee, even in the increasing darkness. He was fuming to someone, "And there we were, just waiting. No orders came—" He broke off suddenly as he saw Ross's white jacket glimmering close by. "Here, maybe you can tell me. You were with Greene. Why didn't he let me charge? I sent for permission and he never even acknowledged the request. I wasn't to engage my dragoons without his authorization, and—"

Ross accounted for his time since leaving Lee in the early morning. Lee shrugged. "Well, Greene will probably tell me later. He must have had his reasons. But it was a wonderful chance. De Chanzy was to explain the exact circumstances to him."

"Where's de Chanzy?" asked Ross. "Winston thought he'd be with you."

"He'll bob up. Men are straggling in all the time. Or Greene may have kept him."

Throughout the night, Ross ranged up and down the column, which was joined from time to time by men who had been sent off on special missions during the day. Nowhere did he find de Chanzy; no one whom he asked had seen him since Lee had sent him galloping off toward the hill south of Reedy Fork Road. Ross tried to reason out probabilities from his own knowledge of events, could only settle on two alternatives. Either he was still with Greene, or he had, in returning from his mission, struck the same bodies of Scots and Hessians as Ross himself. In any event, there was nothing to worry about. If the Frenchman were with Greene, all was well. If he had sighted the enemy in the woods, he was too good a soldier to have run into difficulties. He would have sheered off, attached himself to some American unit; no doubt he was marching with them now, waiting for daylight to rejoin the Legion.

There was a dawn camp at Troublesome Creek, close by the abandoned Speedwell Iron Works. Ross made the rounds of the camp, squinting through sleep-stiffened lids, questioning sentries. By a post of Gunby's men he stopped, peering through the mist at a helmeted man who limped on with the help of a thick staff. He was muffled in a white cloak under which a saber clanked. Ross hailed him. "Hi! You're from Washington's dragoons? Were any of Lee's officers with you yesterday?" He knew the question was a vain one, since it was almost inconceivable that de Chanzy could have been caught up by Washington's men, on the far right of the line. The dragoon, white cloak swishing over the grass, limped doggedly ahead without answering. He was singing to himself in a hoarse, low voice. Ross swore. "Drunken bastard! It'd have served him right if the Guards had snapped him up." Then he started forward, shouting. The man was singing. No doubt of that. But the words!

"Et Tarleton s'en va t'en guerre, ne sais quand reviendra."

Ross shouted again, "Phil! For God's sake!"

De Chanzy limped calmly on, pale but obviously content with the world. "Ah, *te voilà, mon petit!* I learn, back there by the videttes, that you are well. *Baste!* Why do you stare, then? Am I a ghost?" He flung an arm about Ross's shoulder, then amicably prodded him in the ribs with his stick.

"Where the devil have you been?"

De Chanzy spread out his hands. "Where, indeed? That is a question which hundreds of our young men ask, one of the other, this morning. For my part, I supped, late last night, with a cousin, one Georg von Tilley of von Bose's. Our families intermarried during the Thirty Years' War. Later, I make my adieux and come to see how you good fellows do."

"You what?" asked Ross, incredulous.

"As I tell you. I start to deliver a message from Lee, yesterday. All at once, those blue devils of Hessians are about me. My horse, it shies and, owing to my cursed knee, there am I on the ground with a bayonet at my throat. *Il n'y a rien à faire.* To the rear they send me. My knee, it burns like forty thousand devils. I fall down. They carry me. Unaided, I cannot stand. After the fight, I recognize my cousin, von Tilley. It is not strange, for I think I must have thirty cousins in twenty armies. He feeds me and we talk of the battle, over which he does not find himself amused. This cloak he gives me. Then come the Goddams in their red coats. It seems I am *their* prisoner. They wish to hurry me along. I protest. I explain. In short I argue. Not a step can I walk. They bring a litter and carry me off. Under a tree they leave me, seeing well that so complete a cripple as I needs no guard. They ask of me no parole. For a while I listen. Then, being bound by no oath and by no guard, I take advantage of the magnificent darkness, leave my litter and—" he spread out his hands again—"and now, behold me. You must take me at once to Lee and then to Greene."

"Here, lean on me," said Ross. "We'll rout out Lee and you can tell him your story. I—I don't mind saying we were a little worried about you."

"In my conceit, I thought it not unlikely," said de Chanzy. "Hence I took leave of my hosts as soon as seemed advisable. Else I could easily have remained another twenty-four hours among them, listening and observing. As it was, I do not feel that I wasted quite all my time."

De Chanzy had listened to good effect. Webster, in command of the British left, was dying. O'Hara of the Guards was badly wounded. The Scots of the 71st practically ceased to exist as a regiment. Of the Guards, one man in four had been killed or wounded. The Welsh of the 23rd had been badly mauled as had the 33rd. "And I assure you," de Chanzy concluded, "the whole army has few supplies beyond what the men themselves carry. What can Milord Cornwallis do?"

Ross grunted. "He usually finds *some*thing to do, and whatever it is, we won't like it."

"*Ça se peut.* But now, I think, from what I hear we *shall* like what he does. Consider well, my friend, he is stripped like a beggar's ham bone. His nearest base is Wilmington, far away on the coast. He cannot return to South Carolina. He cannot stay where he is, for he would be quite rapidly chopped to pieces. Therefore, while I think no orders have been issued as yet, he will lose no time in starting for Wilmington. Now tell me truly—you think this is of enough importance to engage the ear of our Greene?"

Ross repressed a smile. "Oh, I guess he'll listen."

As the two made their way through the wakening camp, Ross remembered an earlier thought. The retreat to the Dan, he had said, was like the retreat through the Jerseys. At that time he had wondered if a Trenton or a Princeton lay at the end of this. Yes, Guilford Courthouse could be considered a Trenton and Princeton combined. De Chanzy was right. The British—the Goddams as the French called them—would have to seek refuge in Wilmington. And then? He could figure only two courses open to Cornwallis. Either to wait for a fleet to embark his troops and return to Charleston or to march north into Virginia, hoping for a junction with General Phillips. The fleet seemed a remote chance. The march to Virginia would not be pleasant with Greene harrying every step and the Legion in the van of everything.

Greene, with his makeshift army built about a minute core of seasoned, well-led troops, had outmaneuvered, outfought and outgeneraled a first-class British army. But there was more to the story than Greene's mastery. Why had Cornwallis not received the steady flow of supplies and reinforcements on which his very life depended? A good part of the answer, Ross knew, lay in the swift, hard-riding men who followed a frail, limping leader in a charred skullcap, feinting here, striking there, along the chain of posts that led from the South Carolina bases, posts whose only reason for existence lay in expediting the flow of the lifeblood of the main army. Marion, Sumter, Hardin, Shelby, Clarke. Without them, Greene could have been overwhelmed. Without Greene, their strokes could have been mere annoyances. All together, they had flattened the British might between hammer and anvil.

The march to Virginia lay ahead. Now the great partisans could content themselves with routine harrowing, while they watched for news of the last blow, somewhere across the Virginia border, the last blow which would insure the freedom of the South.

X • Along the Congaree

The carriage halted at the neglected earthworks at Monck's Corner, not far beyond the shaky bridge across Wadboo Creek. Dorande sat up, blinking as a sleepy ensign flashed a lantern into the window. The glow lit up her face, and the young officer was instantly alert, bowing and touching his hat. Then he recognized St. Aubin, cool and fully awake on the opposite seat, and bowed still more profoundly. "Sorry, sir. Didn't have an idea. Orders, you know. Each carriage."

St. Aubin inclined his head politely. "Your orders I find most sensible."

By the carriage, Negro dragoons sat their horses nervously, obviously not relishing their night escort duty. The carriage by itself was no bait for a sudden partisan coup, but those supply wagons ahead and behind! They glanced impatiently at the ensign who still leaned on the carriage door, talking with St. Aubin but looking covertly at Dorande. He said diffidently, "I—I suppose, sir, that you were at Cruden's ball."

"But naturally. The journey to Charleston was a small price to pay to assist at that tribute to the victory of your Cornwallis."

"Just my luck to have to miss it." The ensign slid his elbows along the window frame, closer to Dorande. "Hope you enjoyed yourself, ma'am."

Dorande, head leaning against the cushions, said wearily, "I found it as magnificent as the victory which it celebrated."

The ensign tried to prolong the conversation, but St. Aubin cut in politely, "I shall take pleasure in reporting your diligence to your superiors. In the meantime, the road to the Congaree is a long one."

The ensign stepped reluctantly away and the carriage rolled north with the convoy. Dorande tried to sleep, but visions of the great celebration in Charleston flitted before her eyes. There had been fireworks, salvos from the British men-of-war and a great ball at the Pinckney house, now occupied by Mr. Cruden, Commissioner of Sequestered Estates. Men and women had shouted that *now* the war was over. Loyal people would reap the rewards for their steadfastness.

She tried to blot out the scenes, but her ears still rang with the cheers that had greeted Cruden's reading of the dispatch from Cornwallis at Guilford Courthouse. Greene's army in full flight; the British in possession of the ground; the Rebel generals, Huger and Stevens, wounded; the field covered with Rebel dead; Greene's artillery captured.

Her hands clenched tightly. What would now happen to Ross Pembroke? To Francis Marion? Really, it did not matter to her. No doubt all these people who had fought so bravely for a belief would be honorably treated by the victors —all these people who had been good to her during her brief stay in a world that was not hers. Soon, when the seas were clear once more, passage to St. Eusebius would be simple. Her fingers twisted tighter. Yes, the Rebels whom she had known would be honorably treated. Of course. The trailing ends of the gauze scarf about her head tore between her fingers.

Opposite her, St. Aubin felt no need of sleep. Through Cruden's secretary, there had been transferred to his own name the estates of four families whose activities he had been watching up on the Congaree. In the flush of victory, no one would question the evidences of treason on the part of those families which he had produced. With the return of the full power of the Crown, the last sullying traces of democracy would be erased. The state would no doubt be reorganized along the lines of the original grants, with a titled provincial aristocracy. Those titles—Landgrave, Cacique— would be restored. Land would be divided up into the original Baronies. And who would be in better position to profit by that return to former grandeur than himself? In the darkness, his hand touched a small packet on the seat. A Charleston printer had struck off a thousand cards bearing the name "Paul de St. Aubin." Most of the English and all the Provincials took the "de" as an ennobling prefix. Later, he would have cards reading "Paul, Landgrave of the Congaree, Barony de St. Aubin." The way was clear.

There were other matters that kept him in a state of quietly gratified wakefulness. The Crown armies, operating far from Charleston, had commandeered supplies from the civilians. They paid for such seizures in notes on the Crown Treasury, redeemable only at the Claims Office on Queen Street, Charleston, at dates specified. Most of these notes were held by Tories, but a few officers such as Lord Rawdon and McLeroth, were soft-hearted enough to tender such payment to actual Rebels whose goods they took.

Charleston was far and the road dangerous. Many of the Tory holders were very vague concerning their rights in such transactions. Cash in hand, St. Aubin had ridden many weary miles through the country, seeking out those holders. They had been pathetically grateful to him for taking those scraps of paper and paying for them. He allowed himself to smile as he recalled those transactions. He had bought up the claims at discounts running as high as sixty-five per centum, surrendering depreciated local scrip in payment. Well, why not? Was his time worth nothing? And had he not been forced, *parbleu*, to share up to twenty per centum of his legitimate profit with Charleston officials? Nonetheless, even with those deductions, he had been able to deposit with his Charleston bankers a really satisfactory sum in good, fresh-minted British gold. Paul, Landgrave of the Congaree, Barony de St. Aubin. There was another shrewd side to his dealings. No one had objected that he had extended his charitable dealings to a few Rebels who held paper from Rawdon or McLeroth. Such people would still be about after the peace and would remember that the Landgrave, though stanchly for the Crown, had come to their aid in time of need.

Dawn lit up the interior of the carriage and Dorande started, surprised that she had been able to sleep. She looked through the window, saw the new day touching stupendous bursts of azalea banked thick on the slopes, saw the rich buds of the magnolia ready to unfold. The convoy was rolling slowly west and to the north she saw swamp land, the glint of a lazy river. The Santee! It could not have been far from this very spot that she had first seen Ross thrashing through the woods on his great horse in pursuit of Bayne. And north beyond the Santee, beyond the Pocotaligo, beyond the state line? Where was Ross now?

She shook away the thought and watched the river road that ran on past Nelson's Ferry and on to the Congaree. They would halt a few times, she had heard, and spend the night well beyond Nelson's, then strike out again, covering the last miles with no important breaks. The day rolled on under the churning wheels. Opposite her, St. Aubin slept the deep, peaceful sleep of a child. Dorande opened a small hamper, breakfasted daintily on a chicken wing and a bit of lettuce and drank white wine sparingly as she wondered how much farther it was to Nelson's, the first real landmark along the river.

When she had stowed away the hamper, she noticed that the nearest dragoon, magnificent in brass helmet and red jacket, was an intelligent-looking, handsome mulatto. He paced his mount closer on the river side as she beckoned to him, asking, "Is it now far to Nelson's?"

He touched his helmet. "Reckon maybe an hour, Miss."

"Do you know this spot—that is, precisely where we are?"

The dragoon straightened in his saddle and looked toward the river, where a shattered house stood on a bluff. "Don't know many places better. That there house belongs to a Rebel. Maybe you've heard of him. Name of Marion."

Dorande stared at the desolate house, its chimneys sticking up like broken teeth and its shutters sagging. The little brigadier! But for his beliefs, he could be there now, with a whole roof over his head and clean gravel on the drive that led up through live oaks. But for his beliefs—

The dragon went on. "Yes, Miss—folks call him a wicked Rebel. I don't know about that. All I know is, he was mighty good to my people. Most of them that he owned was taken to Charleston and sold to Jamaica planters. But ten-twelve of them hid in the swamps. They come back, when it's safe, and do what they can, clearing fields and propping up doors and such."

Dorande frowned. She might be able to find a way of selling something, to help out those faithful blacks. She remembered black Oscar who had brought her food at Chilyon's Castle, his eyes always on the brigadier—devoted but not servile. Obviously to his master he was a man, not a slave.

The dragoon stayed by the window, pointing out other landmarks to her. A brick house where a creek slanted off to join the Santee—Eutaw Creek, he called it. There were mysterious twin springs nearby that rose, plunged under a marl ridge to emerge again. The waters were famous and convoys often halted there to fill water bottles and buckets for the horses.

The convoy halted and Dorande saw a stream of men heading for a clump of woods with jugs and pails. The dragoon dismounted and adjusted his saddlecloth. Dorande watched idly, while her uncle slept peacefully on. Sun was filtering through the thick brush and trees close by the road. Far in, barely visible in the cool shadows of the trunks, a grayish mass loomed. It was hard to make out details, but the mass seemed to have some form of its own, regular beyond the habit of nature. She called to the dragoon, "Among those trees —yes, I know I see something."

The dragoon looked quickly over his shoulder, then busied himself with his girth, his head averted. "Ain't nothing there, Miss."

"There *must* be. I see it!"

He glanced covertly at her, shaking his head. There was nothing. Maybe a rock, maybe a rotten trunk. Dorande persisted. At last, cautiously drawing nearer, he muttered, "Don't do to talk about such, Miss. In the old daws, white folks bring my people out of Africa. Ten, fifty, a thousand—I don't know —they run away. They settle in the river swamps where white folks don't dast come. That was the old days and white folks all on the coast. My people build villages, like in home country. They live like in home country. The headman, he sets up what white priests call idols." As he talked, Negroid accent and thought grew thicker and thicker. "I know ten, maybe twenty idols they set up in the old days in the river swamps. Ain't really an idol. Just big rock, shaped funny. When the old folks make their prayer for hunting or harvest, they make it in early morning when the sun hit the top of the stone. Ain't any more to it. Just that. White folks come up the rivers, my people keep west. Some got killed by Indians, others join the tribes. Nothing left but the stones along the rivers. Old-time people, they call the stones—" he broke into a string of guttural sounds—"hard to put into white folks' talk, but it means something like 'early stone'—no, that ain't it. Maybe better call him 'the Dawn Stone.'"

"Oh!" cried Dorande. "But I find that lovely—and moving. A prayer to the Dawn Stone, to *la Pierre de l'Aube!* No. It goes prettier in English. I wish someone would cut the trees down around it. I would like to see it."

The dragoon looked startled. "Cut the trees? Ain't none of my people would dast and white folk don't care." He dropped his voice. "But my people, they say if the trees go without a hand laid to 'em, so the first sun can strike the Dawn Stone again, then all big troubles over." He drew himself up, said in his former tones, "I'd be happy, Miss, to bring you a bottle from the Eutaw Springs."

When the convoy rolled on, Dorande dozed again, her sleepy thoughts flowing from Marion's wrecked house to the Dawn Stone of the dragoon's legend. When the first sun strikes the Dawn Stone, all big troubles are over. She slept, and the rumble of wheels was heavy about her. She dreamed that back by the springs, cannon were booming and men shouting. A nameless danger lurked in the trees about the old stone and a man in a white coat rode toward it, unknowing.

She tried to cry out. Then suddenly the man in the white coat was safe, but safe at some price whose nature she couldn't guess. The trees fell away, torn and splintered, baring the stone to the first sun. She settled deeper against the cushions, sleeping soundly.

The convoy moved west along the Santee, through a day of unfathomable peace. The troopers dozed in their saddles or climbed into supply carts where they stretched out luxuriously, their reins hooked over one protruding foot. Foxes and rabbits darted across the road and vivid tanagers streaked across the late March sky. At Nelson's Ferry, Dorande woke, remembering how she had ridden there from Snow Island and the old Quaker who had made the sketch of her. Now there was nothing to suggest that armed bands might sweep down from the Pee Dee onto the sensitive supply route. The ruddy major, chatting easily with her uncle, seemed to have no cares. There were a good many troops about, both British and Tory, but their smart alertness was that of garrison life rather than the field. She ate a little from the hamper again and then, kitten-like, curled herself up.

In the late afternoon, the carriage halted by the river. St. Aubin, out on the road, talked earnestly with three men in Tory green, one of whom held a riderless horse. Then he turned, came quickly to the carriage and spoke through the open door. "I regret, *ma nièce*, that we part company here. I go to Camden, up the Wateree. It is my wish that you press on and beg leave to pass the night with our good new friend, Mrs. Motte, on the Congaree. For my part, I shall rejoin you at Mon Plaisir with little delay. Part of this convoy moves west to Ninety-six, so you will not be alone."

The sun was setting as Dorande sighted the hills of the lower Congaree. She sat up, adjusted her clothes and her bonnet, dusted her face with rice powder and looked out. There on the south bank was the Indian mound where Mrs. Motte had built her new house. As the coach rolled nearer, she made out activity of some sort on the grounds about the house. Perhaps the widow was laying out the beginnings of the formal gardens which the two had discussed. She leaned from the window to see better, but the western glare dazzled her.

The coachman bent from the box to ask if he should go up the main drive or swing in by the north side. The carriage turned a little as he spoke and the shoulder of the hill cut off the sun. Dorande's fingers clutched the sill and she stared toward the house. All along the hill, shirt-sleeved men were digging furiously, carving a deep trench under the direction of an officer of Royal Engineers. Other groups were tugging at heavy logs, up-ending them in the beginning of a high stockade. There was no sign of Mrs. Motte, of her daughters or the household slaves.

Twice the coachman repeated his question, but Dorande still stared. Rebecca Motte's house was being turned into a fort which commanded the road from Charleston and the road from Orangeburg that fed north and west to other posts of the main army. Why? News of Greene's rout was official. But this new fort, the unusual number of men back at Nelson's Ferry?

She looked up at the coachman. "On. We return direct to Mon Plaisir."

The carriage lurched forward as Dorande threw herself into the seat, biting her lower lip. She could only guess that Mrs. Motte's eviction was a first step on the part of the conquerors against a Rebel sympathizer. They were losing no time in showing who now held the upper hand. As to the works, they were probably the idea of some fussy major to keep the troops occupied.

Suddenly Dorande leaned forward, one arm over the sill, calling, "Reliance! It is I, Mademoiselle van Kortenaer!"

The pretty young slave girl stopped, hand to her mouth, as the coachman reined in. Then she burst out, "Glory day! Mis' Motte speakin' 'bout you this mornin'."

Dorande swung the door open. "Get in. Tell me where is Madame Motte? In, I say. There's no one to say no."

Reluctantly the girl got in, perched diffidently on the seat that St. Aubin had occupied, swallowing hard as she answered Dorande's questions. The soldiers had come two or possibly three days before. Reliance was hazy on dates. They had given Mrs. Motte a very short time to leave and had started to work at once. "They wasn't hard men," Reliance concluded. "They was just minded. Mis' Motte, she and me and the little gals, we take what we can an' hit out for the old farmhouse younder. She there now."

The farmhouse was perched on another hill about a mile north of the new building. Dorande called an order to the coachman, who swung the horses along a grassy track away from the rest of the convoy. As they neared the house, Dorande flung open the door, leaped to the ground and ran toward the tall, graying woman who stood by a flower bed. "Ah, Madame! Madame! I see your new house and men about it! What's happened? I was frightened. There is such bad news! Everywhere." Her lips quivered and the restraint that she had maintained through the past days broke.

Mrs. Motte, a good head taller than Dorande, threw her

arms about her and stroked her bright hair. "There, there! No bad news that *I* know of—none that we haven't had before and lived through. Gracious, child, you're trembling. Didn't that uncle of yours give you *any* chance to rest between Charleston and the Congaree? You come right in and we'll have coffee."

"But your house!" cried Dorande. "And—oh, that news from the north!"

Mrs. Motte laughed and drew Dorande inside. "My house is still there. If anything happens to it, why I have this one. As for that battle—why, the Crown's been winning the war by proclamation since '75."

Seated in the bare living room, sipping hot, sweet coffee, Dorande's spirits began to pick up, further bolstered by her hostess's cheery confidence. Setting down her cup, Mrs. Motte made sure that the servants were out of hearing, then seated herself by Dorande again. "Let's face it, my dear. Things aren't good. What's happened in the north, we just don't know. What I do know is this. No one's got the least idea where Francis Marion is, or Sumter, or Pickens. No one's come by here. The Friday boys, the Witherspoons, don't know a thing. It's as though all our people had simply vanished. I don't like it. Usually, we get a hint of some kind. Most always, when things are at their worst, the call comes to rally the countryside. That battle was fought on March fifteenth. This is the twenty-ninth. There's been no call."

Somehow Mrs. Motte's cool appraisal rallied Dorande. Stirring her coffee, she said, "Do not English people hold that no news is good news? May that not apply here?"

"Perhaps," said Mrs. Motte dubiously.

"And, Madame, demand this of yourself. *Why* do men dig trenches about your house? Why do I see soldiers and more soldiers at Nelson's Ferry? Did the men who came to you say nothing?"

Mrs. Motte bristled at the recollection. "Only that I had to go, with just time enough ti throw a few things into a cart."

"*Voilà,*" said Dorande, throwing out her hands. "Men wealthy in good news do not show such haste as that, I think. And consider what you tell me at the door. The Crown wins proclamation battles."

"That was for the servants," said Mrs. Motte. "If they see me in the dumps, they're apt to hit for the swamps. Just the same—what you were saying—" She kissed Dorande. "I brought you in here to cheer you up, and here you are, cheering me."

Dorande smiled. "Perhaps, then, we should stay together. Where are your little girls?"

"Sent to a safe place until I see what those fiddleheads at my new house are really up to."

"Excellent. Then you must come to Mon Plaisir. Janet and I shall be alone there, for a few days at least."

Mrs. Motte nodded emphatically. "Good. Just give me time to throw a few things into a light trunk."

She ran upstairs, leaving Dorande to pace restlessly about the room. Mrs. Motte must have left her best things at the new house, Dorande reflected, noting plain chairs and deal tables that she could see in other rooms through open doors. The slave girls must have snatched at the nearest and most portable objects, regardless of utility. A fragile glass vase stood beside a pair of pattens on the hearth. A telescope lay in a frying pan beside a cowhide bag. Evidently Mrs. Motte had not had time to do much straightening or sorting since her arrival. Absently she picked up a heavy club made of dark wood, then a sheaf of arrows. The arrows were long and heavy with bulbous tips instead of barbs. The tips were thick and resinous to the touch.

Mrs. Motte came downstairs, Reliance after her, carrying a small trunk. Dorande waved the sheaf at her. "Tell me about these, Madame. Never have I seen such arrows."

Mrs. Motte gave a resigned sigh. "A sea captain from the East Indies brought them to one of my brothers, in the days when I was still a Brewton. Lord knows where they come from or why they're here. Reliance's sister Daisy brought them along from the other house. War clubs, flame knives, blowpipes. Those are fire arrows that you're holding. You're supposed to light them and shoot them onto someone's thatched roof and I vow if it weren't my own house I'd send a few through the window of the room where that Royal Engineer animal sleeps. Put them down, my dear, and take this." She held out a short-barreled pistol.

"Oh, but one lies ready charged in the pocket of the carriage, by my side." She gave a tight smile. "My uncle placed it there in case that species of brigand named Marion should attack the coach."

"Then come along. You and Janet and I'll have a good long talk."

The coach rolled on toward Mon Plaisir, beyond McCord's Ferry, while Mrs. Motte talked about the day-to-day doings in the valley of the Congaree. Dorande, listening, kept rubbing the fingers of her right hand, where resin from the oddly headed arrows had stuck.

It was quite late when the coachman opened the door for them by the porch of Mon Plaisir. Dorande took Mrs. Motte's arm. "I know the hour is scarcely *convenable* for a visit, but Janet will be pleased if we roused her for a word at least."

They went down the dark path to Janet's cottage. Dorande rapped three times on the window, then twice. The door flew open and a tall man in a white coat stood in the inner darkness. Dorande put her hand to her throat, crying, *"Mais enfin—"* huskily. Then she stepped back, leaning on Mrs. Motte as Raoul's voice answered, "Dorande! And Mrs. Motte! This is luck. I was just leaving. Come in. I've something to say that you ought to hear."

Dorande stammered, "I thought—I saw only the white coat and thought—"

Raoul dropped an arm about her shoulder. "I'm sorry, Dorande. I wish this were the coat you were hoping to see. It's just a planter's coat that I picked up across the Savannah."

"You—you know where he is?"

Raoul shook his head gently. "I'd love to tell you that he was leading five thousand cavalry down the Wateree. But I just don't know. Where's your uncle? At the house?"

"He said he would go to Camden."

Raoul called, "Janet, dear, there's no reason why we can't show a light. Do light those candles and bring them in here."

Flame glowed in the next room and Janet came in, her dark hair streaming over her shoulders. She blushed as the light fell on her blue silk wrapper and slippered feet. As though to distract attention from her negligee, she asked quickly, "Was the ball very gay, Dorande?"

"No doubt," Dorande answered.

"I wish I could stay here for a while," said Raoul, as he whisked chairs about for the three women. "But time's crowding me. I'll say what I have to say quickly, and then I'm off."

Dorande saw Janet's mouth tighten as Raoul spoke of leaving. She wondered just what lay ahead of him, at the end of his night's ride, of the next. He rode out alone, whereas Ross Pembroke—

Raoul leaned forward. "For the moment, I don't *know* a thing about the north. There's been a battle. Cornwallis claims a big victory. I've heard that Sumter's recruiting in North Carolina and that Pickens has come down to the Ninety-six area. Marion's somewhere along the Pee Dee, they say, but whether he's got a hundred men with him or ten, or two, no one seems to know. Just the same, we're going on here just as though nothing had happened. I've talked with Harden and Cooper down in the south."

"How far south?" asked Mrs. Motte.

Raoul smiled. "Quite far. Now, we've got to assume that even if the news is very bad, the fight's going on. We want to know, as usual, where the enemy is going and why. We'll be pretty well covered in the central part of the state and the east. To the west, it's different. Luckily, it's hilly country and we're arranging to stack beacons on the various peaks. Three to four men will be responsible for each beacon and if, say, Rawdon moves toward Ninety-six or The Long Canes, those beacons will be lit, one after the other. They'll show a long way and give us time—well, to do anything we think ought to be done."

"Such as?" asked Mrs. Motte.

Raoul shrugged. "Time will tell. But I tell you three this—if you see beacons to the south, that will mean that the Tory Thomas Browne's striking up from Fort Galphin."

"And then?" asked Dorande, chin in her hands.

"In that case, even St. Aubin's protection might fail. Go straight to Camden and put yourselves—all of you—under Lord Rawdon's protection. He's a gentleman and you'll be safe. But this Browne! He's waging a war of extermination. I'm sorry to say that some of our people have been as bad as he, and all that's started a precedent of violence that's worse than anything we've seen yet." He rose with a nonchalance that Dorande knew must be assumed. "Janet has a map, showing in code just where the beacons are and who's in charge of them. Dorande, I've tried to keep you out of this, because it's no concern of yours. You *mustn't* get mixed up in what we're doing. But this once, I want you to go over that map with Janet and Mrs. Motte. Men may come here at night, expecting to be told where to go and whom to meet. You see, accidents could happen to *all* the men responsible for a given beacon and then the whole chain would be useless. Replacements for those men would have to get instructions here."

"I do that gladly," said Dorande.

"I only suggest it because your own safety might depend on those beacons—not just our safety, Dorande," said Raoul gravely. "Browne's men—well, I've seen them. You haven't."

Mrs. Motte and Dorande left Janet and her husband in the cottage. Mrs. Motte looked quizzically at Dorande. "You're worried about something, my dear, and I'm sure it isn't Browne's men."

"Perhaps I worry—a little," said Dorande in a small voice.

"Is it over that cavalryman you told me about the other day?"

"It may be. No! I *do* worry. At first I see him as *beau garçon,* a handsome young man pleasant to remember when I go to St. Eusebius. That is all. I see him again. After that—" She shook her soft ringlets.

Mrs. Motte prompted, "After that, you don't think quite so much about your island? And a good deal more about him?"

"I do not know."

"If you don't know, then you *do* know. Your island's more important than he is," said Mrs. Motte firmly. "There's no guessing about a thing like that."

"Perhaps—sometimes—I do know," murmured Dorande.

"Fiddlesticks. If you know, there's no 'perhaps' and no 'sometimes.' From Rhode Island is he? Well, there are fine people up there. Charlestonians have been summering at Newport since the '50s. Just the same, it'd be a new world to you."

Dorande, turning her head to the north, sighed. "I would like to be sure that he was safe. I would not like to sail for St. Eusebius, always wondering."

Mrs. Motte squeezed her arm. "You'll hear that he's all right. Gracious, any man who has come safely through everything since '75 isn't going to get into trouble in a little brush in North Carolina. Now I'm going to see that you have some hot milk and I'll put you to bed myself."

The hushed days crept up the valley of the Congaree where the cloak of uncertainty hung heavy. More than a week passed before St. Aubin returned from Camden. He greeted Dorande, Janet and Mrs. Motte politely, but Dorande noted that his eyes looked hot and angry, that his thin lips were compressed.

Alone in the room that he used for an office, St. Aubin drew back a curtain that masked most of one wall, disclosing a big map of the Carolinas. It had been made for him in Charleston by the Royal Engineers in part payment of a dubious transaction that involved the transfer of wines intended for the army hospitals to the private stores of the officers' mess. The map was marked with colored chalks, obviously indicating boundaries of estates. Spidery lines in red showed the movements of the Royal armies; blue, the American forces.

He carefully ruled a red line from a spot marked Guilford Courthouse, his chalk moving east and south past the Deep, past the Scots settlements at Cross Creek, along the Cape Fear and on to Wilmington. At that coastal city, he shifted his ruler, drew an arrow pointing north past the Neuse and on to the Virginia border. He stepped back to survey his work, muttering a disgusted *"Bigre!"*

With a blue crayon, he traced a thin line that followed the course of the Haw as though in pursuit of the red line. Then he bent the blue sharply south toward the Pee Dee, chalking a question mark as the river was reached. A thicker stroke held to the same course along the Haw, only to curve down over the Yadkin and on west of the Cheraws into South Carolina. He left this mark unfinished, drawing an arrow barb pointing at Lord Rawdon's base at Camden. He smiled sourly. "Two great fools part company! Why does Cornwallis flee to Virginia after his victory? And why does not Greene follow him?" He shrugged. *"N'importe.* Whatever happens, there will be profits for one who is not a fool. All the same, I do not like it. Three swift devils—Greene, Marion and Lee. Where, now precisely *where* will they strike?"

Three weeks later, St. Aubin's carriage trundled slowly along the river road from the west through a waning May afternoon. St. Aubin, his back to the driver, sat absorbed in a mass of notes which he compared from time to time with parchment rolls that rustled dryly as his body gave to the sway of the carriage. Opposite him, Dorande pretended to nap, but her whole body was tense as though each muscle were trying to speed along the lazy wheels.

The long trip, begun in April, had taken her and her uncle to Ninety-six and on into the mysterious western reaches where the carriage had to give way to saddle horses. She had learned a great deal, particularly about the hidden hilltop beacons and the men who would set them blazing to signal hostile troop movements.

But even at the headquarters at Ninety-six where the grave, courteous Tory, John Cruger, commanded, there was a dearth of definite news from the eastern theater. She had learned that Greene's daring invasion of South Carolina had ended in defeat at Hobkirk's Hill just outside of Camden. As after Guilford Courthouse, junior officers were exultant. Now the war was *really* over. Cruger confided to Dorande that he did not share this view. Greene, as before, had abandoned the field, but his army was intact and Rawdon's losses had been staggering.

Then the Tory set her heart beating faster with news which he considered more important than the action at Hobkirk's. Marion and Lee were loose again, had captured Fort Watson on the north bank of the Santee with little or no loss.

Cruger had been ungrudging in his praise of the operation. One of Lee's officers, to offset the lack of artillery, had built a log tower higher than Watson's stockade and filled it with riflemen whose muzzles covered every inch of the enclosure. The post surrendered.

Dorande's mind automatically noted all these details, but her ears hummed with the news that the Legion was along the Santee with Marion. Ross Pembroke would be riding with one body or the other. But what did it matter? Lee and Marion struck swiftly, then melted away—always. At that very moment, both commands might be on the Pee Dee. And, too, the seas might be cleared before she heard of them again and what difference would it make to a girl bound for St. Eusebius?

There had been a brief but rather disturbing interlude at Ninety-six. Just before the carriage had started east, a ragged troop of Tory cavalry had ridden in under a British officer who reined in to stare at her. There was no mistaking the hard eyes and foxlike mouth of Captain Bayne. He had not spoken to her or to St. Aubin, but had dismounted a few yards away where he eyed Dorande coolly, an unpleasant smile twisting his lips. When the carriage finally started, Dorande had glanced back to see Bayne, still motionless and smiling.

Now, in the late afternoon, Dorande smothered a yawn and looked out of the window. The Congaree rolled peacefully along, as meaningless as the eternal spill of sand from the slow-turning wheels. At last the carriage headed up the steep western drive and halted by the porch. St. Aubin handed Dorande onto the steps, excused himself and vanished into his office. Dorande called to the coachman to have a stable boy saddle her tacky and bring it to the steps. Then she flew upstairs, bathed hastily and changed into a riding habit. Janet was staying with Mrs. Motte and the pair would have a bulging pack of new for her. They might even know about the Legion and Marion's men. She could also verify Janet's beacon map by what she herself had seen to the west.

The last button fastened, she gave a quick pat to her hair, then touched the meshlike ring where the white strands were woven and ran down to the porch where her horse waited. She mounted and set off at a brisk canter along the river road that drowsed in the warm sun. The ride was short and she urged her tacky to a faster gait up the last slope that lay between her and the Motte farmhouse. She topped the crest, then reined in suddenly, a hand to her cheek and her eyes wide. In the distance lay the new house in its stockade. Fresh trenches had been dug and she thought she could make out men moving in them. High over the roof floated the Royal colors. But the farmhouse! There must have been twenty or thirty horses about it, held by men in green jackets and crested helmets. Tories!

Uncertainly she turned her horse, wondering if the path of wisdom led back to Mon Plaisir. At least, she would watch for a moment. If Mrs. Motte and Janet seemed in trouble, she could send Tobias to—to whom? The men who might be called on to rouse the local Whigs were surely helpless under this hostile influx. Just the same—

There was a stir about the door of the farmhouse. She saw the horse holders straighten up, look expectantly toward the door. Then she saw Mrs. Motte step out, followed by Janet. Behind them she thought she saw more green, the glint of steel. Her friends were under arrest!

A rather stout helmeted man in green with his spotless white breeches and shiny boots was laughing as he beckoned to someone indoors. Dorande caught her breath as a frail man limped out into the sunlight that fell dead on his dull cap. The little brigadier.

Her breath went out in a glad cry and she gathered her reins. With the first step of her horse the final shoulder of the hill fell away, showing the long sweep to the trenches and the stockade. Off to the left, a small brass field piece slammed in a gush of smoke and flame. She saw the stockade quiver, saw the light ball bounce harmlessly from it. Left and right, infantrymen in green moved forward, dropped into the nearest trenches, began a leisurely fire that seemed directed at the loopholes of the fort. Beyond them, toward the river, lean men in homespun, in buckskin, the men of Snow Island, were leading horses to water, glancing back over their shoulders at the answering spurts of smoke from the fort.

She did not remember using her spur, but all at once the horse was galloping toward the farmhouse. White-crested helmets turned toward her, men shouted and waved. In an instant she was on the ground, Mrs. Motte's arms about her, Janet's. It was hard to talk. Dorande could only say over and over, "Ah, mes amies, mes amies!"

Then, as she recovered her breath, she burst out, "What is all this? Green coats! I feared for you when I saw them."

Mrs. Motte tucked a wisp of curl behind Dorande's ear. "Bless you, child, we're all right. Janet and I are besieging a castle and I must say that's something I never expected to do."

Dorande caught her hand. "Where is he?" The end of the question trailed off as though in fear of the answer.

Janet put her arm about her. "Don't ask me. He's apt to be anywhere. He's tried to stop the water supply of the fort. He's tried to build a tower like the one they used at Fort Watson. I don't know just where he is now, but you'll see him soon enough."

Mrs. Motte said, "Hmph! He's probably gone upstream to try to talk a colony of beavers into coming down here and gnawing away the stockade."

Dorande heard a halting step behind her, turned to find Francis Marion holding out his hand. His dark face softened in a rare smile. "I thank you for disregarding my advice at Snow Island about not concerning yourself with our war. Mrs. Jaudon has told me of all the information you've passed on to her. Also about familiarizing yourself with our beacons."

Dorande colored. "But what I do is nothing. Many others have—"

"Maybe. But they're all natives. In your case—" He broke off as a stout, handsome man with colonel's epaulettes came up. Marion bowed to Dorande. "May I present Colonel Henry Lee of Virginia? Lee, this is the young lady I've mentioned."

Lee bowed over her hand, his glossy helmet tucked under his arm. "Now I *am* honored. Indeed, I've heard of you, not only from the general, but from young Pembroke. You've done a lot to smooth out a very rough road for all of us."

Dorande colored again. "But, Monsieur, I only—all these others—"

Lee smiled and Dorande liked the warmth of that smile, the eyes that were gay and yet somehow gravely steady. "So you want to pass all glory on to the others? Does you honor, I'm sure, but we'll see that you have your share—and it's a big share."

The field piece thudded again and Lee and Marion whirled to watch the flight of the shot, saw it once more bounce harmlessly from the heavy stockade. "Confound it, Marion, that's as tough to crack as a green hickory nut."

"Yes," said Marion, his face impassive again.

"What happened to that coehorn that Pembroke tried to make out of a log? What we need is something to flip shots over the walls and into the interior. By Jove, McPherson would have to surrender then."

"Blew up," said Marion.

Dorande stepped away, looking for Janet and Mrs. Motte. A slim dark officer, tattered silk showing on the facings of his green coat, was bowing before her. "Mademoiselle van Korte-naer? Permit me." His rippling French brought a flush of pleasure to Dorande's cheeks. "Philippe-Georges de la Picon-nerie de Chanzy. At the service of Mademoiselle."

"Mais vous me connaissez, donc?"

"And why not, since fortune permits me to count Ross Pembroke among my friends. He has spoken of you, not a great deal, since, being of the North, he is given to reticence. But enough so that I recognize you at once."

"You know where he is, Monsieur de Chanzy?"

De Chanzy shrugged. "Who may say? It may be that, off in the swamps, he invents engines of war that will turn the walls of Motte into the walls of Jericho. Ah, he is resourceful, that one. Our Greene and our Lee and our Marion esteem him."

He talked on about Ross while Dorande listened happily. Not only was the news of Ross welcome, but it was a deep pleasure to hear French spoken again by someone other than her uncle. She recognized other faces moving about the slope, eyes turned toward Fort Motte. There were the sad-faced Peter Horry and his handsome brother whom she remembered from Snow Island. A James or two, the elder Postell.

Her glance strayed away to the northeast. The sun had dropped below the horizon but a last glow lingered on the crests of the High Hills of Santee, distant but clear. Suddenly she stopped de Chanzy in the middle of a sentence, her whole attention riveted on the far horizon. Was it a trick of the sun? Had a last ray caught some unbroken window hidden off there among the trees?

De Chanzy murmured, *"Mais quoi, donc?"* in polite surprise. Oblivious of him, Dorande still stared at the high lands that lay to the east of the Wateree. Then she ran over the grass where Lee and Marion frowned at the stubborn fort. Without apology for interrupting, she pointed. "Look!"

There had been no illusion. Pale in the lingering daylight, fire flared in the High Hills of Santee, glowed in their northern reaches. Another spot shut up south of the first; a third, south again. Dorande cried, "The beacons!"

The two officers stared with her. Lee exclaimed, "The devil! What does *that* mean?"

"Two things," snapped Marion. "Rawdon's given up Camden. He's coming to the relief of Fort Motte."

It was incredible, thought Dorande. Why should Rawdon give up that cherished base where, by all accounts, he had beaten Greene? Then she remembered that Cornwallis, too, had beaten Greene, a "victory" that had swept the British commander clear out of the Carolinas. Now another dubious triumph must have crumpled the extreme north bastion of the British holdings.

Lee, studying the blazes through a glass, muttered, "Wish he'd waited a little. We can't fight him off and still take Motte."

"No," said Marion.

Lee flushed angrily. "Nothing to it that I can see but to lift the siege. Maybe the two of us can make trouble in Rawdon's rear. Time's short. If there were just some way of getting at the house itself!"

Others had seen the beacons. Mrs. Motte came running out, calling to Lee and Marion, just in time to hear the last sentence. She sighed, looked at her new roof showing over the stockade. Then she nodded as though to herself. "General Marion, if it's a question of setting fire to the house or smashing it up, you go right ahead."

Lee frowned. "Oh—but—really—your house, Mrs. Motte."

"House? Pah! A few boards and shingles and nails. What do they matter?"

Marion inclined his head gravely. "Thank you," he said. "But it's too much."

Mrs. Motte snorted. "Too much? What's your house down in St. John's parish like these days? No. That's mine, and I can say what's going to happen to it. Burn it, blow it up, knock it down with stones. I'll help. No sentimental nonsense now."

Lee studied the stockade and the house behind it. The Royal colors still flew bravely above it, but no return fire came from the loopholes. The garrison was probably watching, conserving its ammunition. Lee sighed. "Burning's quickest," he said regretfully. "Only, will McPherson be obliging enough to admit a burning party inside the stockade? I don't see how we're going to do it. Confound it, Marion, I'm afraid we'd better fall in our men and strike for the swamps."

Dorande stood between Marion and Lee, gently pinching her chin in deep thought. All at once she cried, "Voilà!" turned and raced into the house.

Lee raised his eyebrows. "What's this? Is she going to call on McPherson and ask his permission to set fire to things?"

Mrs. Motte pursed her lips. "You don't know that young lady. She's quite capable of talking McPherson into setting the fire himself. Here she comes, out of the farmhouse. Gracious stars, child, what on earth have you got there?"

Dorande, eyes snapping, held out the sheaf of East Indian fire arrows to Marion. "Messengers to send to Monsieur Mc-

Pherson." She drew a long bow from under her arm. "And this, to send the messengers."

Marion touched the blunt tips, nodding in comprehension. "Barb inside. Outside burns."

Lee balanced the bow in his hands. "That's all very fine, but what are we going to do? Climb the stockade and chuck them across to the roof? I doubt if there's a man in the eastern colonies who knows how to use one of those blasted things."

Marion called, "Peter! Get him!"

Horry vanished, reappeared with a gaunt buckskinned man gliding along beside him. Marion thrust the bow and the arrows at the newcomer, who tested the bowstring with expert fingers. "What do you want me to do with this?" he asked.

"Tell him, Peter," said Marion.

All that day, Ross had been ranging the far bank of the Congaree with Gavin James. Rumor had it that back in the days of the Yemassee War, a field piece had been abandoned in a nearby swamp. Chances of finding it were not bright, Ross thought, and the gun carriage would have rotted into uselessness long ago. But if they could find the barrel, drag it to the slope before Fort Motte and cut a slanting rest for it, he was sure that, with a light powder charge, at least a few cannon balls could be lobbed over the walls of the fort into the enclosure. The ground was hard-packed, he knew, and the balls would ricochet viciously in that small space, thus creating enough of a diversion to allow a storming party of Legion infantry an excellent chance of success.

By sundown both men were sweat-soaked, layered with mud from head to foot, and empty-handed. Gavin James said dispiritedly, "Might as well give up."

"Damn giving up," said Ross. "There are four or five swamp holes toward the Wateree that we haven't touched."

"Getting dark," said Gavin James. "If you want to play Follow-my-leader with those fellows, go ahead. I'll wait till it's light." He pointed to a pool where three alligator heads showed, their eyes blinking slowly.

Ross groaned. "All right. But we start at dawn tomorrow. I tell you, Gavin, just four little cricket-ball lobs over the stockade and McPherson will come running out as though he was chasing a haggis." He looked about the clearing that was completely hemmed in by trees and undergrowth. "Where the devil are we? Where's south from here?"

Gavin James pointed. "That's east there. I marked it when

we came through those trees. I could see the High Hills of Santee."

Ross grumbled, "Can't even see an anthill from here. Take the lead. I've never seen you lose direction yet. And remember where we've been so we can come here tomorrow. Hell and glory! The cavalry's done nothing in this siege. We've got to justify our existence somehow or Lee'll make us eat our horses and carry a musket with the Legion infantry."

They wound on through swamp and clearing, James setting an unwavering course. Flies and mosquitoes buzzed and hummed through the dusk whose silence was broken every now and then by a dull slam from Lee's single gun, far off on the other side of the Congaree.

They emerged at last on the north bank, far higher up than Ross had imagined. Owing to the contours of the land, he could not see the Motte farmhouse, but the fort showed clear in the dying light. "God damn it," snapped James. "They're still holding out. I can see the British flag."

"What I expected," said Ross. "We've just got to find that gun and turn it into a howitzer. Singleton's little grasshopper can't get enough elevation to drop shots inside. And—what the devil—"

From hidden ground on the right, a bright trailing spark arched high toward the fort, sailed well over the stockade and lit on the roof in a quick spurt of fire. Ross slapped his knee. "Old Indian tricks. You know, Gavin, I'd have thought of that myself, if I'd been brighter."

"So would I and the rest of the army. Hi! There's another. Look! Hit ten feet beyond the first. Another. It's spreading. Three separate fires up there."

Ross turned his palms up. "All over. They can't—oh, hell!" From unseen ladders, men of the garrison swarmed onto the roof, began ripping at shingles. He sighed. "It was a good idea, but not good enough. Those boys are out of even rifle range and—" The slam of Singleton's gun sounded as a fourth arrow sailed high. Almost in a single-pulse beat, three things happened. Wood flew from the near gable as a cannon ball slammed into the loft. The men slid for their ladders. A white flag shot up.

Gavin James yelled, "That's done it! Down come the King's colors. Come on. Let's see the end of it. Our horses are upstream a bit!"

Darkness was falling fast as they negotiated a deep ford well above Fort Motte. When they finally scrambled to the river road, the night was so thick that they did not dare move faster than a brisk walk.

"Damn this blackness," fumed Ross. "If I know anything about Marion or Lee, they're mighty apt to be starting right now for a crack at Nelson's or Orangeburg. Would you be able to pick up their trace, Gavin?"

"Wouldn't want to bet on it if Marion sets the pace. Guess we've got time enough, though. It'll take a while to parole the prisoners and that sort of thing. Great day! Things did happen fast, once they started. A pity, though, that Mrs. Motte had to lose her house."

When they finally reached the farmhouse, its windows were dark, but helmeted men in white jackets held torches high about the door. Ross stared at them, blinking in the sudden light. "Look, Gavin! What the devil. Washington's dragoons!"

"Do you mean Lee and Marion have gone? Ask one of those white-jackets."

"No need. See the Legion dragoons, over there by the third torch." He stood in his stirrups, peering at the distant lights from the stockade and the new house. The sallyport yawned wide and men with lanterns shuttled in and out. "There's where we'll find out something. By God, they managed to save the house, somehow."

They made their way cautiously across the rough mile between farm and mansion. At the sallyport, old Sergeant Kuhn was in charge, informing Ross that the "chentlemens *vos bei der Haus, Ja.*"

"See to the horses, please, Sergeant," said Ross, dismounting.

Mrs. Motte must have moved down to the mansion immediately after the surrender. He must find her at once, as it was quite possible that she would have news of Dorande—she or Janet. He was about to spring up the broad steps when Gavin James checked him, whispering, "Who in the name of God is that? Look! Through the window to your left."

At the head of the table sat Mrs. Motte, apparently presiding over a banquet such as he had rarely imagined in his hungriest dreams. At her left, pale but composed, sat a young British officer. The chair at her right was pushed back and a big, heavy-shouldered man in Continental blue and white stood in front of it, a glass in his hand. There was no mistaking him, no mistaking that Grecian nose, those jutting brows or the firm mouth that turned up at the corners.

Ross gasped, "That's the reason for the dragoons, but *how* did he get here?"

Through the open window, Nathanael Greene's deep, steady voice rolled clearly: "—and I know our late foes and present guests will not think that I am gloating when I tell you others that Lord Rawdon *has* abandoned Camden—" a cheer started, was checked by a gesture from Greene "—I may further tell you that he will *not* come near Fort Motte. The instant I saw what had happened, on my arrival, I sent a Tory prisoner, whom my escort had picked up on the road, to inform his lordship that the fort was ours. I further stated that its late commander had done all that a soldier could be expected to do." There were more cheers, which Greene encouraged. A friendly hand reached out, patted the pale McPherson's shoulder. Greene went on, "I was asked to propose a toast. I could not possibly improve on the tribute that Colonel Lee paid to our hostesses. Nor on Colonel Horry's words about General Marion and Colonel Lee. I raise my glass, gentlemen, a soldier who fought us cleanly and manfully, skillfully and humanely. Lieutenant McPherson!"

There was a storm of cheering. Still pale, McPherson got to his feet. His Scotch voice came out slowly, almost painfully. "There's little a beaten man can say. But I'm proud to drink to a general who dares lose a battle to win a campaign, and to the army that stands by him in bright times and black. Will the gentlemen who wear the King's colors rise with me—"

A fresh burst of applause drowned out the rest of his words, died away. On its echoes, a low, rippling laugh sailed out into the night. Ross started. "My God!" he muttered and moved to the right, craning his neck.

There, at the left of Colonel Lee, was Dorande, her dark eyes alight and her color high as she listened to something that de Chanzy was saying to her under cover of the general buzz of voices. Ross could just detect the running lilt of French. She laughed again and her voice came clear to him. His very few words of French were not enough to give him the meaning of what she said, but he was sure that she was replying to some compliment and her reply obviously delighted de Chanzy, who bowed, laughed and raised his glass.

"God's teeth," muttered Ross. "Maybe I was right the first time. 'Pert, railing fribble.' No. That's *not* right. Phil's as fine as they make them. Just the same, what the devil does Dorande find so amusing in what he says? Honestly, Phil hasn't a real sense of humor."

Their laughter died softly away, rose again. De Chanzy seemed to be telling Dorande a story against the noise from the rest of the table. Dark head and blond drew closer and closer, de Chanzy's face animated and Dorande's bright with a anticipatory smile. Ross's irritation grew and he felt a strong desire to bump those two contrasting heads together.

He made a quick gesture. "Come on. I'm going in," he said.

"Hold up!" cried Gavin James. "With all this swamp muck on us?"

"Yes. And a water moccasin in each pocket," snapped Ross, heading for the steps.

As he entered the dining room, a roar of laughter greeted him. He stopped angrily, thinking for an instant that he was the cause of it, then saw that people up and down the table had caught the end of de Chanzy's story, were whooping and wiping their eyes. Then a chair scraped, another. Heedless of surprised glances, Dorande, vivid in a green riding habit, hurried toward Ross, de Chany close behind her.

Ross could only stare at her while she exclaimed, "*Ah, le pauvre!* Ross Pembroke, what do you do to yourself? So pale! So thin!"

De Chanzy broke in, "I tell Mademoiselle, 'Do not worry. I know our Ross Pembroke, who will soon appear.' "

"Why didn't someone tell me about all this?" asked Ross unreasonably, indicating the table. "It's just luck that I got here at all."

Dorande laid a hand on his cuff. "But you *are* here. Now you must pay your respects to Madame Motte and to General Geeene. We have a chair for you, Monsieur de Chanzy and I."

Ross grudgingly made his way along the table, bowing to Janet, acknowledging waves from Lee and Marion. At the head of the table, Mrs. Motte dismissed him with a smile. "So glad you got here. Now run along and take that chair that Dorande's keeping for you."

"Yes," thought Ross. "She *and* Monsieur de Chanzy are keeping it for me. Hope Greene's as obliging us Mrs. Motte."

But the old ironmaster had news for him. The Pembroke family had gone to Boston in '79, according to a letter from the general's brother, and hence Ross's long communications to his father and his sisters had been forwarded from Providence. Their reply would probably come in later. Brown College had managed pretty well to keep its doors open through the war. One of the Butler girls had married an officer of the Soissonais regiment and Philemon Beamish, a town character, had been accidentally locked up by the hog reeve.

Ross tried to hide his impatience. Damn Philemon Beamish and as for the Butler girl, it would be a fine idea if *all* French

officers were compelled by law to marry Rhode island girls—
and no others. He glanced down the table. Dorande and de
Chanzy were laughing again. Hell and death! What chance
would he have to talk to Dorande with Phil chattering away
like an Isle of Pines parrot! He cursed himself for his idiotic
pique at de Chanzy. The Frenchman had obviously been delighted at his return. Gladder, he thought glumly, than
Dorande.

Greene finally released him and he hurried down the
table where de Chanzy bounced up, pulling out a chair for
him. "Ah, *mon cher* Ross. Just now I relate to Mademoiselle—"

From across the room, Lee's voice sounded genially. "Sorry,
de Chanzy. Rounds, I think."

De Chanzy sighed, bounced up again, his saber clattering.
"Misfortune and again misfortune! I am of the guard, you
conceive." He bowed over Dorande's hand, loosing a torrent
of French. Dorande, her eyes dancing, replied at length while
Ross fidgeted.

When de Chanzy had gone, Dorande turned her dark eyes
on Ross. "But I find myself stupid. I forget that you do not
speak French. That was a door which I did not mean to close
on you. You know, Ross Pembroke, you have a good friend
there."

"Phil's fine," said Ross. "Like him a lot. Now I want to hear
where you've been. I tried to find you even before we took
Fort Watson, then I heard you and your uncle were traveling."

"But not so far. Monsieur de Chanzy, only a moment ago,
tells me how you and he—"

Ross laughed impatiently. "I know all about Phil and me.
Not to be abrupt, but I'd much rather talk about *you* and
me."

Dorande dropped her eyes, her long lashes black against
her skin. "I do not find myself absorbing, Ross Pembroke."

Ross frowned, then gave a quick nod. "All right. Shall
we talk about me?"

"I find *that* better. What you have done and—"

Ross smiled to himself. "Well, here's one thing I did. Please
don't think I'm conceited, but I'm pretty proud of it."

Her eyes turned to him. "And that is?"

Ross flicked open the lid of his cartridge box, drew out a
small packet and handed it to her. "Spread it out. It's just
folded."

Dorande's slim fingers unwrapped the oiled silk, then

opened the gauze-mounted sheet. The old Quaker's quaintly faithful sketch lay before her. She colored and her lips parted in surprise. "But this—I do not understand—Yes, I send it to you, being safer than a letter, to tell you I arrive at the Santee. And—and all the time you keep it?"

"Not only did I keep it, I did the mounting myself."

"But why?" Her eyes were still on the sheet.

Ross edged a little closer. "Because, it had begun to tear."

"And again, why?"

"Oh, it was just one day when I didn't have anything else to do."

She turned toward him, startled and a little indignant.

Ross laughed. "You know very well why I kept it, Dorande. You see—I'm talking about myself the way you asked. For the same reason that I named my horse Mon Plaisir de la Congaree. I don't know much French, but enough to translate that two ways. First, it reminds me of the last place where I saw you. Second, it is *mon plaisir* to think of that meeting on the Congaree."

Dorande had lowered her head again and her hands were folded in her lap. Oblivious of the mounting buzz of voices about the table, Ross said quietly, "Do you think of that, too?"

He could barely hear her reply. "Yes. And I was unhappy when I could learn nothing after the fighting in the north." Her hands appeared on the table, lay gently on the fading sketch. "I—I find it moving that you kept this—that you preserved it—on a day when you had nothing else to do."

"And you remember how I carried you off on my saddlebow while you called for help? Your arms were very tight about my neck and when you struggled, your cheek brushed mine."

Eyes still downcast, Dorande whispered, "It was necessary that we act, I think."

Ross leaned forward. "What if I told you that I wasn't acting? That I didn't really *have* to hold you as tightly as I did? You see, I'm still talking about myself. What would you say about me—if I told you all that?"

"Perhaps—perhaps—I would have to talk about myself, Ross Pembroke."

"And if you did, what would you say?"

"I would say—I think I would say—"

There was a sudden clatter of chairs. Mrs. Motte and Janet had risen and the former was making her way toward Dorande with her hands out. "Come along, my dear. We've broken all convention by sitting with the gentlemen this long. General Greene's giving us an escort to the framhouse. This place isn't fit to sleep in yet."

There was nothing to do save to rise politely, to draw back Dorande's chair for her. His sinking feeling was only a little eased as he noted that the corners of her mouth drooped. Then she turned to the table, picked up a flattened bullet with which her left-hand neighbor had been toying and bent over the sketch, writing rapidly. She handed the paper quickly to Ross, smiled and was swept away by Mrs. Motte and Janet.

Ross sat down when they had gone, tingling with disappointment and elation. He looked at the sketch and his spirits gave a leap. Dorande had written on the edge, "*Au capitaine noir*—Dorande—who did not entirely act—perhaps." Ross carefully folded the sketch and tucked it away. Then he sighed. It was likely that Greene, who had left with Marion and Lee after Mrs. Motte and the girls, would want to spend at least another day conferring with his lieutenants. Another twenty-four hours that might give him more time with Dorande. Confound it, why couldn't *he* speak French? Of course, it was quite natural that Dorande found pleasure in de Chanzy's company, listening to her mother tongue. Of course. Anyway, Phil was a fine fellow. Any girl would like him, even if, as in this case, his French gave him an advantage that was downright unfair. What sort of a place was Brown College anyway? Why hadn't he been taught French? He thought of class after class that had been graduated since its founding, ignorant of the most useful language in the world.

A chair scraped beside him and Eggleston pushed a brandy bottle and a glass to him. On the other side, the Frenchman O'Neal was pouring himself a drink. Spurred by the fine brandy, Ross threw himself into the conversation that now ran unchecked by the presence of ladies, superior officers and the prisoners, the latter, under McPherson, having already been started off under parole to join Lord Rawdon down the Santee.

Then the brandy began to lose its fight against the stores of long-accumulated fatigue. There was no lift in it, and its bouquet turned to a salty flatness. God Almighty, but he was tired. He looked along the table. Three or four officers were noisily drunk, but the rest, like himself, drank mechanically with no visible effect. He filled his small glass for the third time, hoping that the alcohol would at least enable him to sleep. He talked mechanically with O'Neal and Eggleston, who answered in kind.

There were voices in the room beyond, where some of the officers had withdrawn. Peter Horry and Hugh were there, Armstrong and Michael and John Rudulph of the Legion, with many others whose tones he could not distinguish. He drank again, was vaguely cheered by feeling his eyelids grow heavier. The voices in the next room turned to a concerted rumpus, mellowed, leveled out into full-throated song. Ross looked up in surprise. Several of those people out there could really sing. The song turned into a melodious chant, grew louder as a strange procession came slowly into the room, led by Peter Horry, who looked sad as a professional mourner. The other singers trailed after him, each holding up a long, lighted candle. Round the table they went, the words rolling out with a fine resonance:

> From noise of Scare-fires rest ye free,
> From murders, Benedicite.
> From all mischances that may fright
> Your peaceful slumbers in the night,
> Mercy secure ye all, and keep
> The Goblin from ye while ye sleep.
> PAST ONE O'CLOCK—and almost two.
> My masters all, Good day to you!

They repeated the last two lines as Peter Horry passed Ross. Ross grinned at him and Horry, almost between notes, bent closer to say, "Get the boys going. We're leaving. Right away."

Ross sprang from his chair. "No!"

"Yes," said Peter Horry, tears dripping from his voice. Then he was gone, the other singers trailing after him, extinguishing their candles as they reached the door.

Ross turned wearily from the table. There was no need to say anything. Horry must have been giving the order as he passed each man. Men who had been previously drunk seemed suddenly sober, rose steadily enough, adjusting helmets or equipment. At the door, Ross found Bill Lovell, the Legion adjutant, who hailed him. "Joint detail—Legion and Marion. Loading up captured carts with supplies. McPherson had oats and flour stored in the sheds by the old farmhouse. Three wagons waiting up there. Take charge of the loading and keep things moving. Marion wants the whole command on the road before daylight and we can't move till the supplies have gone."

"All right," said Ross resignedly. "Know where they're going? The wagons, I mean."

"To the main army, Camden way, I guess. That's not our worry. Load 'em and forget 'em."

The farmhouse was dark and silent as Ross dismounted by the first wagon. A detail of Legion infantry stood sullenly by a rough shed where whitish sacks showed through the gloom. Ross caught a mutter, "Dig trenches all night, get shot at all day, then, by Jesus, load carts all night and march all day."

Another, obviously a British deserter, grumbled, "It ain't the bloody work and it ain't the bloody officers, it's bein' bloody well bloodied about all the bloody time that bloody well bloodies me!"

It was hard to blame the men, for whose surliness Ross had prepared himself. He called as cheerily as he could, "Who's in charge? Sergeant Roche? Here's a bottle of rum. Swallow a charge and pass it around. Then we'll get to work. There'll be another tot all around as each cart's loaded. That's better. Now get going."

The men stepped more briskly, but it was slow, heavy work. The big flour casks were awkward to handle, slipped and shifted in weary arms. Ross sprang onto the cart, helped a sweating corporal to stow them securely. At last the first cart was loaded. It bowled off toward the river and another rumbled into its place. Ross, wiping his forehead, glanced up at the darkened windows, wondering which stretch of wall and roof sheltered Dorande. She and Janet and Mrs. Motte were probably all soundly asleep and were not likely to be roused since the detail was too exhausted to make much noise. He sprang into the second cart, hauling at the sacks as they were passed from below. As the heap rose, he saw that a second-story window was almost level with his eyes as he stood on the final topmost layer. It was at the back of the house and was probably occupied by some favored maid.

The sacks mounted in the last cart. Ross straightened up from a particularly heavy tug and then staggered back against the seat. The window had been raised and he could make out a dim blur of a face, a pair of small hands on the sill. A soft voice said, "Ross Pembroke!"

He recovered himself, felt the final sack push against his ankles. "Dorande!"

A finger lifted and Ross guessed that she was kneeling on the floor, her chin at sill level. "*Chut!* They sleep, the others. You did not shave today, Ross Pembroke!"

The detail had left the cart and were grouped about the sergeant, who was handing out the rum. Ross put a hand toward the sill, but the cart was too far away. "How would *you* like it if the next time I abduct you, I made it in earnest? You better think about that, because that's just what I'm going to do."

There was a gasp in the dark, as Dorande rose in an involuntary movement that gave more than a hint of very thin silk, bare white shoulders and white arms. She vanished with a squeak of dismay, then reappeared more discreetly. Her face came closer as though she were cautiously leaning forward. Her voice was low and rich. "Ross Pembroke, *je l'accueille de tout mon coeur, de tout mon coeur!*"

"No!" cried Ross. "You can't get off that easy. In English! Say it in—"

A whip cracked, the horses lunged forward, broke into a sharp trot, into a clumsy gallop, and Ross rolled among the neatly stacked bags. Clutching at the seat, which the driver had deserted to run by the horses' heads, he shouted, "Halt! Hell blast it, halt!" The rumble of the wheels drowned his words, and the horses plunged on down the slanting road that led to the river. He was tossed this way and that, banged his head against the sideboard, fought his way to his feet, sprawled again as the wagon rocked over a hidden hollow.

The horses slowed down a hundred yards along the river road and Ross, gasping for breath, swung over the side of the wagon, ready to vent his wrath on the driver. He found a hopeless tangle in the dark where sleep-sodden men flashed lanterns in a futile effort to straighten things out. Ross located the key of the tangle quickly, but some fifteen minutes were lost before the wagons rolled on once more.

Rubbing his sides and swearing heartily, he trudged up the long slope that led to the farmhouse. When the walls loomed in the night ahead of him, he saw no movement save the toss of Ree's head as she fretted at her halter. The detail had gone, probably to join the men who were falling in off by the sallyport of Fort Motte. All the windows of the farmhouse were closed and dark. He called softly, "Dorande!" but no voice answered, no glass was lifted. Resignedly he mounted Ree and rode off to join the formation by the fort. What in the devil's name had Dorande *said?* Was there any way of solving the riddle? He closed his eyes, trying to recapture the sounds. He could recall swift, liquid sounds, then at the end something that sounded like *"de too mo cur."* Could that be right? It sounded like French to him, but were those the words? He snapped his fingers. He would reproduce the sounds as best he could to de Chanzy and see if they suggested any meaning to him. De Chanzy? Of course, Phil de Chanzy was one of his best friends, but he remembered the two heads, one dark, the other very fair, bending close at the table.

A horseman trotted up beside him and he recognized the Frenchman with the improbable name of O'Neal. He called to him, "O'Neal! Ferd O'Neal! Listen—does this sound like anything to you?" He formed the words as best he could.

"Perhaps," said O'Neal. "If I heard it once more—" Ross repeated. "Ah—*ça!*" said O'Neal. "I do not quite—but yes, it could be '*de tout mon coeur*'—that is what you wish to know?"

"No!" shouted Ross. "Only part of it. What does it mean?"

O'Neal shrugged. "But many things, my friend. For example, Milord Cornwallis is rash enough to offer me a colonelcy in his army. Then—for my part, I refuse—*de tout mon coeur*, that is, *utterly*."

Ross slumped in the saddle as he rode away. Then he remembered there had been more than just those words. But the easy liquidity of the first phrase eluded him completely. "It might have meant—it could have been—" he reasoned. "Oh, damn and blast and hell! *Why* didn't I learn French?" He rode on, his opinion of the curriculum and faculty of Brown College sinking with each hoofbeat.

XI • The Western Beacon

Paul de St. Aubin walked slowly up the drive of Mon Plaisir through the June heat. At his heels a Negro boy trotted carrying a light fowling piece and a game bag. The master was frowning and yet a faint smile played about the corners of his clean-shaven lips. Affairs were growing more and more puzzling, but at least he had had a good day at the new sport which he had just discovered.

He mounted the steps and glanced down the porch where Dorande was reading aloud to Janet, making a running translation of Rousseau's *La Nouvelle Héloïse*. She laid down the book as she saw her uncle, who came forward bowing. "Ah— Madame—Mademoiselle. My new sport, it went to a marvel! Our neighbor, Colonel Cox, himself spoke of my proficiency. Permit me to lay before you jewels such as you have never seen!" He called sharply to the boy, *"Le gibier, 'cré nom de dieu!"* The boy winced and handed him the game bag.

St. Aubin opened it and poured out a little heap of glowing feathers—ruby red, metallic green, soft brown. Janet cried, "Oh, the poor little hummingbirds! I've found them, too, sometimes. If they're disturbed at night, they get frightened and fly against lighted windows. It always kills them."

St. Aubin crooked a little finger delicately. "You do not comprehend, Madame Jaudon. Of course, one may not *shoot* them. That leaps to the eye since they are so small that the finest shot would tear them to pieces. But my slave, Rex, a clever one, learned to fashion tiny bladders of oiled silk. These he fills with water and seals. Then I load them in this piece with a very light powder charge. I see a hummingbird—" he raised his arms as though holding a gun—"and—*pan!*—another bird—*pan!* The bladder kills them without damaging the feathers." He paused, reflecting. "It could be that a market for these could be created in Charleston. Ah! *Par exemple!* There is one who was only stunned." He picked up a pathetic scrap

231

of bright feathers, holding the throat between his fingers until the faint flutters ceased entirely.

Dorande, pale and angry, got up. "I must go upstairs!" she said huskily, and vanished into the house, Janet beside her.

St. Aubin shrugged. There was no telling what would please women. He had taken the pains to show them the gaudy spoils of his day afield and they turned pale and fled. Women, he decided, were too tender to look dispassionately at death. They had no conception of sport. He made his way to his office, the half-smile now completely replaced by the frown.

Stepping to the wall, he stripped the curtain from the map and his frown deepened. Since the American Greene's seemingly crushing defeat at Hobkirk's Hill north of Camden in late April, St. Aubin had been forced, to his ever-growing amazement, to draw the blue circles indicating American occupation about post after post. There had been Camden, Fort Watson, Fort Motte, Fort Granby, then Nelson's Ferry and Orangeburg. Now with a sigh he let his eye run far south down the map to Forts Galphin and Cornwallis on the Georgia border. News of the double capture by Lee's men had come in late May, but only this day had he had actual confirmation. Reluctantly he drew blue circles about the two strongholds. Galphin was particularly annoying since for years that had been the spot where presents to the western Indians had been distributed. Twice he himself had profited heavily in that traffic.

There were other annoying reports. The Tory commander, Browne, having some Rebel prisoners, had hanged them, then cut them down before they were dead and turned the still-living victims over to a gang of drunken Indians for the latter's own peculiar pleasures. That was bad enough, since such acts would inflame the Rebels still more. What was worse was that Browne's vengeance even extended to the captured horses, which he had penned in a barn and burned alive. Did not the fool know that the Crown was paying more and more for mounts of any kind?

His hand moved west, following a thick blue line that showed Greene's march west to Ninety-six which he was now besieging. From the south a thinner line swung north. Lee's Legion would make junction with Greene at Ninety-six, ready for fresh exploits after its incredibly swift march to Galphin on the Savannah. He started to mark an anticipatory circle about Ninety-six, then checked himself. "Too soon," he muttered. "Milord Rawdon marches to the relief of Ninety-six, they say. What will happen then? Will he once more beat Greene—and give up the post?"

The problem was an interesting one. Greene's army shrank and shrank, fought and lost. Yet—it was certain that had not Cornwallis turned his own guns on British and American troops at Guilford Courthouse, he would have been swept away in a rout that could have cleared the whole South. At Hobkirk's Hill, some American infantry had been unimaginatively handled, Washington's dragoons had stopped too long in the British rear to take useless prisoners. But for these two accidents, Rawdon's whole force of Tories and seasoned regulars might—probably would—have been wiped out utterly.

Two British victories in the field—and to what result? Of all the state, only Georgetown, Charleston and Ninety-Six remained to them. He left the map, his frown deepening.

Upstairs in the middle of Dorande's bedroom stood two big trunks. Deborah, the personal slave whom St. Aubin had assigned to her, blinked as the sun of a hot June afternoon struck into her eye. She ducked her head and smoothed out a coral-pink dress in the bottom of the lighter trunk.

"Reckon you mighty happy you goin' to see yo' folks again, Miss Dorande," said Deborah.

Dorande turned from the east window that looked down the valley of the Congaree. "Such a happiness. It's been long —so long. Now the green dress. Oh, all this is so lucky."

As she held out the green silk to Deborah, she reflected that events had been as unexpected as lucky. Some movements of the fleets and of privateers had cleared the seas at least momentarily. A barque, flying the neutral Portuguese colors, was taking advantage of the lull and was clearing Charleston for Havana in a few days' time. St. Aubin had not only engaged passage for Dorande, but had gone on to Charleston to see about safe-conduct for her, an advisable step in view of her Dutch-French blood, both countries now being at war with Great Britain. From Havana, progress south would be quite simple, although there was a fair chance that her parents might meet her there in Cuba. She would leave Mon Plaisir with the next dawn, which would allow her to reach Charleston with a scant margin of time before sailing.

Her heart sang as she watched Deborah close the smaller trunk, which Tobias would cord skillfully with the other. She had no longer to think in terms of months. In a matter of weeks, rather, she would see her girlish, dark-haired mother holding out her arms to her, would be caught up like a doll by her big, blond Dutch father. Weeks, only!

Her throat suddenly contracted and she stepped to the

west window. The gold and green world of late afternoon swam before her eyes. Weeks? What would happen while that brief time crept past? Somewhere off there, among the tree-choked valleys of the west, Lee and his Legion pressed on to aid Greene at Ninety-six, and Ross Pembroke rode with the Virginian. Her lips trembled and she clutched the sill. By the next dawn, he would still be riding north while grinding wheels would carry her east, increasing the distance between him and the Portuguese barque waiting at the docks below Longitude Lane.

If only this chance had come during the siege of Fort Motte. At least she could have said good-by properly, could have found out if he really meant what he had said about riding off with her on his saddlebow. Why had he vanished so quickly that night? At one moment, she saw him quite clearly in the dark. Then he and the wagon were gone.

She bit her lip. Of course, that had been only gay banter, pleasant gallantry. What did she know of his life? He had ranged through many states and very likely left his heart in one of them. Would he have thought of her again if the tide of war had swept him north once more, into those strangely named areas where there must be many girls and of his own kind?

Now she would never know the answer. And what did it matter? Ross Pembroke was merely an incident in her time of waiting to rejoin her parents. Now that time was past and soon she would reach her original goal. *"Oh, ma mère! Que je suis heureuse,"* she murmured huskily. She caught up a handkerchief.

Tobias's heavy tread sounded in the hall outside. Dorande dabbed hastily at her eyes, gave a pat to her hair and turned as the slave entered, a coil of stout cord looped about his shoulder. "Boxes 'bout ready, Miss Dorande?" he asked.

She nodded without speaking, then turned away. One—two—the lids slammed and keys grated, each sound giving a fresh wrench to Dorande's heart. She beat her knuckles together. *"Que tu es bête!"* she thought fiercely. "It is this that you have wanted all along. Now it comes. You are happy! You must be!"

Behind her, Tobias and Deborah were muttering. Tobias's voice rose in complaint. "Then you go git it! I told you, fotch up that extra bit of light rope when you started. You done forgit it. Go git it."

Deborah went out, grumbling. When her footsteps had died away downstairs, Tobias called in a low tone, "Miss Dorande. Smoke beacons to the High Hills of Santee."

Dorande faced about quickly, heedless of the tears that hung bright on her cheeks. "Beacons? To the *east?*"

"Seen 'em myself." His voice dropped lower and he seemed absorbed in the contemplation of a knot. "Reckon that mean Mist' Lord Rawdon headin' west with his soldiers. Ain't only one place he'd head for, an' that's Ninety-six."

Dorande's lips tightened and for an instant she forgot the trunks and the sea chest. Tobias was right. Rawdon could have no other objectives in mind. From what she had been told and from what she had seen, she knew that Greene, even with the addition of the Legion, had just enough men to have a chance of success against Cruger and his trained New York and New Jersey Tories at Ninety-six. If Rawdon's force were added to Cruger's, Greene's men would be swept away, broken up far in the western wilderness, out of reach of reinforcements and supplies. And then—

Her eyes went back to her trunks again. By dawn, such matters would be of no concern to her as she bowled on toward Charleston and the docks. Besides, Greene's army would *not* be broken up. The beacons would warn him in time.

Tobias muttered, "I'm kind of worried."

"No need. Men will see the beacons in the High Hills of Santee. They will light the other beacons. By midnight, General Greene will learn of the danger and will prepare to meet it."

Tobias shook his head. "I ain't worryin', if all's lit, Miss Dorande. But say mebbe just *one* don't even blink, then how Mist' Greene goin' to know?"

"They will."

Tobias straightened up and rubbed his hands on his breeches. "You ain't heard 'bout the Jobey boys? An' ol' Mist' Twiss and Mist' Randall?"

Dorande felt her cheeks growing cold. Those four were responsible for the beacon between Twelve Mile Creek and the headwaters of Chinquapin Creek, the beacon on Little Wolftrap! If that were dark, the watchers in the west beyond Big Creek would have no warning. Rawdon's advance would roll on, bearing disaster with it.

She thought quickly, her entire mind on the broken western lands. There would be no way of summoning the watchers at the intervening posts between the High Hills and Little Wolf-trap. She knew that, seeing smoke or fire in the east, they would creep to their appointed pyres, light them and scatter beyond hope of anyone finding them in time. What then?

She glanced at Tobias, who waited quietly but obviously concerned. He knew of the beacons and their locations only by hearsay. But someone must light that missing link. Janet! Of course. Janet *must* go. Word could be sent down river to the new house in the stockade where she was looking after Mrs. Motte, laid low with troublesome but not serious fever.

She said briskly, "Tobias, you saddle and go to Mrs. Motte's. Tell Mrs. Jaudon that—" What could Tobias tell Janet? True, she had Raoul's map of the beacons, but she had never ridden through the country. What good would the map be to her in the dark? The country was very thinly settled. There would be few, if any, of whom she could ask the way.

Tobias said, "What you want I tell Mis' Jaudon?"

Dorande glanced out of the window. The sun was dropping fast, but there would be the long afterglow of the June twilight. She rose slowly. "Nothing. It is I who go to Madame Jaudon. Bring my horse to the porch, please." Tobias started toward the door. "*Un moment*," called Dorande. "She must leave quickly. I wish that deerskin bag packed with food and wine. She may not have time, *chez Madame Motte*."

When Deborah returned with the last of Tabias's cord, Dorande had changed into her riding habit. The maid stared. "Great day, Miss. Don' wonder you cry happy, thinkin' 'bout yo' folks. But you white like you seen a ghost."

Dorande shivered. "Ghosts? If I am white, it is because I do not wish there to be ghosts."

She went slowly down the stairs, one hand on the sleek rail, her eyes empty and hollow. By the porch, Tobias held the fairly respectable tacky that she sometimes rode. The deerskin bag bulged on the cantle. Dorande said mechanically, "Thank you, Tobias," and mounted.

Tobias, the bridle in his hands, looked curiously at her. "Sure ain't nothin' I kin do, Miss?"

"Very sure, Tobias. I—I return soon."

The slave let go of the reins and Dorande rode away down the drive. He watched her, eyes narrow and thick lips compressed. He hunched his shoulders and walked slowly off toward the stables.

Dorande kept to the road that slanted toward the river. Her head was bowed and her eyes half closed. Once or twice the tacky stumbled and Dorande recovered herself without looking up. When she came to the junction of the road that led to the Congaree, she reined in, remembering how she had cantered down it to Mrs. Motte's on her return from Ninety-six. She raised her head, drew a long, uncertain breath. Then, with an abrupt movement, she turned the tacky's head *west*, sternly urging the animal to a sharp trot.

The road was easy for some miles, reasonably smooth and

well marked. She felt a new breeze on her cheeks as she came into the hills and dusk fell quickly as the wooded crests shouldered back the last rays of the sun. Soon it was dark and she could only keep to the road by bending low in the saddle and tilting her head to catch the vague outlines of trees against the dimming sky. She smelled charred wood and her horse shied. That must be the Dart's cabin, burned a month ago by a random raider of no particular army or party. She thought she made out vague shapes moving in the clearing that the summer would soon reclaim from earlier cultivation, but they turned out to be meager saplings stirring to the breeze.

She cocked her head and pulled up short. Hoofbeats? Yes, there could be no mistake. She dismounted and led the tacky to the west edge of the clearing, keeping a hand over its muzzle. One rider coming from the east. Or two? She crouched low, covering her face with her broad hat, and was suddenly glad she was wearing dark-colored gloves. No glimmer of white skin would show through the night.

A single rider. He had stopped near the burned cabin and seemed to be standing in his stirrups as though listening intently. Dorande held her breath. Then she gave a sob of relief as a voice, low but carrying, called, "Miss Dorande! Miss Dorande!"

Knees weak with past fear, she ran to the edge of the road, the tacky clopping after her. "Tobias! But I did not tell you to come."

He held out something in the dark. "Figured you'd mebbe need this—seein' you ain't turned east to Mis' Motte's."

Dorande blushed with mortification as she took the tinderbox, complete with all accessories. Even if she had found the beacon, how could she have lit it, lacking the materials? She stammered her thanks, but Tobias was holding out a short, double-barreled pistol.

"But you think of everything," said Dorande, half crying with vexation at her own heedlessness. "I cannot say enough in thanks. Now you must go back."

"Better I stay."

Dorande hesitated, then said, "As you wish. I do not forget this, Tobias. *Allons-y.*"

The night flowed past them on the road that became rougher with each mile. The horses clacked against big stones, stumbled over potholes. Stars were soft and bright now, and it was easier to set a course by catching the treetops against the sky. Now and then they halted to rest the horses while Dorande fretted and watched the sky. By an odd strip of nat-

ural meadow, she bent to test her girth. She heard a low exclamation from Tobias and looked up quickly. Off to the
southeast, but apparently quite close, a new star glowed, a
star that shot up, wavered and shot up again. Dorande cried
out in relief. That star could only be the beacon tended by
the Whittakers and the Breens, the first beacon east of Little
Wolf-trap!

She mounted, calling to Tobias, and set off to the west at
a good pace. They could not be far from their goal now. At the
end of a few miles, she checked her gait. She must begin to
watch very carefully for landmarks which she had studied
from the slow-rolling coach. But then it had been daylight
and she had been traveling east. Everything looked different
in the dark and also she was riding west. If only she had been
wise enough to sit with her back to the horses on that trip.
Then her memory would have held at least something of the
dark country whose contours she was trying to guess.

Twice more she halted, standing in the middle of the road
and slowly facing to all points of the compass in turn. She
remembered that there had been a swift, froth-dappled
stream cutting the highway near the foot of Little Wolf-trap,
but she had already passed at least two creeks that could have
answered its description. On she went again, Tobias silent behind her.

She grew increasingly nervous. What if she had overridden
the hill? High ground loomed right and left but it might end
suddenly with the first crest, fall away into plain and swamp.
She caught the wet breath, the rush and gurgle of a stream,
heard planks ring hollow as she rode over the little bridge.
Could *this* be the nameless watercourse? She looked back at
it. She had a distinct recollection of light guard rails, but the
side of this one was unprotected. She caught a blur of white
wood close by the timbers and dropped to the ground. She
gave an exclamation of relief. There had been a railing of
saplings. Something had ripped it away, leaving only the
splintered butts. Tobias joined her. "This it, Miss Dorande?"

"It—it must be. Now the *sentier,* the path that leads to the
beacon." She looked about helplessly. Unbroken walls of trees
hemmed the road beyond the creek. Yet on the map, the
trail had been clearly marked. She was sure that she had seen,
in the sunlight and from the carriage, gaps in the trees toward
the low crest. Where?

Tobias was making short casts in the dark, first to the
right and then to the left. Suddenly he called softly, "Reckon
I hit something, Miss Dorande."

She ran to him and found him standing by the seemingly impenetrable brush, holding a pair of stag horns in his hands. "Someone done hang these to the trees, figurin' they'd tell someone something." He moved off to the right, mumbling, "Mebbe it's y'ere, mebbe it's y'ere—Lord look down! I'se got it!" There was a ripping, crackling noise and Tobias vanished. He reappeared at once. "Smart ol' trail, headin' plumb up the mount'n."

Panting with excitement, Dorande called, "Lead, then," and plunged after him on foot, her tacky trailing uneasily after her. The mouth of the trail had been hidden by a screen of bushes. She realized that she never would have found it had not Tobias's sharp eye seen the stag horns wedged in a fork and reasoned out their meaning.

The way was steep and rocky. Branches ripped at Dorande's habit, her face, her hands. She labored on valiantly, tugging at the reins. At a level shelf, Tobias decided that it would be better to tether the horses and go on to the top without them. Dorande was uncertain about the wisdom of this, but almost at once the trail grew steeper and narrower, and she knew that the tackies would have floundered helplessly.

Perspiration ran down her face and little, hot, darting pains stabbed at her side. The next beacon to the west was faraway over a level plain and she was not sure that smoke signals from Little Wolf-trap would show at that distance. Suppose dawn were near and the fire flamed in vain.

All at once Tobias stopped. He had taken off his coat and his white sleeve showed clear as he held up his arm. Dorande stepped beside him, staring at a black gulf at their feet. She could not see the far side. Weariness and disappointment brought stinging tears back of her lids. To have come this far, only to stare at a great crevasse!

Tobias was muttering to himself. "Path, he lead right here. Folks made 'at path and folks ain't made it jes' to look down 'at ol' hole. Folks—"

He stepped swiftly and Dorande could see his white sleeves moving first to the right and then to the left, as she leaned hopelessly against the tree. Suddenly she sprang to the left where Tobias was calling, pointing to a huge tree trunk that spanned the gap. Step by step, foot by foot, Dorande followed him to the far side. Then she was on a firm hard path that slanted up and up. Fifty yards, a hundred. She felt cool air on her face and knew that she stood on the summit, close to a huge stack of logs and brush.

With shaking hands she knelt while Tobias held her hat as

a shield for the tinderbox. She struck and struck. Sparks showered onto tinder, onto dry leaves and twigs, flared, died, flared. Slow, blue-tipped flames began to lick upward.

Tobias sprang up. "Back, Miss. Back quick. This-a-way."

She sped after him to the windward side, found herself on a bare, rocky ledge that looked west. On the summit the flames climbed and climbed, fanned by the wind. Dorande turned her back to the blaze and stared into the western night. Stars danced and blurred before her eyes, weird colors showed in the sky. When she closed her lids, stars and colors were still there. When her vision cleared she looked again into the black reaches.

Suddenly both her hands flew up and she gave a low, choked cry while Tobias dropped to his knees, bareheaded. Far, far to the west, a pinpoint of gold glowed, then spread, mounted, ebbed, mounted higher. Dorande leaned weakly against a tree, her lips moving in a silent prayer. Greene's tiny army, west again beyond the distant fire, would have word, and by that word they would live.

Still kneeling, Tobias asked softly, "Our folks gwine be all right, Miss Dorande. You aim for Charleston soon's we git home, Miss?"

Dorande's slim legs carried her on to the downhill trail, but she felt that something had struck her below the heart. She said dully, "To Charleston? No. What need—now?" Even with the greatest of luck in the return ride, it was too late and the Portuguese barque would clear the coast of the Carolinas without its passenger from the Congaree.

Tobias padded on behind her almost reverently. Just to light a fire on a hilltop, his mistress had given up her one sure chance to leave this land of war and terror. He shook his head from time to time, as he repeated the story to himself.

Five days later, Paul St. Aubin, weary and travel-stained, stood before his big map, the blue crayon in his hand. A blue circle now surrounded Ninety-six. With a sigh, he swept his hand clear to the coast, neatly drew another about Georgetown. That little Huguenot devil, Marion, again—the Swamp Fox, as he had heard British officials call him!

With red and blue crayon, he began to trace the routes of the armies, then gave it up. There was no need of showing just how Greene had headed north across the Saluda, the Enoree, the Tyger, after raising the siege of Ninety-six, nor the broken-off pursuit of him by Lord Rawdon, who had ordered the evacuation of that post. Nor could he trace out the march of the Americans' Light Corps south in its vain attempt to head off Rawdon before the latter's move to Orangeburg, which had been deserted by both sides since its capture by Sumter. It was enough to show Orangeburg in red with a blue square somewhere north of the Congaree, but obviously heading for Friday's Ferry not far above Mon Plaisir.

Friday's Ferry. That was uncomfortably close. Or was it? Suppose the incredible happened, and he moved the blue square on and on till it hung above Charleston? What then? St. Aubin shrugged. It could not affect him. He would merely be dealing with a new firm. That he could deal with that or any other new firm, he had no doubt.

He heard Dorande's light step outside in the corridor and, hastily veiling his map, he seated himself behind his wide desk. *Ventre de dieu,* how fresh she looked, despite the suffocating heat that had crept down the valley of the Congaree! In the armies, he knew, powerful men were dying in the steamy air as, in advance or pursuit, they struggled along the dust-blanketed roads.

Dorande said calmly, "You wished to see me, *mon oncle?*"

He spread out his hands. "Always it is a pleasure. For this instant, I only ask myself if perhaps you have comment to make concerning that Portuguese ship that sailed from Charleston."

"No doubt it was a fine ship."

"And you had no wish to test its merits and beauties." He smiled inwardly as he saw a cloud pass over Dorande's face.

"I found other matters more pressing. Of course, out of what is left me, I shall pay any monies which you advanced for that passage which I was unable to use."

"Bagatelles do not interest me," he said negligently. "You would like, perhaps, to tell me what, *précisément,* you found more pressing?"

"Is it important that you know?" said Dorande, rising.

St. Aubin eyed her. What a figure she had! Very like that of the sleepy-eyed octoroon who lived so conveniently now not two miles to the east. He picked up a quill pen, smiling negligently. "Important? No doubt it is not. Events move so fast these days that I see no harm in your knowing that I could guess quite closely at the nature, at least, of your doings." Dorande turned pale and reseated herself, hand to her hroat and her dark eyes wide.

She managed to say, "That you must explain, *monsieur.*"

"*Diantre!*" chuckled St. Aubin. "It surprised you? But you must not take me for a fool. From the first, I know what you do. Strange people ride up here, stranger messages come and go." He raised his hand. "Do not trouble to deny it. Do you suppose I was not entirely aware of the charming widow's history when I arranged that she come here? Do I not know that her husband's most lively ghost comes from time to time to console her?" He chuckled again. "And that most aggressive Tory in white coat and white-plumed helmet who attempted so drolly to play Paris to your Helen? Your words were overheard *before* he carried you off so boldly. Ah, it is so simple when the tongues of servants may be bought along with their ears, when in this droll country in a single family, one brother is Whig, a second Tory and a third whirling like a weathervane. Your white-coated friend, at this moment he attaches himself to the person of General Greene, a fact I learned only today from a certain man who served Greene as volunteer and became disgusted that a New Englander command Carolinians. What have you to say to all this? Or do you wish more detail?"

Cold and trembling, Dorande faced him, her hands locked in her lap. She said with difficulty, "You believe all this to be true. What, then, do you intend?"

St. Aubin rose, bowing. "Only to present my deepest compliments to you for a performance which I have consistently and profoundly admired. *Ma nièce,* you were superb. There were times when I could hardly keep from applauding. Pride filled me as I saw that the same blood bowed in our veins. When I saw the Goddams—your pardon, the milords—swarming about you at good Cruden's ball, I knew that your pretty little ears were taking in more than compliments and I thought, *'Vraiment,* she is more her uncle's niece than her mother's daughter.' I felt—"

Dorande, colder and paler, cut in, "You say all this you believed. Then why—"

He seated himself, smiling. "Why did I not interfere? Why not, indeed? No doubt, in Charleston, you noted many houses unharmed and each bearing on its door a leaden plaque showing the crude outline of a building. Many think that that is a sign of Royal protection, keeping house and owners undisturbed. That is wrong. That plaque shows membership in what is called 'The Friendly Society for Insurance Protection.' You served, up here on the Congaree, as *my* leaden plaque— you and Madame Jaudon."

With numb lips, Dorande murmured, "Your plaque?"

"But what else? There are many Whigs who do not love me, violent people such as abound in this state. Would the worst of them harm this house, knowing that it sheltered two who performed acts highly valued by the little Swamp Fox, Marion, and later by Sumter and even Greene?"

Dorande sprang to her feet, eyes blazing. "So! You have allowed—"

St. Aubin's smile deepened. "Say, rather, encouraged. I think it was well done and you should extend to me a little of the admiration which I hold for you. That is all I had to say to you. I ask no details to add to what I know. For the future—" he shrugged—"I continue to place no impediment in your way. Indeed, if events continue in their present astounding course, I may even assist you."

"No! If I have done what you say, then credit me with doing it because I believed in the people I was helping and what they fought for. I want nothing out of this."

St. Aubin clapped his hands softly. "Magnificent! Thus did I explain myself to the milords who asked themselves why a Frenchman ally himself with the British Crown. Frenchman! What is France to me who have never seen it, whose natives call me 'colonial,' while they brush their snuff from their falls of Paris lace! No! I fight for Paul St. Aubin."

Dorande said coldly, "Then it would be well for one who is *not* Paul St. Aubin to find shelter elsewhere than under his roof."

St. Aubin walked to the door and held it open for her with a low bow. "That, my dear niece, might be found a rather difficult feat. I admire you, you are useful to me. For the time, at least, it would incommode me to have you elsewhere."

She glared at him, then marched from the room, her head high and her lips compressed.

St. Aubin returned to his map, then seated himself, gently nibbling at his thumbnail. How would the tide turn? Greene had almost no army, was always beaten and yet—the better British forces were sapped at their very roots by the needle raids of men like the Swamp Fox. Partisan and regular, each was helpless alone. Together, their efforts at the moment seemed to be spelling out success in big, laborious capitals. *If* that happened—he shrugged. One could at least begin steps that would aid in meeting that event.

He went to a chest that had come up from Charleston with him and began taking books from it, arranging them on shelves. The works of Diderot shouldered those of other liberals, d'Alembert, Rousseau, Voltaire. Montesquieu's *L'Esprit des Lois* showed its fine binding beside a battered copy of Thomas Paine's *Common Sense*, smuggled somehow into Charleston. He stepped back and surveyed the titles complacently. Then from his desk he drew a small packet, stuffed it into his pocket and walked out toward the kitchen house where smoke curled from the chimney.

Brusquely ordering the slaves out, he opened his packet and fed its contents slowly into the flame. One by one the cards bearing the name "Paul de St. Aubin" took fire, crumbled, were consumed. He ground out the last ash and returned to the house, dusting his hands. *"Voilà,"* he murmured. "Behold me, *tout à fait républicain.* If omens change, I may always send Rousseau and the other gentlemen to join the cards and resume my *de.*"

At his desk once more, his thoughts kept returning to Dorande. The time might come when her usefulness would end. She could even be an embarrassment. And in that case? A way must be found to remove her from the scene. Of course, she must not be harmed. An idea struck him. He could easily have her sent through the lines to Charleston, with a brief note to Colonel Balfour citing her activities. Balfour, in pompous chivalry, would do no worse than to see that some British ship conveyed her to Havana or Jamaica, and *enfin,* was that not what she had wished all along? He smiled. An admirable solution, when the time came. It would be well, of course, to —ah—immobilize any people who might be interested in her. To Marion, she was but one of many. Her most logical departure would be regretted. Were there others?

A black footman tapped discreetly on the door. An English gentleman wished to see the master of Mon Plaisir. St. Aubin hastily draped a bright scarf over the new books and turned politely to greet his guest. Then his eyebrows went up. The man wore a battered felt hat, a coat cut from the reddish cloth that the British sometimes used in place of currency to indemnify Loyalists. An ill-kept sword banged against buckskin leggings and breeches.

St. Aubin said, "You wished to see me, monsieur?" Then he recognized the stooped shoulders, the close-set eyes and fox smile, blessing himself for his excellent memory. "Ah, Captain Bayne. Yes, I recall well that in the past you have stopped here on your way from Ninety-six or Camden. *Là là.* The times move. The Rebels have both places and you must find other points for arrival and departure. Be seated and tell me how I may serve you."

Bayne drew a chair to the desk, grumbling. "Bloody awful times. Rebels everywhere. Like slapping mosquitoes in a swamp. They got Tom Browne at Galphin. Sumter caught Wemyss. Bloody fool, Sumter. Wemyss had a list on him showing all the places he'd burned and the men he'd hanged. Sumter burned the list and treated him as a regular prisoner instead of turning him over to the country people. Sumter! Clodhopping peasant trying to act like a gentleman."

St. Aubin sighed. "But, *mon ami*, you people have provided him with so many examples of elegant gentlemen that he may not be blamed for his efforts at emulation."

Bayne looked sharply at him, but St. Aubin's face showed only bland tolerance. The captain grumbled on. "Can't understand things. Some of the best regiments in the army. The Buffs, the 9th, the 7th. And now look at 'em! We control just the ground that our sentries can cover."

St. Aubin said soothingly, "No doubt all that will arrange itself."

"Bloody well better. It's put some of us in a devil of a hole. People like me, serving away from our regiments on command. Men from the Welsh, the Guards. Take me. The 17th somewhere in Virginia with Cornwallis. The pay chest, the records, are with 'em. Devil of a hole."

St. Aubin's eyelids drooped a little. "Regrettable, no doubt, but how does it touch me?"

Bayne laughed shortly. "That's what I'm here for. Look here, our people have been bloody good to you."

"Some may say that I have not been quite useless to them."

"That's all very well. But—I was wondering—dash it all— the fact is, I'm bloody hard up. If I were to give you my note of hand against my back pay—well, how about it?"

St. Aubin shook his head regretfully. "In matters touching the military, I have found it wise not to intervene. No doubt one of your brother officers would be happy to accommodate you."

"Most are as badly off as I am."

St. Aubin leaned back as though in deep thought, then snapped his fingers and leaned on the desk. "Perhaps I have found a way. A trifling service you may render me. As man to man, you know."

Bayne brightened. "Come! Let's have it."

"This concerns," said St. Aubin slowly, "concerns the elimination of one man."

"What the devil are you trying to do!" exclaimed Bayne angrily. "Make a hired cutthroat out of me?"

"Ah, *I* could not suggest such a transformation," said St. Aubin so sweetly that Bayne flushed. He opened a drawer, drew out a small box and opened it. Bayne's eyes widened at the sight of the new-minted gold. St. Aubin murmured negligently, "Fifty golden pounds as earnest money. A like amount to be handed over when proof is presented me that the person in question will no longer be an annoyance."

Bayne said harshly, "You ought to know better than to try to bribe a gentleman." His eyes were still on the gold.

"Ah, perhaps you prefer paper to gold, Captain. Would *this* influence you?" He whipped out a sheet and handed it to Bayne. "I am well informed, as you must know. This is a simple little list of your exploits. Note the entries. 'Burning,' 'Burning' again and again. Nonmilitary 'hanging of prisoners,' 'shooting of prisoners.' Here we find rape and once more and once more rape. This paper would greatly interest, say, Francis Marion. It *could* come to his hands. There are ways."

Bayne went white, then snatched the sheet and tore it into shreds. St. Aubin laughed quietly. "My dear Captain, you do not suppose that I placed my *sole* copy in your hands, I trust. But I assure you that if you see fit to assist me in this small matter, an amount equaling that in the box, together with *all* copies of that sheet, will be placed in your hands. But I am sure that such inducements are little needed, to a gentleman of your standing, especially when I tell you the name of the person whose—ah—erasure will be for the great good. Nonetheless, those inducements will be yours. The man I mean is one Captain Ross Pembroke."

"*Who?*" Bayne's pallor changed to a deep flush. "My God, I'd put *him* under the sod and pay for the privilege."

"With your note of hnad?" asked St. Aubin politely. "No matter. I was aware that you had a slight contretemps with him in this very house, one that you would be pleased to avenge."

"There's more than that," growled Bayne. "He—"

"The details do not matter," put in St. Aubin. "The fact is, for my part, that he has annoyed and continues, when possible, to annoy my niece, to whom I am devoted. That, you conceive, I may not tolerate."

Bayne frowned at his broken-nailed hands. "God damn it, though, he's a bloody tough customer and lucky as he's tough."

"Ah, *mon ami,*" smiled St. Aubin. "You speak of him as an opponent on the battlefield, no doubt. But now, your regiment is gone. You have no true command, I take it?"

"Fossicking about with a troop of Rebel deserters and lukewarm Tories."

"Exactly. Therefore, rid of the cares of war, responsible solely to yourself, you might well arrange, let us say, an ambush, a trap with no other consideration than to bring about a satisfactorily fatal result." He rattled the coin box suggestively. "It does not need to be in battle. On the march, in camp—" He tossed up his hands. "A bold man like yourself could plan such a thing."

Bayne got up. "All right. I'll see to it. Just don't be so damn flowery. I'll need more than this, though. I'll have to break up my troop and just keep two or three of them."

"You foresee no difficulties in undertaking this?"

"Hell, no. The God damn army's in such a scramble that you could march Caesar's 10th Legion with 'em and no one'd know. I've got no one to report to or answer to. How'd you think I managed to get here today, a good march from our nearest post?"

"In that case, I add another ten pounds to this box," said St. Aubin, clinking out more gold pieces, "and hand it to you with much pleasure. With still more pleasure, I shall fulfill the other part of our bargain in due course. Should you encounter Lord Rawdon, commend me to him."

Bayne stowed the gold away. "Rawdon? No bloody fear *my* meeting him. He's found that his health won't stand the climate; *he* says he's going to hand over command to Lieutenant Colonel Stuart and sail on the first transport for England."

When Bayne had gone, St. Aubin paced up and down the room, pursing his lips. Then he opened a strongbox and drew out a sheaf of papers, riffling them carefully over and drawing out several. These he bound with red tape and wrapped carefully, writing in large letters on the wrapping, "These deeds I have held as trustee to safeguard them against the time when I might return them to their rightful owners who sacrificed their property to the cause of liberty." He added an earlier date, signed the paper with a great flourish and returned the sheaf to his strongbox.

In an emergency, the deeds might be looked upon as insurance premiums. If events ran otherwise, the wrapper could be burned. St. Aubin leaned back in his chair, closed his eyes and placed his finger tips together. He reflected on his own progress: a lucky turn of cards when he had been nearly starving in Antigua; his winnings rigorously husbanded and invested in shares in a venture which he dignified with the name of privateering, though less liberal-minded people spoke of piracy; his first dizzyingly profitable deal in sequestered slaves arriving in Jamaica from Charleston, and then Charleston itself and increasing eminence. A gentle smile spread over his face. His hands slid to his lap and he dozed, at peace and carefree.

The marches and countermarches of July had been desperate beyond belief. In a choking pall of heat that hung heavy by day and strangling by night, Ross had ridden with the Legion from the high Enoree to the Saluda, to the Congaree and beyond to the flats about Orangeburg. Swaying with weakness and the vicious heat, he had seen men turn purple and drop from their saddles. There had been odd combats against Rawdon's few horsemen with charges at a slow trot or even a walk, sword-play where blades struck feebly and uncertainly. Hiding in swamps, stirring up the biting grit of sandy roads, men ate handfuls of moldy corn flour. When that was gone, they endured the torture of further heat to boil bits of leather that could be chewed for hours and give the illusion of eating.

Reeling with hunger, fatigue and dysentery, weighed down by the sullen torment of heat, Greene's horsemen floundered into an area of shallow swamps. De Chanzy tumbled from his horse and splashed among the reeds, falling over and shouting in a weak, hoarse voice. Someone called for a surgeon to tend a man whose brains had obviously been touched by sun and fatigue but the Frenchman, dripping and still limping along on a swollen knee, held up three gigantic, kicking frogs. Soon the whole column was diving after frogs, tearing at the sweet flesh before it was half cooked. The smell seemed to spread over the whole countryside and the swamps filled with horsemen and foot soldiers, plunging and stumbling in the undergrowth.

The march was a little better after that. Bellies were no longer quite so empty and griping. Soon the frogs were gone. Delaware Continentals shot an alligator, started a fusillade popping and echoing along every stream. Then the column, a bare half of whose men were even reasonably healthy, found they were heading north again.

Ross rode with a heavy head through which hot pains darted. He tried to gnaw on a frog's leg that de Chanzy brought from his saddlebag. He knew that de Chanzy was shouting something to him, tried to follow while his head thumped and his throat closed against the frog meat that he attempted to swallow. It was something about the British post at Monck's Corner, thirty miles out of Charleston itself. Part of Lee's cavalry, Marion's men and Sumter's had struck the veteran British 9th, de Chanzy was saying, had routed them. Monck's Corner was no longer British. Many prisoners, many horses and wagons. Marion! Sumter! Part of the Legion cavalry!

Ross tried to catch hold of the words, but they slipped

away from him. There was something he wanted desperately to say to de Chanzy. Something about— He heard himself mumbling, "Congaree. May be asleep. Tell me when we come to it. Crossed in dark, last time, going south. Important. Congaree."

All at once he was on the ground with woods and swamp and dusk whirling about his sore body and ringing head. De Chanzy was loosening his collar while Eggleston yelled, "Hi! Surgeon! Surgeon Irvine! Pass the word for Surgeon Irvine. Another fever case!"

XII • The High Hills of Santee

Unit by unit Greene's little army struggled out of the swamps and the dread fever lands. Men from Maryland and Virginia and Delaware, forcing themselves onward, found their lungs gasping in relief as they left the lowlands and fought their way, step by step, to the clean sand and clay, to the cotton and tobacco fields, to the deep oak groves and long meadows of rich grass in the High Hills of Santee. Last of all the regular troops, the infantry and cavalry that followed Light Horse Harry Lee, trailed their wasted troops and companies up among the cool springs and streams where fresh breezes blew. The men threw themselves on the soft grass, unaware when the horse litters went creaking on past them with their cargoes of sick and wounded. They panted, surrendering themselves utterly to the cool peace of the High Hills that smiled down on the sticky valleys of the Wateree and the Congaree.

The soft breezes of the summer passed gently through the room where Ross lay under the merciful anesthesia of fever. Somewhere in the depths of his consciousness he was vaguely aware of those breezes whose touch contrasted so with the endless heat in which he lived. Sometimes, floating a little closer to the surface of life, he knew the smell of fresh-sawn timber and wondered dimly about it before sloughing back into fever depths.

As August came on, he became conscious of alternating blackness and light that marked the passage of night and day, a strange procession of time that had nothing to do with him. His inner life grew more real and he moved in a world of half-dream while his body lay inert on a flimsy pallet. There was cold wind on his face, breaking through the blanket of fever, a cold wind that could only have swept down the valley of the Blackstone from Worcester and the Berkshire Hills far to Rhode Island's west. He laughed as Dorande, a fur cap jaunty on her head, held her hands to her cheeks and faced the snow that came on down the long valley. She'd seen nothing like *that* in St. Eusebius and cried out in delight as snow crystals glittered on her bright hair.

The wind blew stronger, scattered the storm, clouded the hills above Providence. He tried to call to Dorande, and with the effort, the veil of sickness cleared from his brain and he stared up at the sunburned face of Surgeon Skinner who was wringing out a cloth over a bucket of cold water. Skinner grunted in satisfaction. "About time you crawled out of that clamshell you've been living in. If I had a guinea for every time I've sponged your face with cold water, I'd be a damn rich man."

"What's happening?" asked Ross weakly.

"Happening? Well, for one thing, we won't have to call out the burial squad for you after all."

"The war. What's happening?"

"Well, I'd say the war was fine, just flourishing. I wish it'd last forever, just like this. We're all resting and getting fat. That's all. Been a few sorties here and there by the partisans, but that's all."

"Do we move again tonight?" asked Ross vaguely. Something had happened to him, just what he wasn't sure. He'd had a good sleep, though, and could probably mount Ree, if someone helped him.

Skinner shrugged. "All you fever boys are the same. Just blank out. Move tonight? God, no. Nor tomorrow night. You'll probably call me a liar, but this is August fifteenth."

Ross tried to sit up, but a wave of dizziness pushed him back. "August? Fifteenth? Where are we? Where's the army?"

"You're right plumb in the middle of it, sitting on top of the High Hills of Santee."

"It was snowing," said Ross.

"Of course it was. Maybe you thought it was raining brimstone, too. Hell, that's not bad. Poor Cheney of Armstrong's troop had such a God damn strong notion he was trying to put a saddle on an alligator that we had to tie him down, me and Irvine and Sergeant Kuhn."

"Where's de Chanzy?"

"Damned if I know. He's not a patient. Probably he's been out on some of those patrols that Harry Lee keeps going. He was here two nights ago, but you thought he was someone at a college and began scanning Latin to him. Plain as hell. *'Hinc Gaetulae urbes, genus insuperabile bello.'* Go to sleep. I'll have some broth sent around to you when you wake up."

Ross tried once more to lever himself up. "Got to report."

"Lie still, or the only report you'll make will be to Saint Peter. You ought to see yourself. I'd say normally you'd weigh 190. Now, if you scale 160, I'll eat a copperhead from the tail up."

Sleep swept over him, broke, closed in again. In the intervals he became more and more aware of his surroundings. The house that sheltered him had been at least partly burned at one time and new beams and planks accounted for the smell of fresh timber that had entered his consciousness. He seemed to be the only patient in the house, but through the open door into the corridor he had seen a brisk, white-haired woman pass by with quick, birdlike steps. Once or twice he caught sight of a thickset elderly man. No doubt the couple owned the house, one room of which had been commandeered by the army.

On his first day of real consciousness, helmeted men in green jackets clanked in to see him, sternly limited in time by Skinner or Irvine. Eggleston and John Rudulph perched on boxes and gave him news of the war, which was scant. Patrols operated, but the two main armies rested and watched each other, the British being based close to Charleston.

"We've got two Legion patrols out, now. Your friend de Chanzy's with one of them," said Rudulph. "Damnedest man I ever saw. If a corporal and two troopers set out, he wants to go with them. That's all he's done since we got here—ride patrol and try to strike a spark out of your thick head, Ross."

"He's a good man," said Eggleston. "I swear, he's turning into an American quicker than a snake sheds its skin."

Rudulph winked at Eggleston. "Between you and me, he's going to end up by marrying an American girl. That's the only reason he goes on patrol—so he can see her."

"Wish he would," said Ross. "I'd like to see him settle down with us after the war."

"You lose, both of you," said Eggleston. "This girl's not American. You know her, Ross. She lives up the Congaree. Part French, I think."

"She's—*what?*" cried Ross weakly, a cold sweat on his forehead.

"Part French," said Eggleston. "That's why de Chanzy picks only the Congaree patrols to ride with. Been seeing a lot of her." He glanced at Ross, then pulled Rudulph to his feet.

"Let's get out of here. We're exhausting the patient. Come on, or Skinner'll tie us down and pour purges down our throats."

Ross tossed uneasily on his straw mattress when they had gone. De Chanzy and Dorande. What the devil did Phil mean, racing off to see Dorande while he, Ross, was helpless with fever! A nice trick! He began to reason sternly with himself. There—was—no—earthly reason—why they—should—not—see—each—other. None! He had no claim on Dorande. Why, it must mean a lot to her to speak French with someone. And de Chanzy had every right to pay court to her. "He's going to end up marrying an American girl," Rudulph said. *Marry* her? God damn it, why *not*? She wasn't American! De Chanzy, once again, had every right. He must have been lonely as the devil, here in this strange land. Rhode Island was far away, but France was much farther. Good old Phil. Really, Ross told himself, he was glad of his friend's fortune. Only—only—*if* someone had to sweep Dorande off her feet—and Rudulph's remark certainly suggested that—*why* couldn't it have been someone whom Ross heartily detested? Well, his blessing on them both. But his magnanimity did nothing to dispel the feeling of sick weakness that swept over him at the thought.

It was dark when he awoke, and the brisk, white-haired woman was bending over him, a candle in one hand and a bowl of broth in the other. "You can swallow this, yes?" she asked, smiling.

Ross started. There was something in her accent that suggested Dorande's pretty lilt, and the memory of his talk with Rudulph and Eggleston flooded back over him. He said, "You're very good. But really—just now—"

She perched on a stool and held out the bowl. "Drink," she said. "It will do you good."

Reluctantly Ross sipped, found the broth deliciously seasoned, far better than the greasy messes that came to him from the field hospital. The woman smiled again, spoke softly. "For a long time, I wait for this chance. I find we have friends to talk about."

"Friends?" asked Ross, still sipping.

"No less. Before I know your name, I know who you are. One of these friends called you *le capitaine noir*. This friend, months ago, called out about you in a fever just such as you have had and under this very roof."

Ross nearly dropped the bowl. The words sounded like those which Dorande had written on the Nelson's Ferry sketch. The woman went on. "Yes, when they brought you here, a cartridge box fell on the floor and burst open, spilling out paper which unrolled. A very pretty sketch it was, and signed by our friend."

Ross set the bowl down. "Then you're Mrs. Cantey! You're Francis Marion's cousin. Dorande was here when the Tories came. You've got a brother named Rusillon and the Tories smashed your music box!"

"That is true," said Mrs. Cantey. "Ah, those were bad days, but she was brave, that little one. We were moved, Emil and I, when our Dorande told us that true hearts could not be touched by burned timbers. When peace came to the High Hills, we followed it and began to rebuild."

"She spoke of *me?*" asked Ross, his mind swinging back to Mrs. Cantey's earlier words.

"But indeed. And of my cousin Marion, whom she called always 'the little colonel.' But very often of you." She talked on, recalling some fragmentary speech of Dorande's, a reference made long ago to *le capitaine noir,* then told of Dorande's stanchness when Kroysing and the other had come.

"But we talk further of all this," she said, picking up the bowl. "Now you must sleep. And your sketch, I bring it to you as soon as I may have the strongbox key from my brother Emil."

At some unmarked hour of the night Ross was wakened again. He sat up, blinking in lantern light while de Chanzy, limping and travel stained, exclaimed over him in delight. "Only now do I hear, *mon ami,* that you are recovered. A minute, a second ago, I return with a patrol. I do not even pause to see to my horse, whom I groom daily with your own Ree. But I find this marvelous. The good Doctor Skinner permitted that I wake you. But I may not linger, he says. *Baste!* The light dazzles you. I put it out—so." Darkness fell over the room and Ross heard a clatter and jingle as de Chanzy seated himself. "But a little we may talk, at least. And see, my friend, on the last patrol I find a most curious knife for you. My men tell me it must have been made by the redskins, some of whom are skilled in such matters. Like a razor. And light, with a beautiful, sure balance. I shall place it by your bed and in the morning you may look at it. The instant I see it, I think, 'Now that I shall bring to my friend Ross.' "

"Why, that's fine of you, Phil." He felt his mouth growing dry. "By the way, I hear that you are open to congratulations."

"I? To congratulations?"

"Yes. Rudulph and Eggleston told me that you seem

to have found a Madame de Chanzy on the road to the Congaree." He spoke lightly, a hollow feeling about his heart.

"They say that? *Parbleu,* they are optimist. One may admire, one may hope—ah, truly, though, I think one does not hope in vain. My friend, I am quite sure—*sang de dieu!*" He sprang up in the darkness, his arm swung.

Ross heard something whistle through the air. Beyond the open window there was a yelp of pain, something crashed inside the room. There was a blinding flash and a bullet rapped hard against the wood above Ross's head. He cried, "What in God's name—"

But de Chanzy leaped through the window, shouting, "*Au secours! Par ici, la Légion!* The Legion! This way!"

Ross tried to get up, but his legs were too weak. He fell back against the pillow, his heart pounding furiously. What had happened? Panting, he heard shouts in the night, a shot, then more shouts, fainter and fainter.

Silence fell over the High Hills once more. Ross, his head aching fiercely, tried to puzzle out the events. De Chanzy had sprung to his feet. There had been a cry of pain. De Chanzy had vanished into the night, immediately after that mysterious shot that had followed the yell. What did it mean?

There was more light in his room. Skinner was bending over him, asking sharply, "You all right?"

"Guess so. What happened? Where's de Chanzy?"

"Making a report. Damn it, that fellow must have been alert and I guess you owe him your life. Sees there was just enough light for him to see someone pushing a pistol in at the open window, aiming plumb for you. He chucked a knife and caught whoever it was in the hand. The pistol fell to the floor —yes, by God, there it is, just under the sill. The shock of the fall must have set it off."

Ross gaped. "That be damned for a tale! Who'd want to shoot me?"

"Someone who didn't like you, I'd say. Anyhow, you'll have a chance to see him in the morning. Oh, yes. They got him. But not alive. He put up a fight and that old Brunswicker, Kuhn, nearly took his head off with a backhander. Nothing on the body except a couple of British guineas, which is damned funny cargo to find on a ragged clunch like that." He bent and picked up the pistol. "This is quality stuff, too. I'd say you'd pay a good twenty pounds for it."

"Wait a minute," said Ross. "Let me figure this out. Someone tried to fire at me through the window. He was caught and killed. But *why* did he want to wing me? You say there's no identification on the body. Didn't he say anything before he died? Didn't anyone think to question him?"

Skinner held out a mug. "Drink this and don't stew your brains over the whys and wherefores. He was just mumbling when they picked him up. He was cursing someone he called 'Bayne, the bastard.' It didn't mean anything."

Ross sat up. "The devil it doesn't! Bayne! Yes, he'd be quite capable of something like that, bribing some lout to shoot me. Well, it failed. The man's dead and Bayne's out two guineas. Wonder where the devil he got them." He settled back. "All right, Doctor. Give me that slime draught."

The fever poison fled with surprising speed and by the twentieth Ross was able to walk, with most of his old strength returned, through the camps that lined the crest above the Wateree. His first care, having found that de Chanzy was again on patrol, was to report to Lee. Walking easily, he eyed the tents and the shelters of branches that housed the army. The hospitals had been gradually emptying as the good air and water of the High Hills worked their particular cures. But even with such accession of strength, companies and troops seemed pitifully weak in numbers. Few new units had appeared and the old rumor that Anthony Wayne and his Pennsylvanians would march to join Greene had evaporated once again, as it had so often in the past. None the less, such men as there were looked keen and solid, were probably in better shape than they had been at any time since Greene's assumption of command.

He kept on, moving south along the wide ridge. Lee had set up headquarters in a substantial farmhouse close to the carefully selected camp ground of the Legion and within easy reach of Greene, who occupied a mansion belonging to the Laurens family. Men of the Legion called to Ross, infantry-men joining with cavalry. He was both surprised and moved. He had not realized, despite his loose and tenuous post with Lee, that so many men knew him, had been aware of his illness and recovery. It did a little to fill the empty ache that had crept over him since his realization that there was no blinking the fact of a serious understanding between Dorande and de Chanzy.

He had had no chance, since the night of the attempt on his life to hear more details from the Frenchman, who had been constantly on distant duty, at whose nature Ross felt that he could guess. He was not sure that he wanted to hear more of that courtship. He had not realized how deeply he had identified himself with Dorande until the shock of Rudulph's statement and de Chanzy's confirmation.

He turned into the drive that led up to Lee's quarters. There seemed to be more of a stir than usual along the gravel toward the snug house. Groups of Legionaries stood watching the door. Others were bringing up led horses. Off to the left, where the drive swung down to the tracklike road again, a light carriage waited. Probably some local Whig had returned to his farm with the advent of the army and was conferring with Lee about forage for the Legion horses.

He glanced incuriously at the carriage as he passed it. Then he stopped, hands on his hips and eyes blank with surprise. Hanging just inside the carriage window was a deerskin bag, a bag that he had seen for the first time at the edge of the Santee swamps and again hanging to the newelpost at St. Aubin's house.

There could be no doubt about it. Dorande was in the farmhouse, talking with Harry Lee! He drew a deep breath. The only decent thing to do was to march boldly in, offer his congratulations to Dorande and then put her out of his mind forever—or try to. He must tell her, too, what a fine man de Chanzy was, tell her of the place that he had made for himself in an alien army.

Inside the farmhouse Dorande listened in angry incredulity. The stern-faced major of Greene's staff, acting for Lee during the latter's temporary absence, marked his points by rapping on the desk. "The patrol acted far beyond its rights. Mr. St. Auburn holds a pass signed by General Greene. That pass covers members of his household. By virtue of that pass, Mr. St. Auburn was clearly within his rights in ordering his vehicle, which is to be considered as part of his household, to proceed to Charleston."

Dorande, sitting erect, tapped her foot angrily. "The vehicle may go on to the Barbados! *I* do *not* accompany it. I was not in it by my own choice."

"You were in it by Mr. St. Auburn's direction," said Major Sloat curtly. "You are a minor. He stands *in loco parentis*. The two men who accompanied the vehicle are known patriots. Mr. St. Auburn had every right to send you to any destination he saw fit. Even without the pass, we are in his debt. Without a thought of profit to himself, he has secured title to confiscated estates, guarded them and, when he was able, has presented clear title to their original and lawful owners."

Dorande got up quickly. "*My* guards were patriots? *Allez!* Two weeks ago they rode the country, burning patriot homes. I know them. As for Monsieur St. Aubin's estates—"

Sloat raised his hand, his face unyielding. "There is no need for further talk! I regret that I can't please you. I only know my duty. The patrol that brought you here will escort your carriage to the Santee road and see that it proceeds in the direction specified by Mr. St. Auburn."

"You cannot do that! You cannot!"

"I can. I trust, Madame, that you will not make it difficult for me."

A step sounded outside. Dorande cried out, "You send for your guards? No! You cannot make me. I appeal to General Greene, to Colonel Lee, to General Marion. They know me."

"They could only agree with me. The interview is over!" He called, "Sergeant of the guard!"

The door flew open. Dorande clutched the back of the chair, then gave a low cry and ran to the pale, worn man in white who stood in the doorway. "Ross Pembroke! Explain to him! I will not go to Charleston. My uncle, he has sent a letter to Colonel Balfour, telling what I have done. I was helpless. By the river, I see the green dragoons! I call out and they bring me here, to our army. Now this man says I must go on as my uncle orders! Tell him, Ross Pembroke, tell him!" Her slim hands clung to Ross's lapels and she gave a sob of relief as an arm closed protectively about her shoulders. "I will not go. Tell him," she quavered.

Ross stared down at her in amazement, tightened his arm about her as he saw her bright hair pressed against his shoulder. He said gently "It'll be all right, Dorande. Trust me." Still holding her he nodded to the major. "Some mistake, sir."

"None," said Sloat.

"You haven't been here long, Major, or you'd know what Miss van Kortenaer's done for us. As for her uncle—have you seen his pass? Do you know that the signature's genuine?"

Sloat flushed. "Sir, when I require instruction in my duties from a captain, I shall apply in due form."

Dorande clung desperately to Ross and he felt her whole body trembling. He laughed, and patted her shoulder. He was confident that he could deal with Major Sloat, was almost grateful to him for unwittingly placing Dorande in his arms. Then his confidence ebbed. She had turned to him as an old friend, who was acting in the absence of another. He said with forced calm, "Don't worry. We'll find de Chanzy. Between us we'll straighten this out. Come now, sir, I'll make myself responsible for Miss van Kortenaer. If we can't find Colonel Lee, who knows all about her, why don't the three of us go to General Greene himself? Good Lord, man, he knows her, too.

Do you realize that *she* was the one who found the means to burn Fort Motte, that *she* lit that one beacon that warned us about Rowdon at Ninety-six?"

Sloat snapped, "We've wasted too much time. Where the devil's that sergeant?" He clattered to his feet and stamped from the office bellowing, "Sergeant!"

Ross looked about quickly, then caught Dorande's hand and led her through a door at the rear of the room, thinking, "I'm acting 'for and in the absence of' Phil. Just the same—"

The inner room had no other door than that leading to Sloat's office. "This way," he said, straddled the low window and dropped to the ground, where he turned and held out his arms. Dorande sat on the sill, swung her feet about and reached toward him. She was still pale but her eyes were bright. She gave a wriggle, cried out in dismay as she clutched at her skirts that slid back to show round, white-stockinged legs.

She was in his arms for an instant, then he set her down gently. Slowly she let her feet drop, loosened her arms reluctantly. "Afraid of falling," thought Ross. He slipped a hand under her elbow and guided her on along a path that slanted behind the house. "Nothing to worry about now, Dorande. We'll take this path right to Greene's quarters. Everyone there knows you—Carrington and Davie and the rest. Rotten luck, having to run into Sloat, who's just joined us."

Dorande tugged at his arm, brought him to a halt. "I must look at you. Ross Pembroke! What has happened to you? So pale, so thin?" He saw concern in her eyes, a quiver about her lips.

"Just a little fever. Please hurry. Sloat will have found his sergeant and will begin looking for us. Just keep on going. When we get to Greene's, we'll comb the country for de Chanzy. I—I must present my congratulations."

Dorande smiled up at him. "Ah, that one, he lost no time in urging his suit."

The path was smooth and tree-sheltered, but Ross felt his steps dragging. He tried to answer her smile. "There's no better man in the army than Phil de Chanzy. I know you're very happy about it all, but not so happy as he is."

"Happy? But of course I rejoice."

"I suppose you'll go to France with him at the end of the war." His face ached with the effort to retain a smile that battled against the torment of her nearness and her obvious joy.

She gasped, caught at his arm and swung him to a halt. "I? Go to France with Monsieur de Chanzy? Ross Pembroke, what has fever done to you?"

He looked at her in amazement. "You—but everyone says —and just now you told me you were happy and—"

She threw back her head. *"Mais enfin!* Happy, and why not? Did I not present Monsieur de Chanzy to that pretty Claire Long whose father brought her to the Congaree after the fall of Ninety-six? Did *I* not see that they were made for each other? Did I not talk to them both until they saw it too? And you ask me if I go to France with Monsieur de Chanzy!"

A wave of light in which he scarcely dared believe swept over Ross. "Then it's not—"

"Bien, sûr, it is not." Her mouth puckered indignantly. "That *you* could think that I—has the fever taken your memory? Have you forgotten what I told you from the window at Madame Motte's? If you were not so ill, I could shake you! And—you make me say more than a girl ought to say. And because—"

He caught her hands. "And what *did* you say from the window?"

She freed her hands impatiently. "You see? You ask me to say everything! You ask me, that night, what I should do if you rode off with me in earnest. You forget my answer? Then I shall be so *effrontée,* so brazen, as to tell you. I say, '*Je l'accueille de tout moncoeur.' Voilà!* That satisfies you?"

"I know! I know!" Ross exploded. "But what does it *mean?*"

Dorande's eyes widened in amazement. "What does it mean? You did not know?" Her lids slowly drooped and her mouth was soft and tender. "Ah, Ross Pembroke. It means *this!*"

He gave a wild laugh and caught her up as she swayed toward him. Her cheek was soft against his and her lips turned gladly to him, murmuring low, broken words. The green sunlit world spun about him. He said, "I didn't know. I didn't dare hope. Oh, Dorande, since that first time by the Santee—" Her hands were straying over his face and her long lashes lay dark over her closed eyes. The soft roundness of her body was pressed to him, clinging and yielding.

She whispered, "On the Santee—but you were so *bourru,* so gruff."

"I had to be. And you—you tilted your chin and looked as though you were trying to freeze me."

"And *I* had to. You frightened me, and yet— Oh, to think that you didn't dare. *Mon adoré,* there was nothing to dare. I tell you so—and so—and so—"

Shouts from the now distant farmhouse beat in Ross's ears. "The devil! Sloat! He didn't think of the window at first and supposed we'd left by the front door. Now—"

"Now," agreed Dorande, nestling comfortably against him.

"Now we better make for Greene's. Not that Sloat could do anything even if he brought a whole squadron with him."

They threaded along the narrow path, hurrying until the roof of the Laurens mansion showed over the trees. There was a last, breathless pause and then they walked, apart and decorous, up the drive past saluting orderlies.

Headquarters was thrown into a turmoil by Dorande's entrance. Davie, Carrington, William Washington, all the men who knew what she had done, crowded about her. Carrington explained that Greene was expected any moment and as to Sloat's plans, which Ross hastily detailed, they could be forgotten completely. Then Ross saw Davie eying him and Dorande with a sympathetic smile, saw him nudge Washington, saw him murmur to Kirkwood. All at once the room was empty and Dorande turned a surprised look on Ross. "But they are gone! They leave us here."

"Probably busy," said Ross.

"No doubt. Now I place you in this chair. Yes, I insist, since you are *grand invalide*. So. Now, I draw up *this* chair." Utterly content, Ross watched her bustling about like a grave, frowning child. Then she sat beside him, head resting on his shoulder and her hand in his. "Now, when our general arrives, I push my chair, *so*, and we sit proper and *rangés*."

"But he isn't here yet," said Ross.

There was a stir among the guards outside. Dorande quickly shot her chair a good ten feet from Ross's and her hands flew to her hair.

Ross leaned forward, looking out of the window. "Here he comes. The guards are saluting. And—great sizzling snakes! *Who* is that with him?"

Riding blandly beside Greene, in a sky-blue coat and fawn-colored breeches, Paul St. Aubin touched his hat graciously in acknowledgment of the salutes. Ross sprang to the window, Dorande by his side, her hand slipped through his arm. He whispered reassuringly, "Don't worry."

She smiled bravely up at him, but her eyes were clouded.

He repeated, "I say, don't worry. It's a hundred to one that he thinks you're well on your way. He and Greene weren't on the road that goes past Sloat. He can't have heard anything. Step back a little. We don't want him to see us—yet.

The blasted fool! *Why* has he come here? So many people know all about him! And yet—what can be *proved?* He's a French subject and—ah! Listen!"

Greene and St. Aubin had dismounted and were coming up the steps. St. Aubin's voice was clear and firm. "No, *Monsieur le général*, my task was not an easy one, but what would you? Now, as I told you, I wish to find Captain Gray, Monsieur Fesenzac, Monsieur Atherton. Or perhaps your staff could attend to the matter. Their deeds I carry with me, *tout en règle,* but I do not wish their thanks. It is enough that I know these gentlemen to be repossessed of their estates."

Greene said rather stiffly, "Does you credit, I'm sure. I'll be obliged, though, if you'll be good enough to step into my quarters for a few minutes. You must realize that there are a number of questions to answer."

"Mais avec plaisir." St. Aubin bowed. He and the general entered the house and a door across the hall slammed behind them.

Dorande whispered angrily, "Ah, no doubt he has guessed what the questions will be and has his answers well shaped."

"I know. Damn it, he's so slick he could slide uphill. Look here, maybe we both better go in. Greene may need us. You could spoil those answers."

She said uncertainly, "I do not know. There is much that I suspect. But what may I prove? I can show that he entertained Tories and Englishmen. But why not? And for yourself, can you say to the general, 'I *know* that on this or that date he did this or planned this?' "

Ross rubbed his knuckles across his chin. "I could set Greene's mind working. The trouble is, it would set St. Aubin's working too. What's to stop him from saying, 'Yes, I've heard tales like that. I had to hear them in order to do what I did.' So far as I can make out, from what we heard, he's trying to convince Greene that he's on our side, and has actually been so all along—or at worst, benevolently neutral toward us."

"Eh bien, let him. He is bound to stumble."

"And how? You see, things are going pretty well for us and he wants to ride on the crest. Don't make any mistake about it. He's sharp enough to make himself really useful to us. On the other hand, if things go badly, he's in a good position to somersault backwards to the Crown. You wait and see. It's certain that, probably right now, he's making Greene an offer so advantageous to us that he'll *have* to accept. If we begin to lose, he'll clamor to the British that it was forced from him by Greene. He'll yell for an indemnity from the Crown—and get it."

Dorande was silent. Then she said unsteadily, "You—you cannot believe—I mean that Greene would make me—"

"I don't know." Ross's jaws clamped down firmly. "I don't understand local law. It differs in the various colonies, you know. But I've heard that *all* law here puts the family above everything. St. Aubin might claim that he represents your family and has control over you as a minor."

"Does it stand so in the Rhode Island?" asked Dorande.

"No! By Jove, it doesn't and—had I made it clear to you that you're very soon to join a Rhode Island family?"

She tossed her head. "It was I who had to make it clear to you. Just the same— Oh, *could* he? There is one thing, Ross Pembroke—" She turned and started for the door.

"Here," he called, "where are you going?"

"I must know—and at once. If I stand here wondering—no. I must be sure. Come!"

He hurried after her. "But Dorande, you can't burst right into a general's office. It just can't be done!"

"Of course not," said Dorande, her hand on the latch. The latch clicked and the door swung open. Dorande came in quickly, Ross close behind her.

St. Aubin sat in front of Greene's desk, his back to the door. He seemed quite at his ease, while Greene looked up with a troubled frown. He was on his feet at once, holding out a hand to Dorande while he attempted a cordial smile. "This is a very great pleasure, I assure you. You find me rather busy at the moment, but I'm sure that Captain Pembroke will take good care of you until I am free."

St. Aubin turned quickly in his chair, then glided to his feet, bowing, a mocking smile on his face. "This is a most unexpected pleasure." The shock of seeing Dorande must have been great but he masked it completely. "My dear General, there is no need for the captain to concern himself about my niece. We have nearly finished, you and I. She may wait here with us. Then we return together to the Congaree."

Dorande's eyes blazed. "We do *not* return to the Congaree. I shall never—"

St. Aubin raised a languid hand. "Please do not disturb General Greene with academic discussions." He smiled at Greene. "Under the laws of our state, I stand in the place of both father and mother." He turned his bland smile on Ross. "Surely, Captain, General Greene will excuse you from further attendance in this room."

In a wave of hot anger, Ross took a quick step toward St. Aubin. Greene said sharply, "Pembroke!"

Ross fell back, scowling, his fists still clenched. "Very well, sir. But allow me to point out that that man has nothing to say about Miss van Kortenaer, who's going to be Mrs. Pembroke as soon as we can find a chaplain."

A look of relief passed over Greene's face. It vanished as St. Aubin said smoothly, "I think not. Again, as head of the family, I do not feel justified in permitting such a match. How could I explain such mad folly to her parents, whose stewardship has passed to me, pro tempore?" He laughed lightly at the absurdity of the very notion.

Greene was seated at the desk with his head in his hands. Ross said, "Sir, will you allow—"

Greene raised a weary hand. "You know the feeling of the country, Pembroke. I—I hate to say it but— You know very well how careful we've been to subordinate military rule to civil. You know what I'd like to say, but—you know how touchy each state is about its own laws. A clamor like this could be worse than a lost battle." He turned to St. Aubin. "Surely you won't persist in your opposition. I can vouch utterly for young Pembroke. I know his family well—"

"And I," said St. Aubin blandly, "know only my duty to my sister and her husband."

Dorande turned to Ross and buried her face against him. He looked out the window to avoid St. Aubin's stare of cool triumph. His head whirled with a cloud of anger. He barely saw the trees and the bright lawn outside, was only dimly aware of a man in tattered country clothes passing along the porch.

He wheeled toward Greene again, one arm about Dorande. "Sir, you're asking too much. You're giving in too much."

"I know it," said Greene in a heavy voice.

"But I'm not asking a thing, not giving in a thing." He bit down hard on his anger, spoke as evenly as he could to St. Aubin. "Do you really expect that you can keep us apart?"

St. Aubin shrugged. "It is the law, not I. As to my means, I am sure that my friend General Greene will offer me ample aid to prevent the storm that would arise in the event of that law's flouting. General Sumter, for one, would be furious at seeing the statutes of his state set aside by a Northerner. Ah, yes. It leaps to the eye. He and many others. They could well withdraw from the fight. I know the temper of these people."

"But Mr. St. Aubin—" began Greene. Then he looked up, his big shoulders heaving back angrily as the man in country clothes whom Ross had vaguely seen on the porch stepped in. Before the general could speak the countryman drew himself up, saluting. "Captain Jaudon reporting, sir."

His three visitors forgotten, Greene strode quickly to Raoul. "You've news for me? Then please go over it with Carrington. Join me here in fifteen minutes, the two of you."

Raoul's eyes quickly took in the other occupants of the room. He threw one arm around Ross's shoulders, the other about Dorande. "What on earth have you two been up to? Well, we'll talk about that later. General, with your permission, the military matters can wait for a few minutes. I've something else for you and it couldn't be a better time in view of your present company. May I suggest, sir, that Captain Pembroke guard the door while I make another report?"

Puzzled and frowning, Greene nodded to Ross. Raoul placed a chair for Dorande, then, with Greene's permission, took another for himself. "What's the report?" asked Greene impatiently.

Raoul drew out a thick pack of papers from his ragged coat. "The report, sir, has its title on the wrapper. 'The Dossier on Paul St. Aubin.' "

Ross glanced at St. Aubin, who sank back in his chair, motionless and seemingly undisturbed, watching Raoul from under lowered lids. Raoul began, "I've got a whole lot of things here, sir, that touch a good many parts of the state. For the moment, I won't go over them all, but just pick out a few typical ones. The others, perhaps, you'll read at your leisure. Item: St. Aubin, in March of this year, sent an *agent-provocateur* into the Williamsburg District, where the latter raised a force of men ostensibly to serve with General Marion. They were deliberately led into a Tory ambush and massacred."

St. Aubin started to speak, but General Greene held up his hand. "Later, sir. Please go on, Captain Jaudon."

"This was repeated with even greater success north of Ninety-six in January. He financed the Cherokees who came down to join Browne at Fort Galphin. You know what happened there." His cool level voice went on. False evidence had been produced that had led in many cases to families, who were keeping their parole, being imprisoned and their estates turned over to the Sequestration Office. There was a very recent matter of a pass, to which Greene's name had been forged, the pass being held by two notoriously brutal Tories, now in custody of the Legion dragoons. "These, sir, are merely samples. I mention one more item because it touches me very deeply. Monsieur St. Aubin, the next time you pick a hired assassin, find one who doesn't drink. Your Bayne had been tossing guineas about the Orangeburg district, bragging about how he got them and how he would earn more. Keep your eye out for Bayne, Ross. He's after you."

"I know about Bayne," said Ross. He glanced at Dorande, who sat, silent and white-faced, her eyes on her uncle.

Greene turned to St. Aubin, who seemed outwardly collected, although his eyes slid from side to side as though seeking an exit. "Well, sir," said the general, his tones ice hard. "What have you to say to that?"

St. Aubin waved airily, though his hand seemed unsteady. "*Justement*, the sort of thing of which I spoke to you earlier. Yes, I have had to endure much."

Greene's eyes went back to Raoul. "Proof, sir?"

Raoul nodded. "Plenty. Affidavits, sworn statements. You should have remembered, Monsieur St. Aubin, that the type of man whom you hired for your various enterprises was not apt to be distinguished for any loyalty to his employer. Many of them talked freely with me and my friends, under varying inducements." He mentioned several names that meant nothing to Ross.

But their effect on St. Aubin was amazing. He slumped lower in his chair, seemed to turn in an instant into a sapless, wizened old man, shaky and slack-mouthed. His voice was a dry rustle in this throat. "Lies, *mon général*, all lies. Forgeries."

Greene turned slowly to St. Aubin, his face black with anger. Ross watched him. The Greene temper was famous in Rhode Island, and he wondered if the general's mastery of it was about to crack. Greene drew a deep breath, switched about in his chair and leaned his arms on his desk. His face was stern, but calm. The room was very still. Ross could hear the slight wheeze that told him that Greene's asthma had not yielded to Carolina suns. Then he spoke, slowly and levelly. "Mr. St. Aubin, there is enough here to send you to a firing squad. Or, rather, enough to deny you that honor. I sat on poor André's court-martial and sent him to the hangman. Yet *he* was an honorable man. Still, you are Miss van Kortenaer's uncle. I will have no shame touch her even indirectly."

Ross saw that St. Aubin was rallying a little as Greene seemed to be rejecting the death sentence. The general went on. "For her sake, this is what I shall do. A flag of truce will go to the nearest British post. You will go with it, under heavy escort—not that I fear that you could escape from the men I detail, but to protect you from any South Carolinians you may meet. Many of them would shoot you on sight, and justifiably. With the flag, I shall send a letter signed by me, to Colonel Balfour at Charleston and another to Colonel Stuart. Both are honorable men. On reading my letter, which will be based on Captain Jaudon's report and which will include the proposals which you made me, they may do with you as they see fit. I shall make no recommendations. Captain Pembroke, please call the officer of the day to take charge of the prisoner."

St. Aubin struggled to his feet. "No! No! Look—I have good British gold. I know where supplies—"

Greene turned his back on him as the officer of the day entered. "Good day, sir," he said coldly.

When St. Aubin had been literally carried from the office, Greene stepped past the desk and took Dorande's hands. "My dear, I wish I could have spared you this. At least, you can be sure that he'll never trouble you again." He smiled and a great warmth spread over his face. "Now there's nothing to stop you from turning into a good Rhode Islander. Jove! I must write Kitty about this. You'll be neighbors of ours, and let me tell you, I'll see that every soul in the state from the Seekonk to Weekapaug knows what you've done for us down here. Pick your time and choose your chaplain. I'll give the bride away."

Dorande started to speak. Then her lips quivered and her eyes filled. She threw her arms about Greene's blue shoulders and kissed him. He chuckled delightedly. "Well, well, well. Bless my soul! This is— Well, now we'll have to see about quartering you. Where's a good place?"

"She knows the Widow Cantey and her brother very well, sir," said Ross. "They're sort of cousins of Marion's. I'm billeted there now, but I'll move over with de Chanzy."

"Capital," said Greene. "About finding a minister for you, though. That may not be easy. There's not a chaplain in my whole force and with the country upset as it is, it may take days to find any kind of parson."

Dorande smiled at him. "But what do a few days matter, since we shall be together, here in the High Hills?"

"Well," said Greene slowly, "I'm afraid you won't be. You see, I wasn't at all surprised to see your young man here at headquarters, as I'd already sent for him. He must have left home before the order was delivered. Yes, Pembroke, I've got a job for you. It won't take very long and by the time you're back, we'll have some kind of a minister for you."

"Send me, sir," broke in Raoul.

Greene looked at him with quick understanding. "I am

sending you—but to Fort Motte, where *your* young lady is. No, I'm afraid this is for Pembroke only." He turned to Ross. "You're quite well now?"

Ross set his teeth. "Quite, sir."

"Had any chance to follow what's been happening while you were ill?"

"I've a fair idea." Ross felt Dorande's hand tighten on his.

"It's quite simple. The rivers are in flood. Stuart, the British commander's only about seventeen miles away from us, as the crow flies. But the floods have turned the High Hills into a sort of island. He'd have to make a circuit of over seventy miles to get at us. So he's waiting south of the Santee, near Eutaw Springs. Is that clear?"

"Quite," said Ross, wondering how all this affected him.

"And," said Greene, "Francis Marion's watching Stuart. I don't know exactly where Marion is, but he's somewhere to the south of Stuart. In a few days, I'm going to break camp here. I'll make a long swing to the north, to avoid the flooded lands, then cut down to the Congaree, across it and along the south bank of the Santee. In other words, I've decided when and where I'm going to fight, and Stuart's *got* to accept my decision. I want you to start as soon as you can and find Marion."

"I'll find him for you, sir," said Ross, glancing at Dorande, who nodded encouragingly.

Raoul started to speak but Greene held up his hand. "Just a moment, Jaudon. Now, Pembroke, when you find Marion, and I guess that'll be somewhere near Fairlawn, I want you to do some persuading. I want him with the main army when we meet Stuart. I've got to have him. He thinks that he and his men aren't adapted to formal war. I differ with him. Beyond that, a lot of South Carolina militia have come into camp. They're fine stuff, but they've got no real leader. That's natural enough, seeing how torn up the state's been. The one man whom they'll all trust is Francis Marion. Put him in the field with them, and they'll equal any Continental troops I've got. You know our war. You know Marion's. Show him what it'll mean to the army to have him and his men with us. Of course, I'll send formal orders to him later, but I want him prepared for them. You're the one man in the army who can see to that preparation. It's—"

Raoul broke in quickly. "Excuse me, sir. This is something you've all got to know. It's in the military report I've made for you. Marion's nowhere near Fairlawn."

"What!" cried Greene sharply.

"No, sir. He got word that Colonel Harden was in bad

trouble. He's taken two hundred men and gone south to get Harden out of it."

"Any idea where he's heading?" asked Greene.

"Only that it's somewhere along the Pon Pon, well to the southwest of Charleston, sir."

"The Pon Pon? What the deuce is that?" asked Greene.

"It's what some people call the last stretch of the Edisto River, a hundred-mile ride from here at the very least, especially with the rivers flooded."

Greene got to his feet. "In that case, we can't have the least delay. I'll write an order for all the guides and spare horses that you need. Find Marion. Nothing else counts." He turned to Dorande and Ross, who had risen, and took Dorande's hand. "My dear, I'm sorry, very sorry. I'll have Jaudon take you to Fort Motte and you can stay there with Mrs. Motte and Mrs. Jaudon."

Ross put his arm about Dorande's shoulder. "Don't worry. I'll see you at Fort Motte before you've had time to unpack that deerskin bag. I wish—I—well, anyway, I've got to find Marion."

"But, of course! And then—" She looked about, surprised. Greene and Raoul were gone and the outer latch of the door clicked into place. She gave a low laugh and went on, "And then, *chéri*, you come to find me and that will not be so hard as running after the Swamp Fox. Ah, you will see! And there will be a *prédikant*, a minister, for us. Our general will see to that, he and I."

Ross looked down at her a little dizzily. Was it possible? A quick ride to the south, then a north turning that would bring him up the road to the Congaree and Dorande. He caught her to him, swept her off her feet. "It's true, Dorande, it's true! Do you guess a little how happy I am?" He perched her on the edge of Greene's desk. "Didn't you hear me? I asked if you could guess—"

"But not so much as I, Ross Pembroke. Ah, truly I think that the trees have fallen away from the Dawn Stone. You do not know that story? It is one that I shall tell you when you ride up the road to the Congaree—but only one of many. No —I do not tell you now. There is no time. Did not General Greene say you leave at once? So—quickly you go, quickly you return. But—oh, *chéri*, be careful!"

For two days Ross followed a silent guide over a course that bent, twisted, doubled on itself, shot off eccentrically, a course largely dictated by the high waters of the rivers. It had begun by heading north up the Wateree, then crossing at

Ancrum's Ferry and swinging south to the Congaree by Howell's Ferry. From the last point, Ross lost all track of direction and distance and set himself to the one vital task of keeping up with his leader, who always took the rough road instead of the smooth, the dense swamp instead of the broad level savannah.

His body, still weakened by the recent attack of fever, ached with exertion. When he dismounted, his joints were weak and his head swam. But his heart sang and he hummed to himself as swampy miles were left behind. Another ten miles, ten again, a halt for sleep, thirty miles. Then he would pick up Marion's trail, deliver his message and turn Ree's head to the north once more, to the north on the road to Fort Motte and the Congaree.

When the guide suggested slackening his pace, Ross laughed at him, told him to double it if he could. He laughed again when the supply of boiled rice went sour, when maggots were found in the salt beef and the biscuit. Nothing mattered. Nothing except finding Marion was anything more than an incident on the road that led north to Dorande.

There were more sunrises and sunsets as the trail led south and east, skirting the edge of an endless stretch of deep bog land which the guide identified as Four Hole Swamp. It would take them eventually, he said, to the bend of the Edisto and the district known as the Pon Pon. When they passed the spongy expanse where Cow Castle Creek joined Four Hole, they stopped to pick at the bones of a turkey that the guide had shot the day before. The guide, gnawing at a drumstick, frowned. "I'm plumb haig-ridden," he muttered. "Made certain we'd pick up a sign of Marion before now."

"We'll hit him all right," said Ross. "And Four Hole's a fine signpost for the way back. I could get to the Congaree alone."

"Maybe," said the guide, getting to his feet. "Time to be wearin' on."

Late in the afternoon, the guide halted, looked back at Ross. "Maybe they ain't much need of markin' a road home."

"Why not?" asked Ross, brushing away Spanish moss that hung low from a cypress.

"That's why," said the guide, pointing to the soft ground.

Ross could only make out a muddy stretch in the grass. "What about it?" he asked.

"Tories or British. Ridin' tackies. Tackies don't pick up their feet like a good horse. Then there's that bit of red cloth hangin' to that branch." He looked sourly about. "Nope. Maybe we'll fall foul of them folks and home's one place we won't get to see."

Ross dismounted, studied the trampled ground. He could only take the guide's word for the fact that tackies had passed that way, but the bit of red cloth was beyond argument. Color and weave were unquestionably regulation. He looked at it ruefully, realizing that he would have ridden by those signs that had told the guide so much. He cast deeper off the trail. There were a good many branches scattered on the ground, as though a windstorm had swept down Four Hole Swamp. He picked up one branch idly, then stiffened, staring at it. He handed it to the guide. "What do you think of that?"

The guide took it casually. "Cut not many hours gone. 'Bout the same time them fellers went by," he said, pointing to the hoof marks.

Ross gave a sudden laugh and the guide stared at him. Ross kicked through a heap of branches, all similarly cut. "What about all this? Did they stop and cut all these?" He laughed again, remembering the cypress screen that Marion's men had rigged up in a swamp now far to the north. "And look here. Beyond the branches. Marks of ten—maybe twenty horses." He mounted briskly. "Get going. We're close to Marion. Forget about the tackies."

The guide's mouth sagged in chagrin as he stared at the traces that he had missed. But there was new respect in his eyes. He cleared his throat and said, "Well, now, wouldn't surprise me much if we was close to Marion."

Four Hole Swamp slanted sharper to the south as the two rode on. Ross stood in his stirrups from time to time but he could make out nothing beyond the eternal tangle of woods and the endless, sinister crooks, cypress knees rising out of molasses-colored swamp water. Suddenly he gave a shout and whipped off his helmet. Far away to the front of them a single, high whistle trilled out. He threw back his head, answered it. There was silence for an instant, then the sound was repeated, closer.

Ross spurred past the guide, shouting, "I'll take the lead. We're nearing home."

He was surprised at the excitement, the expectancy that filled him as the whistle shrilled out again. It was like coming home, like striking onto one of the fords by Snow Island, far to the north. Men who had ridden with him to the Black Mingo, men who had toiled on endlessly during Tarleton's futile pursuit of Marion appeared among the trees. They shouted to him in welcome that astonishment did nothing to diminish. Then, splashing over a marsh, he saw more men, lines of tethered horses, small, smokeless fires. There were the Horry brothers waving, young Gavin James, John James of the Lake. Ross swept his helmet off in acknowledgment, then clapped it back on his head and swung to the ground, hand raised in salute.

Francis Marion was limping toward him over the rough ground, hands behind his back and dark face as impassive as ever. Still holding the salute, Ross said formally, "A message from General Greene to General Marion."

The brigadier's impassivity melted in a warm smile. He returned the salute sketchily, then shook Ross's hand. "I'm glad to see you. Very glad. What can I do for you and for General Greene?"

"The general wants you to listen to me for about three minutes, sir. That's all." He looked down at the well-remembered figure. The scorched cloak, the rusty sword, the worn jacket and breeches were the same. Somewhere Marion had found a new skullcap, but the old plate of the Second South Carolina was proudly affixed to it. Ross added quickly, "I—I'm glad to be here, sir. I wish I were staying."

"I could use you, Ross," said Marion. "Now tell me about General Greene." He beckoned to Peter Horry, who ambled over, greeting Ross warmly. The three sat on a flat rock. "Go on, Ross," said Marion.

Ross tried to recapture the flavor rather than the words of what Greene had said to him at headquarters and again just before Ross left the High Hills. He described the influx of South Carolinians, their undoubted will to fight, their uncertainty in their leadership and organization. It would take little, he thought, to change them from a dubious asset to a highly valuable one. "It's the general's opinion that only one man can supply that little," Ross concluded. "You're the man. He wants as much of your command as you can muster, but above everything else, he wants you even if you have to come alone."

Marion, who had been listening carefully with his eyes on the ground, was silent for a moment. Then he said, "What do you think, Peter?"

Peter Horry shook his head. "It's not our war. You can do more good hacking at Stuart's communications with ten men than you could standing in line of battle with two hundred. We've agreed on that, Francis."

Marion turned his head. "Can you answer that, Ross?"

"A few months ago I'd have agreed," replied Ross. "Now, I think Greene's right. The two wars can fit together." Horry shook his head, frowning, and Ross went on eagerly. "How about your work with the Legion? You flushed the garrison out of Fort Watson. You laid regular siege to Fort Motte.

And you taught the Legion a lot. I used Legion troopers to take the post at McCord's Ferry, but I used them the way I'd have used your men. And—and—yes! Now I've got you. When I said I wished that I were staying with you, you said you could use me. You didn't talk that way back at Chilyon's Castle. You said then you *couldn't* use me."

"You've learned a lot, Ross," said Peter.

"From you and all your men. I have. But do you think I'm smarter than you and your people? You've learned a lot more than I have, if you'd only realize it." He purposely addressed himself to Horry, talking to him across Marion. "Why, you and the general and your brother and the rest, mixed in with these South Carolinians who know you and trust you—you'd turn them from water into solid rock. When the army meets Stuart, I'll probably be out on the flanks with the cavalry. I won't worry at all about our center if I know you and the others from your state are there."

Marion spoke thoughtfully. "What's Greene's line of march?"

"North up the Wateree, then south to the Congaree and on along this bank of the Santee. It's a huge circle that he's making, but it's the only way."

"I see," said Marion. "This is August thirtieth. It'll take him a good week, counting from today, to get near Stuart. Yes. His plan's interesting. I wish him well with it. Now Peter, you and Hugh better talk with your captains and go over what we've come down here for." He nodded to Ross. "Thank you for delivering the message."

Ross stared at him. "You're going ahead with your raids down *here?* But—why, good God, sir, what sort of an answer can I take to Greene? I can't stress too much how greatly he's counting on you."

Marion looked surprised. "Answer? There's only one answer. I'll join him a day or two before he meets Stuart with every man I can find. I thought you'd understood that. But that's a long way off. We've plenty of time for the work in hand. You know what brought us down here?"

"Only roughly," said Ross.

Marion glanced at Horry. "Tell him, Peter."

Horry stirred his long legs. "It's about Colonel Harden—William Harden, one of the best. The British from Charleston have got him and his men badly penned a little to the south of us. There's a column out, infantry and cavalry, to finish him off. We're going to see that they don't."

"Does Charleston know you're in the districnt?" asked Ross.

"Not so far as we can find out. We're going to get between Harden and this British force under Fraser. Brother Hugh's going to hide his infantry. We'll send the best of our cavalry along the Pon Pon near Parker's Ferry and let Fraser see them. We hope he likes them."

Ross nodded in comprehension. "Like the Tarleton chase."

"Some. Fraser'll chase the cavalry right past Brother Hugh. And Francis wants you to be sure that you lead them well past the ambush. That gives us a chance to—"

Ross's jaw dropped. "Wants *me* to lead them past—but look here, I've got to get back to Greene."

Horry looked sadly at him. "Didn't you hear Francis say he could use you? Why, what on earth did you think he meant except for this ambush? Don't worry about Greene. We'll send word to him and you can be with us when we join him. Isn't that what you meant, Francis?"

"Yes," said Marion.

"But—well, I—I've got another reason. I'm going to be married when I get back. Dorande's waiting and—"

"I know," said Marion.

"*You* knew?"

"Yes. Obvious. But not when," said Marion.

"Then you see that I've *got* to start back. We'd be married now only Greene wanted me to come down here."

Marion folded his small hands over his knee. "I said I could use you. Whether I do or not depends on one man—yourself."

"Yes," said Horry. "She'll wait. Wars seldom do. Now I feel mighty happy, hearing you two are really wedding. She's a fine little girl. Mighty fine. Wonder what she'd advise you to do, right now."

Ross sprang to his feet. "Oh damn it! You can't go putting yourself in her place. It's—all right. If you think I can do the job, use me. When do we start?"

"Midnight," said Marion. "Ambush is set for dawn. I'm greatly obliged to you, Ross. This is important. Now let's have some food."

Light was creeping along the forest road as Ross and Peter Horry led their group of twenty men cautiously on. Off to the left, the waters of the Pon Pon shone dully, then began to glitter as the sun edged over the horizon. Peter laid a hand on Ross's shoulder. "Remember, now. I'm colonel, but you're in command."

Ross shook his head. "We do this together."

"Maybe, but your say's final. Fraser's a regular and his troops are regulars, not Tory levies. You'll know what he's apt to do."

Ross grunted. "No better than you would. However—" He pulled Ree in abruptly, held up his hand. The little troop halted. From the south a new wind brought a faint, irregular drumming.

"Cavalry coming," said Ross. "We'll wait here until we sight them." Peter nodded, eyes on the brown of the road that grew more and more distinct.

The drumming, slow and steady, was closer. Ross straightened. Four horsemen in red jackets appeared around a bend. They were well spaced and riding at ease, their heads turning from side to side as they scanned the curtaining trees on either side of the road. Ross glanced at Horry and then started Ree slowly along toward the red cavalrymen who were obviously a patrol thrown out in advance of a larger body.

One of the British troopers saw him and whooped, pointing. The four men drew together, then one of them wheeled and galloped out of sight, his fellows reining in and waiting. Ross threw up his arm as though in alarm and fell back on Peter Horry and the others while the patrol still watched.

"Friends of ours?" asked Horry.

"Looks that way. They've sent one man back to the main body, probably thinking that we're some of Harden's men."

"Then what'll happen, Ross?"

"They'll come a-booming. Where's that drum?"

One of the detail handed Ross a battered drum from his pommel. Peter watched curiously. "Now I'd wondered what you were going to do with that. Going to beat a charge and scare those boys yonder?"

Ross grinned. "Just going to ask them some questions." He dismounted, set the drum on the ground and laid his ear to its head. At first he could hear nothing. Then the tight-stretched skin began to hum, deeper and deeper. Peter shouted in sudden warning, "Hurry! Here come the rest of our guests."

Ross held up his hand, ear pressed to the drumhead. There was no mistaking that rolling mutter that underlay the lighter tones. He sprang up, kicking the drum into the undergrowth. "There's the answer, Peter. Foot soldiers following the horse. Artillery—two pieces I'd say—following along." He mounted and swung Ree broadside to the road, staring.

A solid wall of red choked the lower reaches of the highway. The troopers were wearing skullcaps and Ross guessed that they were infantrymen turned into cavalry, as Tarleton had used the Welshmen of the 23rd in the retreat to the Dan. A bugle blared and the red wall moved on, first at a trot, then breaking into a gallop.

The detail wheeled raggedly about with shouts of alarm and began flogging their mounts along. Ross, bringing up the rear with Peter, watched them approvingly. Switches rose and fell in mock lashings. Men looked back over their shoulders, then crouched low in the saddles. The illusion of abject panic was perfect, but Ross knew that by a slight slackening of the reins, any man could race far beyond any danger of pursuit.

The leading British troop was getting close. Peter Horry pointed back to it and made frantic gestures to which Ross replied wildly as he fought to keep Ree's gait under control. Some officer, pounding along some twenty yards behind Ross, was bellowing, "God damn you, halt! Quarter, if you halt!"

Ross measured the distance between him and the nearest enemy with a quick glance. Close, but yet not close enough to be dangerous. A pistol smacked and a bullet sang high over his head. He nodded to Peter, who winked at him. Shooting from the saddle at a gallop would do no harm to anyone. Let the pursuit spend its ammunition if it liked.

Suddenly Peter raised his hand, jerked his head to the left of the road. Ross stared in surprise. The forest wall was thick and green. There was nothing to distinguish this particular bit from any other stretch past which he had ridden—nothing save a little trampled ground and a long furrow scored in the turf by Marion, who had used the end of a cut bough to trace this mark of identification.

Ross stood in his stirrups, found that some men were looking back over their shoulders inquiringly. He yelled, "Let 'em run!" Switches rose and fell in earnest. The big horses stretched into a flowing gallop and the trees echoed to the pounding hoofs. Ross yelled again, "Go on! Faster. We've got to lead them clear past! Faster! You've got—"

A ripping crash swallowed up his words and he felt Ree give a sudden bound under him. He let her go on for a few yards, then checked her, swerving her carefully to the right where the trees fell back from the road. As he straightened Ree out from her swing, he gave a shout of amazement.

Behind him, the road was a thick blanket of smoke in which tossed and reared the horses of the pursuit. Men in red, men in Tory green were on the ground. Horses rolled and writhed, lashing out with frantic hoofs. A dismounted officer with a bloody face was standing on the grass, waving madly. Somewhere in the depths of the smoke, those still mounted were obviously trying to wheel, to race back the way they had come, out of reach of the stinging fire from the woods.

Again the volley rang out and when its smoke finally lifted, a handful of fugitives were galloping off to the south while a few dismounted survivors limped after them. He started as Peter's hand fell on his shoulder. "Come on, Ross. Next move is back to Francis."

Ross rallied himself and followed Peter down a path that led deep into the woods, away from the road where the wreck of the British cavalry lay, men and horses inextricably tangled. Ross glanced back. There was no way to estimate the British loss but he guessed that sixty to seventy troopers and officers were dead or *hors de combat*. The shattered remainder would require long refitting and recruiting before they would be able to take the field again.

They found Marion in an open glade watching his men tear down the screen of branches that had been woven across their position. His dark face lit up as he saw the two and he limped toward them as they dismounted. "Thank God you're safe! There were a lot of them and they were coming hard. I was afraid they might run you down before our volley."

Ross asked anxiously, "Did it work all right? I held back our gait as long as I dared."

"Worked perfectly. They had to pass the ambush twice. I sent word to Harden and he'll be on his way south by now. Better mount. We're pushing on for a few miles before we rest."

"Pushing on! But there's infantry and artillery following that cavalry. Wait for them and blow them off the road. It'll be easy."

Marion shook his head. "Easy. Except for one thing, Ross. We started out with only four rounds per man. Most of the boys have just one left. Not enough."

Ross looked at him in amazement. "You started down here to rescue Harden with just four rounds per man!"

"Some had only three. But we had what we needed. There are Hugh's men mounting." He turned to Ross. "I'd be glad if you'd write a little report of this for Greene. Main point is that this cavalry we hit was intended as a reinforcement for Stuart; now Stuart won't get them. That's about all Greene will want to know. I'll tell him anything else that he wants to know when we meet him."

As the column wound on north and west, Ross rode in deep thought. He would report far more than that to Greene. With four rounds per man, Marion had marched over a hundred secret miles, had saved Harden and his men and had shattered Fraser's horsemen. Along the Santee Stuart would look in vain for his cavalry. Without the loss of a single man, Marion had dealt the British commander a crippling blow by the far-off Pon Pon.

The Santee! Ross sighed. He would see the Santee again, would undoubtedly be in action before the chance came to swing away from the army and take the road to the Congaree, the road that led up to the stockade of Mrs. Motte's house where Dorande waited. He closed his eyes. Seven days? Ten days? Two weeks? He touched the worn cartridge box that held Dorande's picture. Time and space would pass away somehow, yielding to the day when once more he would see her dark eyes light up with pleasure, hear her soft voice calling, "Ross Pembroke!"

XIII • The Dawn Stone

With a September sunrise at their backs, Marion and Ross, un-
escorted, rode along the south bank of the Santee. The night
before, the little command had ended its long, winding march
up from the Pon Pon and Ross had expected to run onto
Greene's outposts, if not his main army. But, in the dusk,
road, field and swamp had been empty, silent.

Ross glanced at the brigadier, trying to read some trace of
his own uneasiness in that dark, aquiline face, but Marion
rode on, impassive. Ross tried to take comfort from the
other's calm, but somber questions gnawed at his mind. Had
something gone wrong? Where was Greene? The British
camp was not many miles down the river and if Stuart had
wind of Marion's presence, the position of the unsupported
band of partisans bivouacked back there would be desperate.

Light grew stronger and Ross stood in his stirrups to scan
the tree-masked road ahead. If Greene were off there in the
fading shadows, the first hint of his approach would be the
white crests and green jackets of the legion or the black helmets of William Washington's dragoons. But no plume
waved, no saber glittered along the western reaches.

All at once Marion said in a low tone, "On time!" Ross
stared harder. The road was still empty, so far as he could
see. There were no alert dragoon patrols pacing toward them.
Then he saw that brown and gray moved under the trees,
flanking the highway, that men in buckskin or homespun
were filtering toward him, green sprigs in their hats and muskets or rifles ready. Someone shouted from the woods at the
right and quick-gliding men crowded onto the road while
Ross surveyed them with a professional eye. For all their
alertness, they seemed restless and uncertain as they pressed
on toward Marion. A big man with a sword banging about

his knees caught at Marion's stirrup, shouting, "Is it true? You going to take us into action? That's what they're saying in camp. Is it true?"

Marion, checking his horse, smiled down at the big man. "If the South Carolina militia wants me, I'm here. Now where's—"

A deep shout of relief swept up from the road. Ross caught cries of, "It's Marion! He's taking us in." . . . "I told you! Look at him, there! He's come to lead us!" . . . " 'Twa'n't a damn Tory lie! There he is!"

Marion held up his hand. "Easy, boys. I'll lead as long as you follow, if that's what you want. Now where's General Greene?"

Still yelling, men pointed along the road, their eyes now alight with faith, their uneasiness gone. Marion raised his hand to his cap, smiled again and started off at a fast trot, while the South Carolina militia lined the road on both sides. Ross, following, felt an odd tightness in his throat as he rode past the cheering men.

There was more militia, North Carolina as well as South, and voices suddenly sure and exultant rolled up under the trees. Then there were green jackets and white plumes far ahead and Marion broke into a gallop. Legion troopers recognized him, began to shout as the militia had shouted, opened their ranks to let Ross and Marion pass. Ross found that he was yelling with the troopers, galloping hard after Marion's big sorrel. Trees, rocks, blurred past him.

Then, almost without warning, Marion had reined in, was saluting a big, handsome man in blue and white who let the reins fall on his horse's neck, whipped off his hat and held out his hand. "I knew you'd come," said Greene simply.

"Of course," said Marion, returning his grip.

Ross somehow found it hard to keep his eyes clear as he saw the meeting of the two men who meant so much to the fortunes of the Colonies, two men so different, sprung from the far north and the far south of the country, and yet so oddly alike.

Then the Virginian Harry Lee was greeting Marion flamboyantly. William Washington was trotting up and the swarthy Marquis de Malmédy was bowing from the saddle. The Swamp Fox had taken his rightful place in the battle line of his country.

The group broke up. As the commander passed Ross he clapped him on the shoulders. "I knew you'd bring him. Fine work."

Ross shook his head. "I didn't have to talk. I just said you needed him and—" he shrugged—"the rest you can see for yourself."

"Just the same, I'm mighty pleased with you," said Greene. "Better look for your friend de Chanzy. He's been worrying ever since you left camp. And your young lady's safe and well with Mrs. Motte on the Congaree."

Later, at the head of a troop of dragoons, Ross rode with de Chanzy. Not far down the road, three men paced along, a Virginian, a Rhode Islander and a South Carolinian, their heads bent in earnest talk. Ross pointed to them. "Look, Phil. Lee, Greene and Marion. Now we're ready for anything."

De Chanzy nodded. "Ah, I believe you, we are ready, *mon vieux*. Just last night I talk with our Greene, who spoke much of you. For those three, down there, he holds you to have been the interpreter, making each of them clear, one to the other, where otherwise there might have been misunderstanding."

"*I?*" exclaimed Ross. "All I've done is run errands between them."

"There is more than that, says our Greene. For one thing, when first he came to this state, he distrusted the militia. Their worth you made clear to him. From Marion, long ago by the Congaree, I hear how you explain Greene and his ways to him. To our good friend Lee, you show how his men can act as partisans one day and as regular troops the next. You did not know this? But it leaps to the eye and I will not argue it with you." He settled himself in the saddle. "*Ça.* The pot boils again. Where may we come upon this species of Stuart and his redcoats?"

"Marion says we'll hit him at Eutaw Springs."

De Chanzy nodded calmly. "Then at Eutaw Springs we meet Stuart. Ah, he is never wrong, that one." De Chanzy indicated the little man who rode quietly at Nathanael Greene's right, down the road that led along the Santee to the twin springs that bubbled up by a great brick house.

Under a sweltering sky, smoke rolled heavily through the clearings up to the gardens of the distant brick house by Eutaw Springs. Ross wiped sweat from his forehead as the cavalry of the Legion re-formed after a charge against John Coffin's horsemen at the extreme left of the British line. Through the drifting haze, dragoons rode, now clear in a hot patch of sun, now seeming to float with the acrid smoke while the surrounding woods rang and echoed. Troop commanders were roaring, "From on me! Rally by those trees!"

Ross made out Eggleston, in command of Lee's cavalry for the day. "What orders?" he shouted, his voice hoarse.

"All troops form by the woods. By God, did you ever see a fight like this?"

Ross wiped his forehead again. "Never. Worse than Germantown. Where's de Chanzy?"

"Don't know. Saw him cut down one of Coffin's sergeants in that last charge. Guess he's all right. Pull off to the right. Stay with Armstrong's troops till I send for you." Eggleston cantered off, his horse blowing and wheezing.

Ross rode along the re-forming troops, scanning each group carefully. Then he gave a great shout. "Phil! Where the devil have you been?"

De Chanzy grinned through a smoke-blackened mask. "But everywhere, *mon vieux. Sapristi!* This is warm work."

"You're all right?"

"Yes, but for this devil of a knee which torments me since before Guilford. Nearly do I lose my seat when I fence with a long-legged Englishman. You have news of other parts of the field?"

"Only that Marion and Pickens have made the militia fight as it never fought before. They're as good as the Continentals today. Trouble is, we can't shake Marjoribanks and his grenadiers. They've got a devilish strong position close by the river. Thick growth of blackjack. Washington tried to rush them, I heard. His cavalry got smashed. He's wounded and captured. Hope they don't send *us* against them. Things pretty good, everywhere else. Stuart's thrown his whole force in and Greene's only committed his first line. Or that's the way it was a few minutes ago. That's the trouble with being with cavalry. You charge and things look fine. You reform and charge again and everything's messed up like a highholder's nest. Let's get along here to the right of Armstrong. Maybe we can see something."

From their new position, the field opened out ahead of them. In front, the Legion infantry, partly screened by light woods, was keeping up a steady fire on the British left. "The 63rd and 64th," commented Ross, squinting at the rather tattered red line. "Cruger's Tories are beyond them across the river road. Some in green, some in homespun. Hi! Something's going to happen! See them brace? What's in front of them? Can't see from here."

De Chanzy stood in his stirrups. "Ah—I do not—" Unseen muskets to the left blazed out in steady volleys, then ceased abruptly. A long cheer ripped out. Ross was waving his helmet, yelling wildly. "The Continentals! Greene's throwing them in."

The open space where Cruger's Tories joined the 63rd was suddenly filled with steady-trotting men, their bayonets aslant.

Stuart's whole line bent, crumbled, frayed out at the flanks, was scattered as though by a high wind. De Chanzy pounded Ross's shoulder, pointed east where the road to Charleston forked away from the river road. The narrow brown stretch was thick with enemy fugitives. Clouds of smoke rolled up from a group of wagons. Stuart was burning supplies and records.

A bugle blared. Eggleston signaled with his saber and the Legion cavalry wheeled to the right at a trot past their own infantry that was forming for a rush on the remnants of the 64th.

The move was obvious. Eggleston would circle wide, then swing in hard on the British rear, by the brick house with its palisaded gardens. Ross gripped his saber, closed in on the leading file of Armstrong's troop. The pace quickened, the drum of hoofs barely audible against the raving musketry to the left. Already they were riding into the fringe of the rout. British and Tories were throwing down their muskets. Close by the Charleston road, a huddle of men fled to the shelter of a clump of trees that concealed an odd rock formation. Some of the troopers swung out toward them but Ross ordered them back into line. The fugitives in the trees and underbrush could do no harm.

The bugles blared louder and the Legion swung into line, to meet a sudden wall of red where Coffin's dragoons pounded on in a desperate attempt to shelter Stuart's flank. The crash of meeting was loud in Ross's ears. A gray horse suddenly reared before him, fell as Ree's great shoulders cannoned into it. To the left, de Chanzy and a thin wiry man were circling each other, sparks flying as their blades met.

There were only Legion helmets about Ross, and Coffin's men were re-forming below the brick house whose shattered windows looked down blankly. Again the lines met. A dismounted dragoon fired a pistol at Ross, the bullet rapping through his helmet and creasing his scalp. Ross shouted a warning to Armstrong. If he pushed too far ahead, he would crash into the American pursuit. That would—Ross reined in suddenly. There was no pursuit. The starving, thirsty Americans who had broken the British line had stopped among the tents of the vanquished on the plain in front of the house. They were staving in rum barrels, tearing at chunks of salt meat. Officers stormed and raged at them, struck at them with the flats of their swords, but they were completely out of hand. Hunger and the flush of victory checked them where British bayonets had been helpless.

Already British officers were rallying the fugitives on the Charleston road, urging them on among the tents, linking them up with Marjoribanks's stubborn grenadiers among the blackjacks by the ravinelike river.

Wearily the Legion bugles sang out the recall and the troopers drew off sullenly, retracing their course over the clearing and back into the woods. De Chanzy was pounding his saddle in futile rage. "An instant more! Just one little instant!" he shouted.

Ross, shaken and depressed, shook his head. "Never mind. We'll get another chance. This fight's not over." He looked about at Eggleston, who called to him. "There's Lee off to the left. Go over and see if he has any new orders. I want to sort out the troops. Meet us where we formed the last time."

Ross slapped de Chanzy's shoulder. "Keep your head up. We'll be at them again," he said, and cantered off. Suddenly he gave a shout. By the edge of a distant field he saw Harry Lee, immaculate as ever, talking earnestly to a small man in a battered skullcap who sat a big sorrel. Ross shouted again, "There's Marion!" and rode faster, swinging past that odd rock formation among the trees that he had seen earlier. As he rode, he wondered if all the fugitives had been cleared out of that shelter.

All at once men behind him began to shout. "Ross! Look out! By those trees!" . . . "For God's sake, swing clear. He's aiming at you!" . . . "Get him, someone—there—kneeling in the scrub."

Ross looked over his shoulder. De Chanzy had broken out of line and was galloping toward the trees, yelling, "Ride, Ross, ride! I take him!"

Ross checked his horse, still staring at the clump that looked empty and harmless to him. Then he saw de Chanzy whip out a double-barreled pistol, saw him fire once into the trees, then again. Bushes waved and a stoop-shouldered man in tattered red broke cover. He ran on, as though in panic, dragging a long rifle. He gave a wild cry as he saw de Chanzy, dropped the deadly rifle and tugged out a pistol.

The pistol spat flatly and de Chanzy's horse screamed, reared and fell. Ross forgot about Lee and Marion, spun his mount toward the clump. De Chanzy had fallen clear, was struggling to his feet, his sword out. As he lunged, his bad knee buckled and he fell. His opponent staggered, then picked up his rifle and fired. De Chanzy crumpled, then fought to his feet, his sword licking out viciously just as Ross pulled up by him.

De Chanzy was looking quite coolly at his opponent's body. Ross panted, "By God, Phil, I thought he had you!"

De Chanzy turned a dead-white face toward Ross, forcing a smile. "But it was you he sought. I see him, clear through the trees, aim at you. And so, of course—" Then his knees gave way.

Ross shouted "Phil" and tried to lift him, but there was no mistaking the sag of the body, nor the meaning of the dark red stain that spread and spread over the front of his green jacket.

He stood there, staring down at his friend, his hands opening and closing slowly. He did not look up when Eggleston and Armstrong, followed by a few troopers, dismounted beside him. Eggleston knelt by the Frenchman's body. "Gone?" he asked.

Ross nodded, his dry mouth unable to form a word.

Armstrong growled, "God damn it, I *told* him not to leave formation. No telling what might have been among those trees. Why the hell couldn't he obey orders?"

"Shut up," said Ross in quick anger.

Armstrong laid his arm over Ross's shoulder. "Sorry. He was a good friend of yours, wasn't he? I was just thinking we couldn't spare a first-rate officer. Rotten luck, getting hit like that. Who was it? Some damn runaway?"

"Doesn't matter," said Ross shortly. Unconsciously he glanced down at the body in tattered red. Then he bent over it, with an angry exclamation. There was no mistaking the close-set eyes, the stooped shoulders, the cruel mouth. Captain Bayne had done his best to earn the rest of his money from St. Aubin.

While Ross stared, hands still opening and closing, Eggleston quickly stripped the cloak from his saddle and covered de Chanzy with it. Then he touched his helmet. "Nothing more to do here, I'm afraid. Mount up, everyone. Rejoin your troops."

Ross suddenly shouted, "No! Can't leave him like this. I want five troopers. They can get spades in that little shed in the woods."

"Sorry," said Eggleston. "The fight's not over yet. I can't spare the men or the time."

"Spare the time?" cried Ross. "Phil could spare the time to leave France and fight with us. If you won't give me the men, I'll bury him myself."

Eggleston spoke quietly. "Your orders were to report to Lee."

"Damn Lee! I'm staying with Phil."

Eggleston gathered his reins. "Do you think Phil would agree with your decision, Ross?"

Ross looked once more on the muffled body, then turned and mounted Ree. Then he rode off toward the fringes of the battle where Marion and Lee stared into the smoke-filled dusk. Ross kept on numbly, was vaguely aware of more officers joining Marion and the Virginian, heard Greene's deep voice in earnest speech. Ross halted, sat with his eyes on the ground, heedless of a sudden stir about him, of sharp commands. Again and again, his memory showed him de Chanzy shouting a warning, riding hard to draw off the shot that was aimed at Ross.

A hand fell on his shoulder and he looked dully into Greene's face that was oddly gentle. "I'm sorry, Ross. Someone just told me. You've lost a friend. The army has lost a very gallant soldier. No more duties for you this day."

Ross roused himself. "I'm not quitting. I'm going back for another charge."

"I know," said Greene. "But there'll be no more charges. I'm breaking off the action. Follow along with the Legion. And don't take any chances. There's a young lady with a chaplain waiting for you up the Congaree."

"Someone was waiting for Phil," said Ross.

"And who can tell her better than you? Good luck—and once again, take care of yourself."

Still stunned and hurt, Ross stayed in the field while Greene's army slipped past him in the dusk, heading for the High Hills of Santee. Someone caught at his bridle, led Ree along as the Legion troopers filed by, grim and silent. Unheeding, Ross rode with them.

Far in the rear, Stuart's shattered army held the field of Eutaw Springs but could venture no pursuit, could look forward to nothing save a weary march into the shelter of Charleston, the last remaining Royal post.

In six months, always trading victory for success, Nathanael Greene, Rhode Island ironmaster, had maneuvered British and Tory out of the Carolinas, save for that little strip where the Cooper and Ashley Rivers flowed into the sea at Charleston.

Captain and Mrs. Ross Pembroke had made an early start from Nelson's Ferry, rolling east in the light carriage along the river road through warm October air. Overhead, stars were paling and a vague glow foretold the new day. Her hand tight in Ross's, Dorande said softly, "I wish he could have known that the end is so near. He would have been happy."

Ross nodded, his eyes on the countryside where trees and rocks began to stand out from the gloom. "That's Burrell's plantation, our camp the night before and the night after Eutaw. Yes. I wish he could have known, have known everything. De Grasse has scattered the British fleet. Most of the men holding Cornwallis at Yorktown are French, too. I think you're right. It is the end. He would have been proud."

"He would have been as proud of what his friends have done. The British hold only Charleston and Wilmington."

"Didn't you know? They've even given up Wilmington and Stuart doesn't dare go beyond the Charleston limits. Yes, Phil would have liked all that."

Dorande sighed. "At least, his pretty Claire Long knows." She looked out of the window. "It is still so dark. Will you be able to find it?"

Ross nodded somberly. "Blindfolded, if I had to. Yes, we're getting close. There's a broken musket. Dead horse, still unburied over there. There's the brick house and the gardens. See this level stretch? That's where the British camp was. Now—let me see. Oh, yes!" He called, "Tobias! Stop where the Charleston road branches off. That's right."

They left the carriage, Dorande's arms loaded with a mass of bright blossoms. "But it is still hard to see. I do not—"

Ross took her gently by the elbow. "This way, dearest. I couldn't miss this. Yes, more furrows here. Some of us tried to go back to his grave later, but the British turned their artillery on us. Must have fired half a dozen rounds into the clump of trees. Straight ahead. Here—" He stopped, took off his helmet and dropped to his knees. Dorande knelt by him in the paling dawn, still holding her flowers.

Then she cried, "But the headstone! How could you have put that there?"

"I didn't. Some of the boys came down from the High Hills with it when the fever got me again."

Dorande bent closer. "Oh—there are words. I can't—yes, I begin to read them now. 'Here lies Philippe-Georges de la Piconnerie de Chanzy. Gentleman of France, American soldier. Greater love hath no man.'" Her voice quavered. She caught Ross's hand and, with the gesture, a stream of flowers cascaded over the grave. "Oh, *bien-aimé, that* he would have liked so much. Who wrote it?"

"Harry Lee, of course. Yes, you couldn't describe Phil better than that."

They knelt in silence, hands clasped. Then Dorande reached out, gently arranged the flowers. As she looked up, she gave a low cry. *"Mais, regarde-moi ça, Ross."*

The sun had lifted over the eastern reaches of the Santee and its rays fell full on the tip of the oddly shaped rock whose covering mask of trees and bushes now lay, shot-torn, about its base. The Dawn Stone, now guarded by de Chanzy, was receiving the first light of the sun, in promise of coming peace.